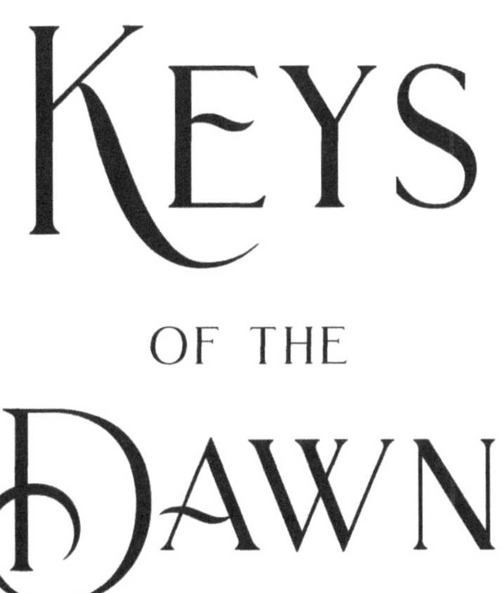

KEYS
OF THE
DAWN

PRAISE FOR THE KEYS AND GUARDIANS SERIES

"Jacklyn is a perfect lead with her sharp wit and just a touch of cynicism balanced with a healthy dose of self-deprecation.
- Indies Today

"Manzano absolutely kills it with characterization in this novel. She makes it so very easy for her audience to picture each of the characters right down to the sounds of their voices…[she] left me no option but to hang on to the edges for dear life and turn pages as quickly as I could."
- Ms. J Mentions…

"The Order of the Key…has enough tropes and traditions to feel familiar and comfortable in the genre, but at the same time enough twists and nuances to read as something fresh and exciting. The characters are tightly drawn, each with their own motivations. The "good guys" and "bad guys" don't blend into amorphous lumps. Even the villains are the heroes of their own stories, at least in their own minds…I highly recommend The Order of the Key for readers of fantasy, urban fantasy, and paranormal fiction, and I am excited to add it to my classroom library to share with my students."
- Jennifer L. Gadd, Teacher and MG Author

"The old saying, 'power corrupts but absolute power corrupts absolutely' rears its ugly head among the members of the Order and the Head of it…various characters in the story were so duplicitous that it was hard to tell the good ones from the bad ones. And that made for a tremendously complicated storyline which was a kick to read. Guess you can call that depth of character. I call it fun!!"
- G. Themann

Indies Today 2020 Finalist
Author Shout Recommended Read 2021
Page Turner Awards Long List

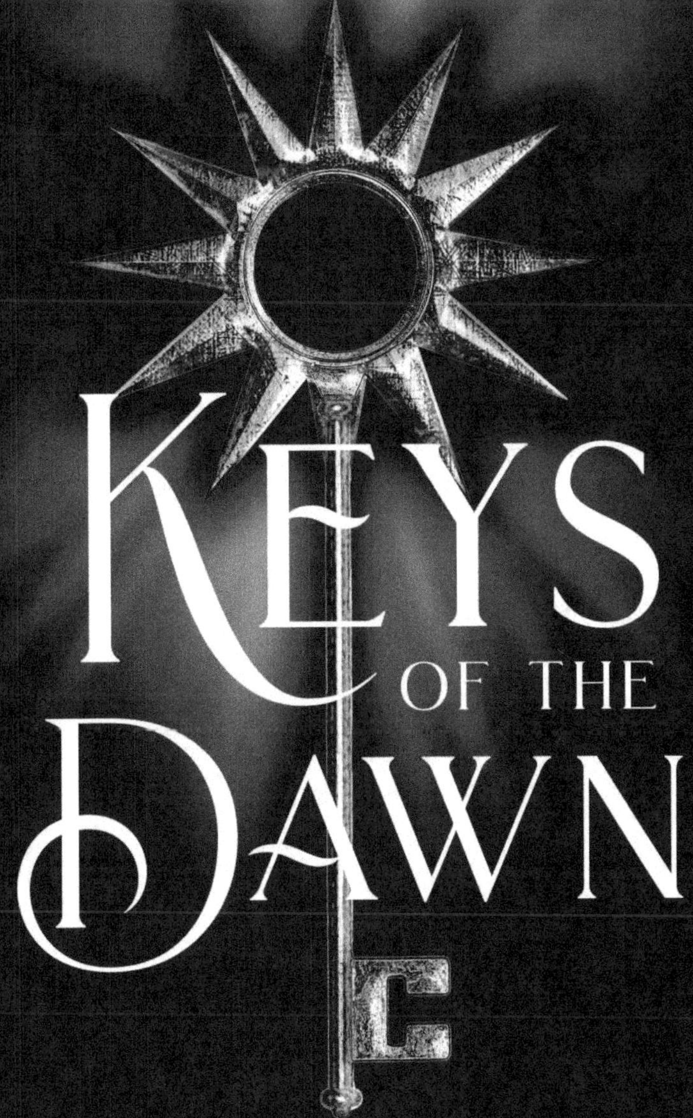

JUSTINE MANZANO
KEYS OF THE DAWN
EVENTIDE BOOKS

Eventide Books
Visit the website at JustineManzano.com

Second Edition: December 2024
ISBN: 978-1-965476-08-6
Edited by Jennia Herold D'lima
Cover Art by Celin Chen
Layout by Celin Chen

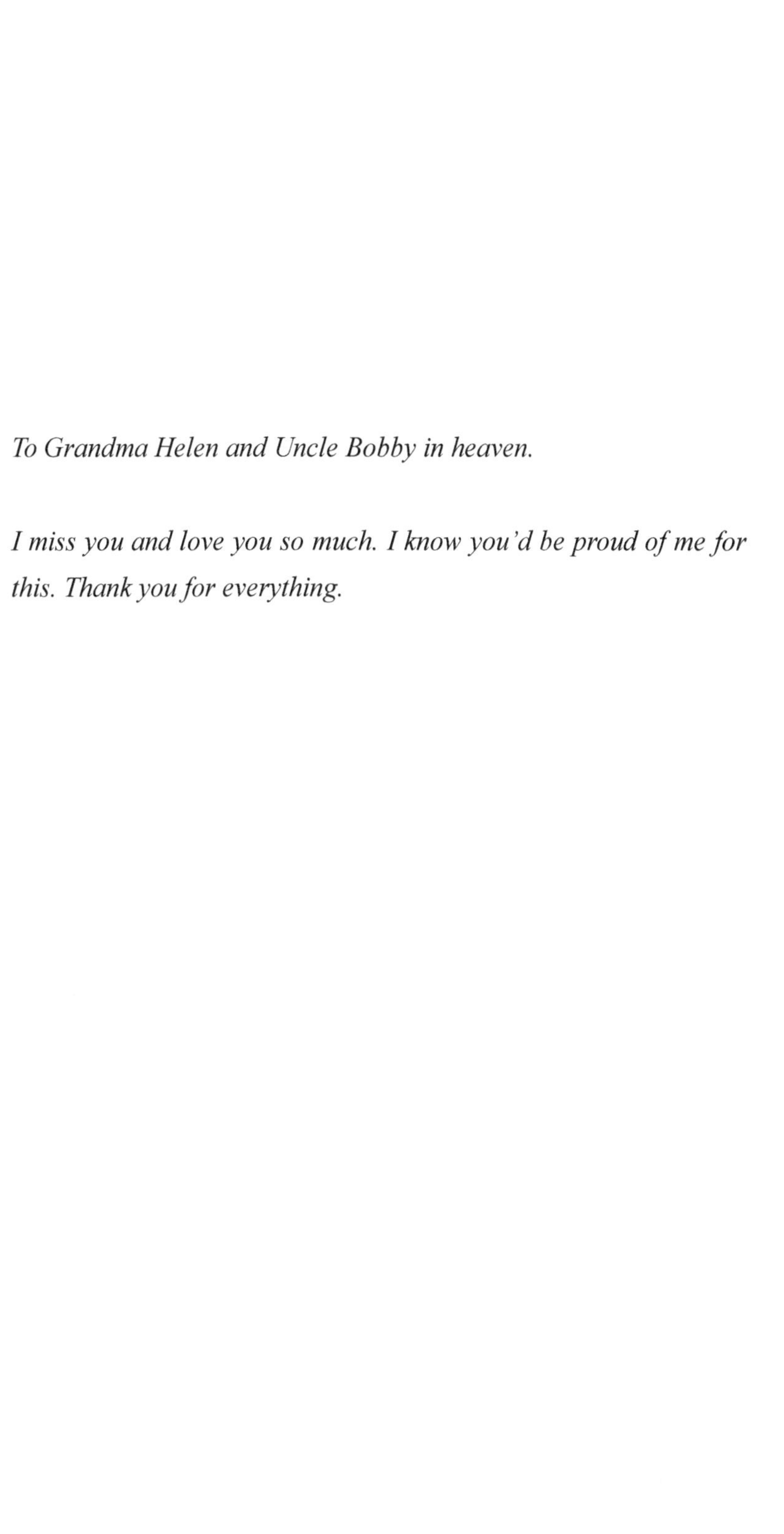

To Grandma Helen and Uncle Bobby in heaven.

I miss you and love you so much. I know you'd be proud of me for this. Thank you for everything.

ONE

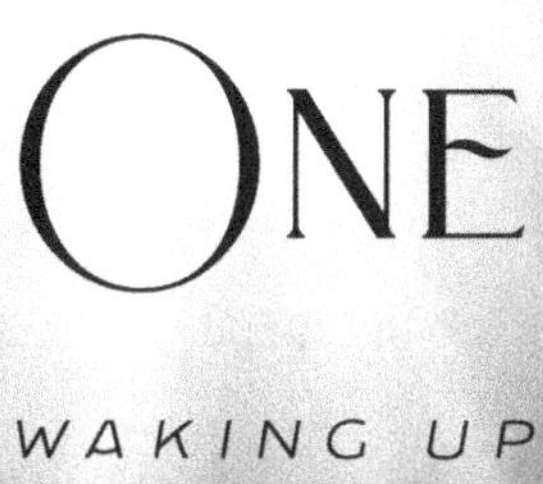

JACKLYN

I sucked in a breath I shouldn't be able to take.

My last memory was of dying and knowing it was a one-way trip, and yet… I was definitely breathing.

And moving. The unique sensation of dropping and suddenly being yanked up, then crashing into something solid. I knew that feeling but couldn't pinpoint where I knew it from, only that the landing was considerably less rough the last time I'd felt it.

A shiver forced me straight into a sitting position. My eyes jolted open to find… darkness. Darkness everywhere. I waved a hand in front of my face and only sensed the movement.

But my Aegis could help.

I closed my eyes and breathed, finding the space within me where the energy lived, my Aegis, the very thing that made me a Key. Deep in my core, the slightest spark kindled to life within me.

Not enough. Not nearly enough.

But just enough for the tiniest flame to flicker awake on my finger, a candle on a birthday cake. And here I'd thought I was done getting older.

I moved my finger around in a circle, stretching my arm as far out as I dared.

Dirt and rubble.

My breath caught and I slammed my eyes shut. I pulled air in slowly, held it for two beats, then released it. Again and again until I felt centered. This time when my eyes peeled open, I discovered this wasn't some kind of twisted nightmarish reliving of being buried behind the estate.

What I was seeing was truly there.

Glass and metal and rock jutted up from every surface. The air was thick with dust.

I had died in the Dusk. I had died to save my impossible clone babies that I loved, despite them being far too old to be my children. I had died with—

My head twisted to either side of me. I was alone.

I tried to push myself to my feet, only for my head to collide with something sharp. Swearing, I reached for the wound and found sticky blood in my hair. I lit another birthday candle flame on my fingertips to see what I'd hit. The ceiling was frighteningly low. I barely had room for more than a hunched, uncomfortable stance, but I rose as much as I could manage.

Now that I was on my feet, I could look in the one direction I hadn't been able to before now. I turned around and a sob tore from my throat.

A scar of dim red light ripped through the floor. It was small, almost like a paper cut in the earth, but it was there, glowing. A Rift I couldn't close with the small amount of Aegis power I was capable of mustering at the moment. Kyp was sprawled across the floor beside it.

The love of my life. The bane of my existence. The man who'd risked it all with me for our children.

Kyp.

And we hadn't even succeeded. How could we have succeeded? It was impossible—a Rift cut through the ground right in front of me. A passageway between the Dawn and the Dusk.

Another sob wracked my body and I fell. Sharp pain jolted up my knees, debris cutting into them, and I nearly cried out, but some deep-rooted instinct stopped me. I'd died in the Dusk, after all. If I made too much noise, I'd draw the creatures here to me. I covered my mouth to muffle any noise that might sneak out.

"It didn't fail."

I started so hard, I banged my head again and had to muffle another scream.

"Sorry," the voice whispered again. "So sorry. I thought you saw me."

This time, I nearly cried from relief. Kyp. Kyp was alive.

I shuffled closer to him. "I did see you! I just… You didn't look like you were…"

"Alive?" he asked, and as I held my flame forward, I saw the slightest upturn to his lips, the patented Kyp Franklin smirk. "Yeah, I didn't really feel alive either. I've actually been awake for a while. Way longer than you've been."

"Why were you just lying there if you were awake this whole time? Why didn't you say anything? Why weren't you looking for a way out?"

Kyp wasn't one to remain idle. Something was very wrong.

His lips twitched and I aimed the light on his eyes so I had a better chance of reading his expression.

Pained. His expression was pained.

"I didn't have any light to see by at first," he said. "But I did what I could. There's a small current of fresh air coming in from the far right of our little bubble of rubble." He snorted a laugh, but it sounded hollow.

Thank God we'd ended up in an air pocket, however small. It was bad enough I always seemed to come back to life while I was still buried. It would be worse if I couldn't move. How would I be able to help Kyp if I was losing my mind in a panic attack?

The finger holding up the flicker of flame shook between us, casting the light in a squiggle that journeyed across his face. I couldn't seem to hold still.

"The good news is, we didn't fail," Kyp said. "The Rift is small. Even if we failed to completely seal it, at least we won't have to force Jainey or Jordan to give their lives to close it."

"That can't be right. I was sure it was closed," I argued. "And where is Cxarana? Dhamyan? If we didn't close it, what could have happened while we were out? If they knew we'd come back, why didn't they take us with them?"

"I don't know," he said, sounding a little breathless. His words came slowly. "I don't. But here's what I do know. We have some oxygen coming in, but the air here is dirty. It's… not safe. There was some kind of cave in or something. I have no idea. I don't know where we are. We don't have food or water. My Aegis is weak and yours probably is, too. But you have to get out of here."

"Just me?" It was warm. It had just been cold a few minutes ago. Hadn't it?

"And the other thing I know?" His eyes lit up. "It's damn good to see your face."

I threw myself forward and wrapped my arms around his shoulders, pulling him against me. He hissed air between his teeth, but buried his face in the crook of my neck.

"Jacks," he sighed.

I melted against him, my fear calming with that one word. We were together. And when we were together, we could manage anything.

His hands slid up my back and into my hair, tilting my head up so his lips could reach mine. The kiss was chaste and sweet, a reunion, a reminder. I ran my hands over his chilled cheeks and pressed a delicate kiss to each of his eyelids. His fingers dug into my hips, dragging me closer.

Something warm and damp spread across my stomach. I jolted, my eyes locking on his.

What the hell?

I reached down between us, the light on my fingertips showing me the slow spread of blood stretching across both of us.

My eyes shot up to his. "You're bleeding."

He huffed a tense laugh. "Yes, quite a bit, actually."

"When were you hurt?" I rasped, struggling to speak against the lump in my throat.

"I… wasn't." He pushed his fingers through my hair, his touch gentle. His thumb brushed my cheek. "It's that wound. The one that got infected with the Senefestrian blood."

I swore. The wound I hadn't been able to heal, even with the full strength of my abilities at hand.

"It wasn't here when I woke up. I think we actually did die," he said. "I think we died and I came back healed. But it just… tore open again."

My heart clenched, and the tiny fingertip flame brightened and widened. "What did you do?"

"I didn't do anything! I was trying to find an exit and it was like a bad set of stitches. It just ripped open. I went from healed to bleeding out and I…" He coughed, again and again. His body pitched forward, his hands not making it up in time to hide the blood that spilled from his lips.

"Kyp." His name pulled out from me in a moan of terror. My vision blurred with tears. I couldn't do this. Not again.

For a while, I was at peace.

For a while, I wasn't fighting for our lives.

For a while, I thought we were going to be okay.

"It's okay, Jacks. We're okay, baby. I love you." His voice broke. "But I can't go with you. You need to get out of here. You can get me help." Sweat broke out across his brow, his breathing became labored, and his skin took on a sickly pallor. He grabbed my sleeve in his hand as though it were the only thing tethering him to consciousness.

"Stop," I sobbed. "I'm not leaving without you."

"You have to!"

I jerked back, my chest tightening. I couldn't breathe.

"You have to, Jacks." His voice softened. "You have to. I can't help you." He smiled that crooked smile and my heart bottomed out. Another ragged cough burst from his lips.

I pressed my hand to the wound. Blood gushed over my fingers. "No, come on, Kyp. Don't die on me." I reached within myself for the healing abilities that came with my Aegis. But I hadn't recovered enough yet. I needed time to recharge. If we had died, it made sense. I was always fragile when I came back. It took time. Time we didn't have.

He slid his hand up my arm to my shoulder and squeezed gently. "Don't do that."

A whimper escaped me, but I took a deep breath and swallowed it back.

"Not dead yet." He gasped the last word, followed by a shuddering, violent series of breaths that ended in one long expulsion of air as he flopped back onto the ground, pulling me down with him.

I knelt beside his body, staring at his glassy, empty eyes. He was dead. It didn't matter that there was a good chance he would come back. What if he didn't? I still didn't know how we woke back up in the first place!

Kyp was right. The air was thick and damp, and it felt like it coated the inside of my lungs. There was no food or water. If I didn't get out of here soon, I could die too. And I might not come back.

You were never supposed to come back. You made your peace with that.

But what if the kids were in danger? What if I could still somehow save Kyp? He'd died so many times only to be jerked back in the way Keys always were. But Kyp had been tortured to death over and over.

Dying and coming back from the dead was excruciating. It took everything out of you. And I wasn't going to let that keep happening to him.

Or me, because screw that.

I crawled toward the area where Kyp said there was air. Wood, metal, and glass debris sliced into my palms and tore through the knees of my jeans as I trudged forward.

When I made it to the far end of the space we were stuck in, I searched for the opening Kyp had detected. I moved my flame along the wall, but instead of the opening, I saw a long piece of metal. Rebar.

Did the Dusk have anything that used rebars? I hadn't seen a lot of it in the short time I'd been there. Still… this looked more like something from the Dawn. Like something from home.

How could we have gotten home?

I considered this as I pushed the rebar against the edge of the walls. After a while, something gave. I used the metal bar to lever something out of the way. A battered piece of pale, flat wood that niggled something deep in the back of my mind.

I kept moving, sweeping aside layers of dust and dirt and grime, chunks of metal and wood. My fingers ached, my muscles shaking, a level of movement I shouldn't be doing so shortly after re-awakening from death.

How deeply buried in rubble *were* we? I worked for hours and just kept uncovering more rubble. An unending pile of metal, wood, and rock, sheets, bedding, and medical supplies. Granted, I was slower than usual, but I'd been doing this for some time and couldn't see the end.

My chest ached. My throat burned. My head spun. The more I moved, the worse I felt.

Pain can't kill you. Not you.

Austin's drawl floated in my head, reminding me to push through. But what if pain could kill me? What if this pain was—

A cough erupted from deep within my chest. One, then another, until I couldn't stop, until I was bent over the mess of rubble I'd dug us out of, blood splashing across the logo on the sheets there.

The air is dirty.

Kyp was right. In what couldn't have been more than a few hours, something here had filled my lungs and made me ill.

A metallic screech sounded from somewhere outside of the walls of our little murderous sanctuary. Something horrific, followed by a rumbling that sent dust and debris raining down on me.

I dropped forward on instinct, covering my head with my hands.

God, Kyp's body was unprotected in that far corner.

I peeled my eyes open. When did I close them? They took a moment to adjust. There was more light somehow, and my vision cleared, focusing on the word written on the sheets I'd pulled from the rubble.

Lifestone.

The sheets came from a Lifestone medical facility. The place that had taken my children. My Jordan and my Jainey. The place that had taken Jainey to a warehouse and held her there, draining her blood. Opening a MacroRift to the Dusk. One that I'd gone through to save Kyp. One that we'd closed from the Dusk. Which meant the growing suspicion building within me was right.

Though we had died in the Dusk, we weren't there anymore.

We were home.

I pushed myself to my feet, but I didn't stop there. I reached within my mind and called out with everything I had.

Jordan!

Jainey!

I'm here!

I'm alive!

I doubted it would do anything. Who knew if they were near enough to hear me or if they even knew to listen? Mind Keys could throw their thoughts to anyone who wasn't blocked, but I didn't have that ability. How would they—

Mom?

They were listening for me. Were they… were they here?

Metallic whirring and scraping sent my senses rattling. I hadn't realized when I'd reached out to them I'd opened my Aegis up wide, and the shrill sound was like a jackknife slamming through each ear.

I fell to my knees again, but this time, I kept pawing through the rubble. My kids were here. They were looking for me. My family. My dad…

The ceiling pulled up and away, flooding my world with light. My eyes burned with it, and I covered them, my filthy hands only making the burning worse.

"Birdie!"

Oh my God.

Dad.

Relief flooded through me, the tension in my limbs seeping away with the sound of my father's voice, saying that name. The nickname he'd given me as a baby.

I shielded my eyes as I peered up. Ray, my father, stood just above me, holding a chunk of the building up over his head with the strength of his Body Key Aegis. On the other side of the opening was the cause of all that scraping metal. Austin, my best friend, was operating a damn forklift.

Behind him, Jordan held Jainey. Drew had a shovel slung over his shoulders. Cass and Zane were leaning out of a crane farther back.

They were here. Our family was here.

"Kyp's back there," I said, wobbling a little on my feet. "He's dead again, but I'm hoping he's still coming back."

Ray jumped down into the pit with me, landing with an echoing thud and the crunch of glass. "You're a right mess, kiddo." That Irish brogue sounded more like home than I'd ever believed it could.

"Pretty sure I'm about to…" Another wobble on my feet and I tipped toward him. My vision dimmed in the corners.

Crap. Not this again.

Warm and solid, Ray lifted me in his arms like the hero I'd

imagined him being when Kyp first told me about him, like the hero he hadn't quite turned out to be.

"I've got you."

"That's good, 'cause…" My lips continued to move, but I didn't hear what I said.

One heavy blink and Ray jostled me hard, an urgent look in his eyes. I didn't know what he was saying. Another heavy blink, and this time, my eyes didn't open all the way.

Another heavy blink and I was gone.

TWO

LIAR

KYP

Kyp was wrapped in warmth and softness, and he melted into the feeling the moment he became aware of it. Sunlight shone upon him, dazzlingly bright despite his closed eyelids. The scent of lavender floated through the air, and he breathed it in deeply, lulling himself into a relaxed state. He couldn't remember feeling this way in years. Comfortable. Peaceful.

He slit his eyes open, hoping to find Jacklyn beside him. Jacklyn had succeeded. He was home at the brownstone, but he was alone in bed. He wasn't alone in the room, though. Jordan perched upon a chair near the bed, his legs crossed, a laptop and notebook balanced precariously on his lap and earbuds dangling from his ears.

His son.

"Jordan?" he whispered, though he hadn't intended to. It seemed that was the loudest sound his voice could make.

His son didn't budge, so Kyp decided to watch him work. Kyp had an eidetic memory, thanks to his Aegis, and he could see all the small ways Jordan had changed, had grown, since the last time he'd seen him.

The kid was the perfect blend of himself and Jacklyn. His eyebrows drew together the way hers did when she was thinking hard. He chewed on his pen and his leg jumped as he worked out whatever problem he was working on. Jordan's hair, black like Kyp's own, fell in his eyes as he leaned forward to write something in his notebook. He was tall and thin, the way Kyp was, the way his family always had been. Slim but fit, without any of Jacklyn's natural softness and rounded cheeks. But his eyes were all hers. Hazel and filled with fire.

Although that was just a memory. He hadn't seen those eyes since before they'd closed the Rift.

How long had they been down?

"Jordan," he tried again.

Nothing.

Was this what it was like to have a teenager? He was only barely not a teenager, and he didn't remember ever being this situationally unaware.

Wait… was this what happened when someone felt… safe?

Jordan's eyes jumped up to his as he yanked his earbuds out. "Dad! You're awake."

Kyp was still a little stunned by the realization that he'd never felt safe enough to be that absorbed in a mundane activity before, and he almost didn't answer. "Hey, Jordan."

"Mom! He's up!" the kid shouted before rushing to the bed and half-tackling him. "Don't either of you ever do anything like that again, got it?"

Kyp laughed. "No guarantees, but I'll do my best."

He flopped onto the bed beside Kyp and rested his head on his shoulder. "So, how are you feeling?"

"Really crappy, honestly," he said. "But I'll get better soon."

"Take it easy on him, kiddo."

Jacklyn.

Jacklyn Madison was freshly showered, her chestnut curls bouncing along her shoulders as she walked, a dazzling smile shining on her face. She wore gym shorts and a T-shirt, and she was stunning.

Or maybe he was just in love. Either way, the sight of her brought him fully back to life.

However fleeting that might be.

"There she is," Kyp greeted. "Where's my little bean?" He was almost afraid to see Jainey. How much older would she look?

"They were all up digging us out until four in the morning, so she's still knocked out." She lowered herself onto the edge of the mattress. The scent of lavender drifted from her, and he longed to bury his face in her hair. He felt like he hadn't seen or held her in ages. Even their moment in the debris wasn't nearly enough.

Wait…

"How long were we down?"

"Year and a half," Jordan muttered. "We've missed you."

Hearing that nearly choked him. A year and a half. They'd been dead for a year and a half, and now they were back.

No wonder Jordan looked older.

"Everyone told us so much about you. We feel like we know

you even better now!" Jordan smiled weakly, clearly trying to cheer him up.

Sugar-coated memories, Kyp was sure. But who was he to correct anything positive Jordan and Jainey believed of him? He'd rather they believed that than the ugly truth.

"How long were you down there before we got to you?" Jordan pushed himself up to a seated position, and Kyp followed.

"Not sure. Couldn't have been too long. Maybe a day." He shrugged. "We were both dead for part of it, so we don't know. I'm not even sure how we ended up on this side of the Rift. We should have been in the Dusk."

"Let's just be glad you weren't," Jordan said. "My Aegis came back about two days ago. I knew something was wrong. I wasn't sure if I should tell anybody. I didn't want to worry them. But then Jainey… Well, when it came back, it caught her off guard. She'd had a lousy day already, and her Aegis decided to help her out without her knowledge. She nearly melted her classmates' brains."

Kyp's eyes bulged. He couldn't imagine the shock they'd felt when their abilities rushed back that way.

"Zane worked her magic to cover it and explain it away as some kind of gas leak," Jordan said. "We figured out that a Rift must've opened. And that's when we thought… what if you came back? We had to see. But we didn't really think it was possible. Not until I heard you call out for me."

Jacklyn closed her eyes, her chest heaving as she inhaled. Kyp waited for her to ground herself before he asked anything else.

"Were Jainey's friends…"

"Nothing a nap won't cure," Jordan said. "And nobody said anything about friends. Kids can be assholes. Especially when someone is different. And even though Jainey doesn't have a perfect memory without an Aegis, she's still learned what she's learned. She isn't anything like the other kids at school."

Kyp frowned.

"Well. That's what Drew said, anyway," Jordan amended. "In school, kids are jerks and pick on people who are different."

Jacklyn nodded, a wry smile on her face. "If it was anything like my school experience, I'm going to have to punt seven-year-olds across playgrounds far sooner than I was expecting."

Jordan's eyes widened. "No, Mom, you can't do that. You'll get arrested."

Jacklyn laughed, and it warmed something still unthawed in Kyp's chest. "They'd have to catch me first."

Jordan looked at Kyp with wide eyes.

"She's joking," Kyp said. "I swear."

She shrugged. "Anyway, Jordan, Ray's looking for some help downstairs. He's pulling the weapons out of storage."

Jordan groaned. "Sometimes it sucks being the muscle." He narrowed his eyes. "Aren't you *also* the muscle?"

Jacklyn smiled. "Yes, but I make the rules, so I get to say this one is yours." She grabbed Jordan's laptop off the chair he'd abandoned it on, but the minute her fingers wrapped around it, a spark flew from it and she dropped it back on the chair with a hiss.

"Mom!"

She swore, shaking her arm out. "It shocked me."

Jordan reached forward slowly, but no spark arced from it when his hand got close. He narrowed his eyes at Jacklyn, then picked it up smoothly. "Maybe it just doesn't like you." He stuck his tongue out at her.

"You would think it would love me, since I made you use it for your homework." She glared at him. "You wanted to train instead. But we don't know how long it will take for us to return things to normal. I'd rather you keep up with your studies in the meantime. You should take your laptop to Zane. That was a bad shock. You're gonna want to make sure it's not busted."

"You could have just said you wanted to talk to Dad alone." He rolled off the bed and landed on his feet, but only just barely.

"I could have…" Her eyes lit with mischief and she swatted at him as he walked by. "On your toes!"

He ducked, but just slow enough that she got in one good poke in the ribs. "Mom!" An involuntary laugh burst free from him with the word.

"Situational awareness is vital, Jordan!" Kyp called.

"Get outta here, or I'll do it in front of Rennie," Jacklyn teased.

Kyp had never seen him move faster.

Jacklyn waited until they were alone to sink down beside him on the bed. "Hi."

"Hi." Kyp barely got the words out before Jacklyn had wrapped her arms around him. Her lips pressed to every inch of his face so quickly he could do nothing more productive than laugh.

"You scared the shit out of me," she muttered in between kisses. "What the fuck was that?"

"I don't know." He shrugged. "Maybe we'll learn more next time."

Her expression instantly darkened. "What? Why would you say that?"

He supposed his time limit on this joyous family reunion had just run out. "I've never understood the patterns of a Key's death. I don't know why some of us come back faster than others. But I can tell you I lied back there in the rubble."

Jacklyn's expression melted into a thin-lipped grimace. "Of course you did. I guess I should be pleased you're coming clean this quickly."

Kyp inhaled deeply and willed his nerves to calm. When he spoke, the words came out a lot less shaky than he assumed his anxiety would allow.

"I woke up much sooner than you. And that wound keeps opening. You see, I died twice waiting for you to get us out. I *keep* dying. And I don't think I'm going to stop."

THREE

KYP

Kyp died a couple more times before he decided he couldn't excuse being locked up in his room anymore. Jacklyn had barred everyone from seeing him, claiming he was extra low on energy.

He doubted they all bought that without argument.

It didn't matter. It had been nearly two days now, and he was through with just lying in bed. He was a man of action, and all this stillness made him antsy.

Kyp rose from the bed and stretched, careful with the side where his skin, currently unmarred, threatened to tear open again.

He could do this. How hard could it be to go out and greet the people he loved dearly, most of whom he almost sort of liked, and pretend he wasn't going to keel over and die at any given moment?

For starters, he needed a shower. His bedroom here at the brownstone was much the same as he had left it, which was much the same as his bedroom had been at the estate. Bare. Why set down roots when you never knew when you'd need to abandon them? And he certainly had at the estate.

Jacklyn didn't share his sentiment, and he'd probably have to get used to her collections if he managed to find a way to stick around.

He'd have to tell everyone soon so he could get on figuring that out.

He gathered up a T-shirt, sweatpants, and boxers, then headed down the hall to the nearest bathroom.

As he approached, he could tell the bathroom door was wide open. A voice muttered from within the room, a familiar voice.

Cass, his dearest friend.

"Today is a really good day." She leaned forward, like she could will the words into her head through the bathroom mirror. She was still stunning, with her rich brown skin and her naturally tight curls. She smiled, but it was tremulous and it didn't light up her eyes the way it normally did. "My best friend is here. Back. From the dead, even. Today is a very good day."

Kyp sighed. "If you're gonna go release a lot of bullshit, you should probably close the bathroom door first."

Cass swore and jolted in place. Her hand gripped her sky-blue blouse just above her chest, and she stared up at him through the mirror blankly for a moment before she whirled around and threw her arms around him.

"Oh my God!" She squeezed him so tight he could barely breathe. "It's you! It's you!"

"It's me!" A laugh forced its way out of him despite his compressed lungs. He dropped his clothes on the floor and wrapped his arms around her, going along with the little dance she did while she hugged him.

She looked worn out. Tired. Her eyes were ringed with dark circles and there was a new crease in her forehead. It implied she'd been stressed out the entire time he'd been gone. He'd seen her just a few days ago for him. But the real year and a half that had gone by counted as the longest they'd ever been apart since they'd met.

She pulled back suddenly, frowning. "You smell foul."

"Thanks, I bled a lot and haven't showered in apparently a year and a half and also, I was dead for a while. Those things tend to lead to poor hygiene. I was coming in for a shower, though."

Cass faltered. "You were dead." She crushed him against her again. "I didn't think you were ever coming back."

He didn't know what to say. He didn't know how to comfort her when he wasn't sure how long he would survive.

He wished he had the words.

"How are you?" He hoped it would be an effective way to throw her off the scent.

"I'm… It was really hard at first." She pulled back. "I had trouble adjusting to life without you, like without the Order. But I had Drew and the others. And the kids. And I went to counseling."

Kyp blinked. "What did that involve?"

"Lying, mostly." She laughed. "But not about the important things. Like my best friend and his girlfriend died, and it was violent and horrible, and now I was helping to raise his kids. And I'd realized my chosen career was not the right career path, and now I was all directionless."

Kyp leaned against the doorframe. "You realized it wasn't the right path? Does that mean you had the option to remain in your original career?"

Cass mirrored him, leaning on the opposite side of the doorframe, her arms crossed over her chest. "What are you actually asking me, Kyp?"

Damn. She always knew when he was talking around something. "When the Rifts were gone… your Aegis… it was really gone?"

Cass tilted her head. "Yes."

"How could you be sure?"

A sigh. "I tried to find you. To talk to you. I guess… I never really had to tackle grief. Not for real. I could always just talk to whoever I missed. But not this time. This time, you were really gone. And it wasn't just you. Mari. Gana. I'm a channeler. And that was just… gone."

The catch in her voice made Kyp's heart ache. He laid his hands on her shoulders. "I'm sorry."

"Not to worry. Everything's fine now," Cass said. "The only thing we have to figure out now is why? How did the Rifts re-open?"

"Jordan said something about having some remnants of his abilities even when the Rifts were closed. But nothing close to his usual abilities," Kyp said. "Is there any way…"

"What? Jordan tripped and opened a Rift?" Cass's eyebrows raised. "Not bloody likely."

Kyp's lip twitched at the very Ray-like comment. "You're probably right." And speaking of Ray… "I should go say hi to the others."

Cass nodded. "Ray's in the kitchen getting Jainey lunch. Go."

He nodded and turned to leave.

"Wait!"

He turned back to her, smiling.

But she didn't return the expression. Her eyes were watery, her hands wringing together as she spoke. "I know you're not the type of person to say it often. And weighty emotions make you uncomfortable. And usually, I'm cool with that. I know how we feel about each other. But this time…"

"I love you, Cass. You're my best friend. And I love you. I do." He owed her that much and so much more.

She let out a sob and tackled him again. "I love you too, bro."

Every time she hugged him like that, he was terrified his wound would reopen. Once he was sure it hadn't, he hugged her as tightly as he could and smacked a huge kiss on her forehead.

"Now that I think about it," Cass said. "You should shower first. I've gotta finish getting ready for school." She swatted him away.

"Hey!" He feigned offense, but he knew she was right. "School?" Kyp walked backward into the bathroom.

"College," Cass said. "For social work. I'm gonna be a grief counselor. Eventually." She smiled, and it was warm. Happy. "I like it. Even if there are Saturday classes."

"Good for you." He returned her smile. "Keep it up. We'll figure out what's going on with these Rifts and set them to rights. So you can get your life back."

She nodded. "Take it easy. You just got here."

But what she didn't know was that he was running on borrowed time.

After a long, hot shower, Kyp felt better. Almost prepared to face everyone.

He strolled down the stairs and into the kitchen, not wanting to startle anyone or face Jacklyn's wrath when she caught him rushing.

"For all that is holy in this world, Jainey, I said no," Ray groaned from where he sat at the kitchen table.

Kyp ducked out of view, peeking in from outside the entrance. Jainey sat at the marble island with Jordan, Zane, Rennie, and Ray. Jainey still had her long, dark curls and her chubby cheeks, but she was clearly taller now and her face held maturity that hadn't been there before.

Someone puttered around the rest of the kitchen, just out of view, their feet shuffling across the wood paneling.

"But Grandpa!" Jainey whined. "Jordan got to see him!"

Jacklyn walked into view and slid a plate of pancakes in front of Jordan and Jainey, then headed back out of his line of sight, probably to the stove.

Ray reached out and pulled her back toward the table. "You. Sit." He headed off in the direction she'd been going. "I get it, I swear I do. But he needs to rest before you go jumpin' all over him." He put plates down in front of Jacklyn and Zane.

Austin trudged over with two more plates and settled in beside Jacklyn. Drew followed with a tray. Balanced upon it was their box of tea bags, a quart of milk, a stack of sugar packets, and huge pots of coffee and tea. "I'm still stuck on the never-ending bullshit. I'm not looking to drop everything and investigate a mystery."

"You're a cop," Drew grumbled, taking the other plate from him.

"A beat cop," Austin said. "Not a damn detective."

Ray followed with his own mug and flopped onto the chair beside Jainey.

It was so domestic, it hurt to look at it, like the sun shining brightly in his eyes. He felt like an intruder in his own family.

"You know, at least your brother listens to me," Ray said to Jainey, apparently ignoring Austin.

Jainey made a show out of rolling her eyes. "No, he doesn't. He just yesses you until you leave him alone."

"Jainey!" Jordan growled. The table jolted.

"Grandpa! Jordan kicked me!"

Jacklyn's mouth opened, then snapped shut when she seemed to realize Ray had been called, not her.

"Jordan!" Ray snapped.

"She'll heal now, won't she?" Jordan narrowed his eyes at her. Rennie shot him a

disgusted look from beside him.

Jacklyn opened her mouth again, but this time, Zane cut her off.

"Thank you for reminding us you're younger than you appear, kiddo."

Jacklyn sank into her seat, bringing her coffee cup up higher, as if she could hide her face

behind it.

Kyp's heart twisted, and finally he managed to make his feet move. "Okay! That's enough of that. You two behaved better than that last time I was here."

Jainey didn't even wait for him to finish the sentence before she leapt into his arms. She was heavier than she had been, and he almost didn't catch her. His side twinged, but he refused to acknowledge it.

"Hey, Bean." He cradled her against him. "Missed you, kiddo."

"Missed you too, Papa!" She patted her hands against his face. "Grandpa wouldn't let me come visit you."

"I'm sorry." Kyp frowned. "But to be fair, I was feeling pretty awful, and I don't think you wanted to see me that way." As he spoke, he walked her back toward her seat.

"Seeing me would have made you feel better for sure," Jainey argued as he dropped her onto her padded seat. "You're all just short-sighted."

"You know, you're probably right." Kyp laughed. He moved around the table to sit down between Jainey and Jacklyn, but Drew stopped him.

"It's good to see your face, man." He held out a hand.

"Good to see you too." Kyp grabbed it, only to get pulled into a quick hug. Once released, he found Austin's fist extended for a fist bump. He was barely looking up from his coffee, but the grin on his face wasn't well hidden.

Kyp gave him a pound. "'Sup."

"Yo."

Rennie grabbed his hand and squeezed as he passed. And then there was Ray.

Ray, who was practically a father to him. Ray, who had saved his life and screwed it up in turns. Ray... who was far too careful when he hugged him, especially on the side where the wound kept appearing.

Dammit, Jacklyn. It looked like she hadn't kept his affliction as secret as he'd asked. But then, he hadn't told her the truth either, had he?

"We're going to talk about this, son," Ray murmured as he pressed a kiss to his temple.

"I know," Kyp responded, his voice cracking as he spoke.

Despite everything, the love in the room was palpable. He had been missed. He had found a family after being destroyed by the one he'd been born into, and it just made his impending death feel even more awful.

Because that was what was happening, whether he liked it or not. They could investigate it if it didn't bother Tex too much, but he couldn't see how they'd discover anything. Cxarana hadn't seemed to know of a cure when they'd discussed Sirin blood and its effects. And who would know better than an Arvokian? Which meant he had time, but in the end, he'd have two choices: either choose to use the Arvokian Death-Bringer Ritual to end this permanently, or lose himself completely.

She was different before she died. But enough deaths and she lost herself.

Ray had told him that about his mother, Lavinia. He hadn't believed him. Couldn't. Because if he did believe, that meant his mother could have been wonderful, and instead had turned into an abusive monster.

He would not become his mother. He would literally die first.

But how would he convince Jacklyn? Was it even possible?

Could he do it without her support?

For now, he ate breakfast. And when he was done, he played recklessly with his children outside behind the brownstone, climbing on the chairs and jumping across them, as one did when the floor was lava.

It started with Kyp, Jordan, and Jainey, and moved from The Floor is Lava to Hide and Seek, but it kept growing as the morning wore on. By the time they went inside hours later for lunch, Rennie had been literally dragged into it by Austin and Drew, and Jacklyn scared them all by hiding under a bench when none of them were looking.

It was a lovely day. Normal. Remarkably so. And for a moment, Kyp almost forgot the Rifts were open again, and he imagined his dream had come true. That he had created a world where they could live in peace.

"Hey, tall Baby Franklin," Zane called to him. "Can you grab me the bread? Austin left it on the top shelf because he thinks I share his crappy sense of humor."

Despite the awful nickname, Kyp smiled. "Sure."

He reached up, and the normalcy ended.

His skin tore, the slice of an imaginary sword. One that had, in reality, been wielded by his mother over a year and a half ago. Senefestrian blood, poisonous to all humans, including Keys, had oozed into the wound and with it, his fate was sealed.

There was no healing this wound.

"Papa?" Jainey called.

Jacklyn swore and Kyp froze. He was still reaching up, but he couldn't bring himself to pull his arm back down.

"'The hell did you do to yourself?"

"Austin, shut up." Drew rushed to his side. "Kyp, what happened?"

A buzz and a beep sounded at the front door, indicating the security system being cleared.

"I'm home," Cass greeted. Her morning class must have ended.

"Cass, your boy is hurt!" Zane called.

A bang and then the sound of footfalls against hardwood floors.

"You managed to break yourself in the five hours I was gone?' Cass asked.

Kyp's eyes slid closed. He should have spoken to her about this in the morning. Finally, he brought his arm down with a grunt.

"You—you're bleeding," Jordan said. Kyp wouldn't look at him. He wouldn't be able to hold it together if he did.

Blood stuck to his T-shirt, running down his side and soaking into his sweatpants.

"Mama! Heal him!" Jainey said, as if she didn't also have the power, as if she didn't remember she could. "Grandpa?"

"They won't," Rennie said. "For the same reason you two haven't moved. You're too busy thinking that's not normal."

"He just started bleeding," Zane said. "It *isn't* normal."

"Yeah, but that's not why Jacklyn isn't healing him." Rennie's voice was cutting. "She's too busy feeling guilty."

"Rennie," Jacklyn warned. Her chair squeaked across the floor as she rose to her feet. "Stop trying to read my emotions. You don't know what you're talking about."

"She's guilty and so is he." Rennie's voice rose to speak over her. "Because whatever is going on, they knew about it and they've been hiding it from us."

Kyp finally turned to fully face them. He didn't know what he looked like, but whatever they saw stopped Rennie right in her tracks. His mouth dried as his family's faces paled. Cass reached forward, and it was like he'd stuffed his mouth full of cotton.

"I just… I wanted to…" He licked his lips. "I wanted a normal day before I explained."

"Explained what?" Drew asked.

"Why don't you all just give him some space?" Ray snapped.

Kyp's vision blurred, twin streaks of tears trickling down his face. He tried to speak, but the words were swallowed by a twisting pain in his side. A groan tore from his throat and Cass gave up any reservations she'd had, stepping forward and offering him support so he didn't have to stand on his own.

Jacklyn appeared before him. He hadn't even seen her move. She stroked his face. "I've got him," she muttered to Cass, taking his weight because she was technically stronger. "It's okay, baby. I told you. We'll figure this out."

"Figure what—" Jordan said.

"Kyp has Senefestrian poisoning," Ray explained, placing his hands on Jordan's shoulders. Zane scooped Jainey up in her arms. Austin wrapped an arm around Rennie.

Drew and Cass shared a pained look.

"Looks like we're all taking some family emergency time off

from work and school," Drew turned to the others as if challenging any of them to question him. "We just went from one mission to two. We need to find out who reopened the Rifts and what they hoped to accomplish. And"—Drew turned back to Kyp and spoke through gritted teeth—"we're going to figure out how to fix this. We're going to find a cure. What we are not going to do is let you die again."

Kyp nodded and rested his head on Jacklyn's shoulder. Cass wrapped an arm around his waist.

Jacklyn offered Kyp a wry smile. "I vote for Drew to be in charge this time around."

Kyp could get behind Drew taking charge. He just wasn't sure Drew should waste the team's time on trying to heal him.

Four

Jacklyn

Drew and Austin followed us up the stairs and into Kyp's bedroom, where I laid him down on the bed.

"Ugh, the sheets," Kyp groaned. "How many times have you changed the sheets since I came back?"

"You're an idiot," I answered.

"An idiot who's dreading making people launder bloody sheets. It's unsanitary," he grumbled.

"I'll have Dad make a Target run."

Kyp smiled, and now I knew he was just trying to distract me. "Not Target. You can get better ones."

"Not if you're just going to bleed all over them," I told him. "Besides, the Target ones are perfectly good, you snob." I sat on the edge of his bed and reached for him, fingers trailing along his jaw. "How do we keep getting into messes like these?"

"We're special."

Austin closed the door, drawing our attention to him. "Sorry to interrupt you two bickering and being all adorable, but I don't want the kids wandering in here," Austin said.

I nodded at Austin. He glanced at Drew, who was already digging in his first aid supplies, tossing a wad of gauze at me. I grabbed it from the air, then pressed it to the wound, soaking up the blood that oozed there.

"She did this to you," I muttered. "One last parting shot from that poisonous monster."

"Which one?" Drew asked. "The Senefestrian or Lavinia?"

"Very funny," I said. "But Kyp already put the Senefestrian down. I'm going to do the same to Lavinia."

"Um… hate to break it to you, darlin', and I know it's been a lot longer for me than it has for you, but didn't you ride her ass like a surfboard all the way down into the Dusk?" Austin laid a hand on my shoulder. "Did she survive that?"

"If I didn't see her die, then she's not dead," I said. "She's way too wily for that shit. If the Rifts reopened, she's behind it. I can almost guarantee it."

Kyp groaned. "Can we not? I'd rather not consider my worst nightmares coming true."

I tossed the soaked gauze to the floor and grabbed another wad from Drew's outstretched hand, applying pressure. It was useless.

The time between deaths was getting shorter. If we didn't act soon, he'd only resurrect long enough to die again.

I'd lose him for good.

"She won't get to you again," I said. "I swear it. On my life. You've already had your last battle with her."

Drew cleared his throat. "What is going on with that thing?"

He knelt on the other side of Kyp, his gaze locked on the swollen, festering sword wound high on Kyp's side. "This should have healed when he died."

Kyp swallowed hard. "It keeps reopening. It's the Senefestrian blood." He gasped for breath. "And it's not just that it won't heal. Been sliced before." He wheezed. "Never hurt like this."

Austin straightened his shirt, like he was trying to look neater. As if that mattered. Based on how gruff his voice sounded when he spoke, he was probably hiding any sign of emotion from Kyp. "Did you try, um, healin' the thing?"

"No, I'm just letting him bleed out. *Of course* I tried healing him!" I crossed my arms over my chest as a shiver raced through my body. "I did it in the Dusk. I've done it here. It won't work." Just to demonstrate, I channeled my Aegis once again, warmth building in my fingertips as I applied them to the wound and begged to be wrong.

"You know it won't work, Jacks," Kyp whispered. "We were stronger in the Dusk and it didn't work there."

I knew that. Of course, I knew that. But I wasn't about to stop trying.

Drew wiped his palms on his turquoise T-shirt. "An Aegis is stronger in the Dusk? Did we know that?"

"Not until we were there, no," I said.

"Interesting." He frowned. "If that wound hasn't healed by now, it isn't getting healed. We have to figure out what to do."

Kyp laughed, a harsh scraping sound. He gripped my forearm tighter, nearly pulling me to the bed beside him. "Or I could just keep dying and coming back to life. At least I come back healed when I do." Another harsh cough sent blood flying from his mouth.

It stained my blue and white checkered button-down, and I watched it spread like fire consuming a sliver of paper. Destruction. It was all around us.

Drew swore and stepped forward, wiping a line of blood from the side of Kyp's lips. A shiver ran down my spine.

Kyp didn't shudder and shake this way from just anything. He'd been through so much that he often dismissed pain. But his face was ashen, and his eyes watered. And he hissed and groaned with each breath. The pain must be excruciating.

"Nah, we need to stop this," Austin argued.

"You'll know when I'm ready to stop when I start turning blue." Kyp glowered at him, but only for a short while before a wave of pain jolted through him, his eyes rolling up into his head. He gritted his teeth. A small grunt escaped.

"Jesus." Austin cringed. "We really need to stop this."

Drew turned a narrowed gaze at Austin. "Yes, thank you, honey. Not really a helpful statement if you don't know how to do that. He's dying *now*."

I nodded, a wave of anguish washing over me, nearly drowning me in its undertow. "He's dying over and over again. And I can't figure out how to stop it." Tears sprang to my eyes.

"We should visit the pocket dimension," Kyp said, eyes hauntingly empty. "The batty old witch will have an answer."

"What?" Austin asked, eyeing the wound with concern.

"Cxarana," Drew said. "He wants to go to see Cxarana. I think he forgot…"

"She's in the Dusk, baby," I said. "We can't ask her."

"I know, I know. Retribution," he muttered, staring off over my shoulder. "You'd like that, wouldn't you? I don't know where he is. I can't. There isn't a solution. There isn't."

I glanced behind me. There wasn't anybody there. Nothing he could even mistake for a person.

"Great idea, little sister," he groaned. "But I can't go back to the Dusk. Cass…"

"I'll go get her." Austin nodded, rushing from the room.

"She's here," Kyp whispered. "Her eyes are here."

"Oh Kyp, what the hell are you talking about?" Drew said, collapsing onto the other side of the bed like his strings had been cut.

"I know. I know. I'll die first," Kyp said with his final breath. And then he was gone again. And I, surrounded by my family and friends, felt so utterly alone.

Drew gently slid Kyp's eyelids closed. "Any idea what he was talking about at the end?"

The question sent fury buzzing through my veins. "Get out."

"Jacklyn, I'm just trying to figure out—"

"He's not a mystery!" I shouted. I knew Drew was trying to help. I knew he wasn't trying to hurt me, that he was trying to spare me greater pain. But none of that mattered at the moment. "He just died. He's dying. He's a person, and he's in tremendous pain every time. I don't care why it's happening or what he was saying. What if he doesn't come back?"

Drew and I had never had much of a chance to get very close. I knew he'd become close friends with Kyp in the year that I was gone, and I knew Austin had been falling for him before I'd… left. But I'd been so absorbed with protecting my children and figuring out my relationship with Kyp that I hadn't gotten much chance to talk to him about anything that didn't involve hatching a plan or mitigating a disaster.

But the moment tears spilled over onto my cheeks, Drew pulled me into a tight hug. "I'm sorry. I'm so sorry," he whispered. "It's gonna be okay. We'll figure this out. We always do."

"We never do," I sobbed. "We suck. We trip our goddamn way into victory if we even achieve it."

"Right. That's true," Drew said, patting my back awkwardly. "We'll make an awful mess out of everything and hopefully keep everyone alive, but we *will do it while figuring out* how to cure him."

I sputtered a near laugh. "God, I hope so."

The door clicked open a crack, revealing a wide-eyed Cass.

"Is he…"

"Yeah," I said, my lungs constricting against the word.

She kept her eyes on me, barely blinking, and it felt pointed, like she couldn't let her eyes trail just to the left, couldn't stand to see Kyp lying there. "Austin said there was some weirdness?"

"Tons of weirdness," Drew said, rising from where he was crouched beside me and moving subtly so Kyp wouldn't be in her line of sight. The gesture was so thoughtful, so observant, I nearly hugged him again.

"Yeah"—Cass stepped into the room and glanced around, only

to zero in on the far wall, the one Kyp had been staring at the entire time—"tons of weirdness."

"What do you see?" Drew asked.

"Just remnants. There was… someone was here."

"Why would they…" I started. "What would the point be? You weren't here. They would just be talking to themselves."

"It wouldn't be the weirdest thing to happen to us." Cass turned her back to me completely. "Keys have reported seeing spirits when they're dying. Nobody knows what happens when you die and come back. But Keys have spoken of visions, of knowing something was going to happen, or of recognizing someone they never met."

My stomach swooped. I had done that. When Ross had first turned on us, I'd known it before I'd been told. I'd seen it. He had stabbed Kyp through his back. But he hadn't. That had never happened. And it happened again when I'd seen Ray comforting me. I saw it when he found me running from the estate. But it hadn't happened until after I'd believed I'd lost Jordan.

My first death. And then a series of deaths in succession. Had they brought me close to death then?

What would happen if Kyp continued to die like this? How close to permanent death was he?

"Can I have a minute alone?" The words squeaked through my throat, which was tight with a lump the size of Austin's home state of Texas blocking it.

"Yes, definitely." Cass was halfway out the door before she'd finished her words.

"What's her deal?" I asked Drew.

"This is probably scaring the crap out of her," he said. "She didn't handle your deaths very well. Anyway, I'm gonna talk to the others. Catch them up on the weirdness." He squeezed my shoulder. "Holler for us if you need anything."

And then I was alone. With Kyp's body.

I took a deep, steadying breath. And burst into tears.

"Honey, when this is over, you and me are going on a trip," I said, squeezing his hand in mine. Maybe he'd remember this too. "We're going to take the kids and go somewhere relaxing. An island? A bustling metropolis? A goddamned yurt? I don't give a shit. But we're definitely not staying here."

He didn't answer. Of course he didn't. Dead people didn't agree to go on vacations.

I swore, loudly and creatively. I punched the bed. Oh god, did I jostle him? What was I talking about? It wasn't like I was going to jostle him awake. He wasn't waking up until whatever mouth that chewed Keys up when they died chose to spit him back out into the world.

I crumbled into myself, drawing my legs up and wrapping my arms around my knees. I buried my face there, closed my eyes, and waited.

My mental struggles had eased, but they hadn't gone away. Time passed around me, and I remained vaguely aware of it passing, but I didn't care. I let it move, swirling past me, like wind blowing leaves. The leaves were my conscious thoughts, and they twirled by me and away, carried on that wind.

Kyp didn't wake up quietly or even slowly, but with a harsh

intake of air as he shot upward. It shocked me out of my thoughts. I watched him from where I'd cradled my head on my knees.

Kyp's eyes darted around in a panic until they finally landed on me. "You okay?" he asked, his voice hoarse.

Was he kidding? Was I okay? The man had just died and then came back to life. Was I okay?

"No, I'm not okay. You died."

"I'm cold. Warm me." He held an arm out and I scrambled over to tuck myself under it. He pulled me against him and I rested my head on his shoulder.

"You're not funny. You aren't helping," I lied.

"It's harder to lose the ones you love than it could ever be to lose yourself. I'm more worried about you and the others. How are you all holding up?"

"You're in pain. Nobody is okay. But I've got a plan." I knew what had to be done. And I would hate every minute of it.

"Ahhh. Coming from you, those are my favorite words."

He didn't even try to hide the sarcasm.

FIVE

JACKLYN

"This is a terrible idea," Ray said.

That should have probably made me feel bad, but then, I was talking to my father, the king of bad ideas, the guy who once started a civil war that wiped out most of the Order, all because he had an idea.

"Well, you know, we ran out of good ideas a long time ago," I said. "If we had any of those, we'd use them." I yanked my work boots onto my feet. I needed to leave, at least for a little while. I couldn't stay in this house and wait to try to heal another wound that wouldn't heal. The futility ate at something deep in my bones. I was nauseated, and my fingers still felt tacky with Kyp's blood. I needed some time away from it before I had to watch him die yet again.

"Okay," Ray said, plaintive, as he inched toward me. "I'm getting ya. But how are we doing this?"

"We know there's an open Rift out there already. We didn't start the fire, but we can light another. We open a second Rift."

"I usually like me a firestarter, but none of my favorites are responsible for lighting this up." He looped an arm around my shoulder. "Which begs the question… Someone has been up to no good. But who?" He scrubbed a hand across the thick stubble on his chin.

"Are you growing that out?" I asked. "Trying to look like an adult?"

He stuck his tongue out at me. "Less mocking my patchy hair growth, more making a solid plan."

I laughed, because I really needed a pick me up. "A Body Key, and you can't grow a beard. Is there no Aegis ability to make your hair grow evenly?"

"No. Sadly, you can't stop your hair from going gray either."

"A shame, really." I walked toward the back door, hoping to get a little air. I didn't think I was ready to go out on the actual street yet. Who knew what would be waiting for me?

"Nice try." Ray followed behind me. "You neglected to mention the rest of the plan."

"The plan is pretty simple. We'd have to split into two groups." I stopped at the back door, yanking at the heavy metal to test it. Our brownstone was a fortress, but I was still as paranoid as Lavinia had made me. "One group would stay here and investigate the possibilities of the open Rifts and protect our world from whatever sneaks through. The other would escort Kyp through the Dusk and keep him safe through all his deaths. They would somehow find Cxarana because nothing in our Ritual book has an answer. Neither does Kyp, and I refuse to accept that this situation is hopeless."

"That sounds dangerous, at least for whoever goes to the Dusk. You don't think taking a journey into the unknown will exacerbate the problem?"

"This isn't a mindless rebellion," I said. "We're opening a Rift to save one of our top soldiers."

"You really believe the Arvokians will know any more about how to cure this than you do?" Ray asked. "The one who helped you in the Dusk couldn't solve it. What makes you think—"

"We're not asking him. We're asking Cxarana. And just because Dhamyan didn't know doesn't mean there isn't any hope of finding an answer."

Ray's jaw clenched.

"Yes, it's dangerous," I said. "But it has to happen." I let go of the door handle and turned to face him again. "Dad, it's Kyp."

He released a heavy sigh, his shoulders dropping. "Oh Birdie, I know." He wrapped me up in his arms, something he did more and more lately. He was glad to have me back, and it showed. Once he realized I would allow it, he wouldn't stop.

Who was I kidding? I buried my face in his shoulder and he held me even tighter. I took a deep breath, filling my lungs with his cologne's spicy scent and letting it ground me.

"You know I'm worried about him too," Ray murmured, his voice muffled by my hair.

"You should go see him," I said. "You're avoiding it. You haven't visited him even when he's been asleep. What's the deal?"

"I... I don't know," he said, backing up to look at me. "I'm scared to lose him? I'm scared to see him that way? My relationship with him is very different from my relationship with you. You and I were on mostly solid ground, but me and Kyp never fixed things. And then he was gone. What if he still hates me?"

"That sounds like a selfish reason not to be there for him." I gave him the kind of look I always did when he was being an idiot. He'd given me plenty of opportunities to perfect it. "I hope you were better for Jordan and Jainey while we were gone."

"So much better." He laughed, tucking my hair behind my ear. "I just considered how you and Kyp would handle anything they threw at me, and I did it that way."

"Parents are supposed to teach their children, not the other way around." My eyebrows raised.

He poked the tip of my nose and I snapped at his finger. A smile flickered on the edges of his lips. "You're wrong, Birdie. Parents have been learning from their children for all time. You look at Jordan and Jainey and tell me you're not flyin' by the seat of your pants at every turn."

"You may have a point there." I planted a kiss on his cheek. "But then, they were a bit more of a surprise than we were. Especially since you literally chose Kyp." A small smack to the same cheek.

"Jordan's out there, by the way." He motioned toward the door. "In case you wanted solitude."

"Nah, just wanted air." I pulled the door open. "More than enough out there for both of us."

Besides, it would be good to get some more time with Jordan. We hadn't had much time to talk. It never felt like there was enough time.

I walked through the security vestibule and out into the perfect spring air. No jacket needed, and despite the sun warming my face, it wasn't so hot that my long-sleeve shirt felt like too much. The freshly cut grass assaulted my nose with the scent of green, of growth and renewal. Despite everything.

Jordan sat at the far end of the backyard, back to the brick wall, balanced on a cushioned wood bench. He'd unfurled a sketch pad across his lap, his legs crossed under him, and his head was bowed over his work. His black hair hung over his eyes and he huffed and pushed it out of the way again.

God, he looked like my memories of Kyp, from when he was only a couple of years older than Jordan was now.

I waited until I was close enough to see the earbuds in his ears, the ones I knew only somewhat worked to dampen the world around him. Jordan wasn't just a regular Key. He was a Skeleton Key, and that meant that while I needed to channel my Aegis, Jordan's Aegis was always active. He just had to keep it under control.

"Whatcha drawing?" I asked. His fingers clenched around the pencil. He drew in short, feathered strokes. The grass of the estate grounds, a different home, a different backyard. "I didn't know you'd ever been to the estate."

"Your memorial is there. We thought you'd want to be buried near Grandma Jaina and Aunt Gana. Even though there was, like, nothing to bury… We thought the memorial should be there, anyway. Symbolic, you know?" He shrugged.

I scoffed. "I hated it there. And Mom and Gana are wherever they want to be. Next time, anywhere else would be preferable."

His hand stilled, and his head shot up until his eyes locked with mine. Hazel eyes filled with fire, the bit of Gana and Mom I saw in him. "Can we not joke about you being dead again while Dad is dying? I came out here to calm down."

Yikes. Me and my stupid mouth. "Sorry. My dark sense of humor is really shitty. I didn't mean to make it worse."

Jordan nodded, returning to his sketching. "I came outside to get a stronger sense of… the vibe. I don't know, the ambience. To help me grasp the outdoor feeling of being at the estate. I just… wanted to draw it. And my memory didn't help."

"You have a perfect memory, just like your father. And that reference didn't help?"

"It didn't feel real enough. I don't know. I needed to feel like I was there, not just remember what it looked like."

"It was a good idea, getting some air." I tried for a smile.

"Yeah, well, my therapist said I should try that. She suggested the drawing too."

"A therapist?" I asked, eyes wide. "That… could not have been a completely honest relationship."

"It totally wasn't." Jordan laughed. "I could talk about grief, but not about rapidly aging. I could talk about just meeting my biological parents, but not about being experimented on by evil doctors. She helped me with the panic attacks a lot, but I stopped going. Like, what's the point? I can't tell anyone about the real problems. Zane even tried to poke around to find out if there was a therapist who worked with people who had an Aegis. There was. Guess who they worked for?"

"Livingston." Because of course.

"Zane backpedaled so fast, there was a Zane-shaped hole in their digital wall. She had trouble covering our tracks. Hasn't even poked at the computer since unless she had to." Jordan put the pencil down and set the pad aside. "We've been trying, but… I don't know if we can fit into the real world. Our Aegis is so much of who we are. Rennie was terrified Officer Austin would end up taking a bullet because he forgot he couldn't just heal."

"Yeah. That's scary." I nodded. "But to be fair, we *are* in the real world. It's everybody else who doesn't know what's really going on."

We sat in pensive silence, and Jordan turned his head up toward the sun.

"Are we going to lose Dad?"

It was moments like these that I wished my children were the actual age they should be at this point, so they would be completely unaware of what was going on. They didn't need more pain in their lives. They were just getting their chance at normalcy. Sure, it would take a while for them to figure it out, but they would be all the better for it.

They all would.

"Jordan," I sighed. "I know you haven't gotten that much of a chance to get to know me, but what happened when Livingston tried to take you from me? I shot out the tires of the car you were in. And when they took Jainey? I went to war. And when Kyp fell in that Rift? I threw myself right in after him. What does that look like to you?"

"Like you make reckless decisions?" He smirked, and it looked so much like Kyp's my heart ached.

"Like I will do *anything* to save my family," I corrected. "And I will. I will fight through hell and back if that's what it takes to save him. Hell, since I came back from the dead and got a second chance at a happy ending, you better believe I'm going to find a way for us all to have one."

Jordan sagged slightly, laying his head on my shoulder. I wrapped my arms around him.

"It's going to be okay," I said. "We're going to figure it out."

"Or you'll die trying." He lifted the pencil and twirled it between his fingers. "That's exactly what I'm afraid of."

He could have punched me in the gut and it would have hurt less. "I'll try to do better this time. We didn't want to leave you."

"I know. I know." His voice was choked. "You had no choice. That's what this world leaves us, right? No good options."

"We do what we can with what we have. That's all we can do," I said. "I know how much it sucks, but that's real life. Not even just our lives. I spent most of my time in the normal world, and it was true there, too. Few people are born lucky enough to have a whole lot of good options. Most people are just trying to get by."

"Yeah… I guess." Jordan shrugged out of the hug. "I'm gonna go inside now."

He looked so dejected with his shoulders slumped, eyes on the stones under his feet.

"Jordan…"

"Nah, it's okay, Mom. I have to go inside, anyway. It's my

day to clean the bathrooms, and it's starting to get late. I should get to work." He walked a few steps away before rushing back and planting a kiss on my cheek. "Love you."

"Love you too, kiddo."

I watched him leave and wished I had better things to say. Some better words of comfort. But I had nothing. I was barely handling any of this myself.

I closed my eyes and breathed in deeply, rolling onto my side so I was lying across the bench. I tried to meditate, to clear my head. Cass had once explained that meditation wasn't actually about having an empty mind. It was actually about acknowledging the thought and moving on from it.

I wished Mom was here, and breathed it away. Saw Gana with a streak of red along her throat, breathed it away. Wondered why Austin talked around me rather than to me, breathed it away. Believed I'd never be enough to comfort Jainey and Jordan through this, breathed it away. Considered using my Aegis to see if Ray had bothered to visit Kyp, breathed it away. How did the Rifts reopen? Breathe. Should I even be alive if coming back meant I put everyone else in danger? Breathe. Maybe that was why Austin couldn't talk to me? Breathe. And why Kyp wasn't really back? Because we shouldn't be here, even if we wanted to be. Breathe. Breathe. Breathe.

"Careful. You'll make yourself hyperventilate." Kyp. "Again."

I peeled my eyes open and blinked. It was dark. When had it gotten dark? How long had I been sitting out here trying to blow my problems away?

I hated losing time, but it seemed it hadn't ended with death, no matter how much more permanent it was this time around. No matter what happened to me, dissociation seemed to be my jam.

"You missed dinner." Kyp stepped forward, closing the distance between us in several easy strides like the tall bastard he was. His footsteps were feather light as they moved across the floor, stealthy even when at peace. All traces of a limp had disappeared.

His dark hair was pushed back messily from his forehead. He was going to require a man bun soon, and I didn't know how to feel about that. On the one hand, it would look hot. On the other hand, it was a douchey kind of hot. But then… sometimes Kyp was just a little douchey, so it might work for him.

Yep, I'd lost the ability to think like a mature human being today. Where were the adults? We had Zane and Ray, but those were slim pickings in the adult department.

Pfft. You're the adult. Let's be real. You always had to be.

The Gana in my head was just as right as the real Gana always was.

"What are you doing out here, Jacks?" He flopped down onto the bench next to me, looping his arm around me. Since we came back, he didn't seem to want to be in a space with me without touching me. Had he always been this openly affectionate? Our relationship had so many ups and downs, it was hard to know. But then, before we'd died, we'd blown the hell out of the walls we'd had up. Maybe it had helped. Maybe this was who we really were.

I seemed to be questioning everything lately.

"Counting the stars," I lied.

Kyp leaned toward me, nudging until I focused on him. His dark eyes zeroed in on mine, his eyebrows raised. "First of all, you're lying because you can barely see anything with all the light pollution in this city."

"Aegis!" I argued.

"Secondly," he continued as though I'd said nothing at all, "if you could even see the stars, you could sit out here all night and never count all of them. It's a pointless exercise. Much like whatever you're actually doing."

"Pointless?" I laughed. Oh, sweet deflection. "It's pointless for me to count every little birthmark you've got, but you've got fifteen. There's one right along the edge of—"

"Why are you really out here, Jacks? Got lonely? Not enough people in the house?" He cut me off with a wave of his hand, his tone solemn and commanding. His words grew clipped, his voice deeper, and just like that, there wasn't any avoiding it.

I sighed and let my head flop back onto the bench. "I can't stop thinking. My head hasn't stopped spinning since we got back. And I can't sleep. I haven't slept in four days and it isn't getting any better. When I fall asleep, I remember..." The cold blackness we came from. The chill of death. "I feel like I'm slipping again. Like that night. I know we made the right choice for them. To save them. But we willingly chose to die. It's terrifying."

"We did what we needed to do."

"Not the most heroic solution—"

"We gave our lives for our kids. And it didn't leave them feeling abandoned, it left them feeling loved. It *was* the most heroic solution." Kyp sighed. "Jacklyn, we've spent the last couple of years doing the best we can, and that's all we can do. We're just sputtering through this mess. None of what we thought we knew is real."

"Weird that these days you're where I started, huh?" I leaned into him. "You were the one who knew everything, and I had no idea what was going on. Now, you're just as lost as I am."

He snorted a laugh. "In some ways, I was just as lost then." He leaned forward, pressing his lips to mine, and I lost myself in him, the pull of his warm mouth, the lull of his gentle rhythm, the soft way his hands pushed through my hair. I deepened the kiss, and his moan of appreciation drowned out the murmured thoughts in the back of my head.

"I love you," I whispered against his lips.

"I love you too." I could hear the smile in his tone, and my eyes opened to find a mischievous glint in his.

"What?"

"I was thinking… We've probably got an hour or two before my body decides it hates me again." He waggled his eyebrows.

It was difficult to hear that and not immediately crumble under the thought of him potentially dying again in an hour or two. But I didn't want to spoil the tease in his words, the way his head tilted in invitation.

It wasn't like it was a chore, anyway.

"You'll have to catch me first." I took off for the house and he followed, laughing, and grabbed for me.

SIX

KYP

"Are you sure about this?" Zane said, as if Kyp hadn't thought this over.

"Are you?" he asked. "Jacklyn's liable to kill you before you can explain."

She was standing behind him, but he could imagine her expression. "I would like to think our friendship has earned me better than that."

"She may not be thinking that clearly," he pointed out, sitting up and fidgeting in the desk chair. Would she warn him, or would it just happen? He didn't want to know it was coming. But maybe he should… "I'm just saying it doesn't have to be you. I could ask someone else."

"I could kill you and it could change nothing," she said. "You could come back and the wound could open up again."

"Or it could reset something?" Even he wasn't sure he believed that. "I just keep dying because of that wound. Maybe if I die before the wound begins to open, it won't open the next time. If I fail, it's simply a chance to rule out another potential correction."

"You're losing it, Baby Franklin." Metal clicked behind him; he knew that sound. She had cocked her gun.

"*I'm* losing it? You're the one who's going to do it."

She sighed. "You're right."

Black.

Kyp's eyes snapped open, a shiver racing through him. Jacklyn sat beside his bed, her arms crossed over her chest, lips pursed, teeth clenched.

It took a minute for his brain to catch up with what had happened. Zane definitely hadn't warned him.

"I can explain."

"You already did. With a letter and everything. And that was supposed to justify having Zane kill you."

"You've done similar things before." He regretted it the minute it came out of his mouth. But it felt right to say. Rewarding somehow. Like it lifted a little bit of the darkness around his edges.

Jacklyn swallowed, her eyes darting away for just a second before meeting his gaze head on. "I was broken when I killed myself to save Austin. I did it and it helped, but it was dangerous and painful for the entire team, and possibly completely unnecessary, although we'll never know."

"It's been a week, Jacklyn. You and the team are digging through books I've already read, looking for something I didn't find when I remember everything." Anger bubbled up within him, a furious rage that heated his blood and dissipated the searing cold death brought. "What did you all imagine I did when I was trapped in that house with that murderous monster of a mother? Did you think I twiddled my fucking thumbs all day? I read every one of those books and I remember all of it. And do you want to know why there is nothing that will give you a hint to where the Arvokians hide in the Dusk? Do you?"

Jacklyn met his ire directly. Her chin lifted in defiance as it always was when faced with something she didn't want to hear. It only made him angrier.

"Why, Kyp?"

"Because the Arvokians gave us all of our information. They. Didn't. Want. Us. To. Know!" He threw a pillow at the far wall, praying for some of this to drill through her thick skull. God, he loved her, but she was so damn stubborn.

And he just…

He just…

He didn't want to die again.

Not again.

"God, Jacks, maybe I came back wrong this time." Tears swelled, but it wasn't fear that brought them on. It was anger. Frustration. Helplessness. His head dropped forward, hair that was greasy with sweat falling in his eyes. "The nightmares don't stop. They blend into reality until I'm not sure what's happening and what are floating scraps of old dreams and memories bleeding through. I'm losing it."

"It's been lost," she said, and though meant as a joke, it failed miserably with the tremor in her voice. She laid a hand on his shoulder and squeezed, her other hand coming up to cup his face, bringing his eyes back to her. She still had that defiant burn in her eyes, but somehow it didn't anger him. This time, it was a promise. "One more day, baby. One more day and if we can't find anything, the mission begins. Can you give me that?"

"Yes," he whispered. "Fine." He tried for a smile. "And who knows? Maybe my plan worked and I reset things, right?"

As it turned out, his plan did not work.

His consciousness returned sluggishly this time, as it sometimes did. He woke with a shiver, but his eyes remained closed. Because no.

No. No. No. No. No.

It didn't work. He couldn't keep doing this.

The scent of mint filled the air, telling Kyp he wasn't alone.

"I know you're back." Ray. It was the first time he'd been there when he woke.

Kyp didn't know how to feel about that. So he went with snark. Jacklyn truly had infected him. "Really? I thought I was doing a pretty good impression of a corpse." He peeled his eyes open finally and glanced at Ray.

He sat facing the bedside table, where he had placed a silver tea tray with two teacups filled with steaming liquid and a matching silver teapot. "I was hoping you'd wake up soon. I brought some afternoon tea." He sounded awfully peppy, too peppy for Kyp's ears at the moment. "How are you feeling?"

"Like absolute shit, Ray." His voice scraped from his throat. "I'm either dead or I'm awake. And just when I think I can finally fall asleep and have a real night's rest, I'm dying again, and we both know how relaxing that is not."

Ray swore under his breath. He closed his eyes and took several deep breaths. "Well, on the plus side, I brought mint tea, because it's supposed to bring energy. Don't know what tea would help with the dying."

Kyp's lips twitched despite himself. "Pretty sure tea won't fix this one."

"Don't knock it till you've tried it. Just need to decide on the right blend…" He trailed off, and Kyp could see him devising a list of ingredients in his head.

"Maybe some Dreviara? We could whip up a nice Death-Bringer Ritual with that one."

Ray's gaze swung to Kyp's, his eyes hard. "Fuck that, son. You're not giving up. You're not ready."

"*You're* not ready."

"No! Damn it all, Kyp. I'm not ready!" Ray slammed a fist on the mattress beside him, then reached out to steady Kyp when it jostled him.

Kyp smacked his hand away. "This isn't about you!"

"It isn't just about you either!" Ray shouted. "Ya damn plank! For the first time, it couldn't be less about me. I hate this. I hate that it's happening and I know you don't believe me, but I can't see you like this. It's breaking me up. But Jacklyn? Jordan? *Jainey?* This is gonna destroy them. So, don't you make it out like I'm the one being the selfish twat here!"

Well. That was unexpected.

Something ugly and desperate filled his throat, and Kyp went with it, forcing his emotions down deep where they could no longer toy with him. He wasn't terrified of dying again. He didn't want to beg Ray for a solution Kyp knew he couldn't provide. He wasn't going to cry. The tears would do nothing to eliminate the crushing feeling in his chest.

"What are you doing?" Kyp asked, and even he flinched at the tone he'd taken.

Ray looked like a wounded puppy, big round eyes aimed his way. "Whaddya mean?"

"You haven't been here since I got back. You've barely spoken with me. Why are you here now?" His jaw clenched painfully.

"I'm… I took a shift when you first got back. I waited for you to wake up and I was proper excited about it too. I missed you and Jacks so much, like a hole in my soul. You don't even know, and hopefully you never will. Losing your child…"

"You didn't much care about losing us for most of our lives, and suddenly it hurts like hell?" Kyp muttered.

"There is a massive difference between knowing somcone is safe and alive and having to be away from them and knowing they're gone forever."

"Not forever, as it turned out."

"Not yet, no." Ray leaned forward. "But think about what you just said. I was just starting to make peace with you being gone, then you came back, and now you're itchin' to leave again? Where's that fighting spirit? The one that completely ignored me when I told you to stay away from my daughter because you believed you could save the world together? Just skipping out now?"

"What? I haven't died enough for you? Haven't been tortured enough?" Kyp spat his words like acid. "I got the point. The message is clear. I don't have to want to leave. Not when this world wants me dead."

Ray's shoulders sagged, his head falling forward. When his gaze met Kyp's, there were tears in his green eyes.

He looked older. Tired.

"Kyp."

"Raymond." He tried for a neutral tone, but his voice shook.

"Son."

It didn't matter that the title wasn't exactly accurate. "Dad."

Ray flopped back into his chair like he'd taken a physical blow. "We're going to find you a cure. And I'm going with you."

Kyp's eyebrows raised. "But Jacklyn won't be coming. One of us needs to stay with the kids, and if I have to be there, Jacklyn will be here in the Dawn."

"I'm not seeing why that would be relevant." He lifted one of the teacups and saucers. He scowled at them when the dishes clattered with the shaking of his fingers. He took a long sip before continuing. "Jacklyn is healthy and will have her own mission. You're sick and need your… You need me more. I'm coming with you."

He couldn't… Ray always put Jacklyn first. And he was always happy for her. Ray was her father, after all. But it hadn't changed the hope in Kyp's heart, the feeling that he'd be chosen by a man who wasn't his father, but who had chosen to serve in that role. And Ray was right. Jacklyn didn't need him here, but God, did Kyp need him.

The words cracked his chest open, tears spilling over his eyes, and he was helpless because of this damn push and pull of death, but he couldn't stop the flood of emotions. "You're sure?" he croaked.

Ray put the teacup down and leaned over, brushing Kyp's bangs from his eyes. "Positive. The kids will need Cass, but Drew can go with us. And Austin. I would say Zane, but there isn't likely to be any tech for her to tangle with." He smiled, his crow's feet deepening, though his eyes shone with tears. "I'm sure Austin wouldn't be your favorite choice, but we need strength to get you around when you aren't at your best."

"Tex is fine," Kyp admitted, the first time he'd ever owned up to it. "It's a good group."

"Damn right it is." Ray clapped his hand on his shoulder. "Now, when's the last time you had a haircut? You look all floppy, and I, for one, won't stand for it… unless you want to keep it that way?"

He thought about it for a moment. He'd always kept his hair a little long, but never this long. This long had started with losing Jaina, Gana, and then believing he'd lost Jacklyn. This long was a sign of tragedy. If he was to attempt a quest to find a cure, one that required hope…

"No. It can go. But not because you said. It's just time." He plucked at the sheet beneath him.

"Thank Jesus!" And with that Irish brogue, it was more like Jay-sus.

Kyp glanced up, and Ray already had a pair of shears in hand. "Wow, really?"

"I was hoping. You look a mite shaggy." He shrugged.

It was such a stupid thing to do, and somehow, so incredibly

Ray.

For the first time that day, Kyp laughed like he meant it.

"I want you to have something," Ray said, his voice solemn as he pulled Jacklyn aside. Kyp watched, his arms wrapped around his center. Jacklyn and the kids were saying goodbye to Ray, and Rennie and Cass were saying goodbye to Austin and Drew. Zane stood beside Kyp, watching Ray with the same trepidation he felt, though probably for very different reasons.

It had oddly been Jacklyn's decision to return to the estate's backyard to do this. They couldn't exactly open a Rift in a stretch of green space in Central Park where anybody could just accidentally step into it.

She still looked antsy as she stood waiting, still hated the estate and everything it represented. And for legitimate reasons. She'd already promised to be on the road heading back to the city the minute they were through the Rift. Time was different on either side, anyway. It wasn't like she could jump in and rescue anyone without hours passing in the Dusk, even if she moved through right after them.

Ray reached into his pocket and produced a chain, the gold faded with age. He unclenched his fist and let the pendant swing free. It looked rather weighty.

The light breeze rippled through Jacklyn's hair as her fingertips brushed across the pendant. "A locket?"

Ray offered her a dazzling smile. "It's got a little secret in it." He opened it. "Looks like a normal locket. Even has a picture of your fella and the tykes. But look." He opened a compartment and though Kyp couldn't see what was there, Jacklyn's eyes told him it was something good.

"You really trust me with that?" she asked, her eyes wide and hopeful.

"You need to keep this on you." He pushed a lock of hair behind her ear. It popped right back out, her wild curls never bending to anyone's will, not even her own. "We don't know what opened those damned Rifts, and I'd be a real shit if I didn't leave you with some sort of defense. There isn't much of it left, but I'm going to try to grab some more while I'm in the Dusk."

He must have given her Arvokian herbs. He'd mentioned needing to get more earlier, and they could be used as a form of defense. It was a damn good idea. One Kyp had been too self-absorbed to come up with.

"Have you ever been in the Dusk?" Jordan asked.

"My first time," Ray admitted, bouncing on his heels. "Gonna be an adventure, to be sure."

Yes, it would be that.

"What about work? It's already been a week, and you said you don't know how long you'll be gone. You're gonna miss a lot," Rennie said. "How will you—"

Kyp's attention ticked to Rennie, watching as she spoke to Austin.

"Ren, I hate to break it to you," Austin said, arm slung around her shoulders. "Until the Rifts are closed again, I don't think any of us will be going back to work or school. It's not safe for any of you to be alone. Not really safe for us, either."

Another thing Kyp hadn't thought of. "Some father…" he chided himself.

"You haven't even had a chance to figure out what kind of father you are," Zane scoffed.

Kyp frowned. He hadn't realized she was that close.

"But you *are* brave," she continued. "Incredibly stupid, but brave."

Kyp nodded. "Maybe sometimes. But this time, it's entirely out of necessity. I'm not going into the Dusk to be a damn hero or anything. It's my only hope of survival."

"Well, I'm counting on you to keep his head on straight," she said, motioning to Ray. "He's gotten better, but he's still him. Don't let him turn this into a crusade."

"Tell that to Tex," Kyp said. "I'll be dead half the time."

Zane bit lightly at her red-painted lip. "Just be careful out there, Baby Franklin."

"Please stop calling me that."

"No can do." She ruffled his newly cut hair. "You're precious." With a wink and a grin, she headed for where Ray had waited.

Kyp stared down at the dew droplets dangling from the blades of grass surrounding his feet.

"Do you have a plan?" Cass sidled up beside him.

"You know I don't." He glanced at her from the corner of his eye. "I saw very little of the Dusk the first time I was there. I have no idea what to expect."

"I really should go with you," she said. "We don't even know what you'll need, and—"

"The Sentinels may come back," he said. The Sentinels were the three spirits that protected the Skeleton Keys: Jacklyn's mother, Jaina; her sister, Gana; and Cass's own sister, Mari. "And if they do, you'll need to be close to Jainey and Jordan. You know that."

Cass sighed. "I'm your right hand. I should be going."

"I'll be okay. The guys will watch my back."

"I know they will. I already threatened them with death if they didn't." She threw an arm around his waist and squeezed. "Stay safe," she mouthed, and then she walked away, probably to scare the life out of Drew.

He turned away from Cass just in time for Jainey to fling herself at him, hitting his stomach so roughly he almost tipped backwards.

"Remember your strength, Jainey," Jordan admonished, though it was soft. He was just behind her, waiting his turn to say goodbye.

Kyp petted her hair affectionately. "I'm okay, but thank you."

"Can't you stay a little longer?" Jainey whimpered, burying her head in his chest. "You just got home!"

"I'm sorry, nugget." He kissed the top of her head. "I'll be back as fast as I can."

"That won't be fast enough." She looked up at him with tear-filled eyes and a pout on her lips. "I thought I was never going to see you again."

His chest tightened and his throat hurt at the sight of her looking so distraught.

"It's gonna be alright, Bean," he whispered. "The whole point of this trip is to find a way to come back to you healthy and whole. And once I'm back, I'll never leave you again, I promise."

"You better not," she cried.

Ray had been right. He was furious at him for the way he'd spoken, and he'd been right. This was his goal. He had to go into the Dusk and he had to find a cure. His little girl demanded it. And that was enough.

Jordan reached over her and clasped him in a tight hug. "Be careful over there. We need you here."

He soaked up their love. Knowing they were waiting for him made all of it easier to endure.

"Okay, okay," Jacklyn said. "Let him breathe a little."

Jordan stepped back, pulling Jainey away with him. "On the plus side, we get a lot of Mom time."

"Lucky you." He grinned as Jacklyn stepped forward.

"I love you so much, you enormously stubborn pain in the ass." She yanked at Kyp's jacket, pulling him in and pressing a hard kiss against his lips. "Be safe."

Kyp cupped her face in his hands, sliding across the soft skin of her rounded cheeks. "I love you, Jacks." One more kiss, this one lingering. He wrapped a hand around her waist and pulled her closer until they were pressed together.

Austin's gagging noises almost weren't enough to make him stop. He was aware they had an audience, but wasn't sure he cared.

He chose not to scandalize Ray and the kids too much and pulled back, but not too much, just enough to press their foreheads against each other. His fingers brushed through her silky tresses and he treasured this moment, grateful for his perfect memory if it meant she would be with him for his entire trip.

"Take care of them." He motioned toward the children. "See what you can find out about the Rifts opening, but try to avoid engaging. If someone has found a way to open their own Rifts, whether it's the obvious option or another, we shouldn't deal with them until we have our full team."

The obvious option. His brother, Caleb. Another one of the kids they'd rescued from Livingston. Little good that had done. Caleb hadn't been happy about any of it.

Jacklyn's lips twitched. "Fine. But if I hear you've taken any unnecessary risks in the Dusk, I'll be bitter."

Kyp smiled, pressing his lips against hers again before stepping back. "I'd expect nothing less." He looked at Jordan. "Your time to shine, kiddo."

He nodded, kneeling down before all of them. Reaching into his pocket, he produced a switchblade. Kyp's instinct was to ask if he carried it with him everywhere, but that was foolish. He hadn't needed to before, when he'd been safely removed from their perilous world, and now it was essential. The last thing he wanted to do was discourage him from protecting himself.

With a wince, Jordan sliced along his wrist, and Kyp flinched, his thoughts gone to that day standing over a Rift, red and black light flickering along Jacklyn's features in a foreign land. Dying over that Rift.

Jordan squeezed the injured arm over the circle they'd created before them, garnet drops falling among the verdant blades of grass. His movements appeared to be practiced, near ritualistic.

Kyp glanced away, only to squint against the sunshine. He clenched his hands into fists, a growl bubbling up inside him that he fought to suppress. He couldn't watch his son bleed himself like it was normal. When he got back, he'd ask Jordan how many times he'd opened a Rift when he'd been in Livingston's hands.

Despite the many times he'd seen a Rift seal, including the most traumatizing of those times, he'd never seen a Rift actually open. As Jordan worked, the wind picked up around them, the normal aromas of grass were overtaken by a sulfuric stench, and a blood red flame-like light emerged from the floor. Then the words spilled from his mouth. Arvokian. Like he was a native speaker.

The grass within the circle flaked away, like ashes from burning paper, dispersing in the wind until only a tear in the Dusk remained. And there it would endure until they returned and he or Ray sealed it.

Creating a Rift was anathema to everything that drove them, but it was also exhilarating. An insignificant amount of his son's blood created a nearly inconceivable symbol of the power of humanity's saviors. His boy had done that. It was a strange, heady feeling.

Kyp glanced back at the abandoned building that had once been his home, a chill running down his spine.

Kyp took one last lingering look at his kids, at Jacklyn.

She smiled and nodded, and it gave him all the courage he needed.

With a returned nod, he stepped through the Rift and into the Dusk, the other members of his team at his side.

Seven

Reunion

Jacklyn

Jainey wouldn't stop crying. It was hurting me, but worse, it was hurting her. She'd thrown up twice. Her head was pounding. I couldn't watch her do this to herself anymore.

She buried her face in my chest and I stroked her hair. She needed a distraction if she was going to get through this. Hell, so did I.

Guilt twisted like a viper in my chest. I shouldn't procrastinate. We really needed to figure out where Caleb was and if he'd been the one responsible for re-opening the rifts. Still…

"Why don't we go out and do something today?"

Jainey hiccupped a sob and shook her head, though all I could see was the puff of her brown curls moving.

I frowned down at her head. "It's okay to cry, but it's not good for you to just sit here feeling awful."

"I don't wanna," she croaked.

"You liked it last time we went out for a mother/daughter day, right?" I said.

"Papa and

muffled in my shirt. "I can't go out and have fun when Papa is hurt."

It did feel weird to try to proceed as normal. "Listen, we can't do anything about it right now. All we can do is hope that Grandpa, and Austin, and Drew will take care of Papa and find a way to help."

She sat up, swiping at the tears in her eyes with her chubby little hands. "You're just procrastinating."

"I hate your vocabulary." I stuck my tongue out at her.

"You're proud of my vocabulary, liar."

"I *admire* your vocabulary. I *aspire* to your vocabulary. But that's not the point," I said. "And I'm not procrastinating. I made a promise to myself when we came back that the mission would never be more important than you and your brother."

Jainey rubbed her eyes and rolled off the bed to look out the window. "It looks like a nice day out."

Her voice was hesitant, but she brightened when the sun shone upon her face.

"Give me a day," I said, getting out of the bed and playing with her hair. "We'll go to the Children's Museum of Manhattan. I looked it up. It's not too far. And you'll like it. Promise."

She glanced back over her shoulder at me, the pout evident. "Fine. But first, I'm getting a glass of water. I'm parched."

I fought against the twitch of my lips as they threatened to form a smile. She wouldn't appreciate that at all.

"You can have a whole breakfast if you want."

"There has never been a brighter place in the history of this Earth, I swear," I groaned to Zane as I looked around at the museum where I now half-regretted begging to bring Jainey.

It was weird seeing Jainey play with other children. She invited playmates, but didn't stick with them long, and as I watched her climb her way up the treehouse in the superhero learning area, I worried. Not for her ability to climb. That, she could handle. I was more concerned about her ability to fit in. My school years had been hard enough.

I couldn't imagine Jainey going through school with the combined weirdness of me, Kyp, and years growing up in a lab. I couldn't imagine being her mother and not stomping onto the playground, fury blazing.

Jainey jumped down off the treehouse like it was nothing, which it probably was for her, given her Body Key heritage, and darted away from the other kids toward a series of colorful, floating scarves. Jainey glanced around the room for a moment.

"Do you see it?" Zane asked.

I did. Jainey was calculating, trying to figure out how the attraction in this new room worked. She glanced from the top of the enclosure to the tiles on the bottom and from wall to wall. And then she rushed toward the center and knelt on the floor.

"Jainey, no," Zane said. Her tone was a warning.

Jainey glanced back at her, her eyes shining with intelligence, and backed away from the center tile to spin and twirl around between the floating scarves.

Zane jutted her chin out, motioning toward the child. "Watch."

Jainey only stalled for a moment before she dove for the center tile and stuffed her fingers under it. I took off toward the enclosure.

"You heard Zane," I said.

Jainey looked up at me with round, innocent eyes. "Yeah, but she didn't mean it. It's a puzzle. This is a test like the ones at the facility. I figured out the answer." She pointed to three specific spots on the floor and two spots on the ceiling. "There are vents hidden in specific locations. The vent control panel is under this tile. I can hear the thrum of the energy."

When I focused, I could hear what she meant—the low-level buzz of electricity moving through the floor. "You're right, but this isn't training. It's supposed to be fun." I heard the distraction in my own tone. The sound of the energy drew my focus.

I placed my palm down on the tile, and the electric hum ended with a click. My vision went purple.

I blinked.

It wasn't my vision that was purple. It was a scarf. I yanked it off my face.

Jainey giggled. "Mama, you're so silly. You told me not to, and then you made them all fall."

"What?" Numbly, I glanced around the room. The scarves had all fluttered to the floor.

I hadn't meant to do that. How had I done that?

I moved my hand off the tile, then placed it back again to see what happened. Nothing. The scarves were vibrant streaks spread across the floor.

Zane's pointy heels clicked across the floor. Why she came to the museum wearing navy blue stiletto booties, I could not understand.

"Back away, please," Zane said. Jainey and I scooted backward.

She crouched beside us, her red lips twisted in a frown. Her eyes narrowed, and she placed her palm down on the tile.

The vents came back online, and the scarves lifted into the air again, sheer strips of red, purple, yellow, orange, and green fabric billowing around us.

"What the hell?" The words dribbled from my lips.

Zane's eyes tripped from the panel to me. "Had to be a coincidence. You can't do that."

I thought back to a year and a half ago when Austin accidentally healed Jordan. Austin, who could only ever heal himself.

"Exactly. That was just really weird timing." I nodded.

"*Really* weird," Zane said.

"Or Mama's magic." Jainey smiled, a small secretive thing. She actually looked hopeful for the first time since Kyp had left.

She got up and sprinted back to the superhero treehouse headquarters, satisfied to run and play in there like something creepy hadn't just happened.

Or maybe it hadn't. Maybe I was just panicking.

"That water exhibit was astounding," Jainey said. She had a skip in her step as she moved down the street toward home. From the time she left the scarf exhibit, Jainey's energy had been contagious. She moved from one exhibit to another, her eyes wide. I hadn't been sure she would enjoy it. She knew so much already. Did she really need a museum for children? But just like I remembered from my childhood with Kyp, it wasn't the knowledge that she took from a place like that. It was the experience.

"Did you see my new best friend?" she asked, cutting into my thoughts.

"What a quick relationship you two formed," I teased.

"Well, she called me her best friend, but I'm probably not going to see her again. The city is ginormous and based on statistical—"

"Who knows?" Zane said, ruffling the kid's curls. "Maybe she lives in the neighborhood."

"She definitely doesn't go to my school." Jainey sighed. "She said she liked my hair. I liked her shirt."

"Was it the color? You like green?" I took her hand in mine.

Jainey jumped up onto the garden ledge, walking along it like she was on a balance beam. "Yeah, but it isn't my favorite. My favorite color is cerulean blue. And her shirt wasn't green. It was sage. They don't teach you colors like that in school."

I stifled a laugh. "Well, no. They keep it a little more simple at first."

Zane snickered. "Jainey hates that."

"Well, behold the Order's queen and princess, respectively." A male voice cut into our conversation.

Zane stiffened beside me. I whirled toward the voice's source.

"I honestly didn't expect you to have the gumption to bring Jainey out virtually unguarded, even though it's good to see her face."

"Caleb?" Jainey screeched. Before I could stop her, my little girl hurled herself into his arms.

Dammit. I'd been procrastinating about figuring out how the Rifts had reopened. The answer had found its way to me instead.

I'd just wanted a nice day out with my daughter. Wasn't that just the way?

Caleb looked different than I remembered. His blond hair was longer and more shaggy. He'd grown broader in our time away. Though not by much. He still had Kylie and Lavinia's genes, and they were both slender. But where he'd been skinny before, he was developing a lean muscular build more like Jordan and Kyp's.

It was still weird to wrap my head around the fact that this kid was Kyp's brother, and though he was Jordan's age and they'd grown up (however rapidly they'd been aged) together, he was technically his and Jainey's uncle.

Caleb caught Jainey easily. "Hey, kiddo. Missed you."

"Kid, I swear to God, high-speed hugs are all you do these days." I sighed. "Hi, Caleb. You remember Zane?"

"Yeah." He kissed the top of Jainey's curls, then lowered her to the floor. "Hi, Zane. Sorry I didn't take you up on your offer." Zane had told me she'd tried to set him up with a new ID and a new life with the others, but he had declined.

I didn't trust this. He hadn't run into us by accident. If he wanted to talk, he could've come to the house. Meeting us here felt deliberate, like a message saying he always knew where we were. It was only paranoid if it wasn't true.

I looked to Zane to find her staring Caleb down. She didn't trust it either.

Caleb looked down at Jainey. "I... Can I talk to you when Jordan is here? I owe him an apology, and I don't want to have to say it over and over."

"You want to come back home with us?" I asked, one hand clenching into a fist at my side. "After everything—"

"We told him our home was always open to him," Zane cut in. "We told him that." She shot me a pointed look.

So, she wasn't happy with my reaction. So what? I had very distinct memories of Caleb shooting me in the chest that could war with her charitable point of view.

"Do you not remember his role in Ray and Jainey's kidnapping? Have you forgot—"

"Jacklyn's right," Caleb said, clear blue eyes just like Kylie's glancing at his shoes. "I hurt you guys. All of you. I acted out of fear and a bit of stupidity. And Jacklyn wasn't there when I said it last time because she and Kyp…" He paused to take a shaky breath. "I didn't have anyone to show me it was wrong. I thought you were evil. I wanted a mom so badly… I didn't even consider I could be on the wrong side until I saw Kylie fighting with you. Then I had one mom on each side and I had to weigh the other things."

"Like me," Jainey said, pulling at one of his fingers. "And Jordan."

"Right. And my brother." Caleb nodded. "But mostly you guys. Because I knew you. I knew how good you were. And if you believed in them… well, could you really be wrong?"

A little of the tension I'd been holding in my shoulders since I'd heard his voice loosened and released. He was just a kid. Like Jordan. Like Jainey.

"Caleb," I started, but he held up a hand.

"You're already showing astounding restraint. I literally killed you."

"True, but it didn't stick."

"You don't have to pretend that it doesn't upset you."

I nodded. "Come on." I waved for him to follow and continued to walk toward the brownstone.

"Thank you, Jacklyn." He fell into step behind me, along with Zane.

I grabbed Jainey's hand and held on tightly. I may be making the decision to trust Caleb, but that didn't mean my brain had left the building. I was supportive, not stupid.

"So, what were you guys up to?" Caleb asked. "Just hanging out? Getting some air?"

"Caleb!" Jainey half-shrieked. I winced. "We went to the coolest place."

"We went to the Children's Museum of Manhattan," Zane explained. "There was this really cool water experiment thing."

"Oh yeah? What was it like?"

I glanced back. Caleb's eyes were lit up, and a smile brightened his face. He actually cared. He actually loved Jainey. How could he be a threat?

Jainey kept up a steady stream of excitable chatter as we walked, and Caleb was completely engaged, asking questions and making her giggle with cheesy jokes.

"We're almost there," I announced, motioning with my chin toward the brownstone. "It's about half a block down."

"Thank goodness," Zane breathed.

I chuckled. "Nobody told you to dress like you were on the way to a fashion show."

"Look, I have an image to uphold," she grumbled.

We'd had this old, affectionate argument since we met. I bounced on my heels, showing off my comfy sneakers, and smirked back at her.

But my look caught something else. Caleb's eyes had gone icy. And my stomach dropped at the sight.

Maybe bringing him here hadn't been the best idea.

I breathed deeply. Zane was no slouch, but I had Jainey and Jordan. They were half-Body Key, half-Mind Key. They had to be stronger than Caleb's half-Mind Key, half-Light Element Key Aegis. And I wasn't anything to sneeze at, either. But we were all rusty. We hadn't been in a fight in a long time.

Still, if Caleb was the enemy, it was better to have him inside our home with all of us than out here where we could be ambushed, right?

Right?

He waited as Zane opened the door and made her way inside. Jainey moved to enter behind her, but she stopped, gazing up at Caleb expectantly.

"Go on, kid. I'll be right behind you."

Jainey nodded and skittered through the door, pushing through the biometric scan before throwing the inside door open. "Jordan!" she screamed. "You'll never guess who's here!"

I winced, then turned to Caleb. "You okay?"

"Is…Where's Kylie?" He looked down at the threshold.

I flinched. "She died. Before we did."

"Then how did you come back when my mother didn't?" he asked.

My heart clenched. "I don't know. I don't even know how I came back. I should be long dead."

Caleb's eyes raked over me, taking stock of me. The sneer twisting his face told me I came up lacking.

"Yes." He turned to walk into the brownstone. "You should be."

A chill ran down my spine and I rushed in after him. I wasn't about to leave him alone with my family after that.

EIGHT

KYP

Just like the first time, it took his eyes a moment to adjust to the lack of vibrant colors of the Dawn. The Dusk was like stepping into a black hole. For the moment, he laid low, still recovering from the tilting, swooping feeling of moving through the Rift and the impact of his body crashing to the floor. He'd fallen through the tear, but was spit back up into the Dusk like sushi eaten after roasting in the summer sun.

The air felt static. His throat burned from inhaling the sulfuric fumes of the tear, and his eyes watered.

"Ray?" he whispered.

"Sssshhh," Ray responded, and he heard the flick of the lighter. "I'm on it."

The resulting flame was enough to open up Ray's Aegis-born sense of sight.

"Here, kids," Ray murmured, lighting candles for each of them. He held up a finger and closed his eyes. When he reopened them, he smiled. "Sound barrier. Now nobody outside of our bubble can hear us."

"Arvokians may still be able to," Kyp said, relieved to speak at his normal volume. "They don't speak English, but Dhamyan spoke into my mind. I'm not sure if that's something he or anyone else needed to work at, or if it just came naturally to them."

"Well," Ray said. "The Mind Block will prevent what it can. My only concern is that it will get in the way of us finding our friends here."

Their friends. The only two people in the Dusk they knew they could trust here—Dhamyan and Cxarana.

"Why aren't we using the flashlights we brought for light?" Austin struggled to get his feet under him. The bigger they are, the harder they fall and all that.

Drew rushed to help him, and Kyp definitely did not find it cute or romantic at all. Drew was the kindest man he knew, and Tex… well, Tex was a bit of a prick.

Kyp still hoped he was okay.

"Everyone here uses natural light to see," Kyp said. "Candles won't stand out as much, but flashlights? We might as well shout 'we're from the Dawn' through a megaphone."

"We just brought them for emergencies, hon." Drew squeezed his arm. "We'll use them if we run out of candles to burn. But let's hope we're not here that long."

Drew pressed a candle into Austin's hand with a nod.

Kyp's side twinged. He gritted his teeth against the pain.

Drew was at his side in moments. "Is it happening again?"

"It's beginning," Kyp acknowledged. It felt good to be honest with him again. It felt good to be honest with himself. "But we have time."

"What's the plan?" Austin asked. "We ain't gonna just stand here in the open and hope Cxarana trips on us while out on a walk, are we?"

Air left Drew's nose in a little puff. "Of course not. We have a better plan than that."

Kyp and Ray winced.

"Right?"

"'Course we do," Ray said. His eyes slid to Kyp's.

"Well, *I* do." Kyp sighed. "If we left things to Ray, the plan would be to cross our fingers and pray."

"Hey, that worked perfectly well that time in San Jose, didn't it, Austin?"

Drew wrapped an arm around Kyp's waist. "What's the plan?"

Kyp glanced around, pushing his memory back to the last time he'd been there. Dhamyan had found him when he'd fallen into the Dusk, wounded and alone. He'd been dropped bleeding into a strange world, blinded and surrounded by predators, and Dhamyan had aided him as they fought through just enough of the creatures to get him to safety in a cave.

He tried to reconstruct the path there in his mind, but they were in a very different place.

"There's a cave. I believe it's over that way." Kyp motioned in the most likely direction. "This Rift is way further beyond it, but that looks about right. It's secluded, but it did the trick of hiding us. We can regroup there. Then I try to figure out how to draw Cxarana and Dhamyan in our direction."

"A secluded cave." Austin clenched and unclenched his fists. "The blinding darkness wasn't enough. We have to cross completely over into full-on eerie territory, don't we?"

"Wouldn't be us if we didn't." Ray's grin looked feral in the flickering candlelight.

Kyp led the way across the Dusk's spongy surface. He hoped they'd brought enough in the way of resources. There was a strong chance they'd have to survive for days without any help from anyone here. Would they have enough food? Enough water?

The Dusk had changed. Last time he'd been there, a dimensional bleed was fracturing the space between their worlds, the even darkness of the sky marred by starlike twinkles that may have been the Dawn, or may have been the pocket dimension where the Arvokians had survived and hid for generations. The tears had healed in the time he'd been gone, the dark blanket of the night sky now uniform.

After some time, they passed a path Kyp recalled vaguely, but he'd been a little busy running and dying then. Crystals jutted up from the floor, reflecting the light from the candlelight and narrowing their path. Mostly a pale green with veins of purple and blue. It looked like fluorite, but not quite. Fluorite didn't have that odd metallic sheen that made the flame's light less like a glint and more like the reflection off cold steel.

He knelt beside the outcropping and found exactly what he'd wished for. A weapon under the guise of a lovely souvenir. A sharp sliver of rock. One that wouldn't be confiscated unless they were in real danger.

"Nifty," Austin grunted as he grabbed his own shard.

"You don't suppose that's a bit too panicky?" Drew asked. "Do we really want to assume there will be violence? We don't know anything about them."

"And that's exactly why we should find something inconspicuous to use as a weapon." Ray grabbed a shard of his own.

Austin moved past him with more grace than a man his size could usually manage. "Let's go. You were leading us somewhere, weren't you? We should hustle."

Kyp agreed, and he put a little more drive into his steps, pushing his feet into the oddly porous earth beneath him. He kept moving until they made it to the outside of the cave. A craggy hole in the base of a rocky hill, the cave would be the perfect place to gain shelter, particularly because the tearing feeling in his side was getting stronger. Just the sight of it loosened the tension in his shoulders.

He moved to enter, only to bump into Austin's outstretched arm.

"No way, Baby Franklin," Austin rasped. "We go first."

"Guardians don't risk their lives for Keys anymore," Kyp said. "I can walk in just fine."

"I ain't never risked my life for someone because they were a Key. Keys got nothing to do with it. Ray and I are the most durable. We'll go in first, scope the place out. Then you and Drew. Once we're sure it's safe." He leaned forward a bit, his breath puffing into Kyp's ear as he spoke. "Way I see it, you can look out for Drew while we're out here waiting. But don't tell him I said that."

Kyp nodded, and Ray and Austin disappeared through the mouth of the cave, the darkness closing around them. The anxious thought that it had devoured them teased his mind, making his heart sink

"The big lug is an idiot if he thinks I didn't hear him," Drew said, filling the space the others had left behind.

"He isn't an idiot. He just knew you'd go with it because you'd want him to check the cave before we entered." Kyp's eyes ticked toward Drew. "Which you did."

Drew offered a wry smile. "Sure. How are you feeling? Cold?"

He wasn't asking about the temperature. They both knew it, too.

"I'm starting to feel questionable. We should probably stay at the cave and let me… go through the cycle… before we do anything else."

"What else were we going to do? You've been quiet about anything resembling a plan. What's the deal? Do you not trust us to understand?" He crossed his arms over his chest, his hip sliding in the opposite direction of Kyp. Edging himself away. His body language sent a clear message.

"I didn't keep it from you to be condescending," Kyp scoffed. "I just barely know what I'm planning. It's more of a sketch than a painting at this moment."

"Kyp," Drew said, a scolding and an acceptance in one word.

"Actually, there's something I've been meaning to talk to you about. Back before we sealed the Rifts, I'd been thinking about it, but then it quickly became unnecessary. But now it's necessary again, so…"

"Kyp, my man, my dude, my bro, stop worrying and tell me."

Kyp sighed. "I can't, because this is a proposal."

"A… what?" Drew asked, one eyebrow raised. "You know, I never thought you saw me that way."

What? Oh.

"Shut up." Kyp slugged him lightly in the arm. "Basically? I don't think I should be in charge anymore. Jacks and Ray shouldn't be either. We're only placed in charge by virtue of our station. And that isn't the way I've ever believed it should be. When we get back, I want to hold a vote and choose the best leader."

"Okay." Drew almost sounded indifferent, which wouldn't do. "What does that have to do with me?"

Kyp snorted a laugh. "I want to nominate you."

Drew started. "Me? Why?"

He couldn't see it. How on earth could he not see it?

"Drew, you're the only one of us that keeps their cool under pressure. You always have the most logical, least emotion-driven responses. And you're incredibly loyal and kind. Just look at the way you pushed Cass and me in the right direction when Jainey first showed up. We were ready to believe she was a mind trick sent by my mother. You were the one who made us see we were being ridiculous. And you did the same thing when I was hiding my… illness."

Drew looked startled. "I… I don't know what to say to that."

"Look, it's not up to me. It's up for a vote with the whole group. I just wanted to ask before I put your name forward. I'm not trying to make you uncomfortable. But I think you would do an amazing job. The Order needs a leader and you would do well. And you wouldn't be alone. We'd help. But…" Kyp placed a hand on his shoulder and squeezed. "I trust you to do this."

"I guess that's fine or whatever," Drew said, pressing his toe into the oddly textured ground. "You can put it up for a vote, but I don't think the Order is in the market for a leader."

Kyp sighed. "They've chosen Ray, then."

"No. They've chosen democracy, you dingus. Is all this just a pretense for your vaguely suicidal bullshit?" Drew asked, his voice tight. "Like you're trying to find someone else to lead for when you're gone?"

A weight settled over Kyp's shoulders. "Ray told you?"

"Ray didn't have to tell him whatever you said or did," Austin's voice came from the cave. "We all know what kinda state you've been in since you got back. Cave's clear, by the way." He motioned behind him.

Something tightened in Kyp's chest and he looked at Drew, who placed a hand on his shoulder.

"It's okay. We're not gonna let you succumb to this. We've got you."

Austin's grunt was punctuated with a nod. "Ray's startin' up a fire. Wants to keep you comfortable when shit starts slidin' downhill."

Kyp stepped forward, but the moment he did, the skin on his side tore open. A freshly drawn wound once again, but an old familiar pain, sharp enough to send him to his knees. He choked for breath, heaving as he fought for control of his body.

His hearing was a vacuum for a moment before switching to a dull hiss. Drew swore, and it broke through, but it sounded about thirty feet farther away than it should with Drew hunched down beside him, his face bobbing in and out of Kyp's view.

He was scooped into someone's arms like he was scarcely the size of a small child. Kyp wanted to chafe at the idea of being carried bridal-style by someone who could only be Austin, but he couldn't spare it much more than a thought before he was placed with an abundance of caution onto a pile of something soft.

"Thanks," Kyp gasped, the word punched out of him by the gentle press of the cushioning between him and the floor. God, he was fucked.

He glanced down at the nest of thin fleece blankets. Austin, Ray, and Drew looked around the cave like they didn't know where to rest their eyes, and it made him smile despite the burning pain.

Red and gold flickered across their faces from the small flame Ray had kindled.

Ray lifted Kyp's shirt gingerly. "It's progressing faster than it did earlier."

"Again," Austin said through gritted teeth.

"Kyp," Drew said. "Whatever you're thinking of doing, you might want to do it now, before you... go."

He grabbed onto Ray's hand and squeezed his pain out through it. Ray grunted, but otherwise took Kyp's pain in the only way he could.

Kyp centered his thoughts on his happiest memory. Him and Jacklyn. He was four, and she was three. The sky was a gorgeous blue, dotted with clouds like the cotton the older members of the Order used to clean bumps and scratches they picked up during battle. They were laying out on the grass in the backyard, and she got him to do something he'd never done before. He hadn't even thought to do it before.

"That one looks like Hector," she said, a pudgy finger pointing toward one oddly shaped cloud. "It's got his nose." She pointed at one part that curved away from the cloud like the top of a cane. Then she giggled.

He didn't giggle. His laugh was rougher, more like a cough or a hiccup. But it only made her laugh more.

They laid there for hours, making each other laugh without really doing anything until the light outside dimmed and one of the older teens summoned them for dinner.

It was one of the best days of his life.

And with that enjoyable memory calming his mind, he reached forward with everything he could summon and screamed out into the far reaches of his Mind Key Aegis, putting out a message that only his old friend Cxarana would hear.

"I'm here, batty old witch," he teased within his mind. *"I'm here in the Dusk and I need your help."*

As the pain tore through him once again, he prayed with everything he had that she'd believe it was truly him. It was quite possible that she wouldn't. Last she knew, he was dead.

But then, by the time she got to them, he'd likely be dead once again.

NINE

JACKLYN

For a moment, I just stood there like a mindless fool, unable to believe the way Caleb had just spoken to me. But if I froze for too long, he would be alone in our home.

I shook off the sick feeling twisting in my stomach and followed him in.

Zane and Jainey led Caleb up the stairs to our main sitting room, the place where we always hung out.

Our sanctuary. A potential enemy within.

I needed an adult. I knew Zane was supposed to be that adult, but…eh.

"Crap!" Zane shouted, then she turned around and gently pushed Jainey and Caleb back before they could enter. "Nope, we're not going in there."

Zane's nose screwed up in disgust and she looked at me like she needed an intense session with a bottle of brain bleach.

"Zane, no," Rennie shouted. She burst out of the room, tidying her ponytail. "Whatever you're thinking, you have the

A little disheveled, a little out of breath, a little… what was that on her neck?

I marched forward and right into the room Rennie had emerged from.

"Mom!" Jordan popped up from the couch. The poor thing was red from his neck to the part in his hair. And he probably deserved to be. "I thought you'd take a little longer." He leaned casually on the end table. It squeaked across the wood floor, sliding into the wall. He stumbled forward and I caught him by the shoulders.

He grinned up at me. His lips were a bit… glossy.

"Sorry. Forgot my own strength for a minute there." He chuckled awkwardly.

"Your shirt is on backwards," I said, tugging roughly at the white tag on his T-shirt's neckline. Gross. Just ew. I didn't need to know this. "Is it time for us to have the talk?"

Horror creeped across his face. "God, please no. Ray already did that and it was bad enough that time."

"He clearly didn't give you the right one, if this is how I find you," I grumbled. "Where the hell is Cass?"

"She went to bed early. Said she wasn't feeling well. She's been acting weird all day." Jordan shrugged. "Guess she trusts us more than you do."

"*She* didn't find her baby making out with a girl that—"

"Don't say it!"

"You're… I was… like… just—" I waved my hands down my body in some approximation of a pregnant belly I never even had.

"I have the intelligence and hormonal maturity of a fifteen-year-old, and I'll be sixteen next year." He squared his shoulders and stood up a little straighter.

"You're just basing your age off of Rennie's."

"He's right though," Caleb cut in, stepping into the room behind me. "That's how old we are. Or at least the reasonable equivalent. Our lives haven't been abnormal enough. We have to live the rest of our lives as though we're babies in teenage bodies? That doesn't seem unfair to you?"

"Caleb?" Jordan gasped before racing forward and throwing his arms around his best friend. His uncle. Whatever the hell Caleb was to him. "I can't believe you're here!"

Caleb huffed a laugh and though he hesitated, he threw his arms around Jordan in return. Caleb just about melted into the hug, like he needed it.

When was the last time this kid got hugged?

"Dude, I missed you guys so much."

"Did you see Rennie?" Jordan asked, pulling back and motioning for the door, a giddy grin on his face.

A smile flickered across Caleb's face, that controlled smile, a Franklin hallmark. "Yep. Couldn't miss her. She made quite the exit."

Jordan punched him lightly on the arm, his smile remaining unaffected. "Shut up." He detached himself from the hug, but kept one arm slung over Caleb's shoulders. "Come on, grab a seat. We have so much to catch up on."

"We do," Caleb said, taking Jordan's cue and lowering himself onto the couch. He shot a glance my way, and it felt pointed, like he was saying *I'm here and your son thinks I belong. You'll have to get used to it.*

Not psychically pushed words, not spoken. Just a feeling. A vibe communicated with little more than a glance.

And then he looked away, plucking at his gray shirt, straightening it like it was a nervous tick, and that awkward shift looked so real I didn't know who I was dealing with anymore.

"Rennie, Zane, Jainey," I called, settling down on the rich brown leather couch and resigning myself to playing Caleb's game—for now.

Jainey was an enthusiastic ball of energy, bounding into the room and throwing herself bodily into the small space between Caleb and Jordan. She landed and burrowed further in until she was safely encased between them.

Rennie and Zane didn't seem anywhere near as excited about Caleb's sudden appearance. Zane's expression was blank in the way that meant she wasn't sure which Zane to be—the overly cool manipulator or the relaxed woman who loved with her whole heart. She sat in the armchair beside where I stood. I leaned on the armrest.

Rennie smiled her usual winning grin, but concern showed in the lay of her brow, in the sharpness of her eyes. Smart girl. She knew something had to be up.

"Not that it isn't great to see you again, Cal," Rennie said. She sat on Jordan's other side, but she held herself up, never quite settling into the cushions. "But when you left, you didn't seem to want to be here anymore. And now the Rifts are open again, and suddenly here you are. Care to share what brought you here?"

Caleb frowned and glanced from Jainey to Jordan. For a moment, he didn't say a word, and in that moment, Zane's fingers tightened on her chair's armrests and Rennie's leg muscles bunched as though she were ready to jump out of her chair to throw herself between the kids.

"I thought that was clear, Ren." Caleb's words were venomous. "You *are* all investigating this Rift, aren't you? I mean, how does this even happen? Only a Skeleton Key can open Rifts. There are only three of us in existence. So, one of us must have done this, right?"

"We didn't do it," Jordan said. "Why would you think we would? We're the ones who want the Rifts to close, remember? We closed them in the first place. My parents *died to make it happen.*"

"Right!" Caleb said, a deranged vigor lighting his eyes. "And yet, here's your mom. Good as new." He waved a hand my way. "I'm sure your dad's good, too."

Jainey's eyes welled up. "Well, actually…"

"Kyp's fine, yes," I cut her off, perhaps a bit too quickly.

Zane winced. Not convincing enough, I guess.

"Yeah," Rennie said smoothly. "He's just looking into some leads on the whole 'Rift reopening' thing, and Jainey's worried about him. But he's going to be fine, Jainey."

Caleb's eyebrow tilted upward. A chill ran down my spine. Such a Lavinia facial expression. One that definitely meant he thought he had an edge over us.

Jainey seemed to catch on, thankfully. She shot a hopeful smile up at Rennie. "Yeah, I know. I just… He just got back, so…"

Caleb nodded. "Of course. You're worried. You just brought him here and now he's off again. You wouldn't want him to get hurt trying to look into something he doesn't even need to."

He sounded so sure of himself.

Could Jainey have reopened the Rift? She certainly had the ability, and she'd always been more self-assured than Jordan. If she'd decided it was the right thing to do, she would have done it without asking.

"What?" She inched closer to Jordan. "I didn't do that. Mama and Papa wouldn't have wanted me to."

My eyes cut to Zane.

"No," Zane said. "I know Ray and I weren't perfect parents while you were gone, but we aren't barbarians, and she's still just a kid. There's no way she would have done that and we wouldn't have known."

"Why are you acting like it would be bad?" Caleb loomed over Jainey. "Aren't you glad? Your mom is back. Some of us didn't get that."

Rennie launched herself out of her chair and scooped Jainey up in her arms. "What are you doing?"

"He's not doing anything wrong!" Jordan stood, protectively inserting himself between Rennie and Caleb. "Come on, guys. This isn't necessary."

Caleb cowered behind Jordan, as though a tall and powerful Skeleton Key had any reason to be intimidated by a petite Guardian with the ability to read emotions.

Unless he did.

Maybe she could see something we couldn't.

Rennie shook her head sorrowfully. Two steps back, and she had lined herself up with me and Zane. She lowered Jainey to the floor. "Of course you'd protect him. You always protect him."

Jordan's expression tightened. "Don't act like you don't care about him too! You know how close we are."

"I do, but something doesn't track here. Unless… Jordan, did *you* open the Rift?"

My head whipped toward Rennie so fast I would have pulled a muscle if I was a normal person. "What?"

Jordan's mouth worked, but no words came out.

"You've been acting weird ever since, like, March," she stated.

"Weird how?" I asked.

"Yeah, Rennie, please. Enlighten us." Zane crossed her arms over her chest. "You didn't tell us anything about him acting weird before now."

"I told Austin." She winced. "He told me not to worry. Said that he'd been through a lot lately. That Jordan would never hurt me intentionally."

"*Hurt* you?" I said. "Jordan wouldn't hurt a fly."

"He led the charge to hurt Livingston," Caleb muttered. "That was a pretty extreme way of not hurting anybody."

Jordan's eyes flashed and he shot a quick glance over at Caleb before returning his attention to Rennie. "He was torturing us. I would *never* hurt Rennie. I *have* never hurt Rennie. Has everybody lost their damn minds?"

Rennie shouted over all of us. "Not like that! Not like that!

Emotionally. And it was an accident! I know it was!" We turned to her for an explanation, and her head drooped forward. "God, that wasn't what I meant. He was just being a little insensitive. Forgetting our anniversary and stuff. It wasn't like him."

"I was distracted," Jordan said, his shoulders sagging.

"With the plan to open the Rifts?" Caleb asked.

He whirled on Caleb. "Okay, man, now you're actually starting to piss me off."

"Answer the question," he replied, his expression flat.

"No. My Aegis started to trickle back to me, and I was scared! I was scared of what it might mean. So I didn't say anything." His voice got breathier as he spoke until he gasped with every sentence.

"Breathe, Jordy." Rennie reached for his hand. "Your Aegis."

He yanked it away and turned to Zane, continuing to talk, but this time he was calmer. "Everyone was just really starting to move on. Aunt Cass was getting better. Grandpa was… He was joyfully stupid again. I didn't want to tell anyone that the world was about to go to hell again. I couldn't."

"Bullshit," Caleb shouted, tears springing to his eyes. "It had to be one of you! It had to be! You're the only ones who had anything to gain!"

Shit. He hadn't opened them. He was just as lost as we were.

"Caleb, I know you're frightened," I said. "So are we. We don't know what's happening either. Now isn't the time to be pointing fingers at each other."

"What did you just say?" Caleb snapped. "I am not one of you!"

"You could be," I said, holding up a placating hand. "Jordan,

Jainey, and Rennie all love you. Kyp wants to know his brother. We can work this out."

"I notice you didn't say anything about you."

I sighed. I wasn't about to lie to the kid. "I don't know you, Caleb. But I could. At the very least, we could work together. I've worked with people I didn't get along with before for the greater good."

"Like Ross?" Caleb asked, his voice going shrill. "Like my mother?"

Kylie. They had the same cornflower blue eyes. When I first met her, I was jealous of those eyes. She was pretty, and I thought she'd catch Kyp's eye. As it was, they were trapped in an arranged relationship pushed on them by Lavinia in an effort to create a Skeleton Key. In a way, by artificially creating a child with Lavinia and Kylie's DNA, she'd created exactly what she'd wanted—a Franklin/Robertson Skeleton Key.

Poor Caleb had been created as a tool for Lavinia. He didn't need to serve that role anymore. He was free of her, and Kylie was long dead. I should have realized he had no reason to open the Rifts.

"You're right," I said with a sigh. "I hated Kylie and Ross. But not in the end. Things changed when we were working together. They weren't my friends, but I respected them." I took a step toward the kid.

He was shaking, his hands clenching and unclenching into fists. His normally pallid coloring reddened. Was he about to blow like Jordan did? He was similarly gifted and similarly cursed.

"How are you back?" he cried, and beside me, Jainey sniffled.

Rennie pressed a hand to her chest, horror written across her face.

"Please," he shouted. "Just tell me. Help me bring Kylie back. You'll never have to see us again. We'll just go. Just close up the Rifts and we'll go be normal and we'll never bother you again, I swear!"

"I'm afraid that's not possible, Caleb."

Kylie. Kylie's voice.

What. The. Hell.

I turned toward it.

Cass stood in the doorway, her eyes flickering from their usual brown to the bright green of the Sentinel to that cornflower-Kylie-blue.

"Hello, Jacklyn," she said, leaning against the wall. "Gana caught me up. Things have gotten even weirder, haven't they?"

I had so many questions. So frickin' many.

Caleb's voice hardened, and tears collected along his lower eyelids. "I don't understand. What the hell gives you the right to use my mother's voice?"

"That's not Cass," Rennie said.

"Yeah, I'm improving on the original." Kylie strutted into the center of the room, wearing Cass's skin. "Mari was a placeholder. Her connection to the Skeleton Keys was only through Cass. Not a close enough connection to keep her as a Sentinel when there was a better option there. And what connection is closer than his mother?"

"What the fuck is a Sentinel?" Caleb shouted. "What is happening?"

This poor kid.

"A Sentinel is the spirit guard of a Skeleton Key," Jordan muttered. "Cass is the only spirit channeler alive, and there are three of us, so they all live in Cass."

"There's Mama's sister," Jainey said, her voice small. "She's Jordan's. And there's Grandma Jaina. She's mine. And Mari was yours. She's Cass's sister. But you didn't have any family close enough that was dead until…"

"Until now." Caleb gasped. He still hadn't stopped shaking. "Kylie?"

"Sorry I couldn't come back," she said, stepping toward her son. "The conditions weren't right. I don't know what the conditions were, just that we weren't in the same place, and that seems to have played into it. It's not Jacklyn's fault and it's not Kyp's. Believe me, if I could blame them, I would."

Caleb blinked hard twice. "I don't…" He backed away from her. "I don't want a ghost." Another step back. "A ghost will just go away when they close the Rifts!"

"Caleb…" Kylie stepped forward again, and Caleb broke into a run, racing down the hall.

"Caleb, wait!" Jordan called after him.

We made it out of the room just as the front door slammed behind him.

Jordan whirled on me. "We have to go after him!"

I looked down the hall.

"No," Rennie said, her voice careful. "He's not ready. We won't get anywhere with him. He needs time."

"But Ren—"

"I know. I don't like it either," Rennie said.

"We won't do it. I will," Kylie said.

Zane grabbed her arm, holding her back. "Rennie's an empath. If she says we won't reach him right now, we won't."

"Right now, he hates us," Rennie said. "We'll only push him further away."

I nodded, but the thought of him out there alone unsettled something deep within me.

"Rennie's right. When he's ready, he'll come to us for answers." I sighed. "Hopefully, we'll have them by then."

If the only three Skeleton Keys didn't open the Rifts, answers were in seriously short supply.

TEN

JOURNEY

KYP

Consciousness returned to Kyp slowly. It started with a voice, one he only heard in his nightmares of his time in the Dusk. The man's words were in another language, spoken in a melody. Arvokian. Familiar, it brought a sense of tranquility despite the terror it was paired with in his mind.

Kyp's heart twitched painfully, struggling to regain its normal rhythm. A chill shook through his limbs. God, he hated coming back from the dead.

Another voice joined Dhamyan's in the darkness, this one far more familiar, bolstering the feeling of safety Dhamyan's voice had created.

"I am unsure," Cxarana said. "We may not have what you seek. I've never heard of anything capable of curing Senefestrian poisoning."

"You see, I call bullshit on that," Austin said. "Whether you know it or not."

"He's right," Drew said. "The Arvokians figured out a way to treat Senefestrian blood and use that treated substance to heal and not kill. That must mean something."

Dhamyan said something else, but he hadn't included Kyp in the psychic circle, on account of him being dead and all.

"I'm going to need you to repeat that," Kyp said, his throat scratchy.

"Kyp!" A moment later, Ray knelt at his side. "Open your eyes, sweetheart."

"I don't want to," Kyp said, and maybe he sounded a bit petulant, but his head already felt like it had been used for a drum solo at a metal concert.

"Most assuredly not," Ray said, dropping his accent like a poorly tailored suit just to lovingly mock Kyp's cadence of speech. "But you don't want to miss Austin's unbearably attractive face, do you?"

"I'll do it for Cxarana," Kyp teased back.

He peeled his eyes open to the flickering of firelight. Cxarana stood directly in his line of sight. She looked the same—her hair the same eggshell white, although instead of being braided across her head, it was now braided down her back the way Dhamyan wore it. Her skin was the same bruise-purple, but her eyes were shinier. Her clothing style had changed too. Gone were the white robes she'd worn as their Arvokian liaison in the Temple. Instead, she wore yellow leathers with brown geometric patterns splashed across them.

It reminded him of a Senefestrian. Another chill.

He smiled through it. "Hello there, old friend."

Cxarana's head drooped, not managing to hide the brightening of her eyes. "It is good to see you breathing, Mr. Franklin." She crossed her arms over herself, a self-hug that told Kyp she'd missed him.

"It's good to see anything at all, honestly."

A quick, efficient nod, and she returned them to the business at hand. "Dhamyan was simply commenting on the effect Senefestrian blood has on the aging of the body's building blocks. Your… cells. I don't understand it. Neither of us are scientists or healers."

"Then perhaps you can take us to someone who is?" Ray asked. "This is urgent. The Rifts have reopened. We don't know how, but we need Kyp in fighting form again in case of an attack."

"The problem," Dhamyan explained, *"is that the scientists are well respected members of the council, and the healers are well respected members of the Arvokian monarchy. And we are not well respected by either."*

"Astounding," Kyp said. "No wonder we get along. I managed to befriend the rebels."

"And yet, it's not the rebels you need," Cxarana said. "After what I did to Zelnick, the council won't be amenable. We need the royal family."

"Was Zelnick acting for the council?" Ray asked.

"Is the royal family in league with the council?" Kyp asked.

"I am unsure," Dhamyan said. *"The council has been making questionable decisions for some time now. The royal family does not agree with their choices, but the Keys stay far out of the reaches of both of them. We try to avoid places where the law holds sway."*

"Off the grid," Austin said. "The way we avoid the law. Hard to explain the supernatural to them."

"And hard to allow them access to the Dusk when we know the nation's governments would likely be as bad as the Sirins." Drew sighed.

"The Keys of the Dusk rebelled against the royal family. We were banished by the kingdom. And I was banished from my intended, the princess," Dhamyan explained.

"I'm assuming that means we should be careful of the princess?" Kyp asked. "She can't be too pleased."

"She has recovered." Dhamyan looked to Cxarana, his forehead ridge flicking up and down. *"Still, I do not have the favor of the others."*

"If it will be dangerous for you, then lead us there and leave," Kyp said. "The last thing I want to do is cause you any more trouble than we already have."

"We will not, Mr. Franklin," Cxarana said. "It's about time I face my family."

Kyp started. "Your family?"

"Yes, dear boy. Much like you were once the crown prince of the Order of the Key, I was the crown princess of the Arvokian royal family."

Oh. So Dhamyan and Cxarana were a couple, if Kyp had understood that look he'd given her correctly. Jacklyn was going to brag her ass off when Kyp revealed that little tidbit.

Dhamyan made a low sound in his throat. *"If we are to travel, we can explain on the way. Especially if we are to get to the kingdom before Kehp succumbs once again."*

Kyp had forgotten he called him Kehp. It made him smile.

"They're Almalas," Cxarana explained, holding out a set of reins to Kyp.

Kyp stared at the creatures. They had the body length and skin type of a crocodile, but they lumbered on two legs, and those legs were large. They reminded Kyp of the Tauntauns from *The Empire Strikes Back*. Just scaly Tauntauns.

He missed Jacklyn. She would have agreed.

"Kehp should ride with Cxarana," Dhamyan stated. *"She is trained well and will best avoid potentially injuring him."*

Cxarana's eyes were fully black, with a fishlike roundness to them, but they still managed to reflect her appreciation as though she were as human as Kyp. "Thank you, Dhamyan. You should take Mr. Madison." She flashed a look over her shoulder at Kyp's absentee father-figure. "Because that will make the ride nice and bumpy for him."

Ray sneered, shoving his hands into his pockets pointedly, like he was restraining himself from another action. He wouldn't dare.

"What about us?" Drew asked.

Cxarana pressed her mouth into a tight line. "Have any of you ever ridden a horse?"

Austin grinned widely. Of course, Tex had horse-riding experience.

Drew groaned. "I'm going to die."

The terrain between the cave and the kingdom grew increasingly mountainous. They'd been on the road for so long, Kyp had acclimated to the nauseating motion and no longer feared he would lose his hold and flop to his death.

Drew used the psychic link that Dhamyan seemed capable of holding with ease for prolonged periods. *"It occurs to me that we may be offered food when we're at the kingdom. What do you guys eat down here?"*

The hesitation from Dhamyan was clear.

"Ah, crap," Austin grumbled. Kyp actually agreed with him.

Dhamyan pushed a hand through the tuft of black hair that fell free from his sleek braid.   Cxarana glanced over her shoulder, her lips tightening in a rictus of a smile. Perfectly genuine smiles looked awkward on her features. This one looked downright dangerous.

"In the kingdom, you will eat a largely plant-based diet. They cultivate large tracts of land, solely for the purpose of feeding their own," Dhamyan explained.

"However, out on the plains where the commoners live, there is some vegetation, but it must be gathered, so it is harder to find. We have to be a bit more inventive," Cxarana said.

"We have great hunting parties. When we're lucky, we feast on a Tralsk or a Senefestrian."

"Is that why your clothes mimic the pattern of a Senefestian carapace?" Kyp asked.

"It does, indeed, help with our hunting. But it doesn't simply mimic it," Dhamyan explained. *"The leather is made from the skin*

beneath the carapace. We must remove the carapace to consume the meat, obviously."

Obviously. Kyp fought to swallow down the swell of vomit in his throat.

"And when you're not lucky. No plants, no Tralsks or Senefestrians?" Drew asked.

Kyp glared at him. *Please, Drew, stop talking.* But Drew was fascinated, and when he was fascinated, it would take actual restraints to stop him. Normally, Kyp loved that about him, but at the moment, he wanted to know much less.

"When necessary." Dhamyan winced, clearly aware of how this conversation was affecting them. *"A Gorvhan is surprisingly filling."*

"Not a great deal of meat, though," Cxarana added. "Like eating a squirrel in the Dawn."

Kyp did *not* want to know how she knew that.

"So, what you're sayin' is, we better pray the royal family lets us eat there?" Ray asked.

Cxarana's strange tittering sound did not make Kyp feel better.

"We have nearly arrived," Dhamyan warned.

"Then we should probably take this time to set some ground rules," Kyp said.

"Ground rules?" Ray asked.

Drew agreed, and Kyp marveled at how quickly that halted any complaints.

"Ground rule number one. You are not at liberty to say anything stupid." He jabbed a finger in Austin's direction.

"Why are ya pointing at me with that crap?" Austin tilted backward like Kyp's finger was offending him with its presence. "He's the daft one here." He turned to Ray. "Don't say anything stupid."

"Feck off, you right bastard," Ray growled.

Kyp stifled a laugh. He wasn't sure when he'd grown to truly love every damn member of this family, but there was likely no going back. He tried not to fear it was a mistake.

That was his mother's way. It wasn't his.

After galloping up a particularly steep climb, the castle came into view in the distance.

It wasn't a traditional medieval castle; however, it was a far cry from the cave. The large building was constructed of polished slate-gray stones. The placement of those stones appeared to have been mathematically chosen, like the pyramids of Egypt. Dug into the blackened earth, a moat hugged the castle's perimeter, the liquid surrounding it the same glowing red of the Rifts. It took a few moments of continued forward movement before Kyp could see the bridge that would allow them passage.

"Does this building not attract the Sirins that seek to enslave your people?" Drew asked gently.

"Many Rituals have been performed around this building, including those that ward it against view," Cxarana explained. "It is virtually indistinguishable from the rest of the environment unless you are allowed, even welcome. Which is rather intriguing. It implies we were expected."

"That could be a good thing," Ray said.

"Or a very, very bad one," Austin said. "And probably nowhere in between."

"Indeed," Cxarana agreed. "To further answer Mr. Clayson's question, in the event of an enemy incursion, openings to the pocket dimension between the Dusk and the Dawn are accessible."

"Aren't all Rifts sealed?" Drew asked.

"No," Ray said. "The closer we get to the castle, the stronger the smell of sulfur—the stink of Rifts."

"The openings can be naturally opened by Arvokians. But they only go so far. Those will only lead to the pocket dimensions," Cxarana said.

"Then how were the initial Rifts between the Dawn and the Dusk ever created?" Kyp asked. "We were taught they were caused by the Arvokians."

"*Nobody truly knows the answer,*" Dhamyan said.

"But we do know what we were told to tell humanity. And it was not the truth." Cxarana leaned back into Kyp. "I am sorry. I could only do so much."

"I understand," Kyp said.

"*Silence even your thoughts now,*" Dhamyan said as they approached the rope bridge, which was woven from some kind of plant stems.

It creaked and swayed worryingly as they crossed it.

Cxarana placed a hand on Kyp's knee. It only slightly helped his racing heart. He was very close to feeling the tearing in his side once again. He had precious little time to convince the royal family to help him before his frailty showed. He hoped it would be enough time to obtain the information they needed.

They made it to the other side of the bridge. Kyp tried not to project his relief too loudly. Austin, however, couldn't seem to ever contain anything. He let out a tiny whoop when the Almala's feet returned to relatively solid ground.

Flowers as bright yellow as daffodils, and as crudely shaped as Venus fly traps lined the path to the royal chamber's entrance. Kyp still marveled at the things that flourished in this place with no sun. His eyes followed the stems of the plants down until he saw where they reached below the blackened earth. This was a strange place, but not without its beauty.

The closed entrance shimmered, then disappeared, and an Arvokian man stepped forward, wearing layers of Senefestrian carapace as armor. *"Greetings Princess Cxarana, Dhamyan, and Keys of the Dawn."*

Kyp steeled himself and ignored the stabbing pain in his side that would soon erupt into a wound. He couldn't afford to focus on that. It was time to get to work.

Eleven

Jacklyn

An unintelligible shout broke through my sleep, and my eyes jolted open before I even knew what was happening. My feet scrambled out from under the thin top sheet I'd covered myself with a few hours ago when I settled down to sleep. I nearly spilled out of my bed, my extra-special coordination not kicking in when I wasn't quite awake.

Another shout. Jordan.

I was out in the hallway and tripping my way toward his door before the rest of the house's occupants dashed out into the hall behind me.

Rennie made it to his room at the same time I did.

"Jordan?" She rubbed her eyes. Her hair stuck up adorably from the top of her braid.

"Mama!" Jainey called behind me.

"Just a second, baby. Zane!" I said.

"On it," she said. I didn't look back. I knew she would see to whatever Jainey needed.

I knocked gently on Jordan's door. By channeling my Aegis, I heard the sheets rustling, but no footsteps. Just in case, I wasn't going to wait for Jordan to answer. I'd woken to a Gorvhan over my bed before and it wasn't worth the risk. I shoved the door open and threw myself into the room, prepared to attack with my bare hands. I probably should have grabbed weapons on the way, but if Jordan was in danger, I wouldn't need them. I still had my fire, and I still had my strength.

Jordan bolted up in bed, terror in his widened eyes. His glassy, unfocused eyes. His chest heaved, a warm glow emitting from below his loose gray Batman T-shirt. He was alone and safe, as long as his Aegis didn't go nuclear on us.

"Jordan, I'm here," I said, my voice low and calm. "You're safe. Nobody is here but us."

"A nightmare," he gasped out, his eyes finally focusing. He was back with me, the glow from his chest dissipating with his deep breathing. He was getting better at pulling himself back from panic mode.

"Another one," Zane said from behind me. "Isn't that just swell?"

"Just dandy," he grumbled back. "But this was different."

I shot a look over my shoulder. "Another one?"

Zane had Jainey by the hand. "He's been having nightmares for… I don't know…"

Cass poked her head in behind her. "Yes, she does. He's been having them since the Rifts closed."

"What?" Rennie looked at Jordan, but he just winced.

"And that's why I didn't say that." Zane glared at Cass.

"Whatever." She shrugged, apparently back to herself since the earlier scene. "I don't think secrets are a good idea when we don't know who is opening Rifts. It's clear we're keeping things from each other and it allows whoever is doing this the space to play us against each other. We can't give anyone that opportunity."

She had a point. Secrets had never served this version of the Order of the Key well. Maybe that was because we needed to get far away from the original Order, which was built entirely from a Jenga tower of secrets.

"Fine, fine." Jordan waved his hand dismissively, such a Kyp gesture that it made my heart ache. "But this wasn't one of those nightmares." He sunk down into his pillows like he wanted to disappear from view.

Rennie took a deep breath, her fingers pinching the bridge of her nose for a moment. When she looked back up, her eyes held less anger and more kindness. "How was it different?"

When they had first started dating, I had asked her to be patient with him. He had the body of a teenager and the intelligence of a brilliant adult, but no real life experience. And here she was, granting him the right to trip up. Hopefully, they'd talk it through later. I didn't want her to just let everything he did slide.

Jordan heaved a sigh before kicking his legs out from under his light blue bedding. "It wasn't like the other ones. Those always start with memories, like being at the facility, or the night we closed the Rifts. And they evolve into something else." He ran his hands over his face. "Usually, they tend to be about me losing control of my

Aegis. Hurting somebody." His eyes slid to Rennie before snapping back to his own knees.

I settled down on the bed near his feet. "And this one?"

"This was oddly… tangible? I don't know." He huffed. "It was cohesive. Like I was being told a story. And Caleb was in trouble in that story."

"That sounds like you're being controlled," Zane said. "Look Jordan, I know—"

Jainey talked right over her. "Or Caleb is trying to tell us that he's in danger. And we need to help him."

"You saw how he was before," I said.

"Distraught?" Cass asked. "Jacks, I'm not his biggest fan, but he's a kid, and he's clearly conflicted."

"And that gives him the right to intrude upon our lives and put our kids in danger?" Zane asked.

"I love how we're *our* kids now," Jordan said. "So who makes the call on this? Mama Jacklyn, Mama Cass, or Mama Zane?"

I rolled my eyes. What could one say when their child behaved just like them? "What happened in the nightmare?"

"I was getting taken in for testing at the facility. It was a bad one. They would test us to see how large a Rift we could create without any Ritual assistance. So they would… they would cut different areas of the body known to bleed heavily, like your carotid, or your femoral… and they would see which one could open or close a Rift the fastest."

My stomach dropped. "This is real. Not part of the nightmare."

Jordan's eyes met mine. "No. Not part of the nightmare." He

paled as he spoke, his hands shaky as he pushed them through his hair. "They always took me to do that. I was the oldest, the flawed test subject." He smiled wryly. "And I could heal myself. So I was an ideal option."

I gritted my teeth to keep back what I wanted to say to that. If I started yelling, I would never stop. The kids hadn't killed Dr. Livingston hard enough. And they'd ripped him into chunks.

"And in the nightmare?" Rennie asked delicately.

"In the nightmare, they decided they'd take Caleb instead," Jordan said. "But Caleb doesn't heal. I tried to fight my way to him, but I couldn't. They took him away. He kept telling me to watch my six. The treasure was in the west. Over and over. I looked behind me and Livingston was there. He told me I was useless and I should go back to where it started."

"Where what started?" Rennie asked.

"He didn't specify. He said I needed my wits to find my way in. If they hadn't abandoned me already. He disappeared behind a door with a lock. But when it closed, my side of the door changed. Vines and weeds, plants, they slithered in and covered it. I was in… like, a concrete parking lot. I looked to my left, and there was a chest with a skeleton key inside. And then I woke up, and you were here."

"Okay," Zane said, her eyes narrowing. "Okay. That sounds like a puzzle."

"I'll get a notebook." Cass rushed out of the room.

"We're rescuing Caleb now?" Rennie asked. "I love him too, but are we sure? This could be a trap."

"Rennie! It's Caleb! He's one of us." Jainey stomped. "We have to protect him."

"He hasn't been 'one of us' for a year and a half!" Rennie yelled loud enough to startle Jainey.

"Hey!" Jordan and I shouted in unison.

Rennie released a weighty sigh. "I'm sorry, Jainey. I'm sorry. I'm just… Caleb made a choice. He rejected us a while ago. And we're going to follow something that could either be a completely random nightmare, or something implanted by Caleb, who has the powers of a Mind Key!"

"It wasn't a random nightmare! Don't you get it?" Jordan snapped. "I can't just leave him alone out there. I never could. Especially not now. He needs us, and we need him, too."

"I know Kylie was pissed when Caleb left, but she's wrong. We don't need him," Zane said.

"Got paper!" Cass trampled her way into the middle of the bedroom and tossed the notebook and pen my way. "And then I realized I could do better and brought your laptop." She passed it to Zane. "We didn't look when he left the first time because he didn't want to be found. Whether he's in danger or not, we should probably know where he is now."

Jordan held his head in his hands. "He is in danger, but you don't believe me."

Poor kid. Even his girlfriend didn't agree with him, and she always seemed to agree with him. I brought his head to rest on my shoulder. Pressing a kiss to his hair, I said, "If I hadn't followed an insane and impossible dream, I wouldn't know you existed. I say we go with it. See what we can find."

"Thanks, Mom." His voice was high and thin.

I petted a hand through his hair. "It's okay. I've got you."

He nuzzled into my shoulder, taking a deep breath before he lifted his head. "What now?"

"Now you tell me about your nightmare again," Cass said. "We'll make a list of the crucial details while Zane sees if she can locate Caleb her way. If the message matches?"

Rennie nodded. "We go."

By the time we talked our way through the story, we had a decent list of clues.

Six (number, six as in six o'clock, back?)

Treasure

West

Where it started

Wits

Abandoned

Lock

Plants (or weeds, or vines)

Skeleton Key

Concrete

Lot

Parking

Cass stared at it some more, this time with a green glow lighting her eyes. She dropped the notebook on the bed and flopped forward onto it. "Not even the Sentinels."

"So we've got nothing," Rennie said. "What about you, Zane? Anything?"

"It should have been easy. A cell phone was obtained by the identity I created for Caleb, but it's locked down surprisingly tight. Hard to track it down," Zane said. "Lots of crosstalk going on. But it's not just that. Everything purchased in his name has been backtracked. Someone is trying to cover all traces of him. But they aren't nearly as good as me. I'm good enough to see it, but not good enough to reverse it. Someone doesn't want him to be found and they're using a technomancer to distort his signal." She looked up, her eyes narrowing when they met mine. "Humor me on something?"

"What?" It was an accusation in a question. I knew whatever it was would be crazy.

"Can you touch the computer?"

"How would that do anything?" Jordan asked.

"Oh!" Jainey said. "Because Mama is magic now!"

"She is?" Rennie asked.

"I'm not magic." I healed people and lifted things and beat up bad creatures and came back from the dead, but I wasn't magic. "Okay, maybe I'm a little magic. But no more magic than I've always been."

She meant what had happened at the museum. With all the excitement today, I'd nearly forgotten about that.

"Touch the computer, Jacklyn." Zane's tone brooked no argument.

I glared at her. What had happened at the museum had been a fluke.

"Come on, Jacks," Cass said. "Touch the computer."

I shot her a look, but I held my hand out to the laptop, pressing it to the space just beside the mouse trackpad. Zane pounded away at the keyboard, her eyes lighting up in the screen's reflection.

"Wait… wait… No, no, no, come on!" She typed furiously. "Jacks, can you give me more?"

"I'm not even giving you anything on purpose," I said. But I felt it. Something in my core, something that felt like my Aegis, but also felt altogether foreign, was feeding into the computer. I closed my eyes and visualized Caleb. I visualized pushing aside barriers between myself and him. Tried to find a way through.

"The Bronx," Zane said. "He's in the Bronx. But I'm having trouble getting a better read on the signal."

I sagged forward slightly. "Dammit." The first time I'd used my Aegis, I'd passed out. This didn't feel much different.

Black edged my vision. Strong arms closed on my shoulders, holding me up.

Jordan.

"The Northeast Bronx," Zane said, excitement lighting up her tone.

Weights hung from my limbs. From my eyelids.

"Enough!" Jordan yanked my hand free from the computer, and it was like fresh air rushed into the room. I could finally breathe.

"I was almost there!" Zane said.

"Not at her expense," Jordan said. "We got closer. That'll have to be enough."

"Maybe we can work through the clues from there?" Rennie said.

I smiled weakly. "Already working on it. Where it all started.

The Northeast Bronx. It's where I'm from. Where Kyp found me when he brought me back to the Order. Give me that list again."

Cass handed it to me while I took deep cleansing breaths, as though it would purge my system of whatever weirdness I'd just experienced.

This time, it made a lot more sense. "The six train runs to the Northeast Bronx. Along *Westchester* Avenue."

"The treasure in the west." Cass frowned. "I wish Kyp was here."

"He wouldn't have gotten it," I said. "He didn't really know my neighborhood. Or Concrete Plant Park on Whitlock. There's an abandoned train station there. It's all in the nightmare."

Zane took the list. "You put that all together because of the Northeast Bronx? Or you pulled that information from the computer when I couldn't even dig it up?"

"I didn't... mean to...?" I shrugged.

"What aren't you telling us, Jacks?" Cass asked.

"I did say no secrets," I said. "But the truth is, I don't know what's happening to me."

"Mama came back stronger," Jainey said. "Right, Jordan?"

Jordan nodded. "But it started slowly. And it's growing."

"Maybe it has something to do with how you and Kyp came back, but Kylie didn't?" Cass asked.

"It's not important," I said. "We find Caleb. We worry about the rest later. One crisis at a time."

And we would. Worry about it. Because I was beginning to wonder what the hell happened to me while I was dead.

Twelve

VIVA LA VIDA

Kyp

There was a time when Kyp had no need to show deference to anyone. In that time, he had been the prospective ruler of the Order of the Key and none of their contacts had dared refuse him anything. But that had all been a ruse. In actuality, his mother had been humoring him in the hopes that one day she would break him, and he would buy into her methods of governing.

Humanity didn't know it, but the Order made a lot of important decisions for them. Sometimes Kyp wondered if that was sustainable. At least the Arvokians had a ruling body that truly served as such.

And the first impression Kyp was giving them was that of a stumbling fool.

Austin caught him by the shoulder and hauled him upward. "Whoa there! Don't pass out on me."

He hadn't been able to help it. He'd felt the cramp that meant his side was less than an hour from tearing open again. This was not going to go well.

Well, that, or they'd have firsthand knowledge of his concerns.

"I'll try, Tex. Thanks."

"No, seriously," Drew whispered. "You look like shit. Are you okay?"

"No, he's not bloody okay," Ray snapped in the same whisper, but with a hiss of anger. "Why the hell would we be here if he was?"

"Quiet," Cxarana croaked.

Sure. Everyone listened to her. But when he spoke? No. Nobody listened to him anymore.

The corridor they traversed was lined with torches. The guard they followed led them to a large open room, lit by several fire pits that cast the entire room in a flickering red light that reflected in the glossy eyes of the small gathering of Arvokians surrounding them.

The guard spoke several Arvokian words that Dhamyan explained to be an announcement of their presence.

In the center of the room, between two large marble pillars, an Arvokian man sat on a stone throne. He was clothed in dark robes, his white hair braided in a crown atop his head, just as Cxarana's had been. His visage was hard, brow heavy, and lips tight.

A stone dais to his right held an Arvokian woman who looked similar to Cxarana. Her white robes trailed past her feet, and the portion that dragged along the blackened earth was smudged with dirt.

A youthful Arvokian joined the woman on the dais. He was smaller in frame than the other Arvokian males Kyp had met, but he had a solid build. He glared down at Kyp and his retinue like they'd come bearing gifts of disease and famine.

Lining the room on both sides, numerous guards stood at

attention, the rigidity of their posture suggesting they were eager for one of them to step out of line. He supposed he would do the same if a group of Arvokians marched into his home.

"Cxarana." The man on the throne spoke.

She stepped forward, her face softer than Kyp had ever seen it. She spoke in Arvokian for a moment. The man nodded sharply.

When he spoke again, he did so within their minds. *"Greetings, Kyp Franklin of the Keys of the Dawn. I learned of your arrival from the spies who keep watch outside of our kingdom. I am King Rhiadon, Cxarana's father, whether or not she chooses to acknowledge it."*

"Hi there, King Rhiadon. I'm Raymond Madison. I understand what's troubling you. I've found my children also struggle with acknowledging me."

Kyp had to grip one hand with the other so as not to literally facepalm at both Ray's lack of decorum and his complete lack of self-awareness.

"He was addressing Kyp Franklin," Dhamyan scolded.

Kyp had to fight down a smile. He knew Dhamyan could pronounce his name.

"Dhamyan, I'm not surprised to see you by my daughter's side in this." King Riadon's brow ridge rose, and it felt less like an acknowledgment of their relationship and more like he considered the man to be a puppy following along after a goddess.

Kyp stepped forward before the man could further insult his friend. *"Please forgive Raymond's insubordination. He means well, but he is not always suited to situations such as this."*

"You have not properly trained your subordinates?" the woman

on the dais asked.

"*Narah,*" Cxarana said within Kyp's mind. "*My sister.*"

Kyp wondered if he was imagining the growl in her tone.

"*These are not my subordinates. The Keys of the Dawn speak to each other as equals,*" Kyp clarified.

"*Of course they do,*" the boy said. "*The humans have lost their way since their leadership changed hands.*"

"*And Merrick,*" Cxarana said. "*My nephew.*"

Now he knew he hadn't imagined the growl.

"*I beg to differ, but that is hardly the current issue, nor is it my reason for coming before you today.*" Kyp straightened and struggled to hide his grimace as the stitch in his side worsened. "*The Rifts between the Dawn and the Dusk have reopened.*"

"*Yes,*" Merrick said. "*We are aware.*"

"*Does this not bother you?*" Ray asked.

"*He means to ask if you could please explain your position,*" Kyp said. "*We are not aware of the Dusk's politics.*"

"*And yet you continue to interfere in them,*" Narah said. She spoke in his mind with less assurance, her voice hesitant and searching. "*We, at least, attempted to understand your politics before we sent our liaisons.*"

"*With all due respect,*" Drew said. "*Your liaisons were only aware of what occurred among the Keys of the Dawn, and not the outside world. Our eyes have been sealed shut by the actions of the council that dictated what the liaisons could say. We wish to understand better. Perhaps we could be of use to each other if we did.*"

King Rhiadon waved his hand through the air and everyone was silenced. *"What is your name?"*

"Andrew Clayson, sir. I'm not a leader or anything. I just wish to find the best solution. My good friend is quite ill. He is suffering from Senefestrian blood poisoning. We've heard there are Rituals we are not privy to, and we simply want access to any of them that may be capable of healing him so we have a fighting chance against whoever opened the Rifts. We know there must be a plot behind this re-opening, and we only wish to come to a conclusion that can help us all. We wish to protect the Dawn, but not at the expense of the Dusk."

Not a leader. Kyp didn't agree.

King Rhiadon grunted and nodded. *"The Dusk is currently in a catastrophic period. We are embroiled in two separate military situations, with no hopes of victory on either side."*

"Father!" Narah's eyes widened, but her mouth remained silent.

"As you well know, our escape from years of slavery was predicated on our escape into the Eventide."

Kyp glanced at Cxarana. Her lips stretched into a smile. "Our pocket dimension."

Yes, that certainly fit the naming convention.

"You have interfered with that," Merrick piped up from his side of the dais.

"We have never interfered with your ability to enter the Eventide," Kyp said. *"Sealing off the Dawn was not intended to do that."*

"You are correct," Cxarana said. *"When my people sought*

escape, they did not understand the concentrated pools of energy that had collected in the Eventide. The modern day Arvokians in the Eventide can't even fathom the power of these ancient Arvokian mages. Their level of power was bred out of us during the years we were in slavery. The mages intended to punch a hole into the Eventide, but accidentally discharged that energy outward, into the Dawn, thus creating the Dawn's first Rifts, and leaking the Eventide's energy into your world. Had the Ritual been done in any other area, or by mages of lesser ability, there would have never been an entrance to the Dawn. Things would have been very different for all of you."

"You have explained more than was necessary," King Rhiadon said, and it may have all been in the translation into their minds, but his tone seemed almost fond.

"Yes, but as one of my Dawn children would say, oh well." Cxarana's eyes sparkled.

"Her allegiance was clear long ago," her sister said, her nostrils flared, chin raised defiantly.

"Those who need to can still escape into the Eventide," Merrick snarled. *"What you fools have done is taken away the distraction of our slavers. The Sirins have redoubled their efforts against us. And worse, your revolution somehow managed to inspire further revolts. Our army is divided!"*

"And so is theirs," Rhiadon said. *"Our only saving grace. The re-opening of the Rifts to the Dawn has only helped us. We cannot assist you in sealing them once again."*

"Can't your Keys help?" Drew asked. *"Where are they?"*

Displeasure rumbled through their minds.

"The Keys of the Dusk are all resistant to King Rhiadon's desire to remain passive in the face of our past actions. They wish to seal all of the Rifts," Dhamyan said. *"I am one of them. We do not align ourselves with the king."*

"Which makes you a traitor within these walls!" Merrick shouted. *"King Rhiadon only allowed this meeting to cater to his daughter's petty whims. We will not work with you because your people are deluded. You crafted an entire class system based upon your Aegis. You're not some evolutionary advancement. You're simply descended from those who were closest to the Rifts when they tore open. Your superiority is merely a gift of accidental proximity. It says nothing of you or your character."*

"Nobody here believes we are anything special," Austin chimed in, hands raised in a placating gesture. *"We just happen to be the only ones standing between the Dawn and the Sirins. The same group that wishes to destroy you. We asked for help, but never for you to treat us as anything more important than you. Or more important than the rest of the people out there."*

"Do not expect to find help in the Keys of the Dusk, either. They are soldiers, but they are not like your Keys. Your line is different. Artificially created," Rhiadon said. *"They will not be able to do what you can."*

A stab in his side nearly brought Kyp to his knees. The scent of rotting flesh wafted up to Kyp's nose. He retched and tipped forward.

Ray caught him around his waist. "No, no, no." His voice held an edge of panic.

For a moment, Kyp had simply been soaking in information to replay in his mind later, and he had forgotten that he was only steps from his own death.

Rhiadon rose from his throne in front of him, his lips a thin line, head lowered and shoulders bowed in. He stepped down from his raised seat of stone and stopped in front of Kyp. *"How old is this child?"*

Kyp opened his mouth to speak, perhaps to say he was not a child. But that was foolish in the face of beings who were ageless.

Ray answered. *"He is twenty. And he has died so many times. Please. I beg you. Give us the tools we need to heal him. He does not deserve this suffering."*

"Ray…" Kyp said, finally summoning enough strength to speak. His heart twisted at the desperation Ray couldn't hide when speaking within their minds.

Dhamyan stepped forward, pulling a thick mound of fabric from a satchel strapped to his thigh, and presented it to Kyp.

Kyp didn't understand, so Dhamyan stepped forward and pressed the fabric to the open wound. Blood spilled down his side.

Kyp took a moment to consider his words before speaking, careful not to offend. "King Rhiadon, this conversation has been extremely enlightening. I'm sorry we couldn't come to a better conclusion for my health, but I do understand your need to keep your culture and your world safe. It's not as though the Order of the Key has always been a group that instills security in the hearts and minds of the people of the Dusk."

"Kyp—"

"No, Ray." Kyp held out a hand, cutting him off before he had the chance to say something foolish.

King Rhiadon reached out with one thin, boney finger and tipped Kyp's chin up. Kyp met his gaze steadily, as he always had with Cxarana. It wasn't easy. His vision swam, the king wavering in front of him as he struggled to keep his face still.

Rhiadon broke their connection and turned toward Cxarana. *"You and yours are our guests. Take the child to rest. I must consider our political allegiances."*

"I understand," Cxarana said. *"Please remember that the Keys and Guardians of the Dawn are indeed mighty. They learn more about themselves and their abilities every day. They could make powerful allies."*

"I will consider this." He caught her hand in his.

"Thank you, Father." She squeezed his hand, then wrapped her arm around Kyp's waist.

"Guards, lead them to the sleeping quarters."

As the guards did as commanded, it was all Kyp could do to catalog the directions in his mind. He could barely keep his legs beneath him. He knew the others were speaking around him, but he'd only just made it through the meeting. The words blurred around him.

Until…

"He's my son in every way that matters. I'd do anything for my children. I don't care what your rules state."

"You are rolling the dice to a gameboard you cannot even visualize, Mr. Madison," Cxarana growled. "I asked you to let Kyp speak."

"And I did. Until he couldn't."

They turned the corner and stepped into a large suite of rooms, with beds of stone and mattresses lined with plush leather, much like the armor Cxarana and Dhamyan wore. It was cool to the touch as Ray settled him down onto it.

Ray turned to get something, but then Austin was there, balling up a sheet from his travel gear.

Kyp might have lost some time. His wound was bandaged, but he was still bleeding through it. As Ray changed the bandaging, Austin lifted his head gently and pushed the balled-up sheet under his head to use as a pillow. He swiped a calloused hand over Kyp's forehead, clearing away the sweat dripping into his eyes.

"Well, this is just dandy. The king better cave and help," Austin grumbled. "Jacks is gonna kill me if I bring this asshole back and he's still dying every coupla hours."

"Austin," Drew scolded from somewhere in the room.

Kyp smiled through the pain. "Relax, Drew. This is just how he shows me affection. Don't worry, Tex. I get it. I think you're swell too."

"Aw, shut up." He ruffled Kyp's hair.

Kyp blinked several times, but each time, his lids took longer and longer to open. He couldn't seem to hold them open completely.

"It's okay, kid," Ray whispered beside him.

When had the torch's fire been doused? It had, hadn't it? Or was he losing his vision? That happened sometimes before he died. Like his brain was shutting down before the rest of his body followed.

The thought made a nauseated panic rise within him and he felt like he was falling. He hated the feeling that his legs were dangling and moving away from him, the way he felt when swimming, the water controlling his limbs better than he did. Frantic, his arm whipped out. "Fight for yourself," Austin said. "Isn't that what you told Jacks? And she came back to ya. Little worse for wear, but still your Jacklyn."

Hearing Austin comfort him made his stomach twist again. Because it meant he made a piteous picture.

"But what if I lose?" Kyp hated the desperation in his voice. "How many times can I fight before I lose? What if I become—"

"You won't." The finality in Drew's tone was a comfort. "And if you did, I'd take you down myself."

Those words made him let go. He trusted Drew to actually do it and do it well.

He allowed his eyes to slip closed, allowed his breaths to slow. Allowed himself to welcome death.

When his eyes re-opened, his body was shot through with a chill, and the torches in the room were lit once again. It took him more than a moment to get a handle on the noise in the room. Shuffling, grunting, and psychic noise that speared through his brain.

And then his eyes zeroed in on something that made him feel like a bucket of ice water had been dumped on him from overhead.

An Arvokian stranger had Ray's wrist in a vice grip.

Kyp threw himself out of the bed, stumbling when his feet hit the floor. Death left him with all the coordination of a newborn foal, but now wasn't a good time.

The room seemed to pause as they all realized he had woken. A group of Arvokian guards had raided their room and were flipping through their things as Kyp's entire party stood on and watched. All their bags had been dumped out, weapons and crystals thrown far and wide.

"Dhamyan, what the hell?" Kyp reached out with his mind. Dhamyan didn't blink. He didn't even look in his direction.

Another Arvokian yanked something out from under Ray's makeshift pillow. An old book or pamphlet. He waved it wildly, speaking in his language with an edge of threat.

"Dhamyan, Cxarana? Someone answer me!" Even within his mind, the words were coarse, scraping across his brain.

Cxarana turned to face him, her eyes even shinier than usual. "My father, the king, is dead. And Raymond just became the prime suspect."

Shit.

THIRTEEN

FINDING CALEB

JACKLYN

The Westchester Avenue Station along Concrete Plant Park in the Bronx had been abandoned since 1937. It was just off the Whitlock Avenue stop on the 6 train, not far from where I lived the part of my life where I was normal. Back when I didn't remember that I was a Key.

It had been overgrown with vines and greenery since before I was born, and the look had only gotten creepier and more overgrown in the few years I'd been gone. The station was decorated with terracotta tiling and had a gothic feel, one that I'd been drawn to as a superhero wannabe.

"We don't have time for a walk down memory lane right now, Jacklyn." Though it was Cass who said it, the green glow of her eyes and her snarky tone told me it was Kylie speaking.

"I'm just trying to figure out our entry point." I swatted a hand her way. It was nearly two-thirty in the morning, and the streets were silent but for the occasional car passing.

"Do you think we should try to climb the gate?" Jainey asked.

I hated that she was with us, but I knew what happened when we didn't keep her close. Zane had strict instructions to take off with her if things went south. But then, Jainey had more than proven her ability to hold her own in a battle.

Who knew what we'd be walking into when we got there?

Rennie motioned to the chain-link fence that came up about a foot over our heads. "An easy climb. Then we could jump to that window and shimmy through."

My eyes narrowed. It was a few feet away. I wasn't sure anyone could make that jump but me and my kids. "That a normal jump for you?"

Her nose crinkled. "Maybe?"

"I'll go first and I'll carry Jainey. Jordan, carry yourself and Rennie over. With your Aegis, you should be able to use your telekinesis and your strength for a boost. Kylie, use your wind and carry yourself and Zane over. Okay?"

Kylie sneered. "Fine. I guess that might as well be the plan."

I took a step toward her. "I know you'd rather be first through."

"So let me," Kylie said. She grabbed my forearm. "This is my son we're rescuing. You never would have let me take point if it was your kids." The desperation in her voice was palpable.

She wasn't wrong. If I was going to execute the plan, I needed Kylie. And I needed her to want to help. "You're right. You and Zane go first."

"Wow!" Her eyes widened. "I'm honestly surprised you gave me what I wanted."

I swatted her in the back to push her forward. She grumbled, but moved.

As expected, the wind picked up around us, buffeting our bodies on all sides as Kylie focused her Aegis.

I stumbled. "Whoa! Could you carry us all over like that?"

"Don't be a fool," she snapped. "I could try, and you could fall." She paused. "Actually, that could be fun."

"Sorry, I thought you'd just gotten good." I lifted Jainey up to rest on my waist and turned my attention to her. "Stay close to me, Cass, Zane, or Jordan. In that order. This isn't your show. Got it?"

"Yes, Mama." She didn't quite roll her eyes, but her sigh revealed her annoyance.

"Don't just yes me," I said. "I'll let you do some Aegis work, but if you're truly in danger, you're out. No questions asked."

"I understand. Promise." This time, her dark eyes met mine, serious in a way her chubby cheeks somehow made adorable.

"Okay, ready?" I asked, glancing at the others, who were already entering the window. "Arms around my back."

She held on like a backpack, and I left for the gate, going up and over in three lunges. The gate shook, metal clanging as I moved. Once I reached the top, I squatted, channeling my Aegis so my sense of balance was perfect. I'd need it.

I darted across the metal rod atop the fence, one foot in front of the other, moving across a width that was thinner than your average balance beam. One step, two, three, and off at a run, moving like the rod might give out underneath my weight, like the floor was collapsing with each step. And… jump.

My hands grasped onto the tiled edge of the windowsill. Jainey squeaked in my ear, her entire body clenching. I could imagine how she must feel. She had no control here, and it must be terrifying.

"Just breathe." I strained to speak as I pulled myself up.

And, as expected, Jordan's hand reached out, his face peeking through the window. "Need a lift?"

"Couldn't hurt." I clasped his forearm, and he hauled me and Jainey up and over.

I stepped down into the station, my path lit only by the ball of fire hovering over Cass's hand, courtesy of either Gana or Mom. Detritus littered the floor, garbage tangled with weedy overgrowth. The air was musty and stale, and I hopscotched my way over the filth until I stood in a clear space with the others.

I lowered Jainey to the floor. "Step carefully."

Cass's eyes drifted closed. "He's here. I can feel him." Kylie's voice returned, her eyes opening.

I shot her a questioning look.

"New powers. Comes with being a Sentinel, I guess." She shrugged.

A hall spread out before us. I added my flame to the light and held out my hand. Beyond an old token counter stood a row of subway turnstiles.

I stepped toward them and right into something that smooshed beneath my feet. Something juicy.

Gross. Please don't be something dead. Please don't be some kind of human waste.

It wasn't. It was food. And it was fresh. Which confirmed someone was camping here.

"Eyes open," I said. "This could be a trap."

Cass and Zane turned to watch behind us as we stepped closer to the turnstiles. They were constructed of wood, not metal, like I was used to. But they were still easy to leap over, something I was way more experienced in doing than I'd ever admit to the kids, and I waved for the others to do the same.

The long hallway branched off into the entrances to what were once the uptown and downtown tracks.

Which way was the right way?

"Were you looking for me?" Caleb's voice echoed through the abandoned station. He stepped out of one of the side doors, waltzing into the center of the lobby. "I've got to say, Jordy, you really understood the assignment." His icy tone sent a shiver down my spine.

"You… you were in trouble. I felt it," Jordan said.

Rennie and I exchanged a look that said it all. On some level, we'd suspected. But would we take the chance there was a kid in trouble and we could have stopped it? Hell no.

"You felt exactly what I wanted you to," Caleb said through clenched teeth.

Scrabbling claws on wood told me there were interdimensionals filling the space behind us as much as the putrid smell of sulfur spoke of an open Rift there. That would have been bad enough if I didn't already know there was something even worse in front of us.

Why set a trap if you couldn't guarantee your prey was surrounded? The sense of foreboding was strong, and I tensed, waiting for an attack from any direction.

"Why?" Jordan's voice cracked with the sting of rejection. "Why would you lie to me? You're my best friend. I would have done anything to help you."

"Because his mother told him to."

That voice.

No.

Lavinia.

She stepped out of the same track Caleb had, looking nothing like I expected. Life in exile clearly hadn't served her well, and she had come out looking feral. Her once flowing black hair had been reduced to an unkempt bob. Green ichor painted her face in rough slashes. Her shoulders were hunched, her knees bent as she stalked forward, dressed in leather-like armor similar to what I'd seen on Dhamyan in the Dusk.

And oh God, was she working with Dhamyan? Had he betrayed us?

"Did I startle you, Jacklyn?" she growled. "How inconsiderate of me."

I shrugged off my surprise. It wasn't easy, but when it came right down to it, Lavinia was just another monster. "Nah, I just thought I'd already killed you. It's all good. Looks like I'll get the chance to do that again."

I couldn't worry about Kyp and the others right now. Caleb was bad enough, but Jordan and Jainey had him matched. Lavinia was a special kind of evil.

"Always so damn confident," Lavinia said. "Strange for a person who lost the last two times we fought."

Anger bubbled in my blood. "I'm not the same girl you fought back at the estate. I could kill everyone in this room and not even break a sweat or shed a tear."

"Jainey, are you crying?" Caleb asked, and he had the nerve to look concerned.

"Don't you talk to her!" Rennie shouted.

"Yes! I'm crying because you chose that mean lady over us! We love you!"

"Caleb, I understand that you're upset," Jordan said. "But this? We aren't the enemy."

"I'm not an idiot! If you don't remember, I'm a Mind Key too!" Caleb growled.

"I never said you were an idiot. But you're misguided. Your emotions are clouding your reason," Jordan cried.

"So are yours," I said, my voice shaky. "So are mine. We should have shot to kill the minute we saw Lavinia beside him."

"You're not killing anyone," Kylie said, stepping forward, her hands held up, placating, as she took a step toward her son. "That woman is not your mother. Not in any way that matters. She tortured your brother. Made his life hell. Tried to murder every single person he loved. I know I don't look like myself, but even a part-time ghost mother is better than that nightmare."

I grabbed Jainey's hand, and her eyes drifted up to mine. "Read my mind," I mouthed.

She squeezed my hand, so I told her the plan and counted to three.

Then I lifted Jainey and hurled her past the Gorvhans and out of the window to my right.

Zane swore and darted for the window, following her. The Gorvhans reached for her, but Jordan held them back with his telekinesis, his brow tightening as he held both his hands out, forcing them to stop in place. Cass leapt into action, fighting her way into the middle of the Gorvhans. She didn't bother to use her sai the way she usually did. Instead, she used the Sentinel's Aegis, Kylie's wind fanning Gana and Mom's flames as she hurled them at her enemies.

That would buy Zane the time she needed to get Jainey out of there. The kid may be powerful, but there was only so much she could do. If Lavinia or Caleb scooped her up, the game was over.

Rennie slid into place between Jordan and the Gorvhans, pulling twin daggers from her boots. She jumped into the fray beside Cass, ducking away from flames and slicing at Gorvhans, the pair managing crowd control so Jordan and I could band together for our main battle.

Lavinia and Caleb. We could handle them together.

We could finish this.

Lavinia smiled, an animalistic grin, her teeth glinting in the fire light. They looked like she'd sharpened them. Before I could attack, she dove for the corridor on the right.

I pulled a throwing star from my pocket and hurled it at Caleb before racing off after her.

"Stay with me," I yelled back at Jordan, pointing to my temple as I moved.

"Goddammit, Jacklyn!" Kylie screeched after me, but I didn't have time to worry about her.

A Lavinia in retreat was a Lavinia with a plan.

I leapt down the stairs after her, channeling my Aegis into my legs to push me off and to absorb the impact when I landed.

Bang. Bang. Bang. Bang. Behind me, something had just rearranged itself as I landed.

I whirled around, expecting to find Lavinia. But she wasn't there. Actually, nothing was behind me. I'd jumped through a doorway, but landed in front of a wall. A wall Lavinia had built from bricks around the abandoned train platform using her telekinetic Aegis.

"What's the matter, Jacklyn?" Lavinia asked. "Is this rescue not turning out the way you expected?"

Lavinia had separated me from Jordan, had trapped me in here with her.

And one of us wasn't leaving here alive.

KYP

"**Y**ou! *You encroached on our world! You murdered our king! My father!*" Narah's slender face twisted with rage.

"Our *father!*" Cxarana yelled, stepping forward to the dais, the same one they had met at just a few hours ago. "*You think I would align myself with anyone who would harm him?*"

"*Besides, we were all asleep when you came in,*" Drew said. "*When would we have killed anyone?*"

Kyp couldn't even bring himself to be properly concerned. He was just so tired. The idea that this would go so incredibly wrong was so on-brand for him, he'd believed he'd talked himself through every possible scenario. Being accused of murdering Arvokian royalty was not one of those scenarios, but he still was not surprised.

"*I would doubt the old one would be capable of killing our king,*" Merrick chimed in. "*Rhiadon was far too great a power to be bested by one as weak as him.*"

Kyp thanked everything and everyone that nobody did something as foolish as taking that bait. He half-expected Ray to pridefully boast of his strength and put himself into an even worse position.

"We have been nothing but respectful of you and your rules since we arrived here," Kyp said, his hands raised as if to ward off their anger. *"We have the utmost respect for you all. In fact, King Rhiadon was kind to us when he didn't need to be and when others would not have advised him to do so. We are eternally grateful to him and have no motive to harm him."*

"Then why was Raymond Madison in possession of this!" Narah slammed down the booklet they'd found under Ray's bed.

At least Ray was blessedly silent. Kyp didn't count on that lasting long.

He stood beside Kyp, head hanging down, expression somber. Some would see this as proof he had harmed the king, but Kyp knew better. It was proof of wrongdoing, but a different one. His careless arguing during their meeting with the king had potentially sealed all their fates, and Ray now regretted his words and actions.

It was too late for regret. Solutions would have to be found. Kyp tried not to allow his search for viable exits into the thoughtline the others could read.

"What even is *that?"* Austin asked.

An exceptional question from Austin. Not bad, Tex.

"That contains the cure to your leader's persistent illness," Merrick explained.

Oh, no. No. Nope.

"If he had that, why wouldn't he have used it already?"

Bad question, Tex. Bad question!

"Who is to say he hasn't? We would not know unless your leader

ceased dying, and he hasn't had enough time alive to determine he hasn't." Merrick strolled around the dais. *"It is only the respect you've shown so far that has kept us from executing you immediately. Dyraxion has mercy on you."*

"Dyraxion has nothing to do with it," Dhamyan said. *"You are all afraid of creating an interdimensional incident… or worse, bringing down the wrath of Kyp Franklin's wife."* He returned his attention to them. *"It is not just King Rhiadon's death they are concerned with. That book is holy. It contains the great higher Rituals of Dyraxion and the other gods. For you to even touch it is blasphemy."*

"Okay, so these Rituals can't be handled by the average person," Drew said. *"And we did not leave our rooms. Even your guards said they bore no witness to us traveling through the kingdom. Is it possible that this book arriving in our quarters is, in fact, the will of Dyraxion or one of the other gods?"*

Kyp swallowed down a gasp. Drew's question was an astute one, and a neat way to get them all out of trouble, but speaking for a person's god was always a bad idea. Kyp even knew that, and he had never lived in the regular human world. Drew had joined the Order as a senior in high school. Surely he should know better.

"You dare to claim knowledge of Dyraxion's will?" Narah's mental voice grew thin and reedy.

"Not at all, Your Highness." Drew humbled himself, kneeling before her and bowing his head. "I am simply trying to put together a feasible explanation. I don't know how the book ended up in our room. Even you can't explain it."

"I can!" Merrick said. *"You are of the Dawn. You have come*

to ask a favor of us. We did not grant that favor. You have decided to take what you believe is yours by force. And your old one has access to abilities he shouldn't have. I've heard this of your kind. Your abilities are artificial. You master abilities at birth that should take you years to master. You are anomalous. With all his additional abilities, your old one could easily sneak by our guards. Who knows the limits of the abilities he could unlock?"

Kyp froze. Unlock things? Anomalous? Anomalous among who? What did he mean they unlocked things before they should have access to them? He didn't understand.

"But I would not," Ray finally spoke. *"Because a boy I took into my care from a young age, a boy I consider a son, was in pain, was defenseless. And I wouldn't leave him alone in a strange land. You seem a decent lot, but other Arvokians have attacked us, and others in the Dusk are our sworn enemies. I wouldn't leave him alone here. Not ever. Not even with the protection of the others."* He turned his attention to Drew, Austin, Dhamyan, and Cxarana. *"Don't take it personally. I've trusted far too many with his well-being over the years. It hasn't proven to be the right choice."*

"It had to be you," Narah said. *"Who else has a reason to harm us this way?"*

"I think the proper question is who does not have a reason." Cxarana started pacing the floor.

Narah's black eyes shimmered. *"You dare?"*

Dhamyan stepped between them. *"You are wrong, Narah. This antagonism between the followers of the Keys and the ruling state is what caused this."*

"Our people were being caught and enslaved by the Sirins! We did what we needed to do to protect our people," Merrick insisted. *"The Keys violated that and endangered our people. They have become traitors!"*

Dhamyan made a rumbling sound low in his throat, almost like a growl, but more inhuman. *"The ruling state holds that title! The Arvokian kingdom is not well-loved. It refuses to choose a side. Those who refuse to take action—"*

"Spare me the ramblings of your human liaison consort," Merrick grumbled.

Heat spread through Kyp, and it was a struggle to hold his tongue. There was never any danger of him murdering King Rhiadon. That little shit Merrick, on the other hand…

"Whoa, whoa," Drew said, holding up his hands in a placating gesture. *"Nobody here wanted King Rhiadon dead. We should be able to work this out."*

"Drew is right," Austin said. *"We came to you for help, but we got why you wouldn't give that help. We figured we'd look for another way."*

"Raymond Madison did not agree," Narah said.

"Raymond Madison is no longer in charge of the Order of the Key." Drew stepped to the front of the group, motioning for the rest of them to fall in line behind him. *"Nobody is. Any large decisions must be approved by the majority of our team. Ray would not have acted without bringing it before the Order for a vote."*

Narah turned to Kyp and Ray, releasing a bitter laugh. *"I'm surprised you would eschew leadership. I thought your kind favored your ritually doctored monstrosities?"*

This again. What was she talking about? Kyp's eyes cut to Cxarana, but she looked away, as though she suddenly found the black spongy floor appealing.

Ray shook his head. *"Doctored monstrosities? None of us have been doctored."*

"Yes, yes. You have no concept of all that you don't know." Narah waved a dismissive hand through the air.

"It doesn't matter who rules you. No assassin would ask permission," Merrick said.

"And what of the Sirin leadership? They would have wanted Father to die," Cxarana said. *"Because it would have left the kingdom in the hands of those with much less favorable opinions on humanity. Like yourselves."*

"You dare to imply I had my own father killed?" Narah snarled. *"Is this a plan for a hostile takeover by the youngest daughter of the king? You brought these humans here to assist in your plan to usurp the king!"*

Austin slapped his hands against his cheeks, letting them drag downward until his lower lids pulled down. *"We did no such thing, lady! And if you think for one second the other Keys of the Dawn won't come looking for us if you hold us, or that you won't be declaring war with the Dawn, you're out of your damn mind."*

"I've heard enough of this!" Narah cracked, her voice going shrill. *"We will further investigate. In the meantime, you are to remain in your quarters. Guards will be posted at your door at all hours and will be ordered to kill anyone who leaves on sight.*

Guards!" She clicked her fingers together.

The guards lining the far wall opened a door. Several more guards streamed into the room, surrounding them on all sides, brandishing blades strapped to the ends of their staffs.

Austin stabbed at Kyp's side with his elbow. "Well, boss. What's your plan?"

"Our plan is that we're going to cooperate," Kyp said.

"They want us to proceed toward our quarters," Cxarana informed them.

The guards led them to their destination, and all the while, Kyp nearly shook apart. He had questions, so many questions about the conversation they'd just mostly listened in on, and he was going to get them.

He waited while the door slammed, only this time he heard locks sliding into place. They were well and truly trapped within stone walls without any conceivable means of escape.

And then he whirled to face Cxarana. She raised her chin defiantly. She knew. The comments of the others may have slid under the radar of their friends, but not his. Though he hadn't understood what they were saying, he had committed it to memory, and now that he had the space to react, he played through it for himself once again.

"A lot to digest in that conversation, huh?" Kyp spoke through gritted teeth. He stalked forward until he had boxed her in against the wall. Everyone allowed him to advance but Dhamyan, which Kyp could respect. But he couldn't allow it to stop him.

"You've been holding out on us," Kyp said. "You're going to

fill me in. Because I'll be damned if I'm going to die uninformed."

Cxarana emitted an odd click, her eyes moving up and away. "You've picked up a few things from your… wife."

"Jacklyn would have already knocked you on your ass, but I'm going to give you one chance first. But only one. I think it's time for you to come clean with us."

Fifteen

VENGEANCE

Jacklyn

My eyes struggled to adjust to the darkness surrounding me. The rubble had fallen in a way that blocked out all but a sliver of light from the window across from the subway tunnel. I'd need to buy time if I was going to stay safe.

I gave my head a little shake, then focused my Aegis into my hands so I could throw a fireball on the floor and light the filth and long abandoned garbage there as kindling.

My hand remained open, empty and cold. This was bad.

She'd done it again, just like she had during our first fight against each other. She'd isolated us, and then she'd nullified my Aegis.

It must have taken her time to prepare. I'd read up on the nullifying spell since then. To accomplish it, you needed to know every potential ability and strip them one by one. She'd found a perimeter and set the trap, and my dumb ass had run right into it.

"You thought you'd harmed me, didn't you?" Lavinia's voice moved through the darkness, the shadow of her willowy body flickering as she moved closer.

The nullified Aegis thing explained my inability to adapt quickly to the change in lighting as well.

"You believed you'd truly ended me this time. But I found my footing. I always do. And I've become something greater in my time in the Dusk."

"This isn't exactly what I expected from you," I said, but even I heard the quiver of panic in my voice as I followed her movements. "I never expected you to release control to a child."

She laughed bitterly. "I don't need to. Not when I finally have a son who wants to follow in my footsteps. A son who understands what is truly important."

I knew her game. She wanted me so consumed with rage that my brain disengaged. It was my rage at her murdering my sister and my shock at losing my Aegis that had tanked me in our first battle.

I breathed in through my nose, out through my mouth.

"Through Caleb, I will have what I always wanted to have. A legacy. And a solution."

When I was sure I located her, I spun and let my fist fly. It connected with her chin in a brutal right hook. "You have nothing."

Her head twisted with the blow. She was closer to the light now, and I could watch as she swiped a hand across her nose, blood smearing the back of her hand. Her eyes dipped from her hand to me before anger and disbelief flared within them. "Just like a Body Key. All brute force. No finesse. You think you can bully me—"

I took a step closer. "You stole my Aegis because you're too scared to face me in a true fight."

I had trained for over a year to become a better fighter. Someone who could fight without my Aegis in tow. I had been in so many more skirmishes since then, with whole rooms full of creatures and vile humans.

I kept reminding myself that this wasn't the same. Still, my nerves reminded me that if it hadn't been for Ray's sudden and shocking arrival, I may not have made it here at all.

"Is that what you believe?" Lavinia asked, the darkness making her features colorless in a way that erased some of the harsh predatory nature she normally possessed. "I only stepped in because Hector and Gretchen weren't good enough to dispatch you. That wasn't an issue with dear Gana, though, was it?"

Cold and unapologetic. About the murder of a thirteen-year-old girl.

She thought she was making a point, but the first time around, it had taken Gretchen, Hector, and Lavinia to take me down. Despite the evidence in my favor, she was a powerful Mind Key, and all my nightmares involved this woman. Her fighting me, tormenting me, killing me. It was time I put a stop to that. I was not weak. I would not allow her to make me weak.

I couldn't let her walk away this time. I had to stamp her out of our lives. This needed to be her end.

Centering myself, I drew from my training. Still, my stomach twisted with the memory of the last time I'd felt so far from my Aegis. It helped that my eyes were beginning to adjust to the darkness.

I heard a rustle in the debris below, the sound of swift footsteps gliding forward in the dark. She'd expect my next move, but I didn't care. I swung a fist at her again. Her arm came up to block, and I grasped her wrist. My ankle slid behind her knee, hooking it and dropping backwards. With a quick pivot, I twisted her arm up behind her back and used her own weight against her until it snapped.

All before she could mount any kind of defense.

I released her and she fell face first. Her head hit the ground with a ghastly thunk that would have made me wince had I been fighting anyone else.

A force shoved at me and I flew up and off her, her psychic touch like being thrown by an invisible hand. That hand tossed me far, and I collided with a subway pillar. Pain radiated through my back and I gasped for air, my lungs having emptied on impact.

Fucking telekinesis.

"I must tell you, Jacklyn, since I heard you fools rustling about outside, I haven't been able to stop smiling." She rolled to her feet and did a hop step across the floor. Gone were the clicking heels, all the composure. She was another monster now, flitting around like the Joker taunting Batman, even as she held her one arm tightly against her chest.

"Jeez," I said when I got my breath back. "A year and a half living in the Dusk really detached you from reality, huh?"

"Have you forgotten the damage I'm capable of?"

I hadn't. I still performed the Mind Block Ritual regularly for that very reason. And though the Ritual held, I could still feel attempts at control slamming on my mental door.

I shouldn't have given her time to gloat, but I didn't have my healing, and I didn't have strength, and my back throbbed from how hard it had smacked into the wall. I pulled myself to my feet, one hand against the pillar for leverage.

"That's the fun thing about this set up. You want revenge?" She drove her fist into my stomach, and my air left me once again. "Well, so do I."

"Liv," I gasped. I wanted to tell her she hadn't just hurt me, she had hurt Kyp. Maybe I wasn't the one to have this fight. But there was something deep within that told me Kyp might fight her, but he would never end her.

And at this point, ending her might be a mercy for all of us.

She swiped forward, something sharp slicing through the air. I jumped back, narrowly avoiding it tearing through my stomach. I squinted at the weapon.

Was that a knife made of bone?

Ew.

Another tilt of her head and I flew off the train platform and down into the tracks. My head smacked into the steel rail, and my vision went red.

Shit, shit, shit. Pain flared, angry and jagged-edged.

Forget the pain. It's temporary. Pain can't kill you. Not you.

Austin's words from when we'd been training together rattled around my brain.

Push through it.

And I really hoped that was still true, despite the way she'd nullified my Aegis.

I pushed my fingers into the grit below me, grabbing handfuls of dirt as I struggled onto my feet. She wasted no time, dropping onto the tracks beside me before I found my footing.

It felt like a freight train had driven through my brain. But I didn't need my brain, and I didn't need my Aegis. I still had that little girl in me, the one who'd been bullied through childhood. The one who had never felt like she had belonged and who never knew why. And she'd been taught to fight long before I remembered what an Aegis was or how to use it. I had instincts.

I thrust my clenched fist at her face, releasing the grit. I wrapped my leg around her ankle and pulled forward.

She wobbled for a moment, but recovered and snapped a kick at my face.

My vision erupted into blasts of light, and my head jerked back. Blood and sweat stung my eyes, and I was shocked I could still feel all of my teeth in my mouth. It felt like they should be long gone.

Despite the way the ground seemed to pitch and sway beneath me, I rose to one knee. The struggle took just long enough that she was on me, swinging another fist my way.

We traded blows, one after another, until blood dripped from my mouth, and my ribs were bruised and achy. I knew she wasn't doing much better. She swayed in front of me.

Her hand wrapped around my throat, but her hold was weak. "Just relax," she hissed. "It will all be over soon."

I chopped one hand against the center of her forearm. She'd grabbed me with her broken arm. Why would she do that?

White hot searing pain exploded across my vision. My hand moved to my side as a reflex, but the bone knife Lavinia'd had earlier was plunged in deeply enough that removing it would bleed me dry, and every move I made with it still within me would only heighten the pain.

Shit. She was going to kill me.

I couldn't let that happen. Jainey and Jordan needed me. Kyp could very well be gone.

Forget the pain. Death isn't permanent. Not for you.

Pain was temporary, but death was imminent. I just needed to make sure she got there first. If I let her live, she would take my family apart piece by piece. And if it meant protecting the people I loved, I'd already shown I wasn't afraid to die.

I didn't get the impression she knew how goddamned determined I could be.

I reached for the front of her top, grasping the leather-like material in my hand and pulling her closer to me. Lunging forward, I head-butted her hard enough to send both of our heads spinning. But I was prepared.

She threw herself back and away from me, which was exactly what I wanted.

One thing I'd learned from my bullying days was that the winner of a fight wasn't always the aggressor, nor was it always the retaliator. It was the person who took control of the battle. And that's what I needed now.

My body was leaden and sluggish. I kicked my foot up with all my remaining strength. Once I had a little more distance, I ripped the knife out of my side. The three-inch blade's jagged edges ripped through muscles, sinew, and skin and scratched along two of my ribs.

My jaw tensed against the sour taste of bile flooding my mouth. *Pain. Is. Temporary.*

"This time, this ends. I'm not letting you go again."

I launched myself to my feet and threw myself forward onto Lavinia and pummeled her face with my fists until they ached. Right. Left. Right. Left. Right. Left. Each hit landed with a deafening crunch.

The ground pitched below me once again, and I dropped to my knees and stopped punching. I needed to get back up.

I did not feel pain. I *could* not feel pain. Every swing of my arms did not send trails of agony into the stab wound at my side, didn't make it feel like it was ripping open even further, like if I didn't stop, my organs wouldn't just flop out onto the dusty ground. My blood was not leaking out, staining that ground. My vision wasn't swimming in front of my eyes. I didn't feel even the slightest bit unsteady.

This fight would not end the way the other had. She would have to kill me harder than last time.

I willed myself upright, but I was too slow. I'd given her enough time to recover.

Her eye socket was broken, if the swelling was any indication. Her nose as well, based on the pattern of the blood on her face. I was sure I didn't look much better, but then, I would heal. And she'd never get the chance to if I had anything to say about it.

Her telekinesis tugged at me again, yanking me up and then driving me back down. My hair whipped around me as I crashed to the floor. A crack, and I cried out. One knee had touched down wrong, and that was my kneecap, definitely moving somewhere it shouldn't. I grunted to tamper down another scream building within me.

"You know I'll win," Lavinia said, blood coating her teeth and dribbling from the side of her mouth. Her words were slurred. I may have broken her jaw. *Poor baby.*

"And you know I won't stop fighting."

I would not feel pain. Pain would not be my end.

Did her internal monologue sound anything like mine?

I crawled forward despite the agony in my leg. The tips of my fingers brushed against something. The knife I'd pulled from my side, carved from bone. My hand wrapped around the smooth handle, and I slid the knife up into my sleeve.

"No!" she snarled.

Another tug. I gripped onto the metal rod that connected the rails with both hands. I refused to let her take me for another ride.

The fasteners creaked, and the metal turned. One rotation.

"What will you hold on to when I pull them out?" Lavinia asked, voice garbled. "Will you grab the rails next?"

She wasn't wrong. What could I grab?

I reached for the third rail with one hand. Something rushed through me, but it wasn't electricity. There hadn't been electricity running through that rail for years. But there was the remnant of power once rushing through it. I could sense the electricity that had once been, the conduit still ripe for use.

That's when I realized Lavinia couldn't know about my recently acquired energy ability. She wouldn't have known to block it. I didn't understand it, but I didn't have to. However the electricity had found its way to me, it was there. There was no room for doubt anymore. My hair crackled more the tighter my focus became.

A zap of electricity shocked along my fingers. It should have hurt. But I just felt open. Free.

I pressed my fingertips to the rail and sent it through the metal and into Lavinia. The electricity crackled through me and into her, my blood heating until it was unbearable. The pain pulled a scream free from the both of us, but it was she who shook with the voltage as it raced through her until she flew backward from the force of the current.

Spikes of pain stabbed through my side and my arm, and my legs gave out whenever I tried to get to my feet. I crawled forward, pulling myself along on my hands and my one working knee to where Lavinia lay on the tracks, twitching. Her mouth was locked in a silent scream, but she stared up at me, eyes focused and determined. She was trying to do something, use her Aegis, but the energy simply wasn't there.

I yanked the knife out of my sleeve. Spots broke out along my vision, but I held on.

I had to hold on.

I could faint later.

I maneuvered her carefully until her back was pressed against my chest and ducked my head forward so I could make eye contact with her. "You with me, Liv?"

The look she flashed at me was the pure fury that burned within her. But it was never as bright as my fire.

"Wonderful. I want you to know this." I bent a little closer. "Kyp suggested I do this Gana's way."

She didn't bother to hide the shock on her face.

I slit her throat. Her blood pooled along the slice, spilling over from the wound, the same way Gana's had. Her breaths choked out of her, thick hissing sounds wet with gore. Her heartbeat pounded and then slowed, each pulse gushing blood further out of the wound. Her skin was pale and clammy. And then the shock slid from her eyes as they went glassy and then dimmed. And all at once, the source of my worst nightmares was gone.

I had taken her life just like she had taken Gana's.

And I had told her it was Kyp's idea.

Maybe I wanted to cut Lavinia deeply in more than one way.

I refused to feel bad about the lie. He deserved some sort of revenge for what she'd done to him for years. It may not be enough, but I would be damned if I left him completely out of this.

Especially because what I was about to do was risky as hell. I couldn't know what Kyp was up to, or even if he was alive. I did know that a Death-Bringer Ritual could reach further than the person it was cast on. That there was no way of knowing for sure how far it could reach, or if it could span dimensions. But once a Key was killed, the Ritual could permanently kill whoever it reached.

I could be killing Kyp with this move.

But the thing that terrified Kyp more than anything was that he'd leave and something would happen to the kids. Jordan was out there fighting Caleb by himself, Jainey was out there with interdimensionals attacking her protectors. If I let Lavinia come back, she would kill them. The only thing distracting her, the only thing standing between her and those kids, was me.

When Kyp had recruited me, he had called me his weapon. But I was more than that. I was a weapon with choices.

Ray had allowed Lavinia to stay alive to avoid looping me into the Death Bringer Ritual. Everything that had happened after — our deaths, Kylie and Ross's deaths, the torture the kids had suffered—it all happened because Ray chose to save me over killing Lavinia.

All I could do was pray to any and everything out there listening that Kyp was either too far away, or was far too alive to be looped into the Ritual. After all, Ray had given me that locket for a purpose.

I reached for the locket hanging from my neck and pried it open. It contained two vials. I sprinkled the Arvokian herb, Dreviara, in a complete circle around her body, the same way Lavinia had once done to me. The herb's spicy scent left my hands shaking, but I pushed for control. I needed to do this correctly.

As I moved, my knee pulled back into place with a click, and the wound in my side began to knit together. The Ritual must have been tied to Lavinia. And now that she was gone, it was gone too. Good, because the more I healed, the faster I could move. I had a job to do, and I didn't know how long I had to do it.

Once I'd outlined her body with the herb, I removed the second vial from the locket. I covered the herbs with the Arvokian blood within it. Then, with a mere snap of my fingers, I lit the herbs on fire. I muttered a sentence in Arvokian, my lips barely moving, but it did the job. Pure white smoke slithered off the burning herbs and into Lavinia's nose like an ethereal serpent. It made its way into her nostrils and out through her open mouth, out through the gaping bloody wound I had made in her throat.

The smoke exited with a blue sheen, just like Ray had taught me to expect, until it dissipated.

I completed the Ritual. She was gone. I had finally attained the vengeance that swallowed my life for so long. Lavinia, the woman who had destroyed a part of my soul, of Kyp's soul, was never coming back.

I had expected to feel lighter. So what was this weight crushing me?

I dropped to the ground beside her, the ground shifting beneath me, dizziness taking hold now that the important part was over.

If you had asked me a few years ago if I would have a nemesis, I would have told you that only happened in comic books and movies.

It had been a long time since I'd allowed myself to enjoy any of the things I enjoyed doing. A long time since I'd bothered popping into a comic book shop or checking out a movie. My normal life was gone, replaced by a reality in which I lived my own adventure plot.

It wasn't nearly as fun as it looked in comics and movies. No ink, no cameras, no amount of compelling storytelling or dramatic recreations could properly express the thrill of a life saved or the pain of a life lost. Nothing could tell you how you would feel about destroying the person who so thoroughly destroyed you.

Vengeance sounded so good in theory.

SIXTEEN

ANSWERS

KYP

Kyp asked for answers, but instead, he got a bony hand pressed to his forehead.

"You're developing a fever, Kyp," Cxarana said, her voice steady. "That is likely the first sign that the Senefestrian poisoning is taking hold."

He swatted her hand away. "Stop that! Stop… *mothering* me. In every sense of the term. I didn't ask for you to distract me. I want the truth!"

For a moment, her hand hung in the air. But when she dropped it, her entire body slumped in a sigh.

"Keys in the Dusk are more like Guardians in the Dawn. They are naturally occurring. Born with one primary ability from their Aegis type," Cxarana said. She glanced over at Dhamyan, who leaned back against the gray stone wall, golden eyes flickering, lips turned down.

Another sigh.

"You understand that the Arvokian liaison meets with every

Key and every Guardian upon their initiation into the Order of the Key, correct?" Cxarana said.

"Of course," Kyp said.

But at the same time, Austin said, "I never did."

"You never did what?" Kyp said.

"I was never initiated," Austin said. "Zane neither. We didn't want anyone picking up on Ray or Jacklyn, so we were totally off the radar."

"I know, and I chose to do nothing about it," Cxarana said.

"Why not?" Drew asked.

"Because I developed a fondness for Kyp that expanded far beyond what it should have," Cxarana explained. "Because I wished to give your team an advantage, and I felt that having uninitiated Guardians would provide it."

"Cxarana," Kyp growled.

"I told you I would assist you as I could. This was one of the few ways I found."

"Dhamyan," Ray said, speaking up for the first time since in the kingdom's throne room. *"What abilities does a Key of the Dusk possess?"*

"A Key is born with one distinct ability. One solitary ability that is part of their complete Aegis. They live with that ability from the time they are born until they reach adulthood. And then the rest of their Aegis starts to develop."

Kyp's stomach dropped with the memory. He'd been struggling, using his and Jacklyn's joint powers to save Jordan and Rennie after a gruesome car accident. And as they were running out of juice,

Austin accidentally bled into the wound and they made a discovery they'd never accepted.

And Zane? He'd never fully comprehended Zane's ability. She could communicate with electronics, but she could also short things out. Did she have two abilities, and he just never categorized them that way?

"Like, say, for instance," Austin said, *"if a guy grew up his whole life only being able to heal himself, but one day, by accident, he discovers he can heal something else? Like that?"*

"Just like that," Dhamyan agreed.

Cxarana dipped her chin. "In the Dawn, there are no true Keys. There never have been."

"Never?" Ray asked. "Then what the hell are we?"

"The product of ancient Arvokian Rituals." She motioned toward Drew. "One that stunts the growth of a Key." Then she motioned to Kyp and Ray. "And another to accelerate that growth."

The anger that had been at a low but steady heat since he'd woken up hit a boil. "The Arvokian Council played god! They're no better than Livingston!" He swung his fist through the air.

Austin caught it before it hit the stone wall. "No broken hands. We've got enough troubles."

Kyp released a shout of frustration, then flopped backward onto the bed he'd claimed the night before." How did they choose?"

"Choose?" Cxarana asked, tilting her head.

"Who we'd be," Kyp said. "Who got the privilege of being a Key, and who..." He locked eyes with Drew, who nodded. "Didn't?"

"When the Rifts opened in the Dawn, those born near the Rift energy were born as Keys. But there were those who wished to suppress that strength in certain types of people. They couldn't completely remove their abilities. So they worked with the Arvokians to suppress the growth of some, and accelerate their own, thus allowing them to retain their, as you said, privilege."

"That bullshit really does climb into everything, doesn't it?" Drew's nostrils flared.

"Far as I'm concerned, there's only two types of people in any of these worlds," Ray said. "Those who care about others and treat everyone with respect, and those who can fuck all the way off."

Drew snorted a laugh and clapped Ray on the back. "Nicely put. I tend to agree. But many people don't."

Drew would know. As a gay Black man raised in foster care, he faced more than his share of discrimination.

"How do we fix it?" Austin crossed his arms over his chest.

"I don't know," Cxarana said. "I know how to perform both Rituals, but I don't know how to reverse them."

"Who would?" Kyp asked.

"We would need the ancient Arvokian's Ritual book," Cxarana said.

"The book that Merrick prick planted on me?" Ray asked. "Because if you don't know it was him behind that little frame job—"

"We know you were framed," Dhamyan said. *"Who did it is at question. But Merrick is definitely a suspect."*

Ray huffed. "Suspect, my arse."

"Where would they stash it?" Austin asked.

"They would likely keep it within Father's sitting room, if they have already appropriated it," Cxarana said. "However, I do not see why this is essential information. We are effectively contained within this room. Even attempting to leave would be equivalent to admitting to murder."

"It would be worth finding a way to break out," Drew said. "We need the Rituals in that book. We need to treat Kyp, and we don't know when he'll get worse. Add to that the fact that we don't know how the Rifts reopened. We may need that full power in our back pocket if there's another threat on the horizon."

"Yeah, but how you gonna get past the guards and the damn boulder in our way?" Austin asked.

Kyp pushed down the anxiety that built in his chest with every minute he got closer to another death. If they were going to do this, they had to do it soon. "Ray could lift it aside. We could fight the guards, but more would come shortly after. So how do we make sure nobody comes running?"

Drew hummed in agreement, then gasped. "Cxarana, where are the bathing chambers in the castle?"

"They are hardly about to allow us to bathe, Andrew," she replied.

But Kyp understood. He looked at Drew and smiled. "Terrifying. I love it."

"Can I offer constructive criticism?" Austin asked.

"No," Drew answered.

"Then can I offer destructive criticism?"

"No, sweetheart." Drew looked up at him with heart eyes. "You can't stop me from taking risks. That's not how this works. And I was kicking ass long before I met you. Particularly at this. Chill."

They were crowded at the door, listening for sounds of the distraction Drew would be causing if Tex could shut up for a damn minute.

Ray stepped a little closer to Kyp. "How are you feeling?"

"I'm holding up so far, but we really need to get moving." Kyp raised his voice a little so Drew and his boyfriend could hear. "Less cute, more action."

"He thinks we're cute together." Austin rocked on his heels.

Drew squirmed in place a little. "Okay, okay, enough. Let me concentrate."

Drew closed his eyes, his brow knitting as he pressed a hand to the boulder. "Cxarana, I need you to… This is going to sound strange… How does plumbing work here?"

Cxarana bared her naturally yellow teeth. "We've adopted some of the Dawn's more rudimentary technology. Piping, water pumps, things such as this. I'm not terribly well-versed. I am a royal scholar. I was to learn about the Dawn, not the bathing chambers." She waved her hands in front of her in a gesture that was unfamiliar, but clearly showed how useless she felt.

"That helps," Drew said.

Kyp smiled at the show of support.

"Just beyond the mountains surrounding this castle, there's a river. An aqueduct system. The bathing chambers pull from the water there." Drew looked up from the boulder. "I'm about to make a mess. I hope you all can swim."

Tex grimaced. "No?"

"You're dating the designated water guy and you don't know how to swim?" Ray asked.

"Is that what you think we're doing, asshole? Going for swimming lessons?"

Kyp didn't like water on his face, hadn't since he was a child and his mother had decided drowning was an acceptable punishment for poor behavior. "Just hold your breath. I'll help you."

Austin frowned. "Not gonna leave me to die, then?"

Kyp grinned. "What can I say? I like seeing Drew happy."

Shouts cascaded down the hall, and Drew rolled up the sleeves of his oversized button-down. "Let's do this. Ray, Kyp? You guys ready to move mountains?"

"It's a boulder, but yeah, sure." Ray shook his hands out. "Out?"

"Yes, and we'll do the rest of the work."

Ray stepped forward and pushed against the boulder, the muscles in his arms and the veins on his neck straining with the effort.

"Tell me this is gonna work," Kyp whispered under his breath. Because it couldn't not work.

He had to get home. He had to get back to them.

The boulder moved. Kyp focused his Aegis on pushing the boulder over to the right with his mind while Drew controlled the flood he'd created. The idea was to pull it back and push it into the boulder with the force of a fire hose.

Austin circled behind him, standing by the boulder, ready to jump out to take down the guards, along with Dhamyan and Cxarana.

The muscles in Kyp's side twisted.

Crap. *Don't panic.* They still had time. He pushed additional Aegis strength behind the boulder.

A great rumbling sound, and the boulder rolled out of the way, the doorway opening to sounds of a struggle. Austin, Dhamyan, and Cxarana rushed forward, with Ray, Drew, and Kyp following behind.

Kyp barely made it two steps out before Ray and Drew were thrown in opposite directions and a force crashed into him, slamming him into the stone walls.

An Arvokian woman with tomato red hair that flowed down to her waist in waves, steel-blue eyes, purple skin, and a feral smile had him pinned to the wall with a knife to his throat before he could blink. "Kyp Franklin. I have heard you are the father of two Skeleton Keys."

The scent of petrichor filled the hallway as the water rushing into the chamber brought moss and weeds along with it.

Kyp glanced up and down the hall, looking for an opening for escape, but the others were preoccupied, fighting along with other Arvokians to defeat the guards.

Her knife biting into his throat told him he was taking too long to respond.

"Who I father isn't really your business, is it?"

God, he really needed to stop picking up Jacklyn's habits.

"Skeleton Keys are my business," she explained.

"Because you'd like to kill them?" Kyp asked, hoping that

wasn't the explanation.

"Not at all, Kyp Franklin," she hissed. "Because I happen to be one."

Seventeen

BOOMERANG

Jacklyn

The sound of gunshots on the streets of New York City jolted me back to awareness. I hadn't been out for long, but it was long enough.

I reached out with my mind. *"Jainey? Jordan?"*

"Mama!" Jainey's voice echoed in my mind.

"Yeah, baby. I'm... here. Stuck behind a brick wall, but I'm here. Are you all safe?"

A slight hesitation. *"Relatively? I'm going to come get you. Please hold."*

She sounded like a little telephone operator. I didn't like that 'relatively.' I wrapped my arms around the ache forming in my twisting stomach. Something fluttered near the ceiling, and I automatically focused my Aegis until I could see the tiled mosaics along the ceiling in the station. I'd meant to lay off my Aegis, hoping to heal my injuries before I jumped back into the fray, but if it was dangerous...

It was nothing. Well, not nothing. A black butterfly moving

through the air. But not a threat.

And not Jainey either.

God, I probably had a concussion.

Now that the fight had ended, I noticed this place was actually somewhat peaceful.

A bang echoed through the space, and my heart stuttered. I was on my feet in seconds.

The Madison-Franklin crew never really left anything peaceful for long.

Another slam.

"Jainey?"

"Shhh, Mama. You'll call attention to us."

Right. Because the banging she was sending through the whole station wasn't doing that already.

"Duck and cover, Mama. I'm coming through."

No hesitation. If she was breaking through, I needed to get the hell out of the way.

I raced around to the side of the staircase and ducked as tightly as I could manage. My side, my arm, my head, my back—they all ached. I covered my ears and pulled all my Aegis power into healing my arm and my side, just to make sure none of it went to my ears.

The bricks that had walled up the exit burst free from the doorway, flying out and hitting the far wall. The crash was deafening, even with my deadened hearing.

"Mama!"

I breathed in some of the dust that was blowing around and immediately started choking.

Jainey rushed to my side, rubbing my back as I struggled to catch my breath. "You're okay, Mama. Just breathe."

I tried not to shoot her a look.

Once I got control of my lungs, I checked Jainey over. She had a few cuts and scrapes, and dirt streaked her face, but she looked mostly uninjured. "You okay?"

Jainey nodded. "Got knocked around. A little discombobulated. You?"

"Very discombobulated. But alive. Which is more than I can say for Lavinia."

"Temporarily?" Jainey asked.

"Not this time."

She placed a tiny hand on my shoulder. "Hey, you did it!" It sounded condescending as hell, but I'd take it.

"Yeah." I punched the air. "Victory!"

"Well, for this battle," Jainey said. "Jordan is still fighting Caleb… and there's even more bad guys down there. We need to go help them now." She tugged on my bad arm. Thankfully, it was healing enough that I didn't throw up when she yanked it.

"We will. But not that way," I said. "We have to start by closing that Rift Caleb opened in the lobby."

"Awesome," Jainey said. "On it." She scrambled out of the debris made by her own explosion, climbing over the stairs and back off the platform.

"Wait!" I followed after her as quickly as my bruised body could manage. "Jainey!"

It was something I hadn't thought about before. There could be

Gorvhans crawling through that Rift, and I had just called Jainey to me. Jainey could have been killed by Gorvhans because I wasn't thinking.

A growl from above got me racing up the stairs. Jainey took it in stride, lighting a fire in the detritus behind the sole Gorvhan who bothered to turn her way, then pushing it into said fire with her telekinetics. The room filled with the creature's ear-piercing screeches and the stench of its burning body, but Jainey's only reaction was a blank stare.

It would be fascinating if it wasn't terrifying.

Three more Gorvhans headed for the window, but they didn't get far. Jainey reached back for my hand and I didn't even think to not grab hers.

She glanced back at me with her eyes wide, and yanked the energy from the Gorvhans, until they were withered husks. It pushed into me, a dark chill swirling along my arms and through my veins, pushing into my core.

She basically fed them to me.

"For you to heal," she said flatly. "You could have died. And we still need to fight."

She motioned toward the window, and I looked through it to find a full brawl taking place under the elevated tracks.

Jordan and Caleb were psychically shoving each other around. Pulling each other away from others they didn't want in danger. The other two Guardians created in the lab had joined in on Caleb's side and were squaring off against Rennie and Cass.

And Zane, two handguns held forward, stood amidst a veritable sea of Sirins and Gorvhans.

Swears erupted from me. Just call me Mt. Vesuvius.

"Like I said," Jainey interrupted my thoughts. "We have a whole fight left." She wiped at her hand, and a gash in her palm disappeared. She'd sealed the Rift while I'd been taking in the mess I'd missed.

"A fight?" I asked. "I'm going to have to go full Hulk mode." I grabbed her hand. "I was going to do that."

She grinned. "Too slow." She hopped up on my back. "Let's do this. I'll help."

"Hold on tight." I gripped her arms where they rested on my shoulders. Channeling my Aegis into my leg muscles, I leapt out of the window and into the fray, Jainey's telekinetics clearing the way for a safe landing in the midst of the crowd.

The battle froze around us and Caleb gasped, a terrible choking sound.

"You killed her."

The battle restarted around us, Caleb, Jordan, Jainey, and me standing still in the center of the chaos.

"You don't know—" Jordan swiped blood from his nose.

"She wouldn't have let her come back alive," Caleb shouted. "You killed my mother!"

"She wasn't your mother," I said. "She didn't love you. She was using you!"

"Fuck you!" Caleb shrieked. "You don't know anything. You're a coward."

"A coward? And you set a trap for us. Not very noble of you."

"You're too scared to gain the power that is your birthright."

"This isn't your dream! It's hers! What do you gain from it?"

"She said we could run this new world together," he cried, tears glistening on his cheeks. "Remake the human part in our image. Choose who we wish to have power and who we wish to be weak. She said we could change everything."

"Look, I'm not trying to argue with you, kid, but you don't know what you're doing."

"And you do? God, you're everything she said you were. An arrogant punk who thinks she's managed to seduce her way to the keys to the kingdom. But life doesn't work that way." He reached out a hand. "I can't do this anymore. You killed my mother, so I'm going to kill your son."

He twisted his hand in the air, and Jordan cried out and fell, his kneecaps cracking against the concrete.

Jainey rushed to his side.

"My legs! He broke my legs."

Behind me, Rennie shouted at the others. "Reilly, let us help you!"

"We don't need your help!"

Metal clanged, and Zane's gunshots rang out, but it was muffled by the ringing in my ears and the words that repeated there over and over.

You killed my mother, so I'm going to kill your son.

Vengeance. It hadn't brought Gana back, and it wouldn't bring Lavinia back for Caleb. And I had just pointed my knife back at myself.

"No, wait!" Jainey screamed.

But Jordan was already being dragged across the floor toward Caleb, his jeans tearing and blood seeping out from beneath him.

Jainey pulled in the other direction, and Jordan fell onto his back, dragging back across the sidewalk.

Jordan wasn't fighting for himself. He was starting to struggle with his breathing again.

I threw a ball of fire at Caleb. I didn't care how much the kids loved him. I wasn't going to let him continue to harm Jordan.

With a swish of each of his hands, Caleb countered with a fierce gust of wind that blew the fire into embers, and another that blew back toward us.

I braced myself, grabbing onto one of the pillars holding up the elevated train station and reaching for Jainey's hand.

The other gust blew toward her with speed.

I grabbed her hand in mine and held on. But she flopped backward, and a rock hit the floor beside her.

A rock.

Caleb had thrown a rock at Jainey's head.

Caleb had knocked my daughter out with a goddamn rock.

The gust of wind calmed, and I rushed to her side. My eyes burned as rage seared through me.

"Jainey!" A slice had opened in the center of her forehead, blood dripping freely along her ashen skin, flowing back toward her ears.

That motherfucker.

The fight continued around me, but Zane and Rennie pushed in closer to keep me safe while I checked on her.

Her eyes cracked open at my call, slices of hazel revealed before her eyelids fluttered closed again. "Mama," she whispered. "What happened?"

"I see what you are now, you son of a bitch!" Rennie shrieked.

I pushed myself to my feet, head jerking up to find Jainey's injury had served its purpose. Caleb had used his telekinetic and wind capabilities to toss Jordan around like a rag doll in the time I'd been distracted.

Jordan was horribly bruised and bloody, his face swollen, bones crunched from the collisions. All in a matter of a minute.

And now Caleb was going to try to kill Jordan. I wouldn't let him. I just had to figure out what to do, and I had to think quickly. Could I do something with my new Aegis ability?

Tension tightened my muscles as Caleb dragged Jordan back to him without so much as twitching a finger. Caleb's Guardian friends glanced back and forth between Jordan and their fights with Rennie and Cass. Cass's opponent, the Black boy with the dreadlocks, swayed in place, his clothing charred and his face bruised. Cass was pulling her hits, but she was too much for him. Rennie's opponent, the redheaded girl, had blood dripping from a cut on her forehead and dripping into her ice-blue eyes. Rennie had her on her stomach, her full body weight pressing her down into the floor. The girl's ability was advanced hearing, which wasn't helping her here.

Zane and the others were locked in a stalemate. I couldn't believe it. The Sirins were fighting each other, standing with Zane as though she were their leader, their guide. Why would any Sirin help us?

Rennie cracked her opponent's head against the floor. "Stay down, dammit!"

"Family," Jainey yelled, looking at the battle around her. She tried to push herself up and away from me, but toppled right back into my arms. "We're supposed to be family."

She looked so pale.

"It's time to end this," Caleb said, his voice steady as he produced a knife from his pocket. "Let the better team win, finally."

"You're lying, Caleb!" Rennie cried, stumbling over the redhead to get closer to him. "Everything you're doing right now is a lie! You still love us. You've just let Lavinia get into your head."

Caleb met her gaze head on. "You don't know what you're talking about."

"Did you forget what my Aegis does?" Rennie asked. "I *know* what you're feeling. I feel your guilt. You feel sick with what you're doing. But you're not evil, Caleb! You're not!"

"What do you want me to do? What do you want me to be?" Caleb asked, and though his teeth were gritted, he sounded desperate. He tightened his hold on Jordan.

"I want you to let Jordan go," Rennie said, stepping forward.

Jordan gasped yet again. The fear in his eyes. There was so much fear.

And that's when it clicked.

He wasn't scared for himself. He was scared for everyone else.

"Mama," Jainey wept.

"I know, baby."

"It's always about Jordan," Caleb said. "Jordan gets a family, gets a team, gets the girl."

"It isn't about Jordan," Rennie said. "I'm asking you to let go of Jordan for you. Look at what this is making you do. You've got a knife to your best friend's throat. You're leading an army of monsters. You threw a rock at a little girl, Caleb. Who the fuck are you?"

Tears ran down Caleb's face. He didn't even seem to notice the way Jordan struggled in front of him. Still, he released him.

Jordan staggered forward a few steps before dropping to his knees. His chest heaved, and he thrust it outward, a warm blue glow lighting him from the inside.

"You're lucky I love Jordan," Caleb snarled. "He's my brother. I need him. But we don't need you." His finger rose slowly until he was pointing directly at me.

A sharp wind rustled through the greenery that crept along the train pillars, whipping up higher and higher.

One of the Sirins fighting on Zane's side shouted a gravel-roughened word, then wrapped an arm around Zane's waist and dove behind a nearby trash dumpster. The others followed suit, the interdimensionals they'd been facing off against chasing after them.

"Move!" Jordan shouted.

The world slowed down around me as I did exactly what Jordan asked of me.

I moved.

Toward him, instead of away.

Holding my hands outward, I slid between him and the others. I knew what I wanted to do, but I wasn't sure I could do it. Either I was about to die, or I was about to do something amazing.

I focused my Aegis on my hands and reached for the energy blast as it left my son.

Energy. It was all energy. And if I could control energy…

The warmth smacked against my palms, but where they were supposed to burn, they vibrated, held aloft by this new Aegis ability I didn't understand. But hell if I wasn't happy to have it right now.

I flexed my fingers, and the warm blue light journeyed up my hands and along my arms. It stopped tingling and started to burn. I slammed my eyes shut and focused on pushing the energy back through my fingers and out.

Shit, shit, shit.

I shook my arms out, pins and needles shooting up to my shoulders. This wasn't working.

My chest ached and shuddered.

I was going to incinerate myself. I didn't know what this power did to a Key.

I couldn't breathe.

If that energy continued its journey toward my core, I could be gone for good.

Like Lavinia.

Like Kyp might have been after I had performed the Ritual.

Kyp.

My memory sparked. Kyp's hand in mine. Our Aegis winding together, giving me the strength to absorb the strength from Govhans and Sirins fighting against us in the estate. The first time we'd ever joined together to fight.

Like Jainey had done on her own earlier. Because Skeleton Keys could do it without help from anyone else.

Skeleton Keys. Like Jordan.

Whose energy I currently held in my hands. It felt familiar. It felt like ours.

But it couldn't stay.

I imagined what I'd done that day with Kyp. The way I'd power drained the interdimensionals, pulling their energy into me. And then I put the process into reverse.

A high-pitched ringing echoed through my ears, my muscles sagging, and it was more like I was dragging my life force out of my bones than eliminating a foreign power from within me.

I'd only been able to absorb the energy of others before. But now, I could redirect it.

I looked to the Sirins and Gorvhans that had been after Zane's sudden and apparent allies.

Bile rose in my throat as I expelled the energy from within me, shoving it out at my enemies.

Caleb was lucky Jordan still loved him. So were the other two lab-Guardians. Because the power that erupted from my fingers evaporated the enemy Sirins and Guardians into little more than steaming piles of ash.

"The child has burned out," a Sirin said, gravelly voice cutting through the din left behind. "And yet, she survives."

"Jacklyn?" Zane shouted, but the words felt oddly distant.

My legs buckled, and I fell awkwardly, my Jainey-gifted strength seeping out of me with no warning.

Rennie dove forward to catch me.

"You… Mom… how did you do that?" Jordan asked.

I wished I had an answer.

Eighteen

STEALTHY

Kyp

A Skeleton Key. Half-Arvokian and half-human. Cxarana had told him that such a being existed, but not that she was still alive, nor that he may stumble upon her in this place.

Soft firelight touched a face that was extraordinary in the truest sense. Like Dhamyan, her eyes held the golden sheen of someone who had evolved to live in nearly complete darkness.

"You're the other Skeleton Key. The first," Kyp uttered, his throat dry. "Cxarana told me about you."

"Yes. I've heard quite a bit about you, as well. And I'd love to chat with you." She moved her knife away from where it rested along his throat. "But right now, we need to move. Narah and Merrick are planning a public execution as a way of joining forces with the Sirins."

She pulled away from him, looking over her shoulder at the others, who had handily taken care of the guards.

Dhamyan said something to her and the head nod that accompanied his words felt like a thank you.

Kyp took a quick inventory of the rest of his team. Drew had a few cuts and bruises, but he leapt when Dhamyan pulled him to his feet, so he still had energy to spare. A cut on Tex's forehead stained his blond hair red, but he looked steady on his feet. Ray was covered in green ichor.

Dammit. They'd as good as declared war against the Arvokian royal family, even if they could prove themselves innocent. A different enemy, but the same unending war.

Kyp sighed.

"Dhamyan tells me you are looking to acquire an important item," the Skeleton Key murmured. "Listen to my instructions. Down the hall to the right, at the end of the hall is a pair of tall wooden doors. These are the doors to the king's chambers. You will find the book you seek there."

"Yes, Lyira," Cxarana said, tension thrumming along her scratchy voice. "I am aware of where my father's rooms are."

"Astounding. Still holding that grudge, are we?" The Skeleton Key—Lyira—laughed, a surprisingly musical sound for the roughness with which she carried herself. She radiated strength. She, oddly, reminded him of Jacklyn.

The thought made bitterness sweep over his tongue. He missed Jacklyn. He frowned at the fascination he felt with Lyira. This wasn't like him.

He felt unsettled. Something was wrong with him.

"Yes. You're breaking."

Kyp looked to Cxarana, then to Lyira, but they continued bickering like they weren't in the middle of a war.

"What did you say?" he asked.

All eyes turned toward him.

"I… spoke of Lyira's careless use of rebel soldiers… and my concern for Dhamyan," Cxarana said, but she watched him keenly, as though she'd just searched for his future in his blood and found a particularly unsettling ending.

"No, you said that out loud," Kyp brushed her response aside. "What did you say in my head?"

"Nothing," Dhamyan said, his lips twisting downward. "I've been guarding your mind. I didn't hear anything spoken there."

Kyp was just so tired. "Of course you didn't."

Was he hearing things now?

"We don't have time for this," Lyira snapped. "Leave with your team for the king's chambers. Once you find what you seek, the library will be your next destination. We will prepare your escape there."

"Great. What's our exit strategy?" Kyp asked. She fiddled with a gold pin at the center of her cloak, an oval with a symbol like two lowercase t's etched into the middle of it.

Lyira stared at him blankly. "I expect you to trust me to handle that."

"We're gonna—" What felt like fire arched along his side, and his hand moved to shield the wound before he could tell it to stop.

"Your charge weakens, Cxarana," she said, and it had a teasing lilt that raised Kyp's hackles. "Expedience is of the utmost importance. There will be fights along the way, and it would be a pity to see him die when you've invested so much in him."

Cxarana's strong, bony fingers wrapped around Kyp's elbow, yanking him upward. He hadn't even realized he'd doubled over from the pain until that moment. She didn't waste any further time on pleasantries, her feet sliding across the floor in the direction of the king's chambers and taking Kyp with her.

"What did you hear back there?" Ray asked the minute they'd put some distance between themselves and their new potential allies.

"Yeah," Austin chimed in. *"Don't remember hallucinations being a part of this whole eternal dying thing."*

"It's happened before," Drew said. *"But he was much closer to death that time."*

"I'm fine. I just misheard. What's the deal with you and the new girl? Should we not trust her?" Kyp shrugged out of Cxarana's grip with a pointed glare in her direction.

"Ask Dhamyan," she growled in response.

"She has never done anything to make me doubt her," Dhamyan said. *"That isn't to say she's a great person. She's… an ally."*

Great. Kyp had stepped into an interdimensional love triangle. Wonderful.

"Okay, what I hear is that we can trust her," Kyp said, picking up his pace to the large double-doors Lyira described.

"The enemy hides within," a voice whispered through his mind. A woman. The same as earlier, but it was the slightest whisper.

Kyp glanced back at the others. Ray nodded reassuringly, motioning for him to open the door. Not looking for the source of a disembodied voice.

God, he really was cracking.

He'd been so close to peace.

Years ago, Kyp had feared finding a Sirin under his bed. When he told Ray, Ray said, "The real monsters don't live under your bed, son. They live in your head." He didn't explain then why he'd looked at Lavinia. It hadn't taken long for Kyp to understand why.

Kyp shook the memory free. Sometimes his mind was a terrible place he couldn't escape.

He pulled a torch off the wall and threw the door open. But he didn't forget the voice's warning.

His eyes found the alabaster marble desk in the center of the room. A royal office space, filled with floor to ceiling bookcases. Books rested upon their shelves—worn, mustard-colored leather bindings constructed from Senefestrian skins, and frayed, well-used pages. Kyp ran his fingers along the back of a chair that faced the desk, seemingly there for a guest to speak with the king.

A choked sound escaped Cxarana as they moved further into the room. She walked around the desk, standing beside what had once been her father's seat.

Kyp reached to place a hand on hers, but the sound of a scuffle had him whirling toward the door. Four guards rushed into the room, all Arvokian wearing heavy and well-shined armor that spoke of a lack of battle. They each carried a sword in one hand and an axe in the other.

The rest of their team was already in motion. Ray expertly caught a guard mid-strike, yanking him forward in an over-shoulder throw. He twisted his wrist, and the guard's sword dropped to the floor. Ray restrained him with a foot against his throat as Drew dove over the guard's prone body, snatching the sword and thrusting the weighted pommel into the head of a pursuing guard. Dhamyan had his enemy on his knees with a knife at his throat. Austin pinned a guard to the floor beneath his knees.

Kyp used his Aegis to quietly close the doors and slide the locking mechanism into place.

"They were behind where the doors stood when we opened them. You should have checked for them," Ray said. "You're off your game."

"I am, once again, average at best," Kyp grumbled. "Apologies if I'm a little distracted by the hole preparing to tear its way through my side."

"Traitor!" Austin's guard shouted, bucking under him.

Austin slammed his head into the ground. "Hush, you."

"No worries," Ray said, cheerfully digging his heel into the throat of his guard. "I cast a Sound Block up around the room before these oafs even attacked."

"Wow." Drew grinned. "Mama didn't raise a fool after all!"

"Don't go talking about my mama." Ray looked down at his guard. "Dhamyan, do the brain connection talky thing." He pointed from his head to his mouth and back.

"For the record," Dhamyan said. *"I can understand some of your language."* He closed his eyes and took a deep breath, then nodded. *"Go ahead. Speak to the guard."*

Ray spoke. *"It's a shame, really. We don't want to kill you, and we didn't kill your king. But we do have something rather important to do, and your remaining royals want to kill us. And we can't let that happen."*

Kyp nodded.

"The royal family has no intent to kill you!" The guard beneath Ray sneered. "Your people couldn't be patient and decided to spill more blood!"

"For fuck's sake, we didn't spill any blood to begin with!" Kyp shouted. "We had it on good word that we were to be killed and we were protecting ourselves."

He slid his eyes to Cxarana. Was it, indeed, a good word?

Cxarana lowered her head and took a long, steadying breath. "Yes, Kyp. She, while frustrating, can indeed be trusted." She sniffled, then lowered her voice so only Kyp could hear. "Don't move. You're bleeding. I don't want them to know."

He hadn't even felt the blood start to seep. He'd been so focused on the battle and the tearing pain in his side.

"It doesn't matter. This whole trip was wasted if we don't find the book."

"Someone else is here," Ray said, pointing to his ear, and then back toward the bookcase on the far side of the office. *"Maybe they know?"*

Ray took Drew's sword and aimed it at the other conscious guard, freeing up the others to move through the room. He was more than capable of dealing with these four, if needed.

Dhamyan stomped toward the back of the room to the far bookcase. He yanked on it, pulling it forward. It had hinges. A secret room.

Dhamyan reached in. Their eavesdropper resisted, but Kyp

caught a glimpse of Dhamyan's fingers wrapped around a mottled purple forearm ringed in bronze bangle bracelets.

Narah.

Another tug, and he'd pulled her out of the room, though she struggled against his grasp. "No! You don't understand what you're doing! These books are nothing. They are nothing!"

"She is mind-blocked," Dhamyan explained. *"I cannot tell if she is lying."*

Drew sidled up to Kyp's side. "You okay?"

Kyp offered him a frail smile. "Getting worse."

He wrapped an arm around Kyp's waist, supporting him against his side. "Lean on me."

Kyp couldn't just slump against Drew; he couldn't show that kind of weakness. But he did lean a little. He reached out with his mind to the guards that remained conscious after their earlier battle.

The guards were not mind-blocked, but they did rebel against the feeling of him in their minds. It didn't benefit them much. He pushed through their mental walls easily.

It was clear they didn't deal often with threats, and based on what he saw within their minds, they were not meant to be on shift, but had come in as emergency coverage due to the death of the king.

They didn't know much. But they did know they were guarding Narah while she gathered important books.

"I apologize, Narah," Kyp said. And in a way, he was. In another way, he was completely done with this. "I did not harm your father, and I think you know that. And I'm sorry I need to take these books from you."

He tipped his head toward Austin, who walked forward to snatch a canvas bag from around Narah's other arm.

"I have no choice. I can't help my people if I can't heal," Kyp said evenly.

Narah threw her head back and laughed. *"You cannot even see it? This selfish belief that only you can protect them is so strong you're willing to trample people to heal yourself rather than let others take over your role."* Her eyes narrowed. *"You think you walk in the light, but the darkness creeps in. It always does with you humans. You cannot be trusted, even with the Dawn."*

Kyp flinched. *The darkness creeps in.*

But the others were more focused elsewhere.

"You want to conquer the Dawn," Drew muttered, his eyes widening.

Goddammit, she wasn't wrong about Kyp being selfish, was she?

"Father would not have allowed you to move to conquer the Dawn," Cxarana said. *"So you killed him."*

"It wasn't her," Kyp said. "It was Merrick."

Narah bared her teeth.

"You sure about that?" Austin asked, glancing in his direction.

"I could be wrong, but I tend to doubt it." Kyp smiled. He was trying to hold on to his confidence, but blood seeped between his fingers.

Narah released a jagged cry, producing a blade from within her robes and stabbing Dhamyan in the center of his chest.

NINETEEN

KYP

A red cloud descended over Kyp's vision, and he reached forward with his telekinesis, throwing Narah as far away from Dhamyan as he could manage. But she held onto the dagger, ripping it free as she flew back. Blood spurted from the wound, splashing onto Cxarana's face and arms as she rushed forward, catching Dhamyan and lowering him to the floor.

With a vicious throat jab to one guard, and a sword pommel to the head of the other, Ray raced forward with astonishing speed. He stopped to give Austin a once over. Then he plunged his sword into Austin's shoulder.

"What the fuck?" Drew shouted.

But Austin understood, pushing out a pained explanation. "I can help heal."

Ray pushed his hands against the wound, which was most assuredly cleaving through Dhamyan's heart, as Austin pulled the sword back out of his own wound with a swear.

Dhamyan was unconscious from almost before the dagger had

pulled free. Worse, Dhamyan was silent within Kyp's mind.

He was dead. He had to be.

"Cxarana, do the Keys of the Dusk return after death the way we do?" he asked, his voice coming out harsh.

"No tampering. No supposed human improvements," she muttered. "They don't come back. It was seen to have… negative effects the Dusk didn't desire for their own."

Of course. If Keys of the Dusk didn't undergo the same initiation process, then they hadn't been subjected to the Ritual that tethered Keys of the Dawn to their lives until the Death-Bringer Ritual was spoken over them. But Kyp had to love that Ray was saying 'fuck death' and trying, anyway.

He'd been stabbed in the heart. Could they really work that fast?

One minute. Two.

Each one dragged on for what felt like an eternity.

The wound still gaped open, the healing Ray and Austin channeled into it only serving to seal the inside. Mortal wounds were always much more difficult to heal. A veritable onion of healing was needed—the most important work was the healing of the organ, but the blood loss and tissue damage surrounding it was just as important in keeping the wounded individual alive. The organ, the connective tissue, the muscle, the fat, the skin, all to make sure the person not only functioned correctly once again, but to make sure they didn't bleed out from the external wound.

And that was it. Exactly why he shouldn't lead. Whenever he tried to take charge, there was so much blood.

"Back up," Ray said to Austin.

Cxarana made a low moaning sound, scratched free from deep within.

"You too, Witch!" Ray shouted. "I can't save him with you in the way." He yanked Dhamyan out of her arms, and she let out a horrible wail.

"Hey!" Drew shouted.

But Kyp understood. Ray was panicking. He didn't like to lose anyone. Instead, Kyp folded Cxarana into his arms.

"Let him work," he spoke into one pointy ear. He'd never hugged an Arvokian before. Her skin was cold and slick. Almost lizard-like. He held her tighter. All the while, both of their eyes were glued to Ray.

"Are you okay?" Drew asked, squatting down beside them. Kyp didn't know when he'd sunk to the floor, but there they were.

"Never felt worse," Kyp answered, his voice flat.

Ray waved to Austin, murmuring something. Austin started chest compressions, and Ray slid in to give him mouth-to-mouth.

Kyp had been right. He was dead. But now that they healed him, they were hoping it wasn't so long they couldn't bring him back.

The crack of Dhamyan's ribs echoed through the cavernous room, and Cxarana let out another hoarse sob.

"They're trying to save him," Kyp reminded her, but even he winced at the sound. He was immensely glad it was Austin and not Ray giving the compressions, as strong as Ray could be.

Fifteen compressions, two breaths. Fifteen more. Two more breaths.

Fifteen more.

One breath, two breaths.

"I've got a pulse," Ray said, pressing his hands to Dhamyan's chest and head. "I'll do the rest."

"I didn't think our biology was this similar," Kyp muttered in awe.

"The basic principles are similar," Cxarana said as she sniffled. "The blood does not contain the same things. The circulation goes through different routes and the nutrients needed differ, but the pump works about the same." She wiped at her eyes, then glanced up at Kyp. "Thank you for the distraction, Mr. Franklin."

Kyp let her slide free from his hold. "We share that need to provide information, Arvokian Liaison." He winked, then turned his attention to Ray. "Can we get him moving? I want to get out of here as fast as possible."

"Wait, where's Narah?" Drew asked.

They all looked around the room, even Dhamyan, who had just regained consciousness and looked confused.

"She hit the wall when Kyp threw her," Drew said. "I was sure she was down for the count."

Drew's head cocked toward the corridor.

"Look, if she's gone, I ain't gonna cry about it. Right now, we gotta gather Dhamyan and get the hell to that library before we can't save the next one," Austin said. "Ray doesn't have much left."

"Fuck, neither do I," Kyp said, rising to his feet. He winced as his side grew worse. "Let's go." He headed for the entry, stepping around the unconscious guards. "I'd like to get home and get healed before Jacks decides she has no desire to love someone who can't fight by her side without chronic death as a side effect."

"C'mon, man," Austin said, "you know it ain't like that."

He knew.

He knew.

But there was always that niggling fear in the back of his mind…

"This way!" Drew shouted from the back room. "There's a passage."

Ray finished helping Dhamyan to his feet. Dhamyan stumbled, and Austin steadied him.

"Thank you," Dhamyan said, reaching out with one hand for Ray and laying his other around Austin's waist.

Ray smiled, grabbing his hand firmly. *"Any time."* He released Dhamyan and followed Kyp into the alcove. Once they rejoined Drew, he stumbled, and Kyp barely managed to hold Ray up.

"Are you hurt?" Drew asked.

"Nah," Ray said, eyes peeling open. "Tapped out on Aegis, though. Just gave the last bit I've got if ya want me conscious." He motioned toward the far wall of the alcove. "The Skeleton Key girl is through there. Path is echoey, but it'll get us there."

A handle rested at the bottom of the wall like the door to a garbage chute. Kyp was sure if he yanked it up, he'd find a path to where they needed to go.

"We've gotta risk it," Drew said. "Ray is fading, Dhamyan is still shaky, and don't think I haven't noticed the blood, Kyp. Austin's shoulder is injured and hopefully will heal soon. Cxarana and I are the only ones still standing at this point."

"They will be able to track us," Cxarana rasped from over Kyp's shoulder.

"Pretty sure they'll know where we're going anyway," Austin said. "Because as soon as we get to the library, we're out of here. Back to the Dawn, fast as we can."

Kyp reached for the handle. "We don't have time to worry about that." He yanked it open. Within was a metal slide that looked as though it was designed for trash disposal. Just a perfectly normal garbage chute in the middle of the Dusk.

Kyp ignored the slicing pain in his side at even the thought of sliding down anything.

"Lyira," he whispered harshly.

"Well done," her voice mocked in return.

Drew jumped in ahead of everyone before they had a chance to question the decision. Cxarana went in next, grasping Dhamyan's hand and pulling him behind her. Austin almost jumped in ahead of them, but he settled for going just after.

And then it was Ray and Kyp. They both hesitated to go down before the other.

Kyp decided to address his earlier heroics. "That was insane. Are you okay?"

Stalling. He was stalling.

"I'm… it was worth it." He shrugged. "Dhamyan saved you. I owed him. Shall we?" He waved at Kyp to follow before disappearing through the door.

Finally, Kyp slid through, his stomach upended by the laws of gravity and the sick feeling of being suddenly and thoroughly without control. Despite himself, his fingers grasped alternately at the wall and at the steadily growing wound at his side, as though he'd be able to hold his insides in if he could just get some purchase.

He came out of the other end, landing, however unwillingly, in Austin's outstretched arms.

"Hey there, Prince Not-So-Charming." His grin stretched until it took up a good half of his face.

He curbed the instinct to punch him in his only partially healed shoulder wound, choosing instead to look around for the source of the smoke that filled his nostrils.

"There you are," Lyira greeted as though it was Kyp alone who had been lollygagging. "I thought you were planning to grow old in the king's chambers."

Austin lowered him to his feet gingerly, a grimace taking the place of his grin. Perhaps it hadn't entirely been a grin in the first place. Perhaps... Austin was worried about him?

Either way, he thrust his chin away from Lyira to what stood beyond the wall of allies that had gathered here.

The room was large, and as was expected for a library, filled with shelves and shelves of books. The problem? Most of them were on fire and a cloud of smoke obscured his vision.

Kyp's gaze flicked to Lyira so fast it made him dizzy. "What did you do?"

"Everything is going according to plan, Kyp Franklin." Lyira stepped into Kyp's space, a pointed finger aimed at his chest. "You let me take care of my world, and you take care of yours, okay?"

Dread spilled through him, but what choice did he have? She was right. He'd already accidentally damaged area politics badly enough.

"You should be more focused on this, anyway." She waved a hand at a tear in the smooth stone flooring, a jagged rip that glowed a bright and angry red. She'd opened a Rift.

She turned her attention to the others. "What are you waiting for? Go! Now! Before they find us!"

"Go through first with Cxarana and Dhamyan," Drew said to Ray. "Come back if anything looks wrong."

Dhamyan's eyes flickered. *We're going to the Dawn?*

"If we wish to stay safe, I believe we must," Cxarana confirmed.

"You trust me so little," Lyira asked. "After I've already helped you?"

"We trust nobody but us," Drew said. "We can no longer afford to."

Kyp's chest felt hot and tight as he watched Ray, Cxarana, Dhamyan, and Austin disappear through the Rift.

"I will let you in on a secret," Lyira said, pulling Kyp even closer until she was sharing his breath.

"What?"

Drew pulled a shard of the crystal they'd found earlier out from a bag on the nearby counter. Apparently, Lyira had gathered their belongings when they'd been tied up with Narah. He drummed his fingers nervously on the stone.

"The books you have aren't the ones you need," Lyira said. She pushed a large tome into Kyp's chest, and he brought his hands up quickly to catch it. "I have marked the page you need to heal yourself. The ones you recovered from Narah contained other secrets of the royal family. But this, *this*, will save your life. Feel free to have Cxarana verify."

Kyp didn't have an answer for her. No words he could come up with would be appropriate.

"One of your bags has the necessary herbs and activators." She offered a shaky smile, then waved away the smoke between them.

"W-why?" Kyp asked. He couldn't wrap his head around it. Why would she want to help him? What did she have to gain? He was almost afraid to move, afraid he would turn around and be back in their room here, trapped and awaiting sentencing.

He'd just met Lyira that day, and she was risking everything. She was giving him his *life* back.

"You and your wife stirred things up down here," Lyira said. She shoved him back toward the opening, her palm pressed flat on his chest as they moved. "Arvokian lives are long and boring. We needed a shake-up."

She pressed a kiss to his cheek and then shoved harder until he was tumbling through the Rift, his hand gripping Drew's sleeve as he went. The acrid burning scent turned into the even worse odor of sulfur as he burst out through the other side.

It wasn't until he was catapulting back up to hit a stretch of grass within the Dawn that he realized he should have pulled her with him. Should have thanked her.

But then, she'd told him not to, hadn't she?

You let me take care of my world, and you take care of yours, okay?

Despite the rough landing, the now throbbing pain in his side, and the way his head was spinning, Kyp opened his eyes and happily greeted the twinkling stars above him. His friends, his family, buzzed around him, rushing to prepare the Ritual that would keep him alive.

He was going to be okay, and he couldn't wait to go home.

A voice whispered through his head as he started to dip into unconsciousness.

"If there is still a home to return to."

TWENTY

JACKLYN

"Jacks?" Zane's voice echoed in my ears, and for a moment, it was all I heard.

The street around us was nearly silent. It always seemed that way after one of these battles. It was as though the supernatural made the natural world cower away.

Rennie helped me sit up just in time to see Cass take off after Caleb and his two Guardian friends.

Damn. A part of me was hoping Jordan's energy had somehow made its way to Caleb, at least.

"Sorry," I groaned as I pushed off Rennie to chase after Cass. She needed to stop. We didn't have another fight in us right now. But I tripped over my own feet and the ground rushed up at me until a sharp, clawed hand wrapped around my upper arm.

I jerked away, lost my balance, and crashed to the packed earth beneath me. A popping tear ripped through my shoulder. Shit. Another injury.

A guttural voice split the quiet of the night, growling out some kind of order in a language I didn't know. I twisted where I lay to find a Sirin standing over me. A Sirin with hair. That was new. Usually they appeared to be bald, but this one had marigold yellow hair spiraling down skin the color of juniper berries. As it moved, I noticed that hair also sprouted along its legs and armpits.

The moment it spoke, Cass stopped dead in her tracks, like a dog yanked back on her leash.

"What the hell?" Rennie leapt to her feet and glanced around her, seeing what I already did.

"It's ancient Arvokian," the Sirin explained. "When you've been forced to do little but serve all day, your nights are eager to be filled. Some of us choose to indulge in exercises to build muscle. Some craft. Some create. Others find whatever we can to learn. I, for one, have a knack for languages."

"Serve?" I asked, pushing myself back up to a seated position with a grunt. I glanced from Jordan to Jainey, making sure they were both okay. Okay was probably pushing it, but they were breathing. Broken, but breathing. Just like Mama.

Cass shook her limbs out, turned, and started walking back to rejoin the group.

"Yes." The Sirin extended a hand to me. "You must be Jacklyn Madison. I am Andaria, leader of the Sirin rebellion."

I took her hand and let her pull me to my feet. "We like rebellions here."

"Particularly if you're rebelling against our enemies," Zane said, emerging from where she and the other Sirins that were helping us had hidden. "Thanks again for your help. We would have been completely screwed if we'd had to do it alone."

"We are glad to help you," Andaria said. "I apologize if the others do not speak to you. They do not know the language. I have worked very hard over the last year to learn it, so I may communicate with you. Cxarana sent me after she met up with your partner, Kyp."

Cxarana. A warm rush of relief spread through me. Cxarana meant trust. And the fact that she had found Kyp meant Kyp had a better chance of succeeding at his mission.

"I imagine you wish to return to your home space," Andaria continued. "May we escort you to your vehicle? We will not take much of your time. But we wish to assist. We will speak to you as we go."

"That would be wonderful," I said, grateful for the assistance. We were a mess. There was no way we could defend against further attack, and we had no reason to believe they would hurt us; if they wanted to, they could have jumped in with the others. Caleb would have destroyed us without Andaria's team.

Still, I wasn't about to let them come stay at the brownstone with us. But a friendly exchange was a good start.

"What about your warriors?" I asked. "Can I assist in healing any wounds?"

Andaria smiled, baring needle-sharp teeth. I assumed it was meant to be friendly. "Please, Jacklyn Madison. You do not currently have any healing energy to give. Nor does your male offspring."

"Her female offspring might," Jainey said drowsily. "After all, we owe you the help."

Zane lifted her into her arms, and Jainey went willingly, laying her head against her shoulder. A few scattered raindrops fell, and Jainey brushed them away from her face, looking irritated.

Suddenly a kid again, just like that.

Andaria spoke into the crowd of Sirins, and a few answered.

"She is asking them if they require healing," Jainey spoke within my mind. *"Their injuries are survivable, and they don't want to waste my energy. I look tired, I guess."*

She did. Hell, she looked bloody. The entire right side of her face was coated with it, and the steady rain that was beginning to pick up was only smearing it further.

"We do not require healing," Andaria said with a nod in Jainey's direction. "I meant no offense, little one. I simply did not want to place added weight upon you. You are but a cub, far too young to be amidst battle."

My heart twisted. "Yeah, well, nobody's ever given us much of a choice."

Air whistled through Andaria's slit nose. "Apologies. I did not intend to offend you either. We are in agreement. The child should not be forced into the situations that have been created for you. This is the fault of the frightening alliance that has been struck between your enemies in the Dawn, the ruling class of the Dusk, and those that follow them."

"The Sirin ruling class?" Cass asked as she knelt to help Jordan to his feet.

Jordan screamed as they lifted him, and to their credit, Andaria and some of the other Sirins that followed her cringed in response.

"Twenty-four rib bones in the human body." Jordan winced. "I think I broke most of them.”

Rennie caught his other shoulder. “At least you’ll heal?”

“Eventually. What can I say? I’m a badass.” A bold statement, considering the way he swayed between Rennie and Cass.

“Just hold on a little longer,” I pleaded. “You stay conscious and we’ll stop and get you some dirty water dogs from the cart on Broadway. Ray said you love hot dogs.”

“Yeah… okay. I do love hot dogs.”

Andaria,” I said. “We really need to get out of here.”

“We need answers.” Cass turned to the Sirin leader. “What did you just do to me?”

“It was an order to temporarily banish spirits,” Andaria admitted. “It was issued in the old language of the Arvokians. From long ago, when they didn’t require Rituals to channel their magicks. I wasn’t sure it would work. I can teach it to you, if you so desire.”

“I’m not sure we have the time for that,” Rennie said. “But perhaps we can meet up again?”

“I would like that.”

“I need to know one thing before you go,” Zane said as they began the slow walk to the car, only a couple of blocks away.

“You okay, kid?” Jordan asked Jainey at the same time Zane asked her question.

Jainey waved at him to shut up so she could listen, and I had to hold back a snicker despite everything.

“Your question?” Andaria asked.

“Who are you?” Zane asked. “Why did you help us? Who did you serve?”

"I'm not sure we should look a gift horse in the mouth," I said.

"Jacks, when your brain starts interfering, ask yourself what Kyp would do," Cass grumbled.

I was sorely tempted to punch her in the head, but I restrained myself.

"The Sirin leadership… likes their servants," Andaria admitted. "The Arvokians serve that purpose for manual labor. Gorvhans behave as beasts of burden. But Sirin females are expected to do any and all other things for the males. We are servants as well. Or, at least, we were."

A Sirin female. I had never even realized that every Sirin we had seen in the past had been male.

"I worked as a historian. A scholar. But my knowledge was only as welcome as its ability to advance the leadership. Though I learned how wrong the leadership was, I never believed I could do anything to stop them. Until I learned of you, Jacklyn Madison. You and your team."

I stopped short. "How did I—"

"You sealed the Rifts! You and your partner, your mate. And your team, your family. You changed the Dawn. You changed the Dusk. And I wanted to change the Dusk as well."

I'd never even considered how this would affect everyone else. My focus had been on saving my family. I knew it had the helpful side effect of saving humanity from the interdimensional threat.

"Shit, Jordan, you're trembling," Rennie cried. She pressed a palm to her chest.

"We're almost there, only a little bit further, sweetheart." I felt like a goddamn villain. I should be healing him, but I didn't have it in me. My body was using all my remaining Aegis to heal itself. I wouldn't be able to do much, and then neither of us would be capable of walking.

"I want to help you," I said, turning my attention to Andaria. "But I'm not sure how best to do that. I'll need some time to think."

And preferably pick the brains of our more strategic members.

"Naturally," Andaria said. "We did not expect your help in return. We offered our assistance freely." She looked away. "Honestly, I wished to meet you. I never imagined we would be able to turn the tides for you."

"You *will* get our help in return. Expected or not." We owed them. And we may just need them again. "Where can we find you?"

"We have been hiding within an abandoned castle on the King's Bridge. Do you know of it?"

I did. Kingsbridge was a road in the Bronx, and the place wasn't a castle, but it looked like one. It had been an armory for the National Guard long ago.

A beep from up the block told me that Zane had unlocked the car with the remote.

"There's our car," I said. "We will come to meet with you. You have my word. We are very grateful."

Andaria said her goodbyes, and we piled into the car to head home.

I glanced over my shoulder to my kids. The more time Jainey got to heal, the more her color returned. Though she was covered in blood, the head wound was nearly entirely sealed. Jordan, on the other hand, looked paler by the minute. Or rather, every part of him that didn't have a bruise on it was pale, and it just made the purple stand out even more.

"Are you okay?" I asked.

"Yep. I'm fine. Please stop asking." He groaned, and his eyes slammed shut, but he flashed me finger guns, because he was a fifteen-year-old idiot who didn't know when he should just stop moving.

"Yeah." My eyes narrowed. "You sure about that?"

He sighed. "Nope." His head dropped back against the headrest and lolled to the side.

"Jordan?" I scrambled forward, but my seatbelt yanked me right back into my seat.

While I struggled to figure out how seatbelts worked, Rennie reached forward and felt for his pulse. "He's okay. I think he just passed out."

Not great, but not terrible.

"He needs the rest," Zane said. "It will speed up his healing." She reached across the car's center console, her hand grasping mine. "Didn't think we'd make it out of there for a minute there, but we did. We did."

"We did," I said. "But at what cost?"

"What do you mean?" Rennie asked from the back of the car. "What's going on with you? You've been off since…"

Apparently, Zane and I weren't nearly as quiet as we thought we were.

"Caleb is on the wrong side," Cass said. "And he's pissed."

"Yeah, but they lost their leader. Lavinia is dead," Jainey said. "And we have new allies."

"We don't know who Caleb has allied himself with. And he now has the fascinating motivation of revenge," I said. "Vengeance powered me for a long time. I know how powerful that can be."

Nobody replied. I stared out the window, watching the raindrops race each other down the windshield, and hoped we'd find the rest of the team safe when we returned.

Twenty One

Jacklyn

Kyp and the guys weren't there when we got home. Nor were they there for the next week. In fact, for a full week, everything was pretty quiet. Nobody tried to attack us, so we took that time to fortify our base against their technomancer. We rested and healed. And we trained. We were seriously out of fighting shape, and we needed to get back into it quickly if Caleb intended to pick up where his mother had left off.

And then, first thing in the morning that Tuesday, the doorbell rang.

I dropped my rather tasty yogurt and rushed to the screen we had mounted on the wall that connected to the camera out front.

Dad. My father waved at the camera, fingers waggling, eyes dancing.

I hit the speaker button. "Why didn't you tell me you were coming?"

"What kind of welcome is that, Birdie?"

Pain in my ass. "What's the word, Hummingbird?"

"That would be kale, Nightingale."

Our code was the one food I'd tried with him that I'd never tried with another person and hated. It was a weird code, but we picked something as random as possible to avoid the chance of it being guessed.

Still…

They had a technomancer. We were speaking through technology. It was better to be safe.

I grabbed a kitchen knife and headed for the door.

"Welcome home?" A smile flickered across Ray's face as soon as the door cracked open. Austin stood behind him with Cxarana and Dhamyan, who were well disguised in *very* human clothes, including hoodies and baggy jeans. Drew and Kyp brought up the rear.

Kyp. Relief loosened the tension in my shoulders, and I sagged a little against the door.

My gaze returned to my father. One simple nod told me they had accomplished their mission. I dropped the knife and threw myself into Ray's arms.

He smelled like cedarwood, which wasn't his typical scent, and I knew he'd bummed it off some stash at the estate, where they'd probably cleaned up before coming here. It was enough to shake me out of the joyous reunion. Or at least the full hug. I pulled back, but Ray kept an arm around my waist.

"Why didn't you tell me you were coming?"

"Sorry, Birdie." Ray grimaced. "Kyp thought it would be a good idea to surprise you."

"Yeah… not a good idea." I waved them forward. "Get your asses inside."

Ray planted a kiss on my cheek before scooting past me. Cxarana and Dhamyan approached next.

"Ms. Madison." Cxarana lowered her head.

Dhamyan glanced over at her, then mimicked her movement.

"Hi Cxarana, welcome back! Dhamyan, welcome to our home. Come on in."

"Thank you, Jacklyn Madison," Dhamyan spoke into my mind.

Austin stepped forward, pulling Drew behind him. "You know it was Ray's idea, right?"

"Definitely not Kyp's," Drew confirmed, squeezing my hand.

"Yeah, that sounds about right."

Austin nudged me with his shoulder and pulled Drew along behind him into his house.

And then it was just me and Kyp.

He pulled a bouquet of red daisies from behind his back and thrust them toward me when he was closer. "I picked these for you."

"Doncha feel special?" Austin shouted back over his shoulder.

"Yes!" I volleyed back before turning my attention back to Kyp. "They're lovely. Thank you." I took the flowers from him. They were truly beautiful, made even better by how thoughtful the gift was.

His lips turned up, but only slightly. "Is that my shirt?"

I glanced down at my clothes, and only then did I realize the state I was in. Kyp's T-shirt, a pair of basketball shorts, barefoot. My hair was tied up in a sloppy bun. I had just woken up. I probably looked ridiculous.

"Yeah." I tucked a loose hair behind my ear. "I'm a bit of a mess. It's been a rough couple of weeks."

He took two swift steps forward until his nose brushed mine. "It was only a few days for me, but… God, I missed you."

Before I could tell him I missed him too, his lips were pressed against mine. I wrapped my arms around his neck as he grabbed for my waist, luring me in to deepen the kiss.

"Hi," he whispered against my lips, his forehead pressed against mine for just a moment before he dove back in for another kiss. "Love you."

I smiled into the next kiss. "Well, hello to you too." I grabbed him by his shirt collar and pulled him in again.

"Enough already," Ray scolded. "You're still on my goddamned doorstep."

Kyp grumbled something very distasteful under his breath, and a laugh burst out of me as I smacked his chest in admonishment.

Kyp rolled his eyes and swatted my ass. "Better go inside."

"I'm gonna get you back for that," I said, and I so fully meant that. "If you're feeling up to it later?"

He smiled wickedly, his dark eyes gleaming. "Nothing stopping me." He pulled up his shirt a little to show me where his wound usually appeared… or to show me a glimpse of those abs. Either way, I wasn't complaining.

"All healed up?" I asked.

"It's been a day and a half and it hasn't reopened yet." His face broke into an uncharacteristically wide smile, and I could see he was struggling to hold it back, to keep his usual calm and serious demeanor.

Screw that.

I threw my arms around him again with a squeal and a peal of laughter.

"You have no idea how worried I was. There was this whole thing here, and I was certain you wouldn't make it out of there, and…"

"Oh, me getting out of there wasn't certain," Kyp said, his deep voice a comforting rumble in my ear. "There was a bit of an incident."

I pulled back, though I didn't let go. "Here too."

He hummed thoughtfully. "Back into the mess?"

"Papa?" Jainey shrieked from deep inside the brownstone.

"Back into the mess." I nodded. We traded one more kiss before we turned and headed back inside.

The team had all packed into the living room, and they watched us expectantly as we joined them. But two people waited at the door eagerly.

"Papa!" Jainey threw herself into Kyp's arms, and it was a damn good thing he was doing better, or he would have been floored. She was small, but she packed a punch if she neglected to hold back.

"Hey, Bean!" He hefted her up onto his hip, knocking foreheads with her before pressing a kiss to hers. "Good to see your little face." He looped his other arm around Jordan's shoulder. "Yours too, kiddo." He pressed a kiss into his hair. "Did you grow while I was gone?"

"Of course not." Jordan rolled his eyes, but he looked downright elated at the possibility. "Right, Mom?"

"Maybe a little," I teased.

"So, how were things when I was away?" Kyp asked, ushering the kids further into the living room.

"Awful," Cass said. "How was your time away?"

"Just splendid," Kyp said, although he cracked a small smile. "I did get healed, though."

Cass released a deep sigh. "Okay, good. That's good."

Kyp found himself a seat with space beside him for me and the kids. "I guess we should get you all caught up since we've… made some waves." He cleared his throat. "We started by looking for Cxarana and Dhamyan and calling upon them for help. But they didn't have the information we sought. Instead, we went where they would. To Cxarana's family, the Arvokian king."

Wait… Cxarana was a princess? When was she going to tell us this?

"Royalty among us?" Zane teased. "Who knew?" She tipped a cup of tea in her direction like a toast.

Cxarana bowed her head in return.

"As I'm sure you can imagine, relying on the benevolence of a group of people I'd never met with values I didn't understand for the only thing that could save me was extremely relaxing," Kyp continued.

Kyp's team took turns cycling through the events of the time they'd been away, and the story unsettled me. I fucking hated the revelation that we weren't natural Keys, that we were enhanced while our Guardian friends had been stifled. I didn't like that someone had decided to take the moment my family was in the Dusk to kill the Arvokian king. And I really didn't like this Lyira chick.

"And you thought it was a good idea to just trust that this brand-new Skeleton Key we knew nothing about would open up a Rift to the Dawn without testing it or anything?" I asked.

Beside me, Cass grunted her agreement. Seemed she didn't care for it either.

"Cxarana vouched for her," Ray argued.

"Begrudgingly," she added.

"Sure, it wasn't the most sound plan." Drew winced. "But it got us out of there and back home."

"And then you just took a book you got from this stranger who Cxarana can barely tolerate, and you did a Ritual you found there because she told you it would heal Dad, but you never saw it before and had no idea if it actually would?" Jordan asked. "Guys… what if it turned him into a Gorvhan?"

"It didn't," Dhamyan said. *"I do not believe there are any Rituals to turn a human into a different species."*

"But what if there was?" Jainey asked

"These were things I did not have to worry about when I was dead," Kyp noted flippantly.

"You're an ass, and that's not funny," I grumbled. "They're right. You had no idea how this would go. It was reckless."

"Well, why don't we hear about how you're doing?" Austin asked. "I'm sure you were chock full of responsibility."

"Caleb tracked us down, but bolted when he found out there was a new occupant in Cass's spiritual routine," I said.

"Who?" Kyp asked through gritted teeth.

"Hello there, Kyp," Kylie greeted through Cass.

For a moment, he just stared. "Kylie. How are you?"

She laughed her usual high-pitched cackle. "Downright terrible. Which you would know if Jacklyn would wrap up the story."

"I just started!" I shot her a glare. "And Caleb asked the obvious question. Why is Kylie a ghost while Kyp and I are running around, causing trouble?"

"Is that a question you got an answer to?" Ray asked. "Not that I'm not thrilled, because I am. That you're alive. Mostly not that Kylie's still dead. But it would help to know why."

"I admire your restraint," Kylie said, her words blades.

"No answers," Zane said, sliding a hand into his. "Only more questions."

Cxarana rose from where she lounged on the couch, her head pressed to Dhamyan's chest. I *knew* those two were a thing. Kyp owed me money… if we'd formally bet on it. Which we probably hadn't. And which probably made no sense since we all shared *his* bank account.

"I… I may possess an explanation," Cxarana said, her voice its usual rasp, but she'd never looked more out of place. Her hair, always braided, hung loosely down her back, knotted in places. She'd lowered the hood on her jacket, but it still looked awkward and out of place with her regal posture.

"You may?" Kyp asked, an eyebrow raised. I didn't blame him for his frustration. "Is this like you *may* have known about the power imbalance in the Order that *you* imposed?"

"It was what your leadership told me must be done," she said. "It never occurred to me to question it until recently. I believed you were aware. This was different. I chose to try something as a precaution without being sure of the outcome. It had never been done before."

"What did you do?" Ray's voice went cold along with my blood.

Cxarana's mouth twitched. "When you asked me to end your lives over the Rifts, to seal them with your life blood, I... I waited until you lost consciousness. And then I bled you into Dhamyan's canteen so I would have your life blood to seal the Rifts. I pushed you both into the Rifts and then poured your remaining life blood in to create the seal. I hoped for a way to save you. I searched for one. I didn't find any answers. However, it seems I may have stumbled upon the solution accidentally, that being nearest to the greatest energy source in the Rifts, being nearest to the Eventide, somehow revived you once the Rifts reopened."

"Any idea how that worked?" I asked, a sense of dread filling my stomach.

"I can only guess. While there, you were kept connected to the power of the Eventide, the power that gifts us all with our abilities. Had I thought of it before, I would have done the same for Kylie Robertson, but it was a last-minute decision. I hadn't believed your gamble would work until I witnessed the Rift sealing. Once I did, I realized I only had a brief chance. I took that chance."

"And it kept us alive," Kyp said.

"It did more than that," I said. "Cxarana, is it possible that being so close to the source of Key energy could have given me new abilities?"

"Abilities?" Ray asked.

"Mama is magic now." Jainey snuggled into Kyp's side. "She can control electricity. She did what Zane does. And she made lightning."

"What?" Austin said. "Badass."

"It's true," Zane said. "She helped me fix a computer issue, believe it or not."

"Not," Drew said.

I flipped him the finger.

"What about you?" I tipped my head back against the couch to look at Kyp.

Kyp shook his head and shrugged.

"That's weird," Austin said. "Why didn't you get any cool gifts? Did whoever hand them out meet you and decide you were too much trouble?" He cuffed him on the arm.

Kyp smacked his hand away, but he huffed a laugh.

Was that… playfulness? Between Austin and Kyp? That was different.

Good different.

"He probably just hasn't accidentally discovered it yet. I'm sure there's something in there," Cass said. She frowned at his interaction with Austin.

Glad I wasn't the only one who was surprised by that.

"Moving on," Jordan said. "Caleb… I think he implanted a dream in my mind. I thought he did it because he needed help, but he was leading us into a trap."

Kyp swore. "I was really hoping that kid would figure himself out and find his way back home."

"So did we," Rennie said. "For now, he's still struggling. But he needs an anchor. He thought he could find it in his mother. But Kylie's spirit in Cass's body wasn't enough for him."

"He teamed up with his other mama," Jainey said, tears building in her eyes.

Kyp tutted, gently wiping the tears from her eyes before his eyes met mine. "Lavinia? She's back?"

I looked away. My throat ached.

"Well, not anymore," Zane deadpanned.

Kyp's head tilted. "No?"

"She led an army against us," Cass explained. "Jordan got trounced. They even hurt Jainey. We were pinned down. And then this group of, get this, Sirin rebels joined the fight. So it looks like we have allies everywhere."

"Yes!" Jainey sat up, rejuvenated by the topic. "And Mama took care of Grandma Liv, so she'll never hurt us again, right, Mama?"

"You took care of her?" Ray asked. "What does that mean, exactly?"

My throat tightened further. "I killed her." I turned my attention to Kyp. "She's gone. Permanently."

"So that's it," Ray said. "Lavinia's dead. Hmmm. I was hoping she'd be eaten by ants. Like, thousands of tiny ants... slowly..."

The group stared at him, but my eyes were all for Kyp. And he was frozen.

"What?" Ray asked. "She'd deserve it! And it would hurt a lot. A tiny thousand searing bites."

Rennie glanced from Jacks to Kyp. "Enough."

"Gone?" Kyp mouthed.

"I killed her. And I did the Ritual," I said slowly. "It's over."

Kyp stared at me blankly.

"She's gone, baby." I reached for his hand.

He let out a strangled sound, his eyes widening, and leapt to his feet.

"Kyp?" I called, but he was already rushing out into the hallway.

He kept walking, talking over his shoulder as he moved. "I'm exhausted from the trip over here. I think I need a nap." He stopped when he made it up the stairs, looking up and back down the hall. I'd never seen anyone look so lost inside their own home before.

He finally chose a direction and stomped his way toward it.

"We should talk about this." I followed him as he passed his own bedroom.

He stopped right in front of my door and turned to face me. "I'd really rather not."

"I get that this is upsetting, but I thought you'd be, at least, relieved." I grasped for the oily feeling in my chest, that thing that didn't feel right about him. "You don't seem relieved at all."

"Neither do you." His eyes narrowed. "Weird, isn't it?" He threw the door open and stepped inside.

"Wait! That's my—"

The door slammed between us.

"—room."

I'd intended to ask him to move into my room when he was healed. I hadn't expected him to lock me out of it.

TWENTY TWO

VOICES

KYP

Kyp couldn't believe he'd managed to make it behind a closed door without breaking down completely.

He didn't know why the words had sliced into him the way they had. He hated Lavinia. He *hated* her. She'd abused him all his life—mentally, emotionally, and physically. She'd ordered Gana's murder and tried to murder Jacklyn. She'd manipulated his children and his brother, and would have killed Jainey if he hadn't stopped her. She was more of a monster than any of the interdimensionals.

So why did he feel so empty?

His chest felt like it was being pressed down, crushed beneath Jacklyn's boot.

She'd killed his mother.

He reached out for the item closest to him, preparing to launch it across the room.

But it was heavy.

It was the Batman bust Jacklyn had brought from the estate. He stopped. He couldn't smash that. Not more than it already had been.

It was Jacklyn's. He looked around the room, turning in a full circle. The entire room was Jacklyn's.

Jacklyn who was probably the only person who seemed to understand him effortlessly, even when he didn't understand what the hell he was thinking.

Jacklyn, who had killed his mother.

Maybe she could understand why he felt this way.

It wasn't so much the idea that Lavinia was gone that plagued him. It was the idea that she would never return. He would never have a chance to show her what he could do. That he was better than she believed he was. That he wasn't completely useless.

"You are good enough," a disembodied voice whispered to him. "She made so many mistakes."

No. He wasn't doing this. Not now.

He dropped onto the edge of the bed and threw himself backwards. His vision blurred as he stared up at the ceiling. He was so tired. So damn tired of not being able to control his emotions. He missed the years he'd had tight control over them. It was as though they had almost been gone until Jacklyn returned and brought them back with twice as much strength.

He missed rationality.

He pressed his palms hard into his eyes.

He didn't know how long he remained that way, but when he'd pulled his hands away, the sunlight coming through the windows had been replaced by darkness and the lights from the buildings surrounding them.

He hadn't been lying when he'd told Jacklyn he needed sleep to handle his emotions. A reset. But he didn't feel like he'd been reset. He felt calmer, but ill. A quick glance at the nearby alarm clock told him it had been half a day since he'd last eaten, and he wasn't anything approaching hungry.

He pushed himself to his feet. He should be happy. The ever-present tension in his side was gone, but his chest felt it instead, like it would tear open, create a new wound. And it was so stupid. Incredibly stupid, when he could still see his mother torturing him to death in his mind's eye.

"All this time, you believed you were trying to destroy her. You were actually trying to prove yourself to her."

"You thought you could change her, and now you'll never get the chance."

"Like you'd win her back to the good side."

"She was a monster. You never stood a chance."

The voices swirled in his mind. He could ask Cass… but he wouldn't. He'd figure this out. He wouldn't talk to Cass until he was sure that it was the dead he was hearing.

That he hadn't just lost his mind.

The concept chilled his bones.

Besides, Cass had looked at him like he was made of porcelain for most of their friendship. The last thing he needed to give her was another chance to see the cracks.

He rolled off the bed. Maybe he should get some air? Air, at least, sounded agreeable.

He could do this. He was fine.

He was fine.

"You're not fine. You need to talk to someone," a voice whispered through his mind.

Fine. He could talk to *someone*. It didn't have to be Cass. It definitely didn't have to be Jacklyn.

He slinked through the door and moved in silence through the empty hallways. The kitchen buzzed with voices and the bustle of people moving around the room. His family. He avoided it as best as he could and made his way out of the back door.

Jordan sat on a ledge beside the planters where leaves spilled forward. His legs were crossed in a classic meditation position, eyes closed. His lips turned up slightly.

He was like looking in a mirror. All the good things about Kyp were before him.

God, did he get bigger?

"You know, they say green is calm and grounding," Jordan said. His eyes never opened.

"Yeah? And what do you say?"

"It's enjoyable."

"Can I join you?" Kyp asked.

"Be my guest."

Kyp lowered himself to the ledge beside Jordan, maneuvering himself into the same position as his son.

"Are you okay?" Jordan asked. "You seem kind of... stilted. Wrong."

"That's about right." Kyp sighed.

Silence reigned between them. Kyp listened to the movement in the leaves, the sounds from within the kitchen that echoed out into the outdoor area. One voice was missing. One loud, boisterous voice.

Jacklyn was worried. She had to be. She was always the loudest voice in the room.

"Will you just be honest with me?" Jordan said with all the impatience of a much older adult. "A ten-ton weight is crushing you and you won't even reach out from below the debris."

"Which one of us is the parent?" His voice was low, but he cringed at the snap of annoyance in his tone.

"Does it matter?" Jordan asked. "You're stressed out. You're not sitting with anyone else. You won't talk to Mom. Why not talk to me? Maybe I can help."

Kyp considered it. He truly needed to take a good look at the twisting feelings in his chest.

"Lavinia's dead," Kyp said.

"Yeah," Jordan confirmed.

"I should be happy."

"You're not?"

"I want to be. I know I should be." He huffed a dark laugh. "Maybe not happy. But I should feel… safe. All my life, Lavinia was my greatest fear. I should feel relieved."

"Maybe it's because you didn't get to face your greatest fear." Jordan turned slightly toward Kyp.

"I *did* face my fears," he argued. "I fought Lavinia before I fell into the Dusk."

Jordan shrugged. "When I faced off with Livingston, it felt amazing. I ended that fear. You didn't get to do that. Mom took that from you."

"She needed it too." He shook his head, but he knew he wasn't quite correct. After years of Lavinia abusing him, did she really need it as bad as he did? He tried to ignore the bitterness that emerged from within at the thought.

"At least in my case, Jainey and Caleb got to help. Although Rennie probably wanted in on that action." His shoulders slumped.

"Caleb. Yeah, I'm sorry about that, kid." Kyp reached an arm around him and pulled him closer, and Jordan let him. "That really sucks. I'm sorry."

"Yeah." He broke his stance, dropping his legs so his feet touched the stone flooring. "I know he's the bad guy now, but…"

"It's the memories." Kyp knew. "There are bad ones, but the good ones are just as vivid."

Jordan nodded. "That's the problem with having a flawless memory."

Kyp slid off the ledge and dropped onto the stone floor. "Calling it a flawless memory suggests there is nothing wrong with it." He leaned back against the wall, one arm slung over his bent knee, his other leg stretched out in front of him. "But really, it sucks."

Jordan mimicked his movements, sitting beside him, again like Kyp's mirror.

"He loves you," the voices said. *"It's a shame you'll only ruin him."*

A chill ran down his spine.

"You'll fail to protect him. There are too many forces against you. You."

"Not just me. Jacklyn."

"What?" Jordan asked.

He'd said that out loud, hadn't he?

"I said I'm here for you. Jacklyn too."

"Such a good liar," the voice whispered. *"An excellently smooth delivery."*

"Yes, and as happy as I am to know I've got you guys, I'd be elated if I didn't have to deal with my Aegis at all," Jordan said. "We've got to find a way to seal the Rifts again. When they were closed, I actually forgot. Not everything, but the pain… It wasn't as sharp. I could breathe again without losing control."

"It's the pain that keeps him safe. It's the pain that keeps him aware." The voice again. *"How will he stay on guard if he forgets what that's like? You could protect him. If you were good enough."*

"Dad?" Jordan said.

Kyp shook the voice free from his head. "Sorry. What?"

"What you need, what we all need, is to forget," Jordan said. "Just a little. We'll be able to face what we need to if we don't remember the reasons we shouldn't."

"He's not wrong. You need to forget why you shouldn't."

Kyp smiled, his heart lightening despite the conflict raging within him. "You know, you're right."

"I am?" Jordan said. "I am. Totally." A huffed laugh. "Obviously."

Kyp rolled to his feet. "Would you like to come inside? Or are you staying out here?"

"I'm good out here for a bit." He smiled. "I'm glad you're feeling better."

Kyp reached down and ruffled Jordan's soft, dark hair. "Okay, message received. You came out here to think, and I got in the way of that. Sorry."

Jordan frowned. "Dad, I didn't say that. I'm glad we talked."

Kyp tensed. "I'm glad too. I didn't mean to make it seem like I wasn't."

Jordan's breath slowly whistled from his nose. "Okay, good."

"I'm proud of you, kid." He waited until Jordan nodded his understanding before leaving him there and returning to the brownstone.

He kept his steps light. He didn't want to alert anyone. It was only a matter of time before they discovered he'd left his self-imposed isolation.

He owed Jacklyn an apology. She'd been doing what he'd asked, what he'd wanted since she'd returned to the estate. Since they'd found each other again.

Even if he had some… misgivings…

He maneuvered his way to the living room to where he'd left the books he'd seized from the Dusk. They weren't there.

Where would they have put them? His desk? They wouldn't be in Ray's room after the way he acted in the Dusk.

It would likely be with Drew and Austin for that very reason.

He was right. The large tome and the satchel of smaller books Kyp had obtained were laid atop Drew's desk. He flipped through the books. He'd need time to translate them before he could find what he was looking for.

A muffled moan sounded just outside the door.

Eyes widening, Kyp shoved one of the slimmer leather-bound volumes into his back pocket and turned to sit on the edge of the desk just in time for Drew to practically tumble backwards into the room. Austin was, quite literally, attached to him, arm wrapped tightly around his waist, lips latched onto his neck.

"Kyp?!" Drew squeaked.

Kyp jumped back off the desk, his hand coming up to rub the back of his neck, eyes dropping to the floor and away from the couple.

"Goddamn, not another one," Austin groaned, detaching himself from Drew and dropping his arms to his sides. He let out a ragged sigh. "I thought you told me it wasn't like that? You promised after Jacklyn…"

Drew pinched the bridge of his nose. "I can't tell if you're being funny or not. But if you're not, we're going to have to talk about your shitty self-esteem."

Austin's brow furrowed, his eyes never leaving Drew.

Kyp's face heated. "I apologize. Deeply. I didn't expect…" The display embarrassed him. Knowing your friends got romantic behind closed doors was something wholly different than seeing it.

Now Austin turned his gaze Kyp's way. He crossed his arms over his chest. "Just…why?" He flushed red.

Drew shook his head. "You two really need to hash out your weirdness one day, I swear." Another weighted sigh. "Kyp, what are you doing here?"

He took a moment to steady himself. The best lies were crafted from truth. "I screwed up." He hated to do this in front of Austin, but he was here, and he wasn't leaving.

"This is new, how?" Austin asked.

"With Jacklyn. I screwed up with Jacklyn."

"In a new and interesting way? Again, I ask…"

Drew placed an arm on Austin's shoulder. "Give him a break, hon." He turned toward Kyp. "I don't think you screwed up. I think you just surprised her. I don't know what she was expecting, but that wasn't it."

"I don't know why I reacted that way, either." Kyp shrugged. "I've been so messed up for so long at this point, and it all surrounded Mo—I mean Lavinia. It was like everything just stalled."

"Grief is a strange thing," Austin drawled. "We all react differently. I even got upset when you bit it. Can you believe it?" A slight smile.

"My relationship with my foster dad was pretty awful, but I still cried at his funeral," Drew said. "It totally makes sense."

"It does?" Kyp raised his eyebrows.

"Of course," Drew said. "It's less about the person and more about the realization that they're never gonna be who you wished they'd been, and knowing that they never will."

Kyp's throat tightened.

Liv had never been a true parent; but he would be a true father to his children. He would do anything for them. And he was starting here.

With this one lie. With this one book in his back pocket. And then the rest. Until he found an answer.

Twenty Three

E FOR EFFORT

Jacklyn

I woke to the scent of citrus and the feel of calloused fingertips stroking my cheek. I snuffled, an undoubtedly sexy sound, as the pillow I laid face down on tickled my nose. My eyelids peeled back to reveal an empty bedside table, and beyond that, a desk filled with neatly piled stacks of books and papers.

This was, most definitely, not my room.

Right. I had fallen asleep in Kyp's room after he'd commandeered mine for whatever over-the-top brooding session he'd required to process Lavinia's death.

It wasn't that I didn't understand he was conflicted. Hell, I was conflicted. But he could have talked to me about it.

"Jacks?" Kyp. His voice was a breath against my ear, hoarse and questioning.

"Hey," I greeted, turning to face him. He lay atop the blanket, head propped up by his hand, looking down at me with sorrowful eyes. "What's wrong?"

He shook his head. "I'm sorry."

"What?"

"I'm sorry, Jacks. I missed you the whole time I was gone. And then I shut you out of my head, of your own room, because I freaked out about something you never would have wanted if I hadn't recruited you for it in the first place." His eyes reddened the way they always did before tears pooled in them. "Every single day I have you with me, I'm still torn about the fact that I brought you into this mess. My idiocy killed your sister. It's the reason you needed vengeance to begin with. And you finally get it and here I am, making it all about me—"

"This *is* about you," I cut him off with a finger pressed to his lips. "Yeah, sure. I'm livid about what she did to my sister. Do you think I didn't care that she tortured my boyfriend for his entire life? I mean, obviously, Gana"—my throat tightened—"meant the world to me. Losing her changed everything."

He petted a hand over my hair, and my heart gave a little squeeze.

"But if you think after everything we've been through, I didn't kill her for you? You're mad."

He swallowed hard. "That's the thing, Jacks. I think I might be."

"Mad?" The last time he'd believed that, Lavinia had been in his head. He'd struggled badly then. This time, he seemed calmer, but the dread in his eyes told a different story.

His gaze slid to the pillow, avoiding mine. "I keep hearing things. Voices."

My breath caught. "Like… like… thoughts? Someone else's thoughts?"

"That's not what they sound like. They're like whispers in the back of my mind. And they… I don't know how to explain it." He squirmed, jostling me slightly. "It's like they're saying things about me. About what I can't do. They're making me doubt myself." His eyes met mine again, and they were blown wide. "Jacks. I'm scared."

My throat felt like it closed up on me. Rarely was he scared. Concerned. At most, he had misgivings. Even if he was actually scared, he didn't openly admit to it. Even when it was obvious.

Whatever this was, Kyp was terrified.

"What if"—he pulled in a ragged breath—"what if this is what Mother went through?" Another. "She died, and she died, and then she broke, right? What if I'm gonna be like her?" He pulled in breaths like he was drinking them from a straw. "Jacks, you've gotta kill me if I become like her. Only you can. It will be just like with her. However you beat her, you've gotta just—"

"Hey!" I cried out. My heart ached with every word he spoke. I took his face in my hands, pressed a kiss to his forehead, a quick peck to his lips. "Hey, no. That is not what's happening here. And even if it is, you know I won't allow it. *We* won't allow it."

"Yeah?" Kyp yanked his head out of my grasp. "You're going to stop it? By doing what?"

"Kyp, you have me, the kids, the rest of our family." I tried to reassure him, but something in me was twisting at his words. Could I do it? If I needed to, if it was necessary, could I put Kyp down?

"She had me! I wasn't enough!"

The words were barely out of his mouth before he deflated. He sagged forward, pressing himself back into my arms.

"Why wasn't I enough?" he whispered into my neck. A shudder

overtook him.

God, if I could kill Lavinia again, I would.

I cradled him in my arms. "It's okay, Kyp. It wasn't anything you did or didn't do. What she did, it was her. It was her fault. She chose the darkness over you. You won't. I know you won't."

A wet sob escaped, tears soaking into my T-shirt.

"I've got you," I said. "I've got you, forever."

"I know," he whispered. "I trust you."

It was funny, and not in the ha-ha kinda way. Ray had asked Kyp to protect me at all costs, but that was what I wanted to do for Kyp. I wanted to hold him in my arms forever, while he cried away all his pain. I wanted to keep him safe from anything that would hurt him. Life had ground Kyp into dust and I wanted to take that dust and find a way to put it back together, just like he'd done for the ceramic bear I'd broken at the estate.

"I love you," I spoke into his ear as he sobbed silently against me.

"I love you so much," he said. "So much that it sometimes scares me."

"Scares you?"

"I lose everything I love," he murmured. "And I've already lost you twice."

"You won't lose me again." I thought about it for a minute, then pulled back so he could see my face. "Kyp, I won't leave again."

"You won't necessarily have a choice." He pushed back the curtain of hair that fell into my eyes. "I'm sorry. I shouldn't have—"

"Don't. You're allowed to feel pain and you're allowed to show it. Don't pull any macho 'sorry for emoting' bullshit on me. Your mother *died.* You don't have to show anyone else how you feel, but you better show me. We're a team. And you never have to apologize to me about how you feel."

Kyp opened his mouth to answer, but my attention shot elsewhere. The door next door clicked closed.

Jainey's room.

That was enough to make me sharpen my Aegis, focus on hearing the sounds from the door. Was she going to the bathroom? Coming back? Or was she up to something?

You didn't have a child like Jainey without expecting her to get into some kind of mischief.

"You need to block—"

That was Kylie. She was advising Jainey to block the sound, and then, just like that, it was.

"Jacks?"

And that was Kyp, who I'd totally just ignored.

My gaze snapped to his.

"I see you've returned," he teased, but it was half-hearted at best.

"Shit, Kyp. I'm sorry. I heard something down the hall." I rolled out of bed and yanked open my dresser drawer.

"What was it?" Kyp moved to follow me, nothing if not adaptable. "You're getting dressed?"

I pulled on my black leggings for ease of movement. "We have to go, now."

"But I didn't even tell you. I made you breakfast." It was very nearly a whine. "Freshly squeezed orange juice and everything."

That explained why I smelled oranges when I woke.

"Well, I want to know why Kylie is talking to Jainey, and Jainey is blocking my ability to hear them."

Kyp's expression darkened. Even with reddened eyes and somewhat blotchy skin, it made him look threatening. "What?"

I reached under my bed once I was dressed and yanked my weapons bag out. "We're about to find out and I'm going to beat Kylie right the hell out of Cass."

I rushed to the door.

"Jacks!"

My hand was already on the knob, ready to turn it, but I looked back at him.

"Wait… I can hear her… her thoughts." His nose wrinkled, eyes narrowing.

"Jainey didn't block you?" That was surprising.

"It's not Jainey… It's Kylie. But that's impossible. I can't read spirits… I can't…"

I breathed in deeply to calm myself. "Are you sure you're actually hearing her?" I winced. "I mean, you said…"

"I know. You're right to question it. Right now, she's just thinking about how badly they need to stay quiet. Which is Kylie being Kylie, because she never actually trusts anything she can't see."

That did sound like Kylie.

Kyp's arms crossed over his chest. "I know that proves nothing. It's probably just all…" His eyes shifted and went out of focus. "Oh no. Oh *shit.*"

"What?"

"That sound you heard… They were leaving the brownstone. She thinks Jainey can help her talk to Caleb." His voice went breathless. "We have to go after them. *Now.*"

"That's what I was trying to do when you stopped me!"

"I know, I know. But we shouldn't just go storming out there. We can use this moment as an opportunity to prove for sure if Kylie is truly on our side. And we don't know if, if what I'm hearing can be trusted." He stepped closer. "We need to test it."

"You want to test it," I confirmed. "While our daughter is potentially in trouble?"

"We'll go. And I'll wake Jordan and the others while we do." He shooed me forward. "So, now? Move. They're heading toward the train station for clues."

"They think he's still there?" I asked.

"At the very least," Kyp said, suddenly rather calm given his earlier state, "they believe they can find a lead."

I nodded. "We'll alert the others on the way." I threw the door open.

Kyp followed me through the door. "Maybe I'm not crazy? Maybe I'm hearing ghosts?"

"Hopefully."

Because, if not, Kylie and Jainey were gone, and we had no idea where they were headed.

Twenty Four

VINDICATION

Kyp

Any fear Kyp possessed over the possibility that he was losing his mind evaporated the moment they pulled up to a parking spot below the abandoned train station. Cass and Jainey were there, leaving the station.

Jacklyn was already unbuckling her seatbelt when he spoke.

"We should follow them. See where this leads us."

Though she had responded with nothing but a flat stare, she hadn't exited the car, and they'd carefully followed Cass's Prius until they'd arrived at a warehouse across the Bronx from where they'd started.

Kyp struggled to keep his heart rate steady as he watched them approach the area. Caleb leaned against a wall, staring ahead as they approached.

Jacklyn gripped his hand hard enough his bones clicked, but he held on just as tightly.

"Can you hear them?" he asked. She nodded, and he connected their minds, eager to take in the information as she received it.

Caleb's voice spilled into his mind instantly. "Mother told me you wouldn't just drop it." His confidence in Lavinia stirred Kyp's blood, and he wasn't sure if he wanted to punch him or comfort him.

"Was that before or after the grave?" Kylie asked, full snottiness on display before she seemed to pull back and realize how she sounded. "She's not your mother, Caleb. Not in any way that counts."

Muscle pain flared through Kyp's shoulder and his back. He tensed, and Jacklyn rubbed a firm hand along his back.

"And you were?" Caleb lobbed back. "You were around for about five minutes before you fucked off and died."

"You act like I drank and drove myself off a cliff. I didn't fuck off and die. Lavinia killed me. Then she decided she'd step in as your mom and you let her."

"This isn't why we're here," Jainey said, and it was still strange hearing a voice so small be the sole source of common sense. "We came here to talk."

"We're talking," Caleb said.

"And not talking like we did last time when you hit me in the head with a rock," Jainey shot back.

HE WHAT?

Jacklyn had left that part out.

Or maybe they were going to tell him, but he was too busy storming away.

"Don't move," Jacklyn told him, yanking back on his hand before he even knew he was moving. *"You'll make this worse."*

She wasn't wrong. Whatever *this* was, his presence wasn't bound to help.

Caleb sighed. "Jainey, I'm sorry about that, but—"

"There's really no 'but' that will work there." She stepped closer to him. "Look, Caleb, war is coming and we want you on our side of it."

He shoved his hands through his straight blond hair, tousling it until it stuck up in every direction. "Jainey, I wanted to. For you and Jordan, for Rennie, I would have done anything. I could have seen a way this could have worked. But that changed as soon as Jacklyn came out of that fight alive. Because I cannot, I *will* not, fight on your side if *she* is there." He jabbed one finger in the direction of the car Kyp and Jacklyn hid within.

He knew.

He knew they were there.

Kyp exited the car, Jacklyn hot on his heels. "You and I have to have a talk, little brother." He stomped his way across the pavement that separated the two warehouse spaces.

Kyp had assumed they wouldn't be noticed or recognized in the large parking lot, which had already begun to fill with early morning workers.

Clearly, he was mistaken.

"Kyp! You're back," Caleb greeted, warm-eyed and friendly. "It's a shame you weren't here last time."

"So I could have seen you brutalize my children?" Kyp's pride kept him strong, but picturing how hurt Jordan and Jainey had been made him ready to tackle the kid.

"Of course not," Caleb said. "It never would have gotten to that point if you'd been here from the beginning. I wanted to talk to you.

I hope whatever was more important was worth it."

Caleb was a teenage boy, just like his son, Kyp had to remind himself.

"Okay then. Let's talk."

Kyp's eyes shifted to Jainey and Kylie-within-Cass beside Caleb. He reached for Jacklyn's hand and felt her energy reach for him.

Caleb took a step toward him. "Truth is… I'm fucked." He glanced from side to side like he was checking to see if anyone else was listening. "I miss my dad. He was kind to me. He cared, and he looked after me. Maybe he would know what to do."

Kylie snorted, but her expression darkened. "I loved Ross more than I could tell you. But he never had any idea what to do."

Caleb glared at her. "He spoke highly of you all. He said he made a bad mistake aligning himself with Lavinia. That he followed love, and it steered him wrong."

Kylie's gaze shifted to the floor.

"I don't want to make the same mistake. So I can't listen to Rennie, or Jordan, or her." He motioned toward Jainey. "I have to eschew the choices that will lead me down that road and make the choice that works best for me."

"So you know Ross made a mistake by following Lavinia, and you've decided you will too?" Jacklyn asked, her jaw slack with disbelief.

"You made sure that didn't matter anymore, didn't you?" Caleb snapped. "You made sure I couldn't follow her *or* you with what you've done. So instead, I'm choosing my own path."

"The best choice for you is with us." Kyp struggled to keep his tone even. "We need you. We'll keep you safe and you'll be a trusted part of the team. We'll rely on each other and we'll stem the tide of the coming war together." He held out a hand. Caleb's mind had been twisted by the authority figures in his life, just the way his own had been. "You do not need to do this, Caleb. Come with us."

"I'll die." Caleb's cheeks reddened. "Do you have any idea what is happening? What is coming? They'll never just let me leave."

"I can't know if you don't tell me." Kyp spoke through clenched teeth. "Can't you see? All we've been trying to do, all our family was trying to do from back when we first closed the Rifts, is protect you. You're in over your head, but we can help."

Caleb's brow furrowed deeply.

"It won't be easy," Jainey said. "But we can do our best to do what's right."

"If I've learned anything over the years, it's that Kyp usually ends up on the relatively successful side," Kylie added, eyes glowing celadon as she spoke through Cass. "Whether or not I'm on that side."

Caleb nodded, a tight, fluttering movement. "All right. Okay. I'll do it. But I'm going to need one thing from you."

"You're our Caleb! Our family!" Jainey answered, clearly cheered by his response. "We'd do anything to get the chance to help you."

Another nod before he lifted his head, gaze aimed directly at Kyp. "Okay. Then kill Jacklyn."

The hair on the back of Kyp's neck rose, numbness prickling his spine. "What?"

Jainey's eyes grew so round, the whites surrounding them were like shiny pearls. "Caleb, no."

Kyp's throat dried to a crusty, wrinkled lump. "You know I can't do that. Nobody needs to die."

Caleb laughed bitterly. "Tell that to our mother."

"You know," Jacklyn drawled, "you're really sad. Grasping onto the idea of a mother, any mother, the way you are. You know Lavinia's a monster, and yet you're fighting for her memory like she ever gave you anything but pain."

Kyp flinched. Jacklyn apologized within his mind, but it didn't matter. The words had hit close to home because of their truth. He wasn't as different from Caleb as he would like to believe.

"Do you think she had nothing to do with the treatments, with the torture you endured at Livingston's hands? She helped plan the whole thing."

"That doesn't matter." His voice was a rasp.

"Doesn't it? For power, she would have gladly sent the Dusk into the Dawn. She would have killed Jainey to do so. And she would have done the same thing now. I was trying to save the Dawn and all of our lives. I'm sorry I didn't go about it in a Caleb-approved way." Jacklyn's voice rose with every sentence.

Caleb's face crumpled. "Vengeance is all I have left now. Vengeance and this war. You killed my mother."

"And she killed my sister. We can keep playing this game of revenge-go-round, or we can stop the damn cycle."

His head shot up, a smirk written across his face. "Then I guess someone will have to give up on avenging you, because it doesn't end here."

A trap. Kyp groaned internally. When wasn't it a trap?

Jacklyn pushed up the sleeves of her saggy gray sweater while sliding daggers free from them.

Gorvhans seemed to melt from the shadows, shrieks rending the air. Kyp motioned the others to join them in a circle formation, back-to-back, just like Mother taught him, with Jainey protected in the center.

The creatures closed in on them, but Jacklyn, brave and beautiful soul that she was, leapt out at them, sliding her dagger into the base of a head, between the ribs of another. And then she pulled her guns free from the holsters on each side of her belt.

Kyp didn't have time to watch what she did next—he had his own Gorvhans to handle—but he turned toward his duty with a smile on his face.

"Telekinetic shield, baby," Jacklyn murmured to Jainey just before the gunfire started raining down.

Kyp used his own telekinesis to shove the approaching Gorvhans back. Once he had some space, he yanked his axe free from where it had been strapped to his back. Heat whizzed by his cheeks as Gana channeled her Aegis through Cass. It alternated with the droplets of water raining upon him from Kylie's contribution.

The trio circled, guarding Jainey. Gorvhans around Kyp exploded in eruptions of brain matter and ichor, others in the flicker of flames and shimmers of smoke, and still others drowned upon water jammed down their throats. The Gorvhans went down easily in a rain of fury.

Which made sense.

They were the easy ones.

"You're not the crown prince anymore, are ya?" An inhuman voice sounded through the crowd, grating and slobbery. A Sirin.

Kyp's stomach dropped. After all this time, it was still the Sirins that got to him, no matter how hard he tried to hide it.

"Nothing to rule anymore," Kyp answered, trying like hell to be as flawlessly flippant as his partner. He swung his axe and hacked through the neck of another Gorvhan with the power of a Yankee slugger.

"And what is a king without a kingdom?" The Sirin stepped past the decapitated Gorvhan, a poor attempt to get in Kyp's space. Kyp pushed back telekinetically, and though the creature strained to keep its footing, it failed, skidding back and scuffing its shoes along the pavement.

"Is he a king or a prince? Pick a lane!" Jacklyn crowed, and the Sirin flew back, the gunshot wound on its forehead spraying Kyp with blood.

Kyp swore at how close the bullet came to him, his hand unconsciously coming up to check for a wound amidst the pounding in his head that seemed ever present in light of all the stress he faced.

Frustration and anger boiled his blood, and he chose to neglect the axe for a moment. He swung out, connecting punch after punch into the next Gorvhan's misshapen head.

"More!"

The axe was just an afterthought, a way of ending them, the

finishing blow.

But they kept coming. No matter how many he killed or how many times he died, they always kept coming.

Fury lit in his veins, goaded by the voices within him, calling for bloodshed. Bones fractured under his hands, blood pooling beneath his feet. Tension twisted his muscles, coiling painfully.

"Jacks, what the hell is Kyp doing?" Kylie sneered, but he ignored her.

A frenzy licked at his heels. His emotions churned like a cyclone, spiraling from him until he didn't know which blood on his hands was his own and which belonged to the creatures lying at his feet. He wanted to burn it all down. He wanted to end it *all*.

A click, or more of a popping sound, and the battlefield was gone. Gray mist surrounded him, but it didn't feel anything thicker or more moist than regular air. Actually, it didn't feel like anything. His limbs felt light, floating.

"Kyp." A voice floated through the air around him. "It's been a while."

His eyes narrowed. *How on earth?* "Janice? Janice Richter?"

Janice Richter had been the last living Spirit Key. She had died when he was sixteen years old, one of the last of Ray's sympathizers remaining in the main group of the Order of the Key. She looked exactly like the last time he saw her. Her light brown skin glowed, and her copper ringlets hung away from her face with the help of a teal bandana, a total mismatch from the cropped peach blouse, purple floor-length skirt, and hiking boots she wore. She'd always dressed like that, a complete mess of colors that shouldn't work together but did. He'd admired her carefree nature. She was the most spiritual person he'd ever known, which made sense.

"What are you doing here?" His words left him in a rush. "How can I… I'm really losing my mind, aren't I?"

Janice rolled her eyes, then stroked her angular jaw line. "Your partner kills your psycho-mama with a bolt of lightning, you start seeing spirits, and you assume you've gone mad? Because last I heard Holden Reinhardt was the last Energy Key, and he's as dead as I am. Neither of us should have passed along our abilities."

She'd always had a way of quieting his heart when he was a child, but he'd pushed her from his mind as an adult. He'd needed to. He'd lost so many people to his mother and to the war Ray had waged with her until all he could do was count the ghosts.

"You're here because you finally figured out how to use what we gave you when you were in the Eventide with us," she said. "You tapped into it and came here to the Spirit Realm."

"Why did you give us anything?" Kyp asked. "We were dead. Permanently gone."

"We knew it wasn't over." A shrug. "But we knew that, if it ever would end, it would be you and Jacklyn with the power to end it."

Jacklyn. "I'm here. What is my body doing there?"

"Do you remember Arcad and Rick?" she asked. "Oh, who am I kidding? Of course you do."

Peter Arkadian and Richard Hutchens. Ray's Guardians for many years. His closest allies, along with Jaina Madison and Karen Zane. They were like uncles to him growing up. Jacks probably remembered them, if she tried hard enough. Arcad had died in the civil war within the Order. Ricky had run with Ray, although Rick's absence certainly told a story. Either Mother or the work they did eventually caught up with him. Otherwise, he'd have never left Ray's side.

"Well, those two took your body into the fight."

Had they been the voices driving him on? It hadn't felt like them. They'd never been that bloodthirsty.

A glint of silver flashed in the air surrounding them, creating a clear window in the fog. For a moment, Kyp's lungs were weighted with the humid mist and he was looking through his own eyes once again. His hand swung the axe, though he didn't make it do so.

And then he was back in front of Janice.

"What the hell is happening to me?" Kyp whispered.

"There is nothing to fear." Janice reached for him, then pulled back, but not before her hand passed through his. She grimaced. "Sorry. We're nearly on the same plane, but not exactly. You'd have to be dead, too."

He nodded, but he felt shaky and wrong. Empty.

"Kyp, you've been given an amazing gift," Janice said, the sky around her changing from gray to blue as she spoke. "You can use this to help yourself and others. Keep your mind open. The spirits will help you. Now go back, but work *with* those spirits who seek to help you on your journey."

Her words chilled him. Was that what he had heard, the spirits trying to help him? "Do the spirits always help?"

"Spirits are drawn to those they care for. They unite with those they are drawn to." She paused for a moment.

"Kyp!" Jacklyn's voice shouted from somewhere outside of this place. Her tone was urgent, almost panicked.

"Kyp," Janice called, regaining his attention. Her expression tightened. "Why would you ask that about the spirits? Has one tried to hurt you?"

"Dad!" Jordan called.

Weird. Jordan wasn't even there.

Janice's voice called after him, but it was further away.

All at once, Janice dissolved, the fog clearing around her, and he could see clearly once again.

Jacklyn's face. Her beautiful panicked eyes and trembling lips.

The axe blade against her neck, scraping there. The blood dripping in red streaks.

His own hand on the axe handle.

Twenty Five

LOST IN TRANSITION

Jacklyn

The interdimensionals just kept coming, no matter how hard we battered them back. Wave after wave assaulted us until I began to fear we might drown in the sheer numbers.

Each blow I made felt numb. No emotion. Just movement. I'd been fighting so long my legs ached and I was running low on ammo. Sweat dripped over my forehead and down my neck. The muscles in my arms twitched from being held in the same position for too long, my handguns trained on the approaching creatures, with only occasional breaks to reload or pistol-whip when someone got too close.

Brakes squealed behind me, and it was almost enough to break me from my reverie. Brakes? Then the thump of several bodies hitting the ground, the crunch of metal and bone. The screech of Gorvhans.

"Need a bit of help?" *Ray.*

Chaos loosed itself upon the battlefield as the rest of the Order of the Key came out swinging.

Across the melee, Caleb sprinted away. I moved to follow. I could leave my post now that the cavalry had arrived. Their presence made the odds feel nearly winnable. And they were until someone grabbed me from behind and pressed an axe blade to my throat. White pain and blood trickled down my neck. My heart slammed in my chest.

They spun me around to face them. My arms rose defensively before I even got a chance to look at the perpetrator, and when my eyes finally settled on the familiar planes of his face, that drumming kicked up even louder.

Kyp.

His eyes glowed an eerie shade of green, all too familiar from Cass's numerous possessions. His face was twisted with virulent hate, lip curled in a snarl.

"Kyp! What are you doing?" I asked, voice taut. But it wasn't Kyp in there. I had no idea who it was, or if it even knew where it was.

"Dad!" Jordan shouted. My tone must have alerted him.

My pulse thrummed in my ears. For a moment, Kyp just snarled at me, like he'd really take my head off.

He rocked on his heels once, twice, as though he was itching to do more.

Then, slowly, the green disappeared and his eyes cleared. The smirk melted from his face, replaced by horrified shock.

"Oh my God." Kyp dropped the axe.

"Thank fuck!" I breathed, reaching up to survey my wound. It wasn't a deep cut. But there had been a blade against my neck. One

Kyp had put there.

"What was I doing?" he asked, his voice hoarse.

I glanced around the parking lot. Dead interdimensionals littered the ground. One of the Order's vans, a hulking brown box of a vehicle, was in the center of the lot. If any interdimensionals had survived, they'd made a break for it and taken Caleb with them.

My gaze returned to Kyp's, finding his eyes pleading with me.

"You were fighting the bad guys." Cass watched him warily. "And then, suddenly, you tried to kill her."

"Bit of an overly-ambitious thing to attempt, considering she and I could stomp your ass," Ray commented. "What the hell happened? Your moves when you fought… that wasn't you out there."

"Spirits," Kyp breathed. "Jacks, I was hearing spirits. I'm a Spirit Key, like you're an Energy Key."

His eyes reddened. He looked miserable. All he'd ever wanted was to be normal. We were getting further and further away from making that a reality.

"That explains a lot," Jordan piped up beside me, "but not why you nearly killed Mom." His voice was low and tight.

"I can probably explain that," Cass said. "It's hard to get a wrangle on spirits sometimes. Particularly when you're new at this. When the Sentinels first showed up, they did whatever they wanted. But I was limited to those three. For Kyp… the spirits he contacts… they could be anyone. And all at once."

"The minute I realized what was happening, I stopped it," Kyp said, but it sounded flat.

"I wouldn't brag about it," Austin said. "You were nearly too late."

"What are you even doing here?" Kyp's eyes narrowed.

"You should be glad we were," Zane growled. "We saved your asses."

"What the hell were you even doing out here by yourselves?" Drew asked. "You shouldn't have been out here alone. And your half-assed way of notifying your team doesn't do you any favors."

"That was my fault," Jainey cried. "I tried to sneak out, and they were just trying to keep up with me."

"I'd say that was more the fault of the adult with you." I shot a glare in Cass's direction, though it wasn't meant for her. "We followed them as fast as we could. Maybe not the wisest move, but I didn't want to lose them while waking you all up."

"We should go." Kyp's eyes flitted to and fro like he expected something to jump out of the shadows and attack him. Which… well…

"We should sort this out right now," Austin snapped. "Can we trust Kyp when he's like this? We saw what he almost did to Jacks, and he led her out here—"

"I'm the one who wanted to go," I said. "And it's not like it's hard to imagine I made an impulsive decision."

"But he—"

"Enough, Austin," Rennie said, her voice faint, eyes locked in a thousand-mile stare. She shook off whatever she was experiencing and turned to Austin. "Leave him alone."

Kyp had gone pale in the face of Austin's anger. I'd never seen that happen before. He wrapped his arms around himself, like he was holding himself together with little more than his own physical strength. He stepped backwards in slow, jerky steps.

"You're okay," I said, laying a gentle hand on his arm. "I know it's a lot, but we'll be fine."

"Will we?" Kyp asked. "What about Caleb? He got away, and he's determined to get in our way. We can't save him."

"I want to help him, but I don't know," I said, dread twisting my stomach. "If he wants to believe he's the hero, I guess that makes me the villain."

The tension in Kyp's shoulders loosened somewhat. "It makes *us* the villains."

"You're right," Jordan said, resignation weighing his voice. "Whatever Caleb was to us can't matter. He's made himself a threat."

Rennie leveled a meaningful gaze on Jainey and Cass. "If we don't start treating him like a threat, he'll destroy us."

"And not only us," Drew said. "All these little dust ups? I don't know if he's trying to warn us or trying to flaunt, but they spell out something dangerous. If he had been out to kill us, he could have done it from the inside. This seems more…"

"Calculating," Ray finished for him. "It's all classic Liv. She may be dead, but she left behind a legacy." He stepped toward Cass. "When Liv first went off the rails, I didn't immediately start a war. I tried, first, to protect her. To shake some sense into her. To change her mind. But her mind wasn't one for changin'. This feels very much the same."

"Ray, what are you saying?" The words sighed out of me. I didn't have much heart for killing a child my son's age. Even if he was trying to hurt us all.

"I'm sayin' I let Liv grow too powerful and gain too much ground before I bothered to pull the rug out from under her." He frowned. "I'm sayin' I don't much like the chance of us risking that again."

"You're saying we kill Caleb," Kylie murmured. I expected fury, but what I got was more like shocked dismay.

"You're saying war," Kyp said with an ugly finality that sent chills through my bones. "Again."

"I don't much like saying that," Ray said. "It didn't work out too well the last time I declared it."

But we all knew that was exactly what he was saying.

And though we tried to reason a way around it the entire ride home, none of us could find a reasonable argument against it.

We were still arguing when we returned to find Cxarana and Dhamyan poring over the books the team had taken from the Dusk.

Cxarana sat on the couch, a tan sweater hanging loosely from her naturally skeletal body, a floral skirt cinched around her waist. It was still so weird to see her in human clothes. Clothes that definitely came from Rennie's closet. Her white hair had been woven into several small fishtail braids that threaded into an artful bun.

If I had to guess, she'd had help with that hairstyle.

Meanwhile, Dhamyan had lifted a pair of sweats from the guys' collection of indistinguishable workout gear.

"Greetings," Dhamyan said, baring his teeth. "Welcome home."

Cxarana's eyes shone, her chin jutting out slightly. "He is practicing your language and mannerisms."

I squeezed Dhamyan's shoulder. "Your English was perfect. Please never smile again. You looked like you thought I smelled bad."

"Do you not?" Dhamyan asked. *"I assumed you had an arduous battle. The odor of sweat is a point of pride to warriors."*

"Thanks?" I sighed, flopping onto one of the puffy chairs in the sitting room.

Kyp flashed a smile at Dhamyan. "Eh, maybe quit while you're ahead."

"I do not wish to halt the learning of your language," Dhamyan pronounced clearly, despite the slight jut of his teeth adding a particular accent to the words. He shook one of the books in front of him. "It is far easier than this horrid collection of swirls and squiggles!"

I snatched the book from his hand as the others found seats around the room. "I thought you'd gone through all the books and hadn't found anything interesting."

"We did indeed find things that were interesting," Cxarana said. "That does not mean we found the answer we searched for." She pointed at the large book. "Many that use herbs that no longer exist, but thankfully had the Ritual that saved Kyp's life." Her spindly finger moved to one of the smaller volumes. "A Doubling Ritual that could be used for replenishing stock, although it can only be done sparingly." She moved to another book. "A Ritual to hide a Rift." Another. "This one being close to Narah makes sense, at least. It contains a method to open a Rift through Ritual means. That hasn't been done since the initial Rifts were opened."

"I'm sorry, Cxarana," Austin said. "I know you didn't want us to be right about her." He wedged his boots off with his feet and let them thunk to the floor, one after the other.

I expected Kyp to glare at him, but he was too busy flipping idly through one of the smaller books to be bothered. Instead, it was Zane who made a face.

"I'll pick up after myself," he groused.

"But then I discovered this book amidst the pile." Cxarana lifted a small book bound with red leather. Ornate patterns lined in gold were scattered across the cover. "I do not know how I missed it on my first review. It was stuck inside one of the other books, but I am certain I turned every page."

"No need to dwell on how you missed it," Kyp said. "Everyone makes mistakes."

"Says the man who once claimed to never make any," Kylie grumbled.

Kyp smiled, the slightest upturn of his lips, but his eyes appeared haunted. "I think we all know I'm well past believing that lie."

Kylie simply nodded. The green faded from her eyes and Cass returned to the conversation.

"So?" she asked. "Anything interesting in this book?"

"That is indeed an excellent question," Cxarana said. "I cannot read it."

"You can't... Wonderful!" I threw my head back against the chair's cushions. "Will this ever end? We're right back to where we started."

"Not entirely," Cxarana corrected. "This is written in the ancestor of our current Arvokian language. It could be the first Ritual book of our people. There are few volumes that haven't been rewritten over time and even fewer people are capable of reading them. Whatever is in this volume is probably considered so dangerous to my people, or to the Dusk itself, that we chose not to translate it as our language evolved."

"And you don't know it?" Drew asked.

"My father did. He likely taught it to Narah, since he sent me off to serve the council," Cxarana said. "Merrick was probably taught by her. There was a line of heredity. I was trained in many things, but never in complex archaic language translation."

"Got a feeling they won't translate that for us," Ray said.

"Ya think?" Rennie rolled her eyes.

"Lyira." Dhamyan frowned. "She knows."

Drew nodded, scrubbing his hands over his face. "We need to go back to the Dusk."

"The last time you went there, you had several people trying to kill you," Zane said. "We need something else. This is just a dialect of Arvokian. Maybe a computer program can translate using your current language—"

"She has a knack for languages," Jordan muttered. He stared at his hands for a moment. When he finally looked up, his eyes were wide and hopeful. "I know who can help us."

"We should track down Lyira," Ray said.

"I swear Jordan was talking." Rennie shot a nasty look his way.

"When we met the Sirin resistance members," Jordan explained, "their leader, Andaria, said she was really good with languages.

Maybe if we provide her with sources, she could translate."

"You want us to trust someone who has worked with us once, who could just report back to other Sirins about what they learn?" Ray shook his head. "That is a bad idea. The Sirins are enemies."

"These Sirins saved my life," Zane argued. "I love you, Ray, but you need to get your head out of your ass. That's like someone meeting Lavinia and deciding we're all power-hungry murderers."

"Or you know, me judging the Arvokians based on Zelnick, when Cxarana and Dhamyan are *right here,*" I said.

"Frankly," Cass said, "it's racist."

"Or… specist?" Drew corrected. "Either way, not good."

Ray stared out into the middle distance for a beat. "Yeah, it's not at all based on the fact that every damned Sirin I met has either tried to kill me, *or actually has.* But fine, I guess I see your point."

"Andaria could have another play," Cass said. "But she did save our lives that day. No doubt. Maybe it's time we made some allies."

"The Order couldn't always be trusted, either." Kyp nodded in agreement. "Maybe what we really need to do is recruit both sides that helped us."

"An army," Kylie said through Cass. "War again."

Kyp glanced her way with a pained expression. "War again."

"First things first," I said, grabbing the tome in question from the table. "If we're going to war, we want to know what weapons Narah and Merrick may have at their disposal. I'm going to Andaria. Who's with me?"

"I'll go," Ray said.

"Hell no," Drew told him. "Not if you'll be causing trouble for the team the way you did in the Dusk."

"Nah, I'll be good," Ray promised. "I want to meet the team that saved the lives of so many of the people I love." He turned to Zane. "If you trust her, I trust her."

"Trust forged in blood," she said. "It's how I learned to trust you as well. Or don't you remember the disaster you were as a teenager?"

I'd heard the stories. They weren't pretty.

"Please don't remind me," Ray huffed.

"I'm going," Austin said. "I'm guessing Zane is in."

I grinned, kicking up to my feet. "The old team. A small contingent, but an effective one."

"Let's go." I waved for them to follow.

Drew cleared his throat. And that was enough to make me feel properly chastised. I turned back toward him, grimacing. "We vote?"

"We vote," Drew confirmed with a nod, the apparent keeper of our tentatively formed democracy. "All in favor?"

They all raised their hands. Zane did a little dance in celebration.

"She loves being right," Ray groaned, but there was a hint of a grin on his face.

"Thank you, guys," Drew said. "I know the answer to that one was probably already obvious. But I don't want us to lose sight of the fact that we're a team. We have in the past. Jacks or Kyp or Ray will say something and we'll just run with it. But if we want to do this right, somebody's got to remind us that this isn't business as usual. We're doing something new."

"Thanks, Drew." Kyp smiled. "That's what I always wanted and I couldn't figure out how to do it. I was too entrenched in the old ways." A little shrug. "That perfect memory thing always makes me stumble."

"And then we catch you," I said. "It's what we do."

I couldn't fight down a smile.

The Order of the Key, fully changed into a true democracy. It was everything I'd fought for when I'd first joined. And if it made Lavinia roll over in her grave? Well, that was just a bonus.

Twenty Six

Jacklyn

The trip to the abandoned armory only took about half an hour, a testament to the lack of true New York City traffic at six-thirty in the evening on a Sunday. We were quiet as we drove, nervous about the risk of allying with the Sirins. None of us could avoid preconceived notions about our newest allies. I may have walked into this spouting Guardians' rights, but even I had never believed there could be Sirins who didn't want us dead. The more we learned, the more we were forced to rethink our prejudices.

But trust was harder and harder to give, and this particular act of trust could do a ton of harm if it went sideways.

The Kingsbridge Armory had been abandoned for nearly twenty years. Built like a castle, complete with corner towers, battlements, and a keep, it definitely stood out in the Bronx. It was just a couple of blocks away from a Morton Williams, for fuck's sake. There was no reason this wouldn't stand out to anyone who was unfamiliar to the area, and it certainly made sense that Andaria had believed this to be a place belonging to royalty.

The streets were still pretty full when we arrived, so it couldn't be as simple as cutting the lock on the fence and walking in.

Austin's eyes went round as he took in the building. "I didn't think anything like this existed here. It looks heavily fortified. What's the entry plan?"

Zane parallel parked the car right in front of the building. "If this doesn't announce us to the folks inside, nothing will."

She wasn't wrong. As soon as we got out of the car, we were greeted by three figures in baggy sweatshirts and sweatpants. The one in the center tilted her head back to reveal she was Andaria.

"Jacklyn Madison," she greeted. "It is good to see you again." She glanced at Zane. "Zane." Her red eyes narrowed. "You've brought two new male companions. Are they to be trusted?"

Ray winced. "Okay, my concerns boomeranging back my way, huh?"

Austin nudged him with his shoulder, a good-natured smile on his face.

"New to you, but not to us," I said. "If we could come in, I'll make the proper introductions. But remaining out here will draw way too much attention our way."

"Yes, of course. But first I must know why you have come here? How can I assist you?"

"We've got a book written in another language," Zane said, "and you mentioned you were good at translating. So we wanted to see if you could help."

Andaria hummed thoughtfully. "Follow us."

We made our way around the fence to the back of the armory

where guards stood, protecting the grounds. Trees lined the area, and Andaria led us behind them. Once we were hidden in the greenery, she peeled back a strip of the fence like she was peeling a fruit and then twisted the metal closed behind us.

She and her guards led us back into the armory through an arched doorway that opened out into a truly enormous space large enough to fit several track fields. I'd run full high school track events in places smaller than this, and the echoing of our steps as we moved brought me back to that feeling of arriving first at an event.

I shook off the thought the moment I pictured Gana arriving with me the way she always did. I couldn't go down that road at the moment.

"Welcome to our home," Andaria said as she pulled the doors closed behind us.

"Oh yeah," I said. "Really homey." I glanced around in absolute awe. The entryway looked lovely, but the rest of the place had clearly fallen into disrepair. Zeroing in with my Aegis revealed chipping walls, crumbling stairwells, and rusted metal fixtures. Just off to the side of the entryway, a small army formed an indoor tent city.

I looked at the others, motioning toward the couple of exits I spotted in the far corners. We still needed to be aware.

"It is quite large, it's true, but it felt the most like our home in the Dusk."

"There's quite a lot of y'all here, huh?" Austin said, and I knew he was mentally calculating how many we could take out if the tides of this turned.

There had to be a couple of hundred Sirins milling about, and they all seemed content and welcoming. As we walked by, they all straightened, pounding fists against their upper thighs.

"It is a salute," Andaria said. "A show of respect."

My heart swelled at the sight. I had started this journey to protect my family and had failed. But now I had a new family. I had continued this journey for revenge and succeeded, but found it wasn't nearly as rewarding as I'd believed. But this—the ability to help those who were disenfranchised by this war across the three dimensions it affected—this was a true reason to fight.

Ray straightened and turned on his heel to face them. He pounded a fist against his upper thigh. Zane, Austin, and I followed.

"Please tell them we thank them for the welcome," I said.

Andaria nodded and translated for her people. They returned to bustling around the tents. She motioned toward a utilitarian desk and three chairs. She sat. Her bodyguards did not. She motioned for us to sit as well. Zane was the only one who did.

"Now, let's see this book you need me to study," Andaria said.

Zane removed the large book from the bag she'd slung over her shoulder.

Andaria's eyes widened when she spotted the book. "Of the Dawn languages, I only know English. And I struggle at times."

"Yes, but that's the beautiful thing," I said. "We're not asking you to translate a Dawn language. We could have gone anywhere for that."

Andaria's prominent forehead tightened, her jaw turning downward as her sharp teeth scraped against her lower lip. "A Dusk language."

Austin took this moment to slide into the one remaining chair. "What we're about to tell you needs to be kept very quiet. If this gets to anyone but the ears at this table, all hell is going to break loose."

Andaria's head tilted. "Where is hell being kept?"

Ray grinned.

"Sorry. It's a turn of phrase," Austin explained. "A figure of speech. Just something we say. What I mean is, it's very important that we keep this between us."

"There is a desk between us," Andaria said. "The book is on it. I shall keep it here."

Austin looked at me, exasperated.

"Andaria, are you messing with him?" I asked.

She grinned widely, teeth like needles. "Perhaps."

Austin groaned.

"Seriously, though," I pressed. "We don't know what we'll find in here, only that the person who killed the Arvokian leader wanted it close. And that person is against us. That's reason enough to keep it out of their hands and in ours. But we have to know what it does, and how we can use it."

She reached out to take the book. "It is… Arvokian?"

"It is ancient Arvokian," Zane clarified, dropping the book into her palm. "Apparently, there's a difference."

Andaria hummed, leafing through the pages. "Do you have anything written in Arvokian that has been translated? Or could be? So I can compare the dialects? I could do it without that, but it would take time. Time we may not have if this book has been copied or memorized."

"Ah, a cynic like me." Ray laughed. "I would like to believe that we got lucky and stole the cornerstone of their plan, but we all know that's not how things work."

"We might have a way to translate Arvokian," I said. "It would involve you and yours working with two Arvokians."

"I would only need one native speaker to read and write with me," Andaria explained. "We wouldn't need to inconvenience two—"

"They come as a pair." Austin's arm crossed over his chest. "And they come with two Order members as well. That is non-negotiable."

A muscle in Andaria's jaw twitched beneath her skin. "You must understand. My people will be made nervous with such strangers here for a prolonged period of time."

When she spoke, her voice was more delicate, which had to be a symptom of her own upset. Still, I wasn't in the mood to argue with her. With anyone. I just wanted one thing, *one thing,* to not require a fight to the death. Or any struggle at all, really. The exhaustion was bone deep, and this day was already too long.

"It is you who must understand. Something is forming here. We have the opportunity to unite warriors from the three dimensions. But so do they. If we work together, we can do what has never been done. We can work together to make it so the danger of the Dusk leaves the Dawn, so the Eventide is the safe home of the Arvokians, so Sirins like you, who want to overthrow their oppressors, are in control of the Dusk." I rose from my seat. "Their armies will be larger, even with us all working together. We need something they don't have, and we haven't found it yet. This book is the first clue we've gotten. Please, Andaria. I know I owe you for saving our asses—"

"You owe us nothing."

"Then I will after this," I said. My stomach twisted. I didn't know what I was promising her. The thought of her agreeing scared me almost as much as the thought of her refusing to assist.

For a moment, Andaria was silent. She moved through the pages of the book slowly. "I will complete the translation with the help of your Arvokian allies. I am already seeing repeating characters and patterns. I even recognize some words that are similar to older Sirin dialects." She peered up from the book. "I believe I can do this. But it will take time."

She shifted uncomfortably in her chair. The sun coming in through the windows made her blue skin shimmer. For the first time, I noticed the scales along the bone ridges on her cheekbones and brows. I'd never looked at a Sirin closely enough in the light. I'd never been this close to a Sirin I wasn't trying to kill.

The thought tore at something within me.

I'd never wanted to kill. But I had certainly grown used to it.

"We do have rules here," Andaria said. "I may seem like the leader, but I am merely the one who can communicate with you. We decide by committee. Because this involves you, I am at an advantage in our discussions. However, I will need to discuss the choice with the others. I say this because our rules, once decided, are absolute."

"What are you trying to tell us?" Ray asked.

Zane glanced at Ray with caution in her eyes. "We will do our best to observe your rules."

A nod. "We only work during the sunlight hours. We rest and associate with one another during the dark hours. I ask that visits to work on the translations only come between these hours, and that you leave upon the arrival of dark."

"Of course," Zane agreed. "It would be ill-mannered of us to do anything that inconvenienced you. However, you understand we are losing time."

"Exactly why you were correct in insisting on the Arvokian assistance. I will likely work later than agreed, but my guests would not be able to stay. It would be disruptive."

It made sense, but something nagged at me. We didn't have the time not to be working around the clock on this.

But then, we also had no idea what was being planned, and until we had an idea of what Caleb intended, we couldn't move forward, anyway.

My hands shook at my sides. I buried them in my jean pockets to hide them. We needed to trust someone. At least if we were choosing the wrong person to trust, we'd have the chance of tipping their hand.

Andaria's eyes met mine. "To righteous war. On our terms." She jutted her hand out at me, her eyes determined.

Despite all my concerns and all the risks, I grasped her forearm the way she had when we'd first agreed to work together. A Sirin handshake.

"To eventual peace."

TWENTY SEVEN

LINGERING DOUBT

KYP

No matter what Kyp did, he didn't feel clean.

The steam in the bathroom had built until it doused everything in a furred haze. The water ran through his hair and over his back, teetering on the edge of searing hot. The woodsy scent of the body wash had gone cloying, but he used more, scrubbing at his body with the shower sponge until it scraped against his skin. Suds and water sluiced over flesh, over muscle, and still he felt the stickiness of sweat, the weight of illness on him.

The wound at his side did not re-open, but was it ever really gone?

His entire being seemed contrite when faced with the idea of his survival. He would feel like he should never have returned, but that would be condemning Jacklyn to death as well, and he couldn't do that. But something about his continued connection to the world of spirits made him feel wrong.

He didn't want to leave. He didn't want to face the outside

world. He couldn't bring himself to close the faucet.

The suds rinsed from his body and Kyp cut off the hot water. He had to get moving. The shower wasn't going to change, and he was wasting time.

Despite all his efforts, he would face nothing new when he left this room. They would still be on the verge of a war they were not likely to win, and that could begin at any time. His brother still wanted the woman Kyp loved dead, and he wasn't afraid to set the world on fire to accomplish it. The cyclone of spirits still spun around in Kyp's mind. His Order, his *family* was still in grave danger, and worse, his children. He had many decisions to make, and he was still unsure of his path moving forward.

The books had provided him with an answer and an idea, but one that did nothing to solve the rest of his troubles, and did nothing to ease the burn of the deception it would force.

The inherent feeling of unease in his life seemed to haunt him. Would he ever find peace? Or would he always be dragged down by the burden of his choices?

You must remain firm. True leaders are not indecisive.

Mother's voice echoed in his mind incessantly, despite his rejection of a leadership role.

The fact that he still couldn't shake her voice, after all she'd done, was nothing short of unbelievable. He knew his internal life was a mess, but he hadn't realized quite how screwed up he was until she died. She clung to the walls of his brain, cutting furrows there with her nails when he tried to forcibly remove her.

A quick towel-dry later and he stood before the misted-over

mirror above the sink, grasping the white porcelain as he struggled to make out his reflection. He looked… better. Not nearly as drawn as he had when he'd first returned. He'd been eating, and his eyes no longer carried the perpetual dark circles they once had.

So why didn't he feel like he looked?

Shaking off the sinking feeling he couldn't define, he threw on some clothes and headed down to the kitchen, finally acknowledging the call of his rumbling stomach. He hadn't eaten since morning.

He galloped down the stairs toward the kitchen. Drew was already in the room, grabbing a granola bar from the cabinet as he headed for the fridge.

"Hey," Kyp grunted, yanking open the door.

"Hey." Drew headed for the exit, but stopped just short of it. "Jacks and her team are back. Starting tomorrow morning, we'll be losing Cxarana, Dhamyan, Ray, and Zane to Andaria's team. They'll be working together to translate that book."

"Oh. Okay." Though it shouldn't, it still shocked him to not be the person everyone came to for the final word. Half the time, they'd argued over every decision he made, but they'd still asked him.

It would take some getting used to.

Drew flashed a knowing smile his way. "You okay?"

"I'm…" He grabbed a bag of grapes from the fridge. "I'm okay. Still getting used to the changes. But that's to be expected, I suppose."

"It is." Drew squeezed his shoulder. "And if you ever need to talk about it, I'm here."

"Thanks, Drew." He filled a small bowl with grapes. "Hey, do you know where Jacks is?"

Drew poked his head back into the room. "Should be in her room, I think."

"Cool. Thanks, man."

Drew headed for the basement to train, and Kyp grabbed his bowl of grapes and took off for Jacklyn's room.

He missed her. He hadn't been himself lately, and though he'd been erratic with everyone, he'd been worse with her. The last thing he wanted was to push her away, but he was breaking down, and he didn't want her caught in the rubble.

He knocked tentatively on her door.

"In!" she shouted, purposefully loud.

God, he loved her.

He opened the door, and there she was, wearing a flannel over a T-shirt and ripped black jeans. Her eyes were closed, her head rested against the back of her desk chair, her booted feet kicked up onto her bed's footboard. Her eyes were lined with bold black eyeliner, her lips a deep wine red.

Captivating.

He closed the door behind him and strolled toward her.

"Is that my shirt?" he asked, plucking at her black flannel.

She hummed, one hazel eye opening. "Could be."

"It looks better on you."

"I doubt that." Her other eye opened, and she smiled, kicking her feet off the footboard.

"You know, I was contemplating asking to move into your room, but then I thought about it and realized that didn't quite make sense.

Your room has nothing but your clothes in it. And mine has all of this." She waved her hand around the room.

The walls were papered in posters of *Buffy the Vampire Slayer*, *Stranger Things*, and *Attack on Titan*. A figure of an *Attack on Titan* character, Levi, sat on her dresser. She joked that the character was Kyp's personality with her Aegis. He was her favorite, which probably said something good about him. Accompanying the figure was a statue of Batman and his Robins. And beside that was the ceramic bear Kyp had once repaired for her. It had been a gift from Gana.

"When did you get your hands on that again?" Kyp asked. "Last I saw, it was crammed in your closet back at the estate."

He didn't mention that it was in her suitcase, which she had packed when she'd still planned to run from the estate with her sister. The night her sister died.

Her smile dimmed slightly, but it was still warm and attentive. "I took it with me when we first left the estate. Seemed I still had a soft spot for you, no matter what I said."

"Imagine that." He stepped closer to her, pushing a hand through her soft curls and drawing his hand downward until he cupped her cheek. "So you want me to move in here?"

She pushed her cheek into his palm, her eyelids lowering to half-mast. "That was the implication, yes."

"How about instead of that, we take the children and run away from all of this?" The idea thrilled him, but his voice remained quiet.

"You want to run?" she asked.

"Only if you go with me."

"That bad?" She studied his face, and he found he couldn't meet her earnest gaze. "Sorry, Kyp. I will not run when the going gets absolutely monumentally shitty. Heroes do not flee."

Kyp poked her in her side. "That's precious. Because we do so well at the traditional hero thing."

She smacked his hand away. "I already ran once, and it turned out wonderfully, right? Have we learned nothing from Ray?"

"How to run?" Kyp made a face.

"We can't leave and you know it." She slapped her palm against his chest. "It's not even funny for you to pretend we can. Once we stop Caleb and avert this war, we get our happy ending."

Kyp's chest hollowed at the thought. She made it sound so close, but there were so many steps between where they were and where they wanted to be. What if they didn't make it? What if they died trying? He wanted something… tangible he could hang onto when everything was going to hell.

He stepped back from her so he could watch her face for the true answer. "If we choose this, there's no going back. We have to be sure. Are you sure?"

Her eyes met his, all steel. "I'm sure. We need to end this nightmare."

He knew what he needed. His eyes traced over her features: her pointed nose, her piercing gaze, her rounded cheeks lifted in a growing smile.

Did he look as desperate as he felt?

"I know we're all dealing with a great deal right now, and I'm aware that this may be the worst time for something like this, but

I reason we could all use a victory we didn't have to pull from the jaws of defeat. More importantly, I feel like you and I should have done this before we died. I feel like you and I should… I think it's important that we…"

Jacklyn's lips were twisted into a smirk now. "Stop dancing around it and say it."

He wanted to, but he could barely breathe thinking about it.

She stepped in so close he could feel her breath warming his lips. "Say it."

"Marry me?"

He couldn't see her lips, but her smile lit her eyes, and her whisper caressed his lips.

"Yes."

Twenty Eight

Jacklyn

"Don't worry so much. You look rather fetching," Ray said, taking my hand so I would stop messing with my hair.

When Kyp said he wanted to get married, I thought he meant, like, next week. I knew he was anxious about what might be on the horizon. But he didn't mean next week. He meant... right that minute.

Within an hour, he had someone mastermind an entire wedding ceremony, and it was all a surprise for me. While he worked, I tried to find an outfit in my closet I could wear to a ceremony. Any ceremony.

Ripped black jeans and a T-shirt was good enough for a wedding, wasn't it?

It better be. I didn't have anything fancier.

"Kyp isn't worried about how you look anyway," Ray said when I continued to fidget with my clothing. "This isn't about all that."

"I know." I dropped my hands to my sides. "It's all supposed to be symbolic."

"It's not just symbolic," Ray grumbled good-naturedly. "You're a fool now? Please. That boy loves you more than life itself. And he's scared as hell. We all feel the danger coming. It's hanging over our heads. He wants to make it official before we all go to war. Not because of some symbol, but because he wants to share that love in front of his family."

I swallowed thickly and Ray's emerald eyes sparkled.

"It's okay to be nervous. But this changes nothing. You two were always tied together. You're just tied tighter now."

"Mama! Mama! Mama!" Jainey dashed to the back door, pulling Rennie behind her.

"We got you something," Rennie said, her voice rushed. Austin popped his head through the door of the kitchen behind her, waved, and rushed away.

So he'd been in on this, too…

Rennie pushed a bouquet of purple hydrangeas into my free hand with a bounce in her step. "You can't get married without a bouquet."

"No, I suppose I can't."

The back door opened and Cass slid through. "We're ready out there." She smiled. "If you are."

I thought about it. Took a moment to toss aside all the weirdness of the moment. My heart felt like it was being pulled along on a string whenever his eyes met mine.

I was never lonely when he was near.

Yeah, I was ready. Hell yeah, I was ready.

"Lead the way," I said to Cass.

Pushing my shoulders back, I followed Cass through the doorway and out into our backyard.

Kyp must have dug up the fairy lights we'd hung the last time we'd thrown a party. They were draped along the ivy-covered walls. Rose petals outlined an aisle over the tiled floor and down to the grassy area. Candles were set along the back wall of the space, ready to take over for the sun, which was just setting. Orange and purple tones settled over the city and provided an almost otherworldly backdrop.

In the center of it all was Kyp, dressed about as casually as I was in his own pair of black jeans, a peacock blue sweater, and black boots. Zane and Cxarana stood on either side of him, Cxarana back in her traditional robes. Jainey and Rennie moved past me and Ray, taking their place in the semicircle our family had made. They all faced us, smiling and bright-eyed, all the people who were still alive that truly made me feel safe.

Only Mom and Gana were missing, but after everything we'd experienced with Cass, I knew they were watching over us.

Kyp took a step forward. His eyes locked on me, and I knew that was my cue. I reached back for Ray, hand bumping against his hip blindly before he gripped it.

"I can't bloody believe we're doing this," Ray whispered. I tensed, but when I glanced over at him, a wide grin had overtaken his face and his emerald eyes sparkled. "My baby girl is getting married."

I wanted to point out that I'd accidentally married Kyp as a toddler in an old Arvokian Ritual, but somehow, that didn't seem right. It wasn't the same.

This.

This was different.

Kyp's lips pulled into a smile, the one he usually reserved just for me, and my heart leapt.

I lowered my head shyly, inhaling deeply and being greeted by the heavenly honey-sweet scent of the hydrangeas.

Ray put a hand on my lower back and prompted me forward, his hand in mine as we moved. It felt like I was floating, like Kyp was just getting closer through no movement of my own, and I had to look down to make sure he wasn't just telekinetically moving me across the yard.

I looked at the faces surrounding us, all smiling. Jordan held Jainey on his hip, and their matching grins told me they were cheering us on. Austin smiled warmly at me, one arm wrapped around Drew's waist. Drew's head was tipped onto his shoulder. Cass's eyes glowed green, and she leaned forward to whisper in Jordan's ear.

Jordan's voice sounded in my mind. *"Cass wanted you to know that Grandma Jaina and Aunt Gana are here with us."*

And just like that, everyone who made me feel safe, both living and dead, was there with us.

"Hi," Kyp said, voice slightly brittle.

"Hi," I echoed, smiling as Ray placed my hand into Kyp's.

Ray pressed a kiss to each of our cheeks before pulling us into a rough bear hug. "I love you kids."

It was like going head-to-head with a boa constrictor.

"Okay, okay, okay, we love you too. Let go." I flailed from inside the hug. Kyp's gruff laugh filled my ears over Ray's litany of complaints.

It was cute, and I reached out and dragged Ray back for another kiss on his cheek before shooing him to wherever he was supposed to be standing.

He jogged away from me, taking his place beside Zane.

When my eyes met Kyp's again, they were a little wild with nerves.

"I've never been to a wedding. So I don't really know what I'm doing here. But I know they're about a couple expressing their love for each other in front of the people they care about most. So I figured the best way to start was to exchange vows."

"Kyp," I said out of the side of my mouth. "I didn't come up with a speech."

He laughed. "You think I did?" He cleared his throat. "When it comes to my emotions, I'm not really good with words. I mean, the first time you told me you loved me, I said 'thank you,' and I don't think either of us will ever forgive me for it."

Cass burst out laughing, her hands scrambling to cover her mouth. "Sorry. All four of us wanted to laugh at you."

Kyp flashed her a look before his eyes returned to me. "I'm pretty sure you disliked me when we first found our way back to each other."

I shook my head.

"At least a little." He chuckled. "I've made so many mistakes, and you've faced them all head on with me. I can't tell you how much it meant to me that you had my back, even when it was hard, even when I was making myself difficult to understand, even when we weren't on the same page, we found a way through the obstacles. And I can't tell you how much it means to me that you continue to stick by me. It means so much to me. You have no idea." His voice cracked, eyes shining more as he spoke. "I told you my dream, and you've been determined to grant it ever since, marching toward it with a single-minded fury and a unity of purpose that I can't help but admire. You stir my soul with your passion and warm my heart with your kindness. I love you more than I have the words to explain, and I will hold you, your safety, your peace, close to my heart and as the direction of my purpose for all of my remaining breaths."

My throat had closed about halfway through that speech, and it wasn't loosening back up. Tears welled up and spilled. My heart swelled, unable to contain the emotion building within. It wasn't just Kyp's words. It was how difficult I knew it was for him to put voice to those words. It was as though he'd turned his soul inside out and shook it out for everyone to see. Knowing he could do that for me… It was so beautiful, it almost hurt.

"Kyp," I tried, but it came out shaky and wrong. I sniffled, swiped at my eyes, and took a deep breath. Then I tried again. "Kyp, it's weird to think that you've known me longer than I remember knowing you. My memories of you from before are few, but my earliest memory is of your face. And then we reunited." I swallowed hard, trying to force my words through. "The connection was instant. You talk about me having your back, but you've been looking out for me, even when it wasn't safe for you. We made so many mistakes. Both of us. But even when things were hard, even when we tried to pretend we didn't, we never stopped loving each other."

Kyp looked down, but I tipped his chin back up so his eyes met mine. "I never stopped loving you." I let my hand slip away. "You struggle with your emotions, like you believe feeling so strongly is a flaw, but I love how much you feel. How wholeheartedly you devote yourself. To me. To the kids. I love how brilliant you are. How you know everything, but it doesn't keep you from taking risks. You are the bravest person I know, and you shouldn't trust anyone, so the fact that you trust me so much means the world to me. I'm not like you. I can't explain it in pretty words the way you, Mr. I'm-Not-Good-With-Words, can, but I love you. There are no words to cover it. You would know. You know a lot of them."

He grinned, another one of those full grins, and his gaze was soft.

"You said all of your remaining breaths, but we already did that. We breathed our last breaths, and we didn't stop loving each other even then. So, I'm going to say as long as I am me and you are you, I will continue to love you with everything I am. My one true partner in everything."

"The love of all my lives," Kyp whispered.

I grabbed his hands in mine, squeezing them tightly.

Cxarana smiled. "You have heard the words of these two warriors."

"And witnessed the love between these two pains in our collective asses," Zane added.

Cxarana's lips shivered in something that resembled a smile. "We join together today to couple the Aegis of these two warriors."

"Now, since they've already managed to do the Ritual before, Cxarana had to add a little something to make it a renewal, rather than a union," Zane explained.

"Dhamyan," Cxarana called.

Dhamyan stepped forward, wearing his traditional hunting outfit, the silver dagger that featured in my memories of our childhood mistake held flat across his palms. He presented it to Kyp solemnly, head bowed.

Mirroring his movements, Kyp took the dagger from him and pierced the tip of his finger with it. Blood bubbled around the wound. He smirked, handing me the dagger.

"Why does everything with the Order involve injuries?" I asked, eyes rolling to the sky as I pressed the point of the dagger to my fingertip. I hissed, the burn of it lancing down my arm. Stupid enhanced pain sensors. I shook my finger out.

"Because," Kyp said, eyebrows raised, "love is sacrifice. It always has been."

"Yes, yes, you are always quite right until you are not, Mr. Franklin." Cxarana's brow ridge jutted outward slightly. "Moving on. Mr. Franklin, Ms. Madison—I would like you to create a picture in your mind's eye. Envision your future together as you press your blood into each other's wounds."

I shot Kyp my best blech face before squeezing my eyes shut and envisioning.

In my head, we live in a place that is not Mission Control. It's a home. A cabin by a lake with wide open spaces in the backyard for Jainey to play in. We get a dog. A Doberman or a Labrador. Name it Trooper, because we're all good little troopers, aren't we? It's just me and Kyp, Jordan, Jainey, and Trooper, but the rest of our family and friends live in the same county, just spread out a little, enough for us to have our own space.

The four of us sit by the lake on purple wooden lounge chairs, a fire roaring in front of us. The kids are telling each other scary stories, but Kyp and I are cuddled under a thick wool blanket. Kyp has an arm around my shoulders, and he holds me close, pressing a kiss to my hair as he tells me stories about his day at work. We have normal jobs. The kids go to school.

We're safe. We're happy. We're healthy.

I pressed my finger to Kyp's.

The rest of the wedding went by in a whirl of emotions, laughter, hugs, stories, food, and a bit of alcohol. Before I knew it, it was nearly midnight, and Kyp and I were alone in the yard, slow dancing to the music in our heads.

It was a perfect day with the people we loved.

A perfect day, and we were married.

My wrists were looped around Kyp's neck, and his hands rested on my waist, holding me close. We swayed silently, staring into each other's eyes.

Kyp glanced around. "Looks like it's just us."

"Looks like," I said, brushing my palm against his face, feeling the stubble starting to break through.

"I get to spend the rest of my life with you," he murmured.

"Like that wasn't already true."

"But officially."

"Which it technically already was."

"Jacks."

"I know." I smirked. "I just can't help myself. You're so fun when you're frustrated."

He waggled his eyebrows. "I'm always frustrated around you."

Oh, really? "Well, we should work on that."

He leaned forward and rested his forehead against mine. The night sky around us, the woodsy scent of his cologne, his warmth. It was all downright dreamy, and I wanted to envelop myself in this world and bury myself in his arms and never let go.

"You are etched onto my heart," Kyp said. "We're so different, but somehow… it's like you've always been sitting on the other side of the scale. There are my difficulties, and then, balancing it out, is you. And I can't tell you how grateful I am."

"I'm grateful for you too," I said. "I'd be even more grateful if you—"

His lips pressed to mine, gently. His mouth tasted like mint and Kyp, and I leaned into him, wanting more. His hands slid up from my waist, moving slowly up my body and leaving me shivering. The kiss deepened, his fingers sliding into my hair, his warm mouth working against mine, and I opened to him, tipping my head to better the angle. We melted against each other, my hands sliding under his shirt, his finding their way to my ass, and oh my God, we were not going to do this right here.

I pulled back slightly. Enough to speak, but not enough to pull my fingers away from the feeling of his back muscles playing beneath his smooth skin.

"Kyp," I whispered. "We really should go upstairs."

He smiled against my lips, kissing me again, like he couldn't quite completely pull away from me. "We'll go to my room. It's closer."

The giggle that slid past my lips was embarrassing. "Our rooms are next door to each other."

Kyp grinned. "Yes, Jacks, but condoms are in my room, and we already have two lovely kids who are more than enough at the moment." He straightened, pulling me up onto my tip toes.

"So romantic." I kissed the tip of his nose.

"I told you, I'm not very romantic." He returned my nose kiss.

I pretended to think about it for a moment. "Ehhhh, it's kind of romantic. You're protecting me."

"But you don't need me to protect you."

"No, but you want to protect me."

My heart swelled all over again. It was a play on what made me kiss him that very first time. It showed so much about how he viewed me. It showed his faith in my abilities, his respect for my independence, and his trust in me to protect someone he held dear. But it was also a show of his desire to care for me.

He twirled me away from him, but kept a hold of my hand, and before I knew it, he was rushing me toward the house. My boots sunk into the earth beneath them, and then pounded along the outdoor tiling.

Kyp threw open the back door, then dropped to a crouch to undo his shoelaces.

"Baby." It was my turn to yank on his hand. "We'll disinfect later. Just take me upstairs."

His eyebrows raised. "Just take you upstairs?" He looked up at me through his lashes, his eyes dark, moving with a predator's grace as he rose.

"You heard me." My heart beat a staccato rhythm against my ribs.

He had me in a bridal carry in seconds, hoisting me up and taking off up the stairs. His lips struggled to meet mine as we jostled with the upward movement. We kissed again and again, his mouth pulling an embarrassingly needy noise from me, his hands tantalizing as they moved over me. When we reached the top of the stairs, he lowered me to my feet without loosening our embrace, his heated breaths husking out against my cheek. He pressed me against the wall at the top of the landing, lips trailing down my neck. I tipped my head back, giving him free reign, a quiet moan escaping me at the feeling of his tongue flicking against my pulse point.

"I'm trying to hold on to some semblance of sanity, and it's difficult enough as it is," Rennie's voice came from down the hall.

I let out a gross little squeal of terror. Kyp flinched so hard he banged his head into my collar bone.

"Could you… not? Like, in the hallway," she added. "For God's sake, your son is right down the hall."

I raised an eyebrow at her.

"In a room that I am going *nowhere* near, obviously." She held her hands up and walked backwards into her room, the door closing and locking behind her.

"And stay there!" I yelled, staring after her.

Kyp chuckled. "You know she locked the door because he's probably already in there, right?"

"I'm… not going to think about that, okay?" I shook the thought free from my head and grabbed his hand, yanking him the rest of the way into his room. I overestimated my own speed.

"Ow, fuck!" My hip smacked into the corner of his desk, knocking a couple of books off a pile on its surface. They hit the floor with a thump.

"Ridiculous," Kyp chided under his breath. "Are you okay?"

"Yeah, sorry." I rubbed at my hip, attempting to soothe the swell of pain.

"You didn't have to actually run, genius."

I shot him the finger and bent to pick up his books. I could feel his eyes on me as I gathered them, painting a sweep of heat along my body.

"Here, let me get that bruise for you." He reached forward to rub at my hip.

I glanced down, feeling my face flush.

My eyes settled on a familiar book at the top of the fallen pile. Arvokian. One of the books from the Dusk.

"Kyp, why do you have this?" I asked. They were supposed to be with Cxarana, ready to go to visit Andaria tomorrow morning.

"Huh?" He glanced down. "Oh right. I forgot I had that. I'll get it to Cxarana before she heads out tomorrow." He rolled his eyes.

"Are you seriously focusing on a book right now?" His voice was thick with desire.

He pulled me up into his arms. His eyes were soft but dark with promise, and when he kissed me that time, I melted against him. He led me to his bed, our bantering silenced by the warmth and love between us.

It wasn't until we settled down for sleep later that I realized Kyp said he forgot he had the book. But he had a perfect memory.

Kyp didn't forget anything.

TWENTY NINE

KYP

One week of wedded bliss. That was all Kyp and Jacklyn got before things started going downhill.

No, that wasn't accurate. It started going wrong the morning after, but Jacklyn had valiantly tried to pretend it wasn't. Something was on her mind. But she wouldn't express it, and Kyp was too determined to pretend everything was fine to push. The time would come all too soon for them to work through any issues.

They could just pretend to be content for a few moments, at least.

But sparks still erupted whenever her skin brushed his, and Kyp wondered briefly if it was all paranoia. Perhaps everything was fine between them. Perhaps he was incapable of being content.

Perhaps he was only moments away from sabotaging it all.

The real trouble had started that morning when Cxarana had slammed her way through the door, followed by the protective entourage Drew had sent with her, and Andaria, who came with several Sirin guards of her own.

Within moments, they were all crowded in the sitting room, waiting for what Andaria had to say.

"First of all, I want to introduce myself to the half of you I'm not already acquainted with." The Sirin spoke politely in accented English, slurred slightly by the gravel in her tone and the clumsiness of her razor-sharp teeth. Her red eyes shimmered in the artificial light. "My name is Andaria. I am the contact between your people and mine. And in that, I am forced forward to be the negotiator. Because brokering a truce has now become a matter of life or death."

"Hit us with the bad news, friend," Austin said, his smile friendly even when his eyes reflected a challenge. "Better we know now than waste time."

"I have discovered the plan of the Arvokian royalty." She swallowed hard. "The book you pilfered contained a series of dangerous spells."

"Ancient and evil Arvokian blood magic," Cxarana supplied, tugging at the tips of her white locks. "The likes of which haven't been used in generations as far as we were aware."

"That sounds… not pleasant," Jordan said.

"No kidding," Rennie breathed. "Can't you feel the anxiety? It's coming off them in waves."

Jordan frowned, then blanched as he locked onto the same feelings. Kyp followed suit.

Rennie's empathy was her only ability, so it was always at the forefront. For Jordan and Kyp, it sometimes took balancing out other Aegis-borne abilities to zero in on that one.

Jainey shivered, and Kyp knew she'd come to the same

conclusion. Something was very wrong.

"This isn't what we thought it was," Zane explained. "This entire time, we'd assumed Caleb was working with the Sirins, and the Arvokian leadership had expressed the desire to work with the Sirins." She nodded in Andaria's direction. "Those that oppressed Andaria's people, I should clarify."

"Doesn't matter what we thought," Ray chimed in. "Because we were wrong."

Kyp's stomach bottomed out.

"The Rituals they were accessing are parts of a process," Andaria explained. "I have not been able to translate what they must do to set it in motion, but I have uncovered how it ends."

Dread pooled in Kyp's stomach, churning and swaying like waves in a storm. His hand reached for Jacklyn's unbidden. Her strong fingers wrapped around his, firm and reassuring. Ready to fight.

Always ready to fight.

Andaria's bone-ridge brow furrowed. "If the Arvokian leadership accomplishes what they set out to do, they will pull the Dawn and Dusk into the Eventide. Our worlds will cease to exist."

"Narah will take her place as the leader of the known world," Cxarana supplied. "The Arvokians will be the strongest beings and the rest of you, Dawn or Dusk, will be forced to bow."

Jacklyn tugged at the circular ring on her black hoodie's zipper. Up and down. Up and down.

Nerves.

Her nervousness never failed to make *him* nervous.

"Cxarana, Dhamyan," Drew said. "There are others like you. Like Lyira. Do you think we can gain their help?"

Kyp's shoulders slumped forward, fatigue weighing him down until he could barely hold his head up.

He was twenty years old. He felt so much older.

It probably didn't help that he was married with two kids, but those were the things that made his life more buoyant while everything else fought for its chance to pull him down into the depths of his mind.

"I would have to go to the Dusk and speak to them," Cxarana said.

Drew shook his head. "You haven't finished translating yet."

"It doesn't matter," Andaria answered, her chin jutting forward. "This is bigger than the Keys of the Dusk. It is bigger than our Sirin uprising."

"She's right," Jacklyn said. "The Arvokian royalty and the council must be in league with each other. The council hadn't wanted the Rifts closed, and Narah having the books implies they're on the same page."

"The royal family used to work with the council, simply by appointing the liaison." Cxarana motioned at herself. "They were each allowed to operate independently. The council was to deal with relations with the Dawn and Ritual advancements, while royalty ruled. But my time in the Dusk revealed a growing schism between them. We didn't get close enough to be sure, but I never believed they would work together."

"King Rhiadon may not have," Kyp offered. "But that may have changed, with Narah and Merrick in charge."

Cxarana grunted her agreement.

Jacklyn lowered her head into her hands, scrubbing them up and down her face. When she looked up again, resolution shone in her eyes. "We need them. All of them. Any Arvokians who will side with us, and … we need the Sirins. We need an alliance. With the interdimensionals."

Jordan wrapped himself up in a self-hug, a motion that made Kyp want to reach across the room and hold him. He didn't, only because he knew it would embarrass the kid.

"For all we know, Zelnick was the only Council member in league with Lavinia," Drew said. "He, alone, might have had an ulterior motive."

"We should investigate," Cxarana said. "Visit the council house."

"What I'm hearing is that we need to go to the Dusk again," Drew said.

"Me too," Jacklyn sighed. "But I'm not liking that I'm hearing it."

"And what about Caleb?" Ray asked. "Are we just forgetting about him? He figures he knows what he's playing at, but he has no idea. He's just a kid."

The mere mention of him sent fury like fire through Kyp's veins. "A kid who has nearly murdered Jordan and Jainey."

"A kid who hasn't known anything but pain since he was made," Rennie answered. "He went through everything Jainey and Jordan did, but he lost more. Ross was like a father to him and Lavinia killed him. She killed Kylie too. And when he turned to her instead, Jacklyn killed her. He wants a mom so bad, he's willing to avenge the monster he had left. And he has the backing of a bunch of interdimensionals to do it."

"We need to help him," Austin said. "She's right."

"Thank you!" Kylie spoke through Cass.

Ray pushed his fingers through his dark curls. "So, how do we help him? I doubt he has any idea what he's gotten himself into. If the entire plan is for the Eventide to devour the Dawn and the Dusk, nothing they could be promising Caleb can be true."

"And it won't be worth the risk for him either," Zane said. "But would he listen to us?" She stood beside Ray where he was sitting, leaning against him with her elbow on his shoulder.

"Not a chance." Jacklyn sighed. "I killed his mother. He's not going to listen to anything we have to say as long as I'm on your side." She launched to her feet. "The only way to save Caleb is to defy him, ignore him, and fix this from another angle before he gets any stronger."

"So we go to the Dusk," Kyp rose. "If we do that, we'll need more firepower. We barely made it out last time."

Drew nodded, his face pinched with worry. "We'd have to abandon the Dawn and bring all our troops to the Dusk."

"We face having to overcome the Arvokians and the Sirins if they don't agree with us," Cass said.

"Yeah, that doesn't make me feel secure about this whole thing," Jordan said.

"I don't think we're gonna feel okay here either, Jordan." Jainey sank into the cushion she sat on, her hand fisted in her nightgown.

"Some of us will have to go to the Sirins, some of us will have to go to the Arvokians. But all of us must go to the Dusk," Drew said.

"If we do this," Kyp said, "it will be a declaration of war." He didn't want this choice. He had too many poor ones on his head and he needed to… he needed to rest. Especially with what he knew came next.

Drew's eyes met his, and he nodded sharply.

A strange clicking noise emitted from Cxarana. "Do you understand exactly what you're courting? We will leave the Dawn defenseless. Permanently. We do not have the numbers or the strength we will need to take my people down if they are united under this purpose. And the Sirins will not likely believe us enough to align with us."

Jacklyn paled. "But… what about Kyp and me and our shiny new powers? And did you count that we have two Skeleton Keys on our side? Three if you count Lyira!"

Jordan nervously picked at a pimple that had been forming on his chin. "I think Cxarana is saying we're not enough. Even with that."

Rennie elbowed his hand away. "Yeah, it certainly feels that way."

Kyp turned to Cxarana and met her glossy, blackened gaze head on. "So you unlock us."

This was what he'd been looking for. The edge they needed.

"You've already *been* unlocked," Cxarana said sternly.

"Them," Kyp corrected. "You have to unlock the Guardians."

Drew choked on an inhale. "Can she… can you do that?"

"No," Cxarana said. "The Ritual requires the blood of a child. Someone fresh… unsullied."

"Rituals for virgins only?" Zane grumbled. "Blah."

"What if Senefestrian blood was added? Treated properly. The way you've used it in the past for healing salve." Kyp's heart slammed in his chest. The suggestion was invigorating. "Treated with Phylifian root and Drongian herbs, Senefestrian blood heals. I don't know the exact amounts, but the difference can mean accelerating growth to the point of advanced aging, as in the children, or it can heal wounds."

By the time he'd finished, his family stared at him with varying levels of intensity.

"How did you know that, child?" Cxarana asked. She hadn't used that name for him in a very long time.

Kyp's chest lightened. "I read through all the books that were written in modern Arvokian. I wasn't sure what information, if any, we would need, but I hoped…"

"That's why you had that book," Jacks trailed off, her voice hoarse.

That's what had been bothering her. The book. She hadn't trusted his response. Guilt swooped through his stomach.

"From which book did you obtain this information?" Cxarana asked.

"*Theories of Ritual Alchemy*," Kyp responded, struggling to keep the tremor out of his voice.

"Theories." Cxarana chewed on the word, and it appeared to

leave a sour taste in her mouth. "It may not work. It hasn't been proven."

Kyp sighed. They needed to do this. He had sworn he would protect his family. Sworn. And he would. But he would never be able to accomplish that goal if they were swallowed into the Eventide.

And if they weren't, all of them would be in a better position to maintain their safety.

When he finally spoke, his voice was quiet, overpowered by the usual sense of foreboding that always filled him when he was rolling the dice on an idea. His heart sped up again. "Cxarana. Not a single thing I've tried has been a certainty."

Jacklyn's hand bumped his. He hadn't realized his hand was balled into a fist until she pried it open with her strong fingers and clasped it within her own. He welcomed the comfort.

"The last mission I jumped into with that kind of surety was the mission to recover Jacklyn, and that didn't turn out to be nearly the spectacularly well thought out idea I had believed it to be." He squeezed her hand. "I haven't allowed myself to consider anything certain since then. It has all been a risk. All a potential disaster. But risks must be taken." He rubbed at the back of his neck with his other hand. "This is a good one. If we have to go to the Dusk anyway, why not hunt down a Senefestrian?"

"Incredible," Cass said through gritted teeth. "Because the last one didn't kill you enough times."

"Cass, you know that doesn't matter." His words were strangled. "You were never the only one of us ready to lay your life down for the mission. I've always been willing to do what must be done."

"I know that." Tears welled in her eyes. "Don't you think I know that? Is it so bad that I don't want to lose my best friend?"

"We're gonna lose Papa again?" Jainey cried.

"Not if I can help it." Jacklyn rose beside him. "We go to the Dusk, we try to broker peace with those that can help us, and we hunt a Senefestrian, or we do nothing and see how we survive in the Eventide. I don't think this should be up for debate."

"Are we sure we should bring the children?" Zane asked.

"You volunteering to stay home with them?" Austin countered. "Because I thought you'd want to be part of the action. 'Specially if Ray will be with us."

"The kids need to come with us," Drew said.

Kyp slid his thumb over Jacklyn's knuckles.

"The last three times we rushed into battle and left a portion of our team at home, what happened?" Drew said. "The first time killed Gana. The second time killed Ross and got Jainey and Ray kidnapped. And then there was the train station debacle. We walk into that trap again and we deserve what we get."

"We go in together," Kyp said. "What's the plan from there? Jordan and Rennie can hold their own. How do we protect Jainey?"

"Hey!" Jainey scowled. "I can hold my own, too."

"Come on, kiddo," Kyp said, his heart tightening as he imagined the scenario. "*I'm* too small to fight a Senefestrian."

"You still killed one," she said triumphantly.

"And died trying," Kyp volleyed back. "Can we not?"

"Can you try not to sound so damn nonchalant about your own death?" Cass snapped.

"I'm not!" He hadn't meant to shout. He took a deep breath to cool himself down. "I'm not, Cass. I'm trying to avoid losing anybody else."

"We split into two groups with even power differentials," Drew said. "However, Jacklyn should not keep all the kids. We screwed up last time. We thought she was safe here, so we left all of them in her care, but Jainey would have been screwed if it hadn't been for Andaria and her team. We need better balance this time. Jacklyn, you take Jainey, Rennie, Cass, Austin and Dhamyan to the Arvokians. Austin was probably the least offensive in our team for our entire visit. You need to work with them. I will take Kyp, Ray, Jordan, Zane, Cxarana, and Andaria, and go try to rally up a Sirin army."

"And you're set on that?" Ray asked. "I don't know if I love the idea of sending my daughter to a place we barely made it out of alive."

"Fifty percent of the reason we barely made it out alive was because you couldn't keep your damn mouth shut," Austin said, crossing his arms over his chest.

"She'll be okay," Kyp said, sliding a proud smile her way. "She's tougher than most of us."

"And once we're at each assigned location, we do what we can to ascertain the location of a Senefestrian," Drew said. "We stay connected through our Mind Keys, and we do not approach until we're one united team."

"If we're doing this, no packing light like last time. We can't trouble ourselves with bein' non-threatening," Austin added. "We need to be fully armed."

"So we're going to war," Cxarana said, raspy voice grave.

For a moment, everyone was silent, heads dipped down in thought. Kyp's gaze slid to Jacklyn.

Her eyebrows pinched in concern, lips quirking as she thought. And then her eyes hardened, determination blooming behind them as she fixed her mouth into a straight line, her chin lifting and jutting outward in a challenge to the world.

"War was declared a long time ago," she said, voice sharp. "If we're going to be viewed as starting anything in this war, let it be the final battle. Let's end this."

Kyp's eyes darted along the Order he had created with Jacklyn as they cheered in response, and he remembered why everything had changed when he met Jacklyn. She was going to change the world.

She was going to change everything.

And all he had to do was hold on to her when it was done.

JACKLYN

In my defense, it had seemed like a good plan until we were all in the Dusk and had gone our separate ways. And that's when I remembered that the source of my most recent nightmares was wrapped up with the pitch darkness found there.

It's where I'd watched Kyp bleed out. Where I'd said goodbye to my family. Where I'd tried to make peace with my death.

I wasn't at peace with it. I didn't want to die young or die a hero. I wanted to survive this, and I wanted a future. I wanted the normalcy Kyp wanted.

Never was there as big of a "be careful what you wish for" than my old desire for an exciting life.

"You okay in there?" Austin asked, bumping me with this shoulder.

His teal eyes reflected the light of the fireball floating atop my hands. They sparkled with excitement, way more excited about the potential of going to war than I would've expected from him. And they were nearly all I could see of him.

"I'm worried about the other team," I admitted despite myself. I trusted them all to be able to look out for themselves and each other, but this was enemy territory and they were about to broker peace with the faction we'd been fighting against for generations.

We picked our way across the spongy ground of the Dusk, avoiding a particularly vicious looking bush with spiked branches.

"Don't worry, darlin'." He grinned. "Ray won't get into too much trouble with the others there looking after him. Jordan can probably kick his ass."

I laughed, perhaps with a tinge of nerves I couldn't help. Austin cracked, letting out a whoop of a laugh that had the rest of the group hushing and scolding us in seconds.

"Sorry."

"There are guards stationed nearby," Dhamyan said. *"It would be best to start by alerting royal security that we are in their territory, rather than let them discover it on their own."*

"Agreed." I took a deep breath. *Here we go.*

Another shoulder bump rocked me, Austin's attempt at comfort.

"I would feel a lot more comfortable about all of this if I could get GPS down here," Rennie grumbled.

Jainey snorted.

I was fine without GPS. I had my guns, my daggers, and my powers were slightly elevated here. That was all I needed.

The guards Dhamyan moved toward were well-armed, dressed to the nines with a mixture of iron and leather armor in an unfamiliar pattern of red spots. It was a reminder that many of the creatures of the Dusk never ventured to the Dawn.

Dhamyan raised his arms in a gesture of peace. *"Excuse me."* He translated Arvokian so we could understand it within our minds. *"I am Dhamyan, a member of the Keys of the Dusk. I wish for an audience with Queen Narah."*

One guard, more brutish than the other, stepped forward with an imposing stance. *"You dare to come here and surrender yourself to our queen for your crimes?"*

Dhamyan squared his shoulders, meeting the challenge head on.

That wouldn't do. We needed supplication to get to Narah, not a dick measuring contest.

"Dhamyan, stand down. Translate." I slid between the two warriors, keeping my back straight and my chin held high. I was also a warrior, but I was sure to inject the kind of deference I thought the situation needed. "Sir, my name is Jacklyn Madison, a Key of the Dawn. I am here with new information about your enemies and with wishes to barter a truce. I understand if you do not wish to bring me before your queen after the way things went the last time my people were here, but I assure you, that situation was never our goal. If you must, feel free to guard her with as many soldiers as necessary to make it possible, but please, we must speak with Queen Narah immediately."

Another guard stepped forward, a large woman with thick arms and the build of a Viking shield maiden. Her jaw was dainty but sharp, her eyes steel, her stark white hair braided intricately into something that resembled a gaudy king's crown. *"You will surrender your weapons."*

"No damn way," Austin grumbled.

I held a hand out to stop him and met the steel lady's gaze head on. "We will. However, it would be lying if I didn't remind you that we are Keys and Guardians of the Dawn. My Aegis is a weapon all its own. So you can have our blades, but you do not leave us defenseless."

Steel Lady stared down her nose at me. *"Bold of you."* But apparently, my boldness was admired. She ordered a few soldiers to summon the queen, the others circling us and gathering our weapons as we waited.

In a short while, Queen Narah joined us, surrounded by a retinue of new guards. She closely resembled her sister, but her hair was darker.

"Queen Narah," I greeted. "Despite everything, it is a pleasure to meet you."

Dhamyan translated for Narah as she glanced between the two of us, beady eyes twitching.

"I doubt that is true," Narah said. *"The last time I saw one of your kind, I nearly killed him."* She motioned to Dhamyan. *"And your intended nearly killed me."*

"Ehhh, we're Keys. It happens all the time. Water under the bridge."

Dhamyan turned a glare my way.

Right. Shit. It didn't happen to them all the time.

"I mean…" I cleared my throat. "I suspect you won't try that again once you hear what I have to say."

"Honestly, I am not in the position to concern myself with the likes of you," Narah said, wringing her hands. *"My son is missing,*

and the fact that you have appeared alongside the event has raised my suspicions of your lot even further. My meeting with you is more about us questioning you on your whereabouts than any conversation you wish to have."

Wow. Ray truly screwed this up, hadn't he?

I peered back at Austin. "Any ideas on where her son may have gone?"

"Not a clue. I thought he would be itching to take over as soon as his father died. She seemed to accept his complaints about humanity. If I didn't know better…" He trailed off, his voice hardening when he found his words again. "Tell her of the plans against us."

Austin was serious. I didn't know what he hoped to accomplish, but I followed his lead. "As you know, we borrowed some books from you on our last visit."

"I wasn't aware you intended to return them."

"Oh, you can have them back as soon as we're done with them. We only took them to save Kyp."

"Lies! Your father is not what he purports to be, nor are his kin, by blood or by bond." Narah snorted. *"I know what they search for and I know how desperate you are to attain it, but I shall not hand you this victory."*

"A victory we would find through the books."

"Mama." Jainey tugged on my sleeve from behind me.

"Sssh. She's busy," Rennie admonished.

"Let Jainey speak," Gana warned.

Maybe Jainey perceived the situation better than I did.

"Ah, is that it? Did they hold the child over your head?" Narah

asked. *"I'd heard your generation of Keys were far less likely to heed the council without a great deal of... motivation."*

"The council." I turned to look at Jainey for an answer, and tried not to feel too ashamed of having no damn clue and looking to a child, however intelligent, for help.

"She thinks we're on the Arvokian Council's side, Mama," Jainey said. "And I think she hasn't chosen their side, after all."

Beside me, Austin grumbled.

Oh crap. Oh crap! I got it now. The entire time, when Narah was trying to keep the books from us, she thought she was hiding the secret Ritual from the council. And she was willing to kill Dhamyan to keep it from them.

"We're not on the council's side. Whatever you believe, Narah, you're wrong." I practically stepped over my own words as I tried to get it all out. "I'm actually wildly against them. When we took those books, we only wanted a cure for Kyp. When your father didn't provide one, we were willing to steal, but never to kill. We don't know who did that. But we did find something important in those books besides the cure. We know what the council intends to do. And we want your help to stop it."

Narah's mouth worked soundlessly for a moment. *"You wish to stop it? What exactly do you wish to stop?"*

I glanced over my shoulder at the others. How much should I say? What if she couldn't be trusted?

Narah's guards stepped closer to us, tightening the circle.

"The council plans to turn everything inside out," I said, after a moment. If she couldn't be trusted, we were well and truly screwed already. "Make the Eventide swallow the Dawn and the Dusk. Destroy our homes. That about right?"

"Correct, yes, but not complete," Narah said, eyes narrowed. *"They do wish to make the world a place where they are most powerful. But from there, they wish to subjugate the humans, the Sirins, and anybody else who gets in their way. The Eventide would be ruled by them, and with the use of the ancient Arvokian Rituals, nobody will be powerful enough to stop them."*

"Then we won't allow it to get that far," I assured her. "Do we know if the council knows the ancient language of the Ritual?"

"Master Zelnick may have. He was one of the oldest and wisest of the council." Narah grimaced. *"Are the rumors true? Did my sister bring him to his end?"*

Master Zelnick. "Yes, she did. After he helped to open a MacroRift between our worlds with the blood of…" My mind spun. "Wait. Why would he want to open a MacroRift?"

Austin shivered. "He was starting the process. Can't turn something inside out without something to push it through."

"It kept growing," Rennie said, her voice small.

Jainey nodded, pressing her head to Rennie's shoulder. "Every drop of my blood made it bigger and stronger."

Cass facepalmed. "I can't believe I didn't see it sooner. Stupid!"

I placed a hand on her shoulder. "No time for beating ourselves up. What is it?"

She shook her head. "Jacks, remember back when Gana grabbed all that data off Lavinia's computer. We were looking through it and found Lavinia taking orders from someone?"

"Yes…"

"What were they trying to create?" Cass led me.

"A Skeleton Key." *Shit.*

I could still feel the weight of the gun in my hands when I aimed it at Marcelo, fighting to keep him away from my daughter so I could free her from becoming a sacrifice to the MacroRift. I shook my hands out to release the build of adrenaline.

"We sealed it." Cass took a step closer to Rennie and Jainey. "They'll be looking to open a new one."

"Lavinia believed him," I said. "She said they were bringing a Senefestrian through so they could gather their blood to continue rapidly aging the Skeleton Keys. But Zelnick never seemed to care about the Senefestrian coming through. He had bigger plans. This was what he was doing. But Lavinia had no idea."

Austin scratched at his beard. "Jacks, what are you saying?"

"That the council has been playing us. All of us. Even the deal between the Sirins and the Order! Narah, when did Zelnick join the council?" I asked, excitement and terror burning a hole in my stomach.

I was cracking this. This was a mystery that *I* was going to solve. Kyp was rubbing off on me.

"Zelnick joined the council when my sister moved into her place as the liaison between humanity and our people." Narah's voice was thin and reedy. *"What does that have to do with anything we're discussing?"*

Puzzle, puzzle. Where is the puzzle?

"Cxarana became liaison right before Kyp was born," I explained to the others. "And how old is Lyira?"

"Only a few years older than Kyp," Dhamyan answered, jaw clenching. *"What is this ceaseless questioning?"*

"Oh, nothing, just building a timeline in my head. Because something switched the plan. Prior to this, the plan was to help the humans against the Sirins they had accidentally allowed to travel between worlds by opening the rifts. What changed?"

Cass gasped. But it wasn't Cass. I glanced back at her and her eyes were lit with a green glow.

"That was not the plan. Not for the council." Mom spoke through Cass. "Or at least not the only one." She adjusted her clothing, an old habit from back when she had a body of her own. "It was the horrible discovery your father made that initially turned him against the Order. The Sirins would collect a tribute from us. Something with an Aegis. But it wasn't for them. It was for some other being. And it needed a creature with an Aegis."

Jainey's nose crinkled in disgust. "They were already experimenting. Like they did with me."

I crossed my arms over my chest. "Until the first Skeleton Key was born. And then the plan changed. Zelnick found his way into the council. And his plan needed Skeleton Keys. So he altered the deal so they could create one."

Silence reigned while everyone digested that for a minute.

Then Austin let out a string of curses that made even my eyes widen.

"They enlisted Caleb to kill him," Kylie said, her voice barely above a whisper. "They convinced him he's going to be powerful and promised him he'll get revenge against Jacklyn. All he had to do was help him. But they're going to bleed him out to open another MacroRift."

"Why would they need to do that?" Narah asked. *"The one you closed reopened long ago."*

That was impossible. There hadn't been a Rift there when I came back. I would have noticed that.

"How did you think *you came back from the dead?"*

I tried to push my mind back to that day, to waking up in the mostly collapsed warehouse. Kyp was awake when I woke up and…

My mind clouded. I shook my head like it would make the feeling go away.

That felt familiar. Like way back before the Order, when I'd see things like Gorvhans in my mind, or have dreams about running in the woods with my father, and my mind would cloud and I'd shake the thoughts loose…

How did I not see that? Why couldn't I remember going through the Rift from the Dusk? Someone had to have taken me there. And how would I have not seen the Rift on the other side?

But I did. I did see it. I just didn't remember it.

"It reopened?" Jainey's shrill reply interrupted my train of thought. "How large?"

"At least as large as it was before," Narah said. She looked at the guards surrounding her, who had previously just been observing. They were all shifting on their feet, glancing at each other. *"I assumed you knew. But then, I had assumed you had been the cause."*

"So Caleb is the literal Key to growing the portal further."

Rennie frowned. "God, who knows how much Skeleton Key blood they would need to open the Rift all the way."

"Maybe all of them." Cass's horrified gaze hooked mine.

Austin swore. "Where is your brat, Narah?"

"My son *is no Skeleton Key,"* Narah replied, her lips twisting into a snarl.

"No, but I bet he'd love to get his hands on one," Austin said.

"What are you implying?" Narah snapped.

"When we met, Merrick was hateful toward humans in general." Austin's jaw fixed, his words escaping through clenched teeth. "This whole thing is heating up, and they know it. And now your son is missing?"

Narah snarled and was about to say something, but I held up a hand and she stopped, turning to glare at me.

"Forget about that. What is being done to locate your son?"

"The guards are searching up to the edges of our kingdom. Once we've determined he is not within our kingdom, we will have to organize search parties to enter Sirin territory as well as the Dawn." Her gaze went hard. *"That would not be good for you or for them."* Her black eyes glistened in the light of the fire that rested within my palm.

"Listen, I wouldn't blame you," I said. "My children were stolen from me by the council. I died to protect them. But we're all going to die if we don't solve this larger issue. So we'll help search for him on the way, but I need you to tell me where Lyira is. We need to join forces if we're going to stop the end of the damn world."

"Lyira?" Narah asked. Her jaw loosened, her eyes widening.

"She's the leader of the guard."

Now it was Dhamyan's turn to swear.

Austin's eyes flashed with concern. "What is it?"

"As the leader of the guard, she would be protecting the prime members of the Arvokian leadership," Dhamyan explained.

"Wouldn't that be Queen Narah?" Rennie asked. She gnawed at her lower lip as she waited for the response.

"Do you see her here, child?" Steel Lady asked, not unkindly. *"No, the leader of the guard protects—"*

Shit. I knew the answer.

"The Arvokian Council."

TAKE ME TO YOUR LEADER

KYP

"The blood of the ancients," Andaria said, gravelly voice and unique accent distorting the words. "Does that mean ancient Arvokian?" She walked side-by-side with Cxarana, the book they translated balanced between them. They didn't seem remotely concerned with looking where they were walking, despite the rocky uphill terrain, nor did they seem to need light to read. Kyp was directly behind them and couldn't see two feet in front of him.

"I suppose it could mean that," Cxarana replied to Andaria's question. Her head tilted. "I think you're missing the superlative on this word."

"This is mind-numbing," Ray leaned forward to whine in Kyp's ear.

"This is necessary," Kyp corrected. "I understand that they are arguing semantics, but it is necessary. You want a proper translation, don't you? This is what we need to win this thing."

"We need a helluva lot more than that, my boy," Ray grumbled. "We need luck and a right feckin' army, and we aren't getting that."

"The blood of those most ancient." Andaria scribbled something in her book. "I'm unsure what that means."

Cxarana emitted a clicking sound from the back of her throat. "We should translate first. We can worry about the meaning after."

"We're entering Sirin territory." Andaria slipped the book into her satchel, red eyes cautiously flitting around in the darkness.

Sirin territory was marked by a narrowing of the trail on which they tread, the hills rising high on either side of them. When the trail widened again, they came upon a clearing where a Sirin village had taken root. Stone huts lined the clearing. In the center, a large creature, a Tralsk, based on its brush-like gray fur, was being hacked apart by a broad Sirin wielding two knives the size of Kyp's head.

"What in the ever-loving fuck," Drew whispered under his breath as they all bunched up close, ready to protect each other from whatever they'd just walked into.

The light of the fire from Drew's torch glinted off the giant knives. Kyp suppressed a shudder.

"We're totally going to die here," Jordan muttered.

Kyp wasn't going to say it, but…

"No," Ray reassured the kid with a hand on his shoulder. "This ain't where my journey ends, and you don't stop breathing while my heart's still hammering away. No chance."

Jordan smiled.

His words were a relief to Kyp as well.

The Sirin growled, a noise that tore from his throat, and several Sirins emerged from the huts, wearing the crumpled vestiges of clothing worn in the Dawn. Kyp had always found it bizarre, the way Sirins had taken such an interest in the culture of the Dawn.

"This is the Glr'kandan," Andaria explained. "The… the guard stand. They work out here, scouts on the edge of Sirin territory."

Kyp steeled himself against his fear. Someone would need to approach them if they wanted to get anywhere. What would Jacklyn do in a situation like this?

He knew exactly what she'd do. He stepped forward, plastering on a cheerful smile. "Excuse me. Could you take me to your leader? Please."

He winced the minute the words were out of his mouth.

Ray snorted. "Shame Jacks wasn't here for that one."

"You've got some massive balls on you, son," the Sirin with the giant cleavers said, his words garbled and wet-sounding. "If you think you and yours have come to take the fight to us, you're out of your damn mind."

Andaria marched up between them, shoving a hand into Kyp's chest hard enough to make him choke. "Please excuse him," she said. "Nobody is here to fight anyone, Abbath. I came to you first because I knew you wouldn't kill me. We simply wish to speak."

The Sirin, Abbath, eyed her suspiciously from head to toe. "You knew that, did you? Where have you been?"

Drew stepped forward. "We would really love to get out of your hair so you and Andaria can catch up. But we're in a bit of a time crunch. Can we speak to your leader? We need to discuss a common enemy."

"You wish to assassinate our leader?" Abbath asked, his voice raising enough that the rest of the Sirins closed in tightly around him.

"If we did that, you could just kill us," Drew pointed out.

"Yes, but our leader would still be dead," the Sirin answered.

"You have more than one leader," Andaria spoke up. "And you know that. But you're

purposely playing word games. You know I wouldn't come to you without reason. I know I'm not wanted here."

A low rumble passed through the clearing.

Kyp's fists clenched. He'd heard a rumble like that before. It happened whenever a woman dared to speak while the big boys were talking, and it disgusted him. He knew it wasn't up to him how other cultures behaved. It wasn't his business if it wasn't his culture. The reasonable side of him understood that.

The less reasonable side of him, the side that had been hunted by Sirins in the past, the side that was trying to pretend he hadn't been terrified of them all his life, the side that suspected he could relate more to Andaria than he could to the men, wanted to lay waste to the entire clearing or die trying.

Andaria glanced around uneasily at the crowd and took a step back to be couched in the protection of her new friends.

"Your leadership is grouped in a family structure," she said, her voice cracking slightly. "We wish to meet with the Circle. The heads of the families."

"We don't wish to weaken your forces," Drew said. "Actually, we need you at your full strength. We wish to go to war against a group of Arvokians attempting to destroy our worlds."

Abbath's brow ridges shivered. "Indeed? They could never do

that. They know the kind of damage we can cause."

"And you have no idea of the Ritual they've gotten their hands on." Kyp stepped forward. "Two years ago, a Sirin representative came to the Dawn and asked if we could come to an agreement. That agreement was in service of something I could never align myself with. Now, I'm turning the request to you. We could align, and we can change everything. Or we can stand alone and perish."

"You can keep trying to convince me until your words run out, but I'm not the one you need to convince," Abbath grumbled. "I won't take you to see them. That can't even be done. We don't all live within walking distance of wherever the hell you show up." He stepped closer. "It takes a Ritual to communicate with the Circle. That might be more within my doing. And that way, if they tell me I should just kill you all, I'll still be able to do it."

"Guard up," Kyp shot through the line to Jordan. Jordan's head bobbed in response.

"I guess that's reasonable," Drew said. "We didn't bring our entire team to you, either."

"Not right here," Abbath said, his smile revealing a frighteningly sharp needle-like grin. "But they are all in the Dusk, aren't they?"

Blank stares were the only response.

"I can scent the delightfully enticing aroma of humanity anywhere." His teeth were slick with drool.

Kyp fought to stifle the gag that nearly tore out of him.

"Enough, Abbath," Andaria stepped forward, voice soft. "You must hear what they have to share."

"Oh." Abbath took a step closer. "You run away and come back here aligned with the damn enemy and you think that earns you the right to a voice? Are you out of your damned mind?"

"The only reason you haven't killed them is because of me. Don't act like you hate me." Andaria's voice stayed soft, but her words were firmer. She glanced around at the rest of them. "You are a fool. You remain a humble servant to the Circle as though they are doing well for us. But what do they do? They ensnare our own with addiction to the drugs running through the veins of humanity. Make them indebted to those who run this… this farce of a world. Just because there are more Sirin men does not mean you all should lead. It just means you have the force to keep us from challenging you. But your former underlings are rising against you. And we will prevail. The least you can do is give us the opportunity to mourn your sorry turn at rule."

Kyp's breath caught in his throat. *"Be ready to retreat."*

Abbath didn't move, his red eyes wide. "Andaria…"

"When was the last time you saw Father?" she whispered. "Is he still trading his most prized possessions for the chance of consuming humanity's fluids? He traded Mother, our home, me. Every single bit of sustenance you bring home. You're hiding your meal from him right now. We can cut him off from his source. We can end what they have brought here through the Dawn."

Abbath's eyes lowered, his gaze flitting to the side. His blue skin was shadowed, lit only by the torch in Drew's hand.

"I would have come ahead, but I didn't think you'd want to see me. Still, you were more likely to listen to any of the others who work for them," Andaria said. "And it might not be safe to do this.

Perform the Ritual. Please, just make them listen."

Abbath glanced back and forth. With a grunt, he tilted his head toward a nearby hut. Collecting his plate of carved beast, he shouted back at the others in his native language, then walked into his hut, pushing aside a curtain made of an ivy-like plant.

Drew motioned for us to follow him.

The hut was small, constructed from a collection of the reeds the Arvokians used to construct bridges and sticks like bamboo sprouts. The walls were covered in reflective surfaces, enhancing the light of the few candles that rested on several surfaces.

It was a clever set up, one that reminded Kyp of the personhood of even the Sirins. In fact, this whole trip had been a revelation in that regard.

They weren't monsters. They were sentient. The differences were just so apparent that it was easy to overlook the similarities. The Sirins lived in a society that had been overtaken by what was essentially a multi-national drug cartel. But it wasn't without hope. The Arvokians were corrupted by their own abilities. The Gorvhans and Tralsks were not that different from really creepy lions and tigers. The Senefestrians were like a race of dinosaurs that survived.

Dinosaurs…

The translation! *The blood of the most ancient.* They needed Senefestrian blood.

"I hate you," Abbath grumbled to Andaria. "You think you're so damn smart."

"I'm very smart." Andaria perked up, a smile breaking across her face that was almost endearing. "And you can pretend it doesn't bother you, the way we're living. But I've been able to see right through you since we were little."

"So you say." Abbath waved her off, but his jaw twitched. "Let's get this over with." He reached for a clay pot containing several twists of gray, leafy roots and oddly colored flowers. He plucked the leaves from the roots and the petals of one crimson flower.

He crushed them between thick, clawed fingers and spread it in a square on a small wooden table. Reaching into a basket beside him, he pulled out a small vial of clear purple fluid. He dribbled the fluid over the herbs.

He turned his attention to Jordan. "Boy. You wield fire?"

Jordan glanced at Kyp, then wiped his hand on his jeans and held it out to him. "Uh, yeah. Yeah, I do."

"Light the herbs." Abbath looked at him like he was a fool.

Jordan did as requested, then glanced over at Drew. His eyes were wide, eyebrows raised, and his mouth turned down. The very definition of puppy dog eyes.

"I wasn't going to make you talk to them," Drew said, squeezing Jordan's shoulder.

For a moment, the faint sounds of insects and birds overtook the clearing as everyone fell into cold silence.

One by one, Sirins appeared before them; their frames varied from broad to lean, but all were muscled and distinctly masculine. The final one was clothed in a golden cape with a single loop of gold adorning his head. They shared the same blue tinge to their skin, the same burning red eyes, the same mouthful of sharp teeth and brow ridges. But they each appeared distinct in a way Kyp hadn't really paid attention to enough before, except for when he'd met Marcelo, the one Sirin he'd known on a first name basis. He'd made mistakes, lumping them all in together, treating them like they were all monsters. They looked like monsters to him, but that was just based on how people from the Dawn appeared. For the people of the Dusk, Arvokians and Sirins were more normal than Kyp's human appearance. It would do him well to remember that.

"Why do you call for us?" the one in gold spoke in the familiar slurred voice all Sirins used when speaking English. As he spoke, Kyp noticed that each of the Sirins was projected to them with a shivery silver sheen surrounding them, signifying their lack of substance.

"My lords, I am Abbath, loyal servant of the Crelnik house. I have been approached, on our very own land, by the prince of the Keys of the Dawn and his entourage. I have been asked to summon you all here in mind. In body would have been too long for the urgent message they wish to impart to you."

"Why would you believe we would wish to speak with them? Why haven't you destroyed them already?"

Kyp pushed his consciousness forward into the conversation. "With all due respect, if you refuse to heed our warning, you are fools. Years ago, one of your people requested an alliance from me. What he wished from me was not something I could give him. Today, we are extending the same offer. We would like to ally with you for a specific purpose."

"And what would that purpose be, fool boy?"

Drew cleared his throat before launching into an explanation of their current situation. Once he reached the part about stopping the Arvokians, the leader cut him off.

"And once the threat is defeated? What then?"

"Based on the situation and the treaty we would be putting forth, I would expect us to be able to meet civilly to discuss a change in the current policy. One that will allow humans, Sirins, and Arvokians to live in a way we can all be content with."

The leader scoffed. "Why are you doing that?"

Drew frowned. "What?"

"Speaking to me like you have respect for me?" he asked. "You do not."

Drew opened his mouth to answer, but he was cut off.

"We know the meager amount of remaining Keys and Guardians among your number. Your former leader did well to inform us of his treachery." His chin jutted in Ray's direction. "As well as its effect on your numbers. You do not have the higher ground here to negotiate any kind of deal. Your army is lacking."

Ray grabbed onto where Kyp and Drew's hands met. "And yet you keep losing to us."

Andaria shouted something at them.

"Don't you yell at me in languages I can't understand," Ray shouted back. "You want to scold me, you do it like a warrior, ma'am." He glanced at the floor. "Sorry."

The leader leaned forward in his chair threateningly. The part of Kyp that had been taught to loathe weakness and to bear no weakness within himself couldn't help but applaud Ray's move.

If the Sirins weren't afraid of them, why go to such lengths to protect themselves? If the Sirins weren't afraid of them, what else did they have planned once they stopped this current crisis?

The leader smacked his hand down on the arm of his chair. "You will receive no support from us."

The other members of the Circle, who had simply been nodding and frowning through Drew's entire explanation, now cheered.

"And for your hubris," the leader added, "you will be killed. Abbath, destroy the—"

Jordan smeared a hand through the herbs, putting out the fire with one hand, while he drew a dagger from the inside of his jacket with the other. It was pointed toward Abbath faster than Kyp could blink.

"Don't move a muscle," Jordan warned. "I have enough strength to burrow this through your chest like a very long, bladed bullet. I really don't want to, but I will."

Kyp's heart swelled with pride. Jordan was older and stronger, and ready to fight for their cause. But there was no need.

The look Abbath gave him wasn't carnivorous or vicious. Instead, he held his hands up in retreat, his head lowered as if in deep sorrow.

"I will not harm you," Abbath said. "Andaria and I have not always agreed on anything, but she does not lie, and if she believes this threat is coming, it must be stopped. The Circle is refusing to see reason. Working together on this will not just protect the Dawn, it will protect the Dusk. Their decision is foolish." He shook his head. "Please don't misunderstand me. I have no loyalty or kindness toward the Dawn. My heart and my sword belong to the Dusk."

Andaria stepped forward, fury brightening her eyes. "Abbath, it's time."

"I fear you may be right," Abbath rumbled.

"Jordan," Andaria said. "We need your help."

Jordan glanced back at Kyp quickly, then back at Andaria. "What do you need me to do?"

"I want you to help us connect with a different group. The leaders of my team," Andaria said. "Can you also reach out to people in the Dawn from here?"

Jordan scratched at the back of his neck. "Um, yeah. With Dad's help, probably." He leaned in to Kyp, whispering, "That last one took a bit out of me."

Kyp squeezed his shoulder lightly, calloused fingers catching on the edge of his leather jacket. "What will you tell them?"

"That we're done waiting," Andaria said. "Today is the day we rise. We were willing to try to end things amicably, but their reaction to this threat proves their inept leadership. By the end of this fight, the Circle will die and our resistance will rise."

Drew nodded approvingly. "Sounds very motivating. We can't back you up in the initial attack. We'll be spread too thin. We have to attain the Senefestrian blood if we want the power boost we'll need."

Abbath grunted. "They should be easy to find. They're at the site of the MacroRift, waiting for it to grow to the proper size once again, so they can make their escape into the Dawn. If you're going there, you should be careful."

"Wait." Kyp held up his hand, his stomach plummeting. "That

Rift was small. It kept on growing?"

"Yes," Andaria said. "Just like the translation said, 'the wound in the world will reopen with the blood of the ancients.' I cannot believe I didn't see! The blood of the ancients must be what reopened the MacroRift."

Kyp's chest ached. "The Senefestrians. The wound in the world reopened, just like my wound did. The moment I stabbed that Senefestrian over the MacroRift, I gave them what they needed for the next step of the plan. We have to get to that Rift."

The wound had reopened. And Kyp had allowed it to stay that way.

THIRTY TWO

CRIME SCENE

JACKLYN

The cavern we entered was vast and silent, save for the rhythmic dripping of water in the distance. Though the next right turn would lead to the Council's war room, we weren't there to battle, so we had to remain quiet. It didn't help that our small and tidy group was now joined by Narah and five of her armed guards. Although, that would help if we got caught.

We walked in a tight circle, my Aegis combining with Jainey's to cover as much noise as we could and keep our approach unheard. Our individual spheres of influence were large, but combined, they were even better and we couldn't afford to take any chances.

The battle with Zelnick had been hard won. The war room could hold up to six Arvokians of his superior strength and ability. Or it could hold a hint as to where we could find them. We wouldn't know how snoopy our snoop would need to be until we knew if they were inside.

Something bat-like fluttered around the ceiling of the cave. It was more insect than mammal, more like a giant flying cockroach, but with wings like leather.

I was *really* sympathizing with Bruce Wayne at that moment. He understood it was the bats we should fear.

The thing emitted a weird croak, and I startled.

Austin let loose a low chuckle, still whispering despite my sound block. "Isn't this lovely? And still, I'd rather do this than have to negotiate with the rat-bastards our boyfriends got stuck with."

I grinned, allowing the opportunity for friendly conversation to ease the dread pooling in my guy. "Mine is my husband now, sir. When are you gonna make it official with Drew?"

Austin huffed a laugh. "Assuming he gets out of his mission alive, and I get out of mine?"

My breath caught. We wouldn't fail. We couldn't. The entire dimension was on the line.

My family was on the line.

I couldn't lose Austin. I wouldn't.

"Well, it would be hard to marry you any other way," Rennie chimed in from behind us. "Can you guys adopt me when you get married?"

The smile he sent back her way was warm and bright. "You bet, kiddo. Just you wait."

"You didn't answer my question," I teased.

We continued forward for around fifty feet before he spoke up again. "This has to be over. I can't do this for much longer." He bumped my shoulder with his. "We had a taste of peace, you know? Not having to fear for each other every day. We had a family, and we didn't have to do anything alone, just like it is now, but we didn't have the lingering fear that we were about to destroy something with the wrong decision or we'd have to fight some kind of battle to the death."

"So much for that," I said. I knew how he felt. I hadn't been eager to jump back into the fray myself, and I hadn't been alive during the period of peace. We were all just so exhausted.

"I want a peaceful life now. I don't want to ask Drew to marry me just to have him die." Austin frowned. "Sorry. That's probably a bit insensitive to say to the married chick."

I shook my head. "No worries. You could go. If this isn't the end, you can take Drew and go back to that peaceful life. And when we're done, we'll join you."

"I don't think Drew would want that," he said. "Besides, I'd never leave you to go through this without me. We see this through to the end." He smiled, his teal eyes sparkling in the firelight.

I offered a fist bump his way. "To the end."

He bumped his fist with mine, miming an explosion as he pulled back.

Narah muttered something to Dhamyan, frustration evident in her tone.

"Is she judging us?" I asked, poking ahead at Dhamyan, who walked in front of us with Narah.

Dhamyan chuckled. *"She asked if you're always so talkative. I will tell her you are."*

"Yeah, well, you try having the weight of all the worlds on your shoulders all the damn time. I bet you'd want to distract yourself, too."

Narah whispered something.

"She said silence implies thought." The mirth in his tone was evident through the connection.

Rennie's foot snagged on a root that had grown partially up along the floor. I grabbed her elbow to steady her. My fire wasn't tipped in the right direction.

A gasp ripped free from Cass, way up in the front, where Gana's fire provided light for the guards.

One of the guards shouted in Arvokian.

Dhamyan quickly translated. "He's calling for Narah."

She rushed forward, and I followed, holding out a hand to Austin to tell him to stay behind with Rennie and Jainey.

Only a few steps closer and the odor of iron assaulted my nostrils. Blood waited for me. And a whole helluva lot of it.

I pushed to the front until I was side by side with Narah. She gripped the stone wall to keep herself standing, her fingers slipping at the blood streaked even there.

Dead. One. Two. Three. Five. Eight. Eight Arvokians.

"Austin, don't let the kids come over here!" I shouted, but it was in vain. Even without coming in, Jainey and Rennie knew. Jainey read it in my mind and Rennie read it in my soul. They both retched outside, Austin and Cass whispering comforting words to them.

The blood dripped from the walls and congealed in pools that merged with each other on the floor.

"Are these the members of the Council?" I asked, cautiously picking my way across the room. I cataloged each of their horrified and enraged faces as I passed.

"It is," Narah answered, her mental voice unable to hide her anguish.

"Who would do this?" Austin asked.

"Are the girls okay?" I asked.

"With Cass." He shrugged.

"Why do they ask foolish questions?" Narah hissed. *"Who else could it possibly be? It is obviously the Sirins, declaring war against our kingdom."*

"It is not the Sirins," Dhamyan argued.

Austin knelt beside one of the bodies, some poor bastard who had landed face down in a pool of blood during the struggle.

Narah smoothed her robes as she approached Austin, streaks of blood marring the pure white. *"It must be the Sirins. Who else would do such a thing?"*

Clasping the dead Arvokian's shoulder, Austin turned them so they laid on their back.

"We were negotiating a deal with the Sirins," Dhamyan said. *"Unless that completely failed…"*

The Arvokian's face was half-coated in the blood he had lain in, and it dribbled back into his hair like syrup once he was lying on his back. He clutched something in the hand that had been pressed beneath him.

I stepped forward, my boot pressing prints into the congealed puddle surrounding him. "Do you have fingerprints? A way of tracking evidence?" I tore my gaze away from the dead Arvokian's face, twisted in agony, and looked at Dhamyan.

He stared back blankly.

"How do you know who committed a murder?"

"Examine the circumstances. Look for the weapon. Determine an alibi."

"DNA? Fingerprints?" I grabbed his hand and yanked it toward me, my fingers running over the tips of his much broader ones.

"Jacklyn Madison, I must ask that you—"

"You don't have fingerprints," I said.

"Huh. Didn't think of that," Austin said.

I didn't say what I was thinking. I couldn't. They wouldn't see it the same way I did. A fingerprint, clear as day, was pressed into the blood caked onto a circular gold pin about the size of the dead Arvokian's palm.

Which meant it was a human. Or a Sirin. Did Sirins have fingerprints? There had never been a reason for me to check.

I peeled back the dead Arvokian's fingers and pulled the pin free, turning it in my hands. It was a golden oval shape. At its center, there was a symbol carved into the middle. It looked like two lowercase t's.

I displayed it for the rest of the room. "This look familiar to anyone?"

Narah took the gold pin from my hand. Her hand shook, and a chattering sound seemed to rattle loose from her. Dhamyan rushed to her side and plucked the pin from her fingers. His eyes widened, his mouth gaping open.

"This is the symbol for Lyira's faction of the guard," Dhamyan said. *"Lyira and her soldiers massacred the Council.*

I swore. The Council wasn't our enemy anymore. Lyira was.

A Skeleton Key with an army.

"Narah?" Dhamyan said, his voice brittle with caution. *"Where is Merrick?"*

Another strange chattering noise tore free from Narah. *"He went missing earlier today."*

"What does this have to do with Merrick?" Austin asked.

"I am not certain as of yet," Dhamyan said with a deep sigh. *"But Merrick's disappearance must be connected."*

"Why would you draw that conclusion?" I asked with a deep sigh.

"Because Merrick and Lyira are betrothed."

THIRTY THREE

KYP

"Well, that didn't end the way I expected, but at least nobody important died," Drew said with a sigh once they'd cleared enough space between them and Abbath on their way to the MacroRift. "Can you connect to Jainey and Dhamyan and see how their meeting went?"

Kyp reached for Jordan's hand, Ray guiding them across the cracked dry land of the Sirin side of the Dusk while they worked.

Before they'd left, Abbath and Andaria worked through whatever differences they had. Apparently, Andaria's wasn't the only revolutionary group at play here. Andaria's wanted the Circle's rule to end with righteous vengeance. Abbath's tried to heal the system from within. It seemed Andaria had finally gotten them to bend in her group's direction. With Jordan's help, Andaria had reached out to the team in the Dawn and sent them after the Circle. The rest of her team in the Dusk would assist. Meanwhile, Abbath's group was journeying with Kyp's team, planning to help them with whatever lay ahead.

It was a lot to communicate, and he felt better sharing the darker details with Dhamyan, rather than Jainey.

That was the right decision. Dhamyan sent him a horrifying update of what he and Jacklyn's camp discovered.

Kyp had tried to shield Jordan from the most gruesome parts of the recap, but the problem with communicating within someone's mind was that pictures and words were difficult to separate.

"I knew I didn't like her," Ray pronounced upon hearing what had transpired.

Kyp made a thoughtful noise. "I liked her."

"She fancied you a bit too much. You could have stood to fancy her less, in my eyes." Ray glared at him.

"I came home and married your daughter, didn't I?" It came out sharper than he intended. He softened the next sentence. "It doesn't matter, anyway. She isn't an ally, as it turns out."

"Her guard is strong," Cxarana said, a hush in her tone. "I am not surprised her unit managed to lay waste to the Council. Especially with her in charge of protecting them for as long as she was. She likely knew all their weaknesses."

"I wonder how long she planned such an attack," Drew said. "Although I'm much less surprised about Merrick's involvement. He was prickly from the start."

"He was a little prick," Zane said. "There! I fixed it for you."

Kyp chuckled, and it was that very thing that made him realize Jordan did not. He nudged him with his elbow. "You okay, kiddo?"

He glanced up at Kyp, his eyes glistening in the firelight. "Caleb went evil. Now Lyira. Are me and Jainey going to go evil, too? What if that's what Skeleton Keys do?"

"Jordan—"

"Don't just brush it off as untrue. Fifty-fifty odds don't bode well." He sighed. "Dammit, could this get any worse?"

"Sure it can, love, just give it a minute." Ray clapped him hard on the back.

They moved through a path of gnarled trees, their branches sharply pointed. They reached toward them, like grasping fingers.

"Not funny," Drew scolded.

"Not funny," Ray said. "Fucking inspirational, I tell ya."

"What he *means*," Zane corrected, "is that you never say that while on a mission. It's a curse. It can and will always get worse. You've been through enough to know that by now."

"I guess."

Whatever Ray had been trying to do there, it had failed spectacularly.

"You're not going to go evil on us," Kyp said. "Caleb made a choice. And Lyira did the same."

"What about your mother?" Jordan asked.

The tree-lined path seemed to narrow. "What about her?"

"Ray said she died one too many times and came back wrong?"

Kyp frowned, a shiver racing down his spine at the mention of her.

"I'm sorry, Dad. That wasn't cool."

"You can ask me anything, Jordan," Kyp said, fighting through his own discomfort. Ray used to do that for him when he needed it. Mother hated him questioning, because it meant he had a mind of his own. He wanted to encourage his children to think independently. "Ray believes what he believes. I'm not so sure. I don't know if it matters."

"How could it not matter?" Jordan asked.

That was a much easier question to answer. "Because I love you. And I'm never going to let you die."

It was a bit of a cop-out. But it was the truest response he could offer.

Jordan's glowing smile in response would likely be something etched into his soul for the rest of his time.

"Oi! They made it!" Ray gained a skip in his step. Kyp followed his gaze to find a group of Arvokian guards leading some shadows at the other end of the wooded path. Kyp trusted Ray's vision enough to know that if he was happy, it was Jacks' team he saw.

Jacks. Just thinking that she was near lit something warm within him. Something like hope.

Ray could joke about Kyp's limited interest in Lyira all he wanted. Was she an attractive woman? Sure. Kyp was a man. He had eyes. He could look. But he didn't want Lyira. Or anybody but Jacklyn.

Jacklyn was his always. Nothing else mattered in comparison.

He would do anything to protect her and the family they had created.

Anything.

Their groups collided in a sweet reunion. Drew rushed to Austin and Rennie. Cxarana surprised him, running not only to Dhamyan, but to Narah, comforting her about Merrick. Narah apologized to

Ray. Jacklyn and Jainey hugged Ray. Jordan kissed Rennie. Zane drew Andaria into the crowd as she greeted Jainey and Jacklyn, keeping their newest friend company. And Cass found Kyp.

"Hey." She smiled, joining him where he hung back, watching the reunion from a distance. "What do you make of all these revelations?"

Kyp thought about his response, the slightest tilt of his lips greeting his best friend. "Fear. It can be quite the motivator."

"So you think Lyira is afraid?" she asked, falling into step beside him as he closed the distance between himself and Jacklyn.

"I think Lyira is, and Zelnick was. Afraid of the Sirins. Afraid of what harm could come to their own. The Sirins were oppressing their people. The Eventide is the only place they feel powerful." He met Cass's gaze. "They're bending the world to make sure they stay strong in the face of danger. Not the only people we know who have done that."

Kyp was completely aware of the irony of his own words. He would not acknowledge it.

He grabbed Cass's hand and squeezed. "I'm glad you're safe."

She smiled. "Me and all my other passengers?"

"You," Kyp said. "They're cool to have around. But none of them are you." A quick kiss on the cheek and he dashed forward, scooping Jainey up in his arms.

"Hey, booger." He crushed her against him, and she squealed. She was like happiness in a bottle for him. "You good?"

She wrapped her arms around his neck. "It was scary in the Council room." Her hazel eyes were wide and glossy, her words choked with oncoming tears.

"They let you see that?" He tried to ignore the way his blood heated at the thought.

"No, I did not *let* her see that." Jacklyn. Arms crossed. Eyes that matched Jainey's, blazing with fire. "She's a telepath. It was an overwhelming sight. We were probably shouting it in our brains loud enough for you to see it."

"You're right," Kyp said. "I didn't mean it like that."

"Protective is good," she answered. "But don't be an ass."

Seeing her there warmed his soul. It would be blissful if they weren't in the wrong dimension.

"Papa, put me down and say hello to Mama," Jainey advised.

"You could tell I wanted to say hi to her, huh?" He grinned at the little girl, whose raised eyebrow showed her impatience with him. "How very perceptive."

"Oh, hurry up." Her tiny pink tongue poked out at him.

He made to grab it. "I'll be back to cuddle you again in a minute." He lowered her to her feet, then turned his attention to the love of his life. He was in her space in two wide strides.

"Hey." She smiled shakily.

He tracked her from head to toe, noting the blood caked on her boots. "You okay?"

"I'm not hurt," she said, but her voice cracked.

He pulled her into his arms and held her close, one hand in her curls. He inhaled her scent at her neck—strawberry shampoo, leather, and the tang of sweat. This cost her so much. Every time she had to kill, every time she watched others die, she lost a bit of herself.

He wished he'd never brought her into this. But he didn't know who he would be if he hadn't.

"I know," he whispered against her ear. "I love you."

"I love you too." She released her words on the end of a sob. It was eternally surprising to him that even after all this time, it crushed her as much to see enemies die as innocents. She'd wanted everyone to believe she'd lost that at some point, but he knew it was still there.

"We're together again now." He pulled back, taking her hand in his. "With the might of the Sirin rebels and the Arvokian guard on our side."

"Together. Someone once said we were stronger that way."

"Did they?"

"They think they're so smart."

"They are."

They held each other's serious gazes for just a moment before they both cracked, laughing and leaning into each other.

"Mom!" Jordan threw his arms around both of them. Kyp scooped Jainey up to join the hug just moments after. The four of them pressed their foreheads together. This was what family felt like.

A growl sounded in the distance, rumbling through the air around them.

"Kyp," Cxarana called to him. "There's your Senefestrian."

For a moment, Kyp kept his eyes screwed shut, shutting out everything but the feeling of his family close to him, his wider family close and just beyond. If he was honest, he wanted to stay there like this forever. For he knew, however things went from this point on, they would lose something, somebody.

One way or another, after this battle, nothing would ever be the same.

"Okay." He stepped back from them. "Let's go hunt some dinosaurs."

Thirty Four

Kyp

The ground shook beneath their feet as they resumed their movement toward their target. Abbath had said there had been a Senefestrian trying to get through the MacroRift, so they knew where they needed to be.

The journey there was swift.

"What the fuck?" Jacklyn breathed. Scaffolding now surrounded the MacroRift's location.

Dhamyan led them into the mountain range where he'd met both Kyp and later Jacklyn, so long ago, hiding there until they had a plan settled.

"The Circle converted it into a…" Andaria fumbled with the words. "A tourist place. You could pay to visit the Dawn. For those who weren't yet addicted to the drug. And hopefully to create that addiction within them."

"Like the Dusk's very own Ellis Island," Jacklyn said. Her mouth twisted in thought. "But… with drugs."

"And behind a paywall," Zane added. "So not out of the kindness of their own hearts."

But that wasn't the worst of it. The cracks in the ground were far beyond the limits of the walls containing it.

"It's big. Bigger than it should be," Ray said. "Why hasn't the Senefestrian just gone through? What's stopping it?"

A screech rent the air. It was answered by a long rolling growl.

And then another. And another screech.

Kyp's blood froze in his veins.

"Holy macaroni," Austin said.

"There's more than one of them," Cass said, all her voices coming together in a symphony. "They could tear through to the Dawn any minute. We have to stop them."

Drew nodded, his brows drawn. "Dhamyan, translate. Queen Narah, are any of your guards as skilled as you in Rituals?"

"*Yes,*" she said, her voice sharp. "*One of my guards. Shayral.*"

"Okay, great. Cxarana, I want you to lead the others. What do you need to unlock the remainder of the Guardian's abilities?"

"A droplet of blood," she said, her voice rushed. "Just as I do for the initial pledge."

"Can you collect those now?" Drew asked.

"Guys." Jacklyn looked up. Small particles of light dotted the black of the sky.

Stars? But that didn't happen in the Dusk.

"Two dimensional bleeds in one lifetime," Austin grumbled. "Who woulda thought…"

Dread bubbled through Kyp's stomach. They were really doing this again, weren't they?

"I—I can," Cxarana said, her eyes glistening as she surveyed the pseudo-stars above. "I brought vials." She slid her tote from her shoulder.

"Let's work quickly," Drew said. "Before this Rift opens farther."

"Zane, go first," Drew said, motioning for her to go to Cxarana. Meanwhile, he stepped over to Andaria. "Stay with them. Keep working on the translation with the help of the others. We need to crack the Ritual and its remedy."

Drew moved on to Dhamyan. "Work with Jordan and Andaria to get a message out to the Sirins and the rest of Narah's Guard with our location. Once you're done, assist the others in whatever way you can."

"And the rest of us?" Jacklyn asked.

"We go in," Drew said.

And that was where Kyp was going to have to draw the line. "Wait." He swallowed hard. He wanted to jump in and dole out orders. He wanted to correct Drew on his strategy. But the truth was, he wasn't wrong. The smartest idea was for them all to run in, half of them with guns blazing. But that left the Guardians in the most vulnerable state. And wasn't that exactly what they swore they would no longer do?

"May I make a suggestion?" he choked out.

Drew's lips twitched, but Cass let out a full giggle. "That was hard for you, wasn't it?"

Jacklyn bit down on her lip in an effort to stifle a full grin. Austin bumped Drew with his shoulder. Ray and Zane gathered the kids up in a squeeze.

A moment of levity before entering hell. Kyp was glad he could provide it.

"Our Dusk contingent will be largely unguarded, if even some of the Guard are busy working on Rituals," Kyp said, struggling to find the best words to use that wouldn't make anyone feel slighted or untrusted with the mission at large. "We could use a group watching their backs out here."

"Fair point," Drew conceded. "Who do you suggest stays here?"

"You and Austin, Jainey, Cass, Zane, and Rennie." Another deep breath. "And I suggest Jainey and Rennie remain outside of the main battle even after the Senefestrian blood is retrieved and abilities are unlocked."

"You're sidelining me?" Rennie snapped.

"Your powers weren't limited by a Ritual," Kyp rushed to respond. "You shouldn't have any of this. You were artificially created."

"I was trained to fight," she responded, her jaw going rigid.

"You were marked for death," Kyp corrected. "You all were." He motioned to the Guardians. "And it wasn't fair. It never was, but at least we can give them stronger tools to fight with. But empathy can't win wars."

"Maybe not," Rennie said through gritted teeth. "But it can tell me how much of a goddamn fraud you are."

"Ren," Drew said, but Rennie kept on going.

"You have no idea what you're doing. Lately, your brain is a constant churn of sickening emotion. You don't even believe any of us will make it, but you want me to stay here for what? Me being here won't protect Jainey."

"That's about enough out of you, kid."

Austin stepped between Rennie. Kyp hadn't realized he'd stepped in closer.

What had he been thinking? Was he trying to intimidate her? Was he going to fight her? The thoughts inside of him had taken on something feverish and wrong, and he could see himself reaching forward and snapping her neck.

That wasn't him.

"Rennie, tensions are high right now," Austin said, placing a hand on her shoulder. "None of us are doing too good upstairs. But he is right. Things get out of control in there and if you and Jainey want to throw your hat in the ring, we ain't gonna stop you. But you should definitely start out here. The element of surprise will work way better for you." He turned to face Kyp and took a step closer. "I'm gonna give you a pass because you've literally died for us before. But loom over her like that again, and I will crack that dense skull of yours, ya hear?"

Kyp swallowed thickly. "You'd be right to. I'm sorry, Rennie. I'm just…" He didn't have an answer.

"Yeah, I know," she said softly. "Okay."

Jordan's eyes searched him, like he didn't recognize him. Kyp didn't dare look at Jainey or Jacklyn.

"Why do I have to stay outside?" Jainey asked, her voice shaky and worn.

"Because I don't want your blood anywhere near the MacroRift they made you open," Kyp answered and was met with no resistance. He took breath after breath to calm himself. His hands were shaking and he could not go into battle in this condition.

"Okay, that decides it," Cass said, "although I think I disagree on being out here, but I'm good with the idea of having Kylie's Key-level strength out here, protecting Jainey."

"Even if it means you won't be there protecting Jordan or Caleb?" Zane asked.

"Jordan can take care of himself," Cass said. "And Caleb…" Kylie's voice broke through. "I'm not sure there is any saving Caleb."

Jordan's fists clenched at his sides.

"Jacks," Drew said, stepping closer to her. "When I met you, I never thought I'd say this next sentence, but of the Keys, you're the one with both a level head and battle experience."

Ray shifted on his feet uncomfortably, his arms crossed over his chest.

"I expect you to call the shots in there," he continued. He turned toward Kyp. "And I expect you to be our broadcast signal keeping everyone apprised of the situation. Can I trust you to do that?"

"Your confidence in me is staggering," he responded, struggling to find his equilibrium. "I've got it."

The four Keys gathered their chosen weapons and headed for the MacroRift.

"What do we do once we're in?" Jordan asked as the Keys began the trek along the cracks in the ground.

"We play that by ear," Ray answered, his voice detached in

a way Kyp hadn't heard in quite a while. Everyone seemed to be slotting themselves back into battle mode.

Red light spilled like blood from each of the fissures in the ground, and Kyp pushed down the memory of Jacklyn with this very same red reflecting in her eyes, tinting her face as she bled into the MacroRift. His stomach twisted.

The first fissures they walked past were spidering cracks. But as they cautiously advanced, the fissures became jagged tears that threatened to buckle as they moved. At least they didn't need the light from the fire in Jacklyn and Jordan's hands anymore.

The longer they went, the more difficult the journey became and the shakier the ground below them got. Kyp reached out to grip Jordan's hand in his. Ray had already grabbed onto Jacklyn.

When they finally reached the entry door that would allow them through, they found it unguarded.

"Why wouldn't they—" Jacklyn didn't get to complete her question before the erratic movements in front of her caught her attention.

Surrounding the Rift, the Sirins who once guarded this entryway were locked into battle with hissing and screeching Gorvhans, who were racing for the opening to the Dawn.

In the center, with one foot each in the MacroRift, three Senefestrians fought each other for entry.

"You wanted Senefestrian blood?" Jacklyn asked, a smirk thrown over her shoulder at Kyp. "I think I know how you get it."

"Oh?" Ray asked.

"How do we fight creatures like that, but keep ourselves from getting hurt?" she asked. "Distance."

Kyp felt a smile pull across his face. He knew what she meant. It was crazy, but he could do it. He had to do it.

He'd just never tried anything like it before.

Closing his eyes, his mind reached out for the closest Senefestrian. It was a strange thing, entering the mind of something so primitive and exerting his will over it, replacing its drive. If he allowed himself to ponder the differences between the two minds present, it would drive him even more insane, so he focused instead on the things they had in common.

The need for survival.

To the Senefestrian, survival was on the other side of the Rift. He felt that palpably. Here, it was hunted. Here the Senefestrian was hunted by Arvokians and Sirins alike. Senefestrians were cannibalistic, each other's hunter as much as the other interdimensionals. The Senefestrian was afraid.

It turned its head up to the ebony sky, now dotted with spare sparkles of light, and roared. It felt Kyp's intrusion into its mind. But sadly, he couldn't let it loose in the Dawn.

But he could keep it alive.

And that was where they found their common ground. A being would only allow control if it wasn't crossing a line. Mother couldn't control Gana to make her harm her own sister. She couldn't control Kyp to get him to drop it when he believed she was attempting to kill Jacklyn. It was why his father, Hector, had been such a disappointment. He had been able to break her hold to protect Jacklyn when it wouldn't cost him much, but not when it would cost him his place in the Order.

A being would let you control it if you could make it trust you.

That was how he had accomplished any control he had ever held. Even that one time…

Jacklyn didn't want to think he would control her. So she never did. And it haunted him still.

This creature would only bend to Kyp's will if it trusted him to get it out of this alive.

And so it must be treated with compassion and tenderness.

Kyp showed it what he needed. He needed it to win against the other Senefestrians. It would have humans backing him up. Hunters. And if it accomplished its task, they would help it to escape.

The creature turned toward Kyp so the eye on the side of its head faced him. Its triangular head towered high above them all. Its yellow skin had the familiar geometric print of brown shapes across its hard carapace. It stood on armored spiked legs, each step cracking the unstable earth beneath them.

Its thin, cat-like pupils settled on Kyp, and he felt its acknowledgement. The creature reared back on two legs and drove one spike-like leg into the eye of the Senefestrian beside him.

"Jordan, help me," Kylie's voice came from behind them.

"Cass?" Kyp hissed, but he couldn't break his concentration. Not now.

"I heard your plan," Kylie said. He could practically hear her shrug. "It was a stupid plan, though, so I amended it."

Jacklyn swore.

"Telekinesis it from the body," Kylie explained. "And I'll

control the water in the blood."

"Can't look away," Kyp muttered as he helped the creature through dodges and bobs to avoid the counter-attacks of the other two Senefestrians. "Does that make sense to you?"

"She's got a repository for the blood," Ray said. "Looks like a plan."

"Nice thinking, Kyle," Kyp said. At Kyp's order, the Senefestrian parried the attacks of the others long enough for Jacklyn and Ray to pick up their side of the attack.

They stepped forward, yanking the hoods of their jackets up over their heads and pulling their turtlenecks up. They had come prepared to fight a Senefestrian, and they'd covered themselves to avoid Senefestrian blood getting into any wounds.

"Let's go, honey," Ray said, waving Jacklyn forward.

They yanked shotguns free from the holsters on their backs. In unison, they fired on the two rival creatures. One shot. Two shots. Again and again. Echoing sounds Kyp felt down to his feet. Pieces of the carapace flew from Senefestrian arms, legs, thorax. Jacks and Ray stepped forward with each movement, and Kyp took the opportunity to use his Senefestrian to plunge holes in their exposed spots.

Jordan got to work. With his eyes clamped shut, he removed the blood from the wounds, droplets of red floating free in the air above them. Then Kylie stepped in, yanking on the droplets and forming them into ribbons that floated through the air. With Jordan's help, she funneled the streams of red through the air and into the jar she held in her hands.

More gunshots rang in the air, and it was nearly enough for Kyp to miss Kylie's murmur.

"Jainey, now."

"What do you mean, Jainey?" Kyp shouted, his mind warring between the mind of the Senefestrian and his own concern for his daughter.

"She's just using telepathy from their spot. She got the jar."

He nodded. "Time to pull the trigger on this."

"Shit," Jacklyn cried.

Kyp followed her gaze, but he couldn't see what she did. What he did see was the way her gun's aim shifted to a point behind the creatures.

Someone else had joined the battle.

Kyp guided his creature through spearing its pointed legs into the soft underbelly of each of its enemies. In its mind, he felt the flesh tearing away, its legs clawing its way through skin, sinew, and scraping against bone. Blood splashed from the wound, black ichor flying forward.

And oh God, it was going to hit Jacks and Ray. Had they been wounded yet?

They had both turned their attention away from the Senefestrians, moving toward whatever waited behind them, and though they ducked low, the blood rolled off their leather jackets in rivulets.

He prayed to whatever or whoever was listening, from whatever faith he had left, whatever this damn war hadn't taken from him, that they had no lingering open wounds, no scratches, and that none were still to come in the fight.

Piercing screeches returned as the Senefestrian tossed one of its enemies onto the Gorvhans and Sirins, who were busy battling each other. It crashed to the ground, sending everyone off balance.

Jacklyn spilled to the ground, but Ray caught her by the elbow, dragging her back to her feet.

The gravelly sounds of the Sirins shouting orders filled Kyp's ears, along with the melodic Ritual chanting of Arvokian. Ray shouted gruff orders, sending Cass around one end with Jacklyn. Ray rushed in on the opposite end of the circle, Jordan following closely behind him.

The Senefestrian, now the only one still alive, turned to acknowledge Kyp. It leapt over the mangled bodies of its enemies, rushing through the front of the structure and ruining the steel-fortified bamboo walls.

It galloped toward him, its feet hitting the ground, clacking over the rocks, and squelching through the soft ground. It moved at a speed that made Kyp's blood freeze and his breath stutter. He bit down on his lip so hard he tasted iron.

"Please. Stop."

The reaction that flooded his mind was a whine not unlike the sound a puppy would make when accused of some injustice.

The Senefestrian stopped in front of him, head bowed, cat-like eyes aimed down at him.

"You've seen what my people can do with only small guns. On the other side of the Rift, there are bigger guns. You would be hunted there too, and you would die. Run. Run where you know how to hide."

The response was a series of pictures and thoughts and formed words, but it seemed to understand him.

"I'm sorry I had to use you to protect my family. The others will be too busy to hunt you right now. Go. Be safe."

It leaned even further forward, the point of its head tilting down. Kyp felt the farewell across the connection.

He hadn't expected the kindness, though at this point, he should have learned better. He reached out gently, his hand petting across the thick carapace, a gentle touch in thanks for its assistance. The Senefestrian leaned up into his hand, for a moment shedding all its normally destructive tendencies.

It chuffed, then took off back the way they'd come, past the camp they'd set up for the Guardians.

As it disappeared from his view and into the darkness, something else came into view.

The rest of the Order. They were heading toward him. And Kyp watched, captivated.

Zanc led the way, electricity crackling from her fingers. That was new. As was the glowing aura surrounding Cass. Drew flew forward on a gust of air, and Austin ran with an enhanced speed Kyp had only ever seen in the Madisons.

Energy Key. Spirit Key. Light Element Key. Body Key.

His idea for the Ritual had worked.

And just in time, it seemed.

Jordan shouted, enhancing his voice until it boomed around Kyp.

"Mom, no!"

Kyp didn't wait to respond.

THIRTY FIVE

CRUMBLING

JACKLYN

"Get the fuck away from her!" Jordan's voice screamed through my mind and into my ears as he yanked Caleb off from where he'd tackled me, knife burying deep in my stomach.

It wasn't like Body Keys felt pain more than normal people or anything. That little asshole.

Jordan's fingers were wrapped in Caleb's collar, lifting him high enough that Caleb's toes barely brushed the floor. For a moment, it looked like he would say something, but he shook his head instead, hurling him toward the army of Arvokians and Sirins that stood behind him.

And at the back of that line, stepping down from a back entrance we hadn't known about, a pair of Arvokians.

I didn't have time to wallow in my pain. If I stopped moving, I'd die here. I pushed myself up to a seated position just in time to see Ray get trampled by the rest of the army on the other side.

I scrambled to my feet, but the knife was still lodged in my stomach, and it felt like I was burning alive there, like I imagined fire felt to people who couldn't wield it. My knees gave out, and I hit the ground with a jolt I felt all the way up to my jaw.

Electricity cut through the air, zapping the Sirins who'd been poised to tear into my father. A whoosh of air blew my curls across my face, and then Ray was gone.

"What the fuck?" I whirled, trying to rise again to find him, but Austin was on his knees beside me, pushing me back to the floor by my shoulders.

"Hey, hey, hey," he said, flexing his fingers. "Stay still. I'm gonna yank out that knife so you can heal up, yeah?"

"Wait, Ray—"

"He's safe," Austin interrupted. "And Kyp is helping Jordan fight. And his plan for the Ritual worked. We're all—"

He yanked the knife free from my stomach and a scream tore from my throat.

"—fully unlocked and enhanced Keys. Sorry. If I warned you, it woulda been worse."

I sneered at him, but I threw a fireball over his shoulder into the face of a waiting Sirin, knocking it backwards and onto the waiting tip of Drew's sword.

"I can heal you, if you need," Austin said, glancing between the two of us like we were angels for rescuing him. Like we all didn't do it for each other all the time.

"I'll heal soon enough. Help me up?" I needed to get back into the battle.

"Let me," he urged, glancing around at the rest of the battle, obviously struggling with holding back.

"No," I stressed. "You can't overuse your Aegis. You're used to some Aegis ability, but not what Keys have. You'll drain yourself if you use too much and then you'll be no good to anybody."

A thunderous crash had us both ducking and covering our ears. It wasn't that close to us, but it wasn't far.

Damn it. Why was war so fucking noisy?

Austin finally gave in on not healing me, grabbing my hand and yanking me up along with him.

To my right, Ray and Zane fought through a stream of approaching Sirins with little more than their Aegis, a shotgun, some knives, and, in Zane's case, an assault rifle. To my left, Kyp, Drew, and Cass fought through Arvokians with swords, axes, and Aegis abilities. Across the expanse of the open Rift, Caleb and a younger Arvokian had Jordan pinned down. All while an Arvokian with ruby-red hair watched on, taking it all in.

That had to be Lyira. Not a single Arvokian we'd seen here had that color hair.

A member of the Arvokian Guard rushed at me, proof that I was taking too long assessing my situation. I didn't even bother wasting bullets.

"Nap time." I reared back and swung the butt of my shotgun across his cheekbone. It connected with a crack and he sunk to his knees.

I needed to get to Jordan's side of the fight, but battles raged on either side, and a Rift lay in the middle. I didn't have time to fall through.

"I'll get you over."

Jainey.

"Don't look for me. You'll give away our position."

Our. So she and Rennie were both ready to jump into the fight.

"I'll telekinesis you over. Protect Jordan. Running jump."

I remembered the time I jumped out of a window and trusted Kyp to float me into a window and just ended up smacking my head on the window frame.

I frowned, but ran toward the MacroRift, anyway.

A Sirin stepped in front of me, but was picked off by an arrow to the eye. An arrow? Andaria's crew used arrows. Backup had arrived, and wherever they were, they were picking the enemy off from afar.

I leapt over the Sirin's body and kept running until I reached the last of the solid ground, and then I diverted my Aegis energy into my leg muscles and shot forward, determined to make most of the jump on my own.

A push against my back was my sign that it wasn't all my Aegis that put me over. Jainey helped, and I was going to do what she asked in return. Not like I wasn't, anyway.

I barely landed before I pulled my gun from its holster and pointed it square at the space where Caleb's head met his neck. "Move and Jordan will be cleaning your brains out of his hair for hours."

Caleb froze, but even more noteworthy was the way the Arvokian froze.

"Hi, Mom." Jordan offered a fragile smile. Red bloomed along his eye from the punch Caleb had just thrown, but it healed just as quickly.

I pulled another gun from the holster on my left and aimed it at the Arvokian boy. "Now listen. I've had enough of death. Particularly the death of people my son cares for. So you're both going to back the hell away from him, and we're going to talk this out."

"I don't care for him," Jordan said, motioning toward the Arvokian. "You can kill the fuck out of that guy."

"You are a lousy excuse for a warrior," the Arvokian volleyed back.

Between his place with Lyira and his superior way of speaking, I figured out who this guy must be. "Merrick. Great to meet you. Your mother is very worried."

Lyira moved closer as we spoke.

"My mother has limited vision. She got a glimpse of what we had planned and turned away."

"I'm sure she's lucky you didn't kill her like she did to the Council," I said, motioning at Lyira with my chin.

"She is my mother," Merrick said, as though that clarified anything. "I wouldn't harm her. She would come to see the truth when the Eventide overtook the other realms, and she rose to be the queen of an all-powerful race."

Jordan scooted to his feet, making his mama proud. I trained him well. He walked around the outside of the three of us, planting himself between myself and Lyira.

"Do you really believe Narah would retain leadership?" I laughed. "Did you trust Lyira to give that to her? With the power she has? She intends to lead. And if your mother doesn't get in line, she'll kill her."

"You know a lot about that, don't you?" Caleb growled. "Killing mothers."

"Maybe I do," I said. "I know a lot about betrayal, too." I lowered my guns. Jordan was out of immediate danger and back on his feet. And I preferred to keep my firepower ready for Lyira. "Lyira worked for years as the head of the Council Guard. And then she and her warriors slaughtered the Council. It was brutal, even to me."

"She wouldn't do that," Merrick muttered.

I tossed Merrick the pin we'd found at the scene of the crime. "She would. She did."

"It doesn't matter," Caleb shrieked. "None of it does, as long as you're dead!"

He lunged at me, but I blocked, pushing him back. A flurry of battle erupted around me. "You want to tear the world down because you're alone?" Blocked a punch. "You're not the first person." Another. "You're not even the only person here."

I punched him in the stomach. "Do you know what I did when Lavinia got my mother killed in battle and killed my sister?" A right cross. "I didn't wallow. I started the fuck over. I found people." Another punch. "And when I finally got my revenge, do you know what it did?"

The wind kicked up around me. "It did nothing!"

"Shut up!" The wind spiraled around him, lifting him off his feet.

A flash of fire zoomed by me, engulfing the structure's bamboo wall. The fireball had been Jordan aiming at Lyira, but Caleb's wind had thrown it off course.

I couldn't leave Jordan alone to face Merrick and Lyira while I worried about Caleb. We needed back-up. I groped for Jordan's hand, but the wind between us held me back and away.

I couldn't reach him.

"Call Dad! Call Cass!" I gasped, but Caleb stole the breath from my throat, just as Kylie had once done to me. Jordan shot me a quick look, but he was caught up, one arm catching a sword strike against his own aimed by Merrick, and the other holding Lyira back telekinetically.

I couldn't tell if he heard me.

Caleb rose above us, and Lyira smirked and lifted Merrick along with him.

Jordan swore. We didn't know what Lyira's Skeleton Key Aegis contained. But now we had a better idea. At least one side was Light Elements, so she could control air and water. The other still remained to be seen.

The ground rumbled and split apart beneath our feet. The pull of Jordan's Aegis yanked me through the wind and dragged me to him before I could plummet into the Rift.

With a flick of Lyira's wrist, more of the ground split beneath us, and I realized exactly what the balance was. Half Light Element, half Dark Element. That meant she'd have control over air, water, earth, and fire. All powerful weapons to have in an Aegis, and they were all at our enemies' disposal.

"Lyira! Caleb! Merrick! Enough!" Kyp spoke behind me. I wasn't sure where he was. I was hesitant to take my eyes off the three enemies before us.

"Kyp! I'm sorry, but I hope this has been a good lesson in not trusting people." Lyira genuinely looked excited to see him. "Not that you'll survive long enough to use it."

"You're killing your own! For what purpose?" Kyp asked, his voice hardening as he approached. He had to be using his abilities, because this entire portion of the ground was torn chunks of earth now. Jordan and I struggled to balance on the one I had. "We could form a treaty. There is no need for further bloodshed."

"Bloodshed? You want a treaty?" Lyira snapped. "Do you think any of your petty squabbles even matter? Gorvhan blood, Sirin blood, Key blood, Guardian blood. Arvokian blood. It's all the same to me. And do you know what blood does?" Lyira smiled. "It seals Rituals."

The screams of battle swirled around them, carried on the wind Caleb had created. It got more and more tumultuous as time went on. Whipping through our hair, stealing our breath, leaving Jordan and I clasping at each other to keep ourselves from toppling off of the small bit of ground we stood on, and into the Dawn.

"It doesn't matter," Caleb mouthed. "Blood seals Rituals. But not all blood." He sought Merrick out, but Merrick stared off into the distance.

My leg exploded in pain. I hadn't seen the rock coming, but Lyira had managed to send one careening into my knee.

"Caleb, please," Jordan cried. *"You don't want this. You can't want this. We were like brothers. We could still be."*

Caleb's expression collapsed. *"But your mother—"*

"—would take you in like you were her own." Jordan looked

over at me and I nodded.

I didn't like Caleb. But I did feel terrible for him. And I hadn't liked Kylie or Ross, but they had eventually become allies. Maybe without all this pain and terror, we could find a way to work. Be a family. The way Caleb needed.

A splatter of blood splashed against the wall, but I couldn't turn to see where it had come from. Panic flooded me.

"That's what you get, ya right bastard!"

Dad. Okay, that was reassuring.

"In the Eventide, the Arvokian race are the most powerful beings in creation," Lyira said.

She smiled, despite the blood splashing, the booming noises, the fetid odor of charred flesh. "And as the only Skeleton Key that is Arvokian, I am uniquely suited to lead my people and unify the world under my power. I've earned this. I *deserve this.*"

"Lyira," Caleb said. "I think maybe you should stop this."

"Caleb?" Merrick's head snapped to face him.

More of the rocks crumbled away from beneath their feet. I clutched Jordan's hands in mine.

A shout echoed through the hall.

"Lyira!" Was that Narah? Her words were followed by a flood of Arvokian, and Dhamian was unfortunately unable to translate.

I wouldn't look away from Lyira. I couldn't risk an attack from any of our trio of potential enemies. I had to trust the army of Arvokians and the others to protect my back. Or hope that my spider sense would tingle when it was needed.

"Your arrogance is unparalleled."

Kyp. Relief sped through my heart. He'd been a tad too quiet for too long.

"What makes you better than any other Arvokian? Any other Skeleton Key?" he asked. "I should have seen this. I believed you were helping us. But I should have seen how clearly full of yourself and what you believed was the right thing to do."

"Caleb, please," Jordan begged within our minds again. *"Nothing is worth the end of the world."*

"But... but Jacklyn..."

"Lavinia would have killed me." I needed to make sure my point got across. I needed to impress upon him how damn serious I was. How determined.

How could I do that? What could I say?

I had to make him see I was serious. That he was important, that I would take a risk to protect him. I tore my eyes from Lyira, and locked on to Caleb's tear-filled eyes.

"When I met Lavinia, I tried to like her. I tried to please her. But she wasn't who I believed she was. And you can ask Kyp, there was no pleasing her. You know Lavinia trapped me there to kill me. She wouldn't have left that room until I was gone. And it was the second time she'd trapped me in a fight to the death. What should I have done? How else could I have handled it?"

"You relegated me to the role of a freak for far too long, Narah!" Lyira's words broke through the psychic conversation. "The Council believed I wasn't worthy of anything but guard duty. Zelnick was the only one who saw more in me."

"Zelnick saw all the Skeleton Keys as pawns." I allowed my gaze to flit between Caleb and Lyira. "A science experiment he wanted to duplicate. Someone entertaining. He saw me as entertaining, too. It wasn't a good thing for me, as it turned out."

"The council and the kingdom saw the potential of corruption in you!" Narah shouted from safer ground. "Had I a choice, I never would have agreed to your betrothal to my son."

Caleb made a choked noise, even in his mind. *"Betrothal? It was all a lie."*

"But Cxarana handled that for me." Lyira grinned. "She's very helpful. She even brought the perfect murder suspects to the castle."

Merrick's jaw tightened.

"You killed King Rhiadon," Kyp said. "Of course you did."

"This didn't have to be this way," Narah said. "Forces were amassing, Sirins were rebelling. We could have worked together to each have our own places of power."

"Yes, I could do that," Lyira said. "Or I could move you all exactly where I need you. Which has worked out pretty well for me."

I had to get to her. I knew it. Whatever she was working on was already in effect. We were missing something.

I wrapped a hand around my dagger.

Jordan leaned into me. "She'll kill you."

"Then she better be faster than me."

But I wasn't planning on throwing the dagger. The dagger was the distraction. The direction I wanted her to believe I was taking. The real method of her destruction would be my latest parlor trick.

Caleb and Lyira were keeping the wind blowing. And that wind harnessed something I could now control.

Energy.

I closed my eyes, focusing my Aegis on feeling the wind around me, on finding the place where that push centered itself, where that magnificent work of nature formed, and then, even when my hand plucked the dagger from its strap on my waist and poised to throw it, I redirected the energy back. Behind me and away from us.

"I am tired of being considered some runt, not Arvokian, not human, not even a Key. But I was always better than all of it. The only one fit to lead you all. Narah! How does it feel to know that the person you relegated to guard duty is the person who turned your own son against you?"

My dagger should have blown away, but it wouldn't. Despite the stumbles I heard the wind cause around us, my dagger flew true.

She did see it though, and raised one hand to block it.

It stabbed through the center of her palm. She was fast. But not fast enough for me.

She smiled, a vicious light in her eyes that belied her otherwise cool facade.

Caleb glanced between me and Lyira, horrified.

"How does *that* feel?" I snapped.

"Painful," she admitted. "But Key blood is Key blood, as I said." She yanked the knife free from her palm, then shook it out over the Rift. Once.

Twice.

She flipped the knife from her hand, edge over edge.

Jordan yanked me down, ducking out of the way, but the knife wasn't aimed at me.

It swerved around me, carried on a single blast of wind.

I whirled, following the path of the knife as soon as it made its way around me. It sunk directly into Narah's throat.

Merrick bellowed a stream of invective. Caleb was already moving. I tensed. But Caleb wasn't coming for me.

He lunged at Lyira, tackling her to the ground. "You lied! You lied! You lied!" Each word was punctuated with a punch to her face.

Lyira didn't try to fight back, and Merrick didn't come to her aid. He was frozen in place, staring at his mother. Cxarana bent over her, and Jainey rushed to her side, resting her hands on Narah. Dhamyan hovered closely beside them, and the Kingdom Guard surrounded them.

Jainey wasn't supposed to be in the middle of this war zone.

And that's what this was. The war had spilled far beyond the space within the structure. Farther than I could perceive from my position. All I could see was row after row of Sirins and Gorvhans and Arvokians battling each other. I knew there were humans among them, but I could barely make them out amidst the larger armies native to the Dusk.

While I still watched the battle, searching for a way to get to Jainey, a way to find the others in this mess, the ground beneath my feet bobbed and dipped.

A quick turn revealed Lyira had gotten a hand free from her grapple with Caleb. When she pressed it to the ground, the chunks of earth we were all balanced on disintegrated beneath us.

"Protect Jainey," Jordan shouted, telekinetically pushing Kyp off and away from the Rift, just moments before we went tumbling through the Rift and back to the Dawn.

THIRTY SIX

KYP

The sheer number of warriors between Kyp and Jainey was constricting. One child and his wife had been sucked through the Rift with their three largest enemies. The other child was in the center of the warzone. The rest of his family was scattered throughout this mess of battle. And he had to make it through to Jainey.

Jordan's directive to protect Jainey seemed a lofty goal indeed.

You'll never manage it.

Spirits, voices in his head? Kyp wasn't sure which, but he didn't need this crap right now.

He shoved through the warriors fighting around him, like they were insignificant, because at the moment, they were. He needed to get through to his child.

You're going to lose her. Everything you've done will be for naught.

An explosion of pain in the side of his head sent him tottering to the left. He caught his balance and turned to find a Sirin rolling across the floor to grab a recently abandoned sword on the ground. Kyp spun his axe with a twist of his wrist, preparing to do some damage.

A blast of water ripped past Kyp, flooding the Sirin's nose and mouth. Electrified, the water sparked as it hit the creature, sending him down to the ground.

Kyp whirled to find Drew and Zane working together and zapping as many Sirins as they could reach. Just behind them, Austin lifted a rifle to put a bullet in the head of a member of Lyira's guard.

"How many of them do ya reckon we'll have to put down before this is all over?" Austin asked.

"Better question is how many we'll need to put down before we can get to Jainey," Kyp said.

Austin looked like he'd just sucked on a lemon. "Whaddya mean? They were supposed to stay outside!"

"They didn't," Kyp answered, telekinetically pushing an approaching group of Gorvhans back and into a wave of Sirins. "And I didn't see Rennie anywhere."

"Fuck," Austin growled.

"Drew, what should we do?" Zane asked, shooting out another zap of electricity. "Without the opposition leaders present, I'm not sure what we're fighting to accomplish anymore. This will not be over any time soon. We need an end game."

"An end game starts with our regiment in one place," Drew said. "Ray, Cass, Rennie, Cxarana, Dhamyan, and Andaria. Once we're reunited, then we choose our next steps."

"Cxarana and Dhamyan are with Jainey. And Narah. Who may

already be dead by now," Kyp admitted. "Lyira stabbed her in the throat. Jainey rushed in to heal her. Hopefully, she succeeded."

"Can't say I'm her fan, but I hope you're right." Drew sighed, flicking another rush of water from his palms. It lacked the pressure of his usual offensives. "Truth is, we need an out. At least temporarily."

Kyp heard what he didn't say. Aegis energy was running low. They were running out of time.

"Don't overtax yourself," he advised. "Axes and swords work just as well."

"And guns," Austin chimed in, blowing the head off another Arvokian. "Now, can we find our kids?"

You'll never get to them in time. You'll never get to Jacklyn in time.

Kyp's head ached, but he engaged his Aegis, reaching out to his team and hoping for a response. He didn't get a verbal response, but their positions lit up in his mind like a map. Which meant they were all alive. He projected his new knowledge to the others, and they were good to go.

The good news was that Rennie was with Cass and Andaria. Since he knew Jainey was safe with Dhamyan and Cxarana, they headed for their other kid first. Besides, Kyp was pretty sure Austin would turn that gun on him if he suggested anything otherwise.

He just wished Rennie and Jainey had listened to his orders. But that would be too good for his blood pressure.

Drew closed his eyes and a blast of wind pushed away everyone in our path. The red sea of warring interdimensionals, and they walked through it, soldiers fighting against the wind, struggling to hold on to their stances. Drew wobbled as he ventured through, and Austin held him up.

Kyp and Zane exchanged a worried look. There wasn't much fight left in Drew. They'd have to keep an eye on him.

After a few minutes, Rennie came into view. She swung around effortlessly, escrima sticks gripped in her hands, reaching forward to poke one into her Arvokian enemy's stomach. When he pitched forward, she crashed the other into the back of the Arvokian's head. She moved fluidly, and Kyp found he was proud of how far she'd come in the time he'd known her.

Andaria's back faced Rennie, and she slipped forward, her bo staff sliding between her hands and over her fingers, striking the head of her Sirin enemy, then sweeping the legs out from under him. The next enemy Sirin swung a sword, but she blocked it, bending her arms to let the staff absorb the blow, before she ducked and spun out of his way. She dropped the staff from one hand, swung it around his throat, and grabbed it with her other hand, pushing up into his larynx.

They continued to advance, which brought Cass into view. The Ritual had amplified her Aegis more than the power of the Sentinels normally did, and she glowed, luminescent from the spirit energy around her. She blasted the approaching army with fire, water, and wind.

It was all so frustrating. He wasn't sure the Gorvhans even knew what they were fighting about. They saw humans and attacked. They saw the fellow Gorvhans they'd oppressed, and they attacked. They didn't care that Lyira would destroy them if given the chance, or they weren't aware.

All the different opposing groups had just ballooned this into a nightmare where nobody knew what they were dying for.

Drew cried out, and Austin didn't hesitate. He tackled the Sirin that had bitten down on his shoulder, tearing his teeth from Drew. Austin shoved the Sirin to the ground. "Fuck. This. Shit." He battered them with his fists until they stopped fighting back. Blood sprayed onto his fist and face.

Zane swept in to check on Drew, leaving Kyp to hold off any oncoming attackers.

"Take cover, friends!" Ray's voice shouted from over his shoulder.

Kyp didn't have time to doubt. He'd known Ray for long enough.

"Tex! Get Drew!" He grabbed Zane around her waist and yanked her backward. Her eyes went wide as Kyp covered her body with his own.

A moment later, Austin and Drew landed beside them. Just in time for the flash of light to temporarily blind him. The boom of the explosion assaulted his ears. A wave of heat, followed by a rain of debris and something else Kyp didn't want to name, swept over them.

"You okay?" Kyp asked, struggling to blink his vision back to normal.

"I'm good," she said, although she had a scratch across her cheekbone he hadn't noticed before. It was probably the least of their worries.

She gently pushed him off her, scrambling to her feet before whirling in the direction of Ray's voice.

Kyp turned to the others, who were already getting to their feet, thankfully safe.

"You alright?" he shouted. He wasn't sure if the clanging of swords and the general rush of movement around him blocked out the sound of his own voice, or if the damned grenade Ray had thrown into the mix impaired his hearing. "Any of that blood yours, Tex?"

Austin was literally dripping blood, and it had smeared all over Drew's dark blue shirt, which was torn where the Sirin had bit his shoulder. He leaned on Austin for support. Kyp hated seeing him, seeing them like that.

He was a warrior, but he wanted to go home.

"Not enough of it's mine to be cause for worry." Austin jerked his head toward where Zane was getting right up in Ray's face. "Somebody's in trouble."

"And he should be." Kyp rushed to join her.

"We don't even know where our allies are and you're creating explosions?" Zane asked.

"Where is Jainey?" Kyp asked. "If you don't know, no higher power will be able to protect you, I swear."

"Jay-sus walked, give me a little credit. Of course I know where the little love is. I know where they all are. I was just with them." Ray smiled, a spark in his green eyes. "Let's go meet up with them. They've holed up close to the Rift. I was told to blow my way through." He jutted a thumb behind him. "They're going to help."

Cass, Rennie, and Andaria emerged from the shadows.

Austin and Drew joined them. "Good to see your faces."

Kyp squeezed Cass's forearm before turning his attention back to Ray. "Told by whom?"

"Cxarana." Ray swallowed hard. "She just became queen."

"What?" Austin asked. "What happened to Narah?"

"Lyira threw a knife at her," Kyp said. "Hit her in the throat. But didn't Jainey get there? Why couldn't she heal her?"

"There was poison on the tip of the knife," Ray said. "Something she cooked up with a Ritual as well."

Drew swore wholeheartedly.

"Did you see Jacks and Jordan go into the Rift?" Kyp asked.

"Wait, whatnow?" Zane asked.

It was like something had shaken free within Kyp once his anger dissipated. "They fell in. And they're there with Lyira, and Caleb, and Merrick." His breath quickened. "We have to get there. They're trapped with them."

"They're trapped with Jacklyn." Ray pressed a hand to his shoulder. "You know that girl. They're trapped with *her*. Besides, Cxarana is pushing us toward the Rifts. She has some kind of plan or something."

Kyp swallowed, allowing himself to take comfort in Ray's words for a moment. "Wait, does Cxarana even have the say here? The monarchy shared leadership."

"With the Council. All of whom are now very dead. As is the Sirin Circle, although that was done by the rebels. If our allies can keep up the momentum, the Arvokians and the Sirins will be under new leadership soon enough," Ray said.

"Cool, whatever," Rennie said. "Fuck interdimensional politics.

My boyfriend is on the other side of that Rift." She glanced at Kyp. "I think we can agree on that, right?"

Kyp smiled, but it was a fleeting thing.

"Not to mention we need to get this damn Rift closed soon." Drew pointed at the sky.

The dots of light in the Dusk had torn through the canopy and were now strips of light. No wonder it had gotten a bit easier to see. The torches surrounding the enclosure had been lighting the way, but he'd left the enclosure a while ago. He should have questioned it, but Kyp hadn't had the presence of mind.

Kyp's head swiveled as he took in their surroundings. The explosion had been enough to temporarily give them some breathing room and blow back the surrounding armies. Just far enough. However, troops were starting to cautiously make their way back to their tract of land.

"C'mon," Ray said, breaking through Kyp's observations. "Let's do this."

The path to the others wasn't clear, but they couldn't let that matter. One by one, each of them fought through their surrounding attackers with guns and blades, with punches and kicks, and when they had little other choice, with Aegis attacks. They needed to conserve their Aegis, they knew it, but the battle wasn't allowing for it. Drew was already running very low. They were trying to stagger use, but every time they got down a rhythm, someone got a bit too close or a weapon was knocked out of a hand, and suddenly, Kyp needed to telekinetically push, or Zane needed to electrocute.

They only had so much fight left.

Still, they made their way through, their movements mechanical and urgent. He got lost in the constant slash and push of battle, his focus burning on one goal.

And then he was through. One second, he was hacking away at a Sirin, and the next, it had fallen and Jainey was in his arms. He caught her on instinct as she wailed his name.

"Hey there, Peanut." Kyp cuddled her close. "Good to see you safe."

She pressed her face into his chest and held on to his jacket with both hands.

Cxarana and Dhamyan greeted them quickly before Cxarana issued orders. "Dhamyan, tell the rest of our army to fall back and take the allied Sirins with them. Get them away from this Rift." She inhaled sharply. "Raymond Madison, on Dhamyan's word, please issue another one of your destructive explosion devices. We need a show of strength if we are to garner any respect from our opponents."

The rest of the Order and its allies took their places insulating Drew, Kyp, Jainey, and Cxarana from anyone who neared the Rift.

"We need a plan," Drew said. "This won't begin to reach its end until we can prove the leaders of these factions are dead."

"Motherfucker!" Ray shouted, jumping aside, and an Arvokian guard came barreling toward Kyp. She wore Lyira's crest.

He swung his axe up and brought the handle down against her temple, then returned to the conversation. "Even if we do prove Lyira's death, that may not be enough."

"We can't do that if we don't kill her." Drew sighed.

"She's on the other side of the Rift," Cxarana said. She jutted her chin forward, and though there were tear tracks in the dirt on her cheeks, she plowed forward. "Take the Order and leave this place. Find a way to seal this Rift and never return."

"What?" Jainey cried. "But what about you?"

"My dear sweet child." Cxarana reached out, running a hand along Jainey's curly mop of hair. "This war won't end until it's ready to. It's been, in many ways, going on before you knew of it, and though it has hit a fever pitch, it will likely continue in many ways beyond this day. But now that factions of Sirins and Arvokians are united, we now have something we never had before. Numbers. And unfortunately, you can provide little extra to that."

"But we made it worse," Kyp said. "We stirred up trouble."

"Tensions were rising before you returned." Cxarana pressed a hand to Kyp's face. "You know I care deeply for you. But this battle is not yours to end. You can't come in and save an entirely different world's problems. It is the problem of your kind. Many of humanity's battles—"

"No history lessons, please," Kyp said. "I don't need them. I need you."

Grief choked him. Cxarana had been a part of his life since he was a child. He may not have loved the gift she had given him, but in making him a Key she had given him so much of the life he now led.

"You do not need me, Kyp Franklin." She smiled, toothy and wide. "You are your own man. Our people punched our way into your world and then expected you to find a way to correct the problem."

Another explosion.

"We controlled humanity's champions and forced this war between Dusk and Dawn to continue far longer than was required."

"Not you," Kyp said.

"No, not me. But now that I can see it all for what it is, how can I not try to correct it?" she asked. "You are all my children. My exquisite family. I must make this right."

"But—"

"No, Kyp. I have the power to do this now, however ill-gotten. And I will. You can't fix our problems. And we can't fix yours. Go. Save your world. Save the Dawn. And live as you always should have."

She handed him the pack she'd carried through the Dusk.

"Live a normal life, Kyp Franklin." Her eyes reflected the flames surrounding them. "Good luck to you all."

Kyp's tear-blurred eyes locked on hers. He would miss her. Batty Old Witch. When had that nickname for her he'd had back before this all began to become fond?

"Long live Queen Cxarana," Kyp said, and behind him, his entire group echoed the sentiment.

He reached forward with the arm that wasn't holding Jainey, and crushed Cxarana's bony frame against him, pressing a quick kiss to her hair. He moved toward Andaria next.

"Farewell. Accomplish reputable goals." She bobbed her head in acknowledgement.

Kyp had to smile at that. "You as well, Andaria."

She leaned forward and whispered in his ear, something he didn't have time to process before Dhamyan's voice entered his mind.

"*Kehp.*"

Dhamyan stood behind him, arm extended. They grasped each other's forearms, converting the greeting into a hug.

"*Thank you for all that you've done,*" Dhamyan said.

"*Thank* you."

Dhamyan nodded, motioning with his head toward the MacroRift. Kyp followed his direction. With his throat burning with unshed tears and his baby crying at his hip, he led his team back home.

THIRTY SEVEN

JACKLYN

I couldn't breathe.

I'd crossed through Rifts four times now. The first time, I'd had Lavinia as a cushion. The second time, I'd been dead. The third, I'd jumped in knowingly. But this time, I flew up out of the Rift, only to crash unceremoniously onto the rubble of the warehouse we'd returned to life in just a short time ago, and it had knocked the wind out of me hard.

Air whistled through my dry, split lips. Couldn't remember when I'd gotten that particular injury, but I'd go with it.

I wasn't the only one down for the count, either.

"You alive over there?" Jordan asked in my mind. It nearly made me laugh. Even his mind-projected voice sounded wheezy.

"Barely," I shot back.

What little light existed in the remains of the warehouse was a sharp red from the MacroRift I'd landed just in front of. The Rift emitted a dull roar, like ocean tides smacking against the rocks. I wondered if anyone else could hear it, or if it was just me.

Biting back a groan, I turned onto my side. There were bound to be rock-shaped bruises all over my back. That was going to make me irritable. I channeled my Aegis into healing my body. I could fight without my Aegis, but I couldn't fight like this. I needed to be fresh again. I mentally advised Jordan to do the same.

"Already healing a broken arm. Don't like that we're in a room full of rubble with a Skeleton Key that can control rocks."

Earth, fire, wind, and water. Her Skeleton Key combo united all the elements. A scary combo. But I had… fighting skills? And I could run away really fast. It was better if I didn't end up blowing my entire Aegis just to walk again. Then I had a lot more cool stuff.

Lyira thought she was doing something smart when she dissolved the ground beneath us, and perhaps she was. Or maybe it was the last gasp of an idea. But what she'd actually done was put us in a unique situation. If Lyira had just had as bad a fall as we had, we had nothing to worry about.

I was smart not to count on it.

"I've always wondered what was so special about the Dawn," Lyira said. She sounded rather aloof for someone who had just been thrown through dimensions. She must have had a much better landing.

I tried to figure out where she'd risen based on the sound of her voice. She wasn't far, maybe about fifteen feet away. But that left me with the question of where Caleb and Merrick were. And which side they were on.

Not to mention that, while I could communicate with Jordan, I couldn't actually see him.

Alright. Enough healing.

I pulled myself to my feet, the strain evident in my voice. "The Rifts have been open since before you were born. Hell, you could open your own. You didn't have to start an interdimensional war just to come for a visit."

"Do you truly believe that?" She kicked at a chunk of concrete. "King Rhiadon kept me close at hand. I was too powerful to be trusted without a tight leash. Shame about his grandson, though."

She leaned down, pressing her palm to the ground. The rubble on the floor clattered around violently. A large slab of concrete flipped over to reveal Merrick, his limbs and neck twisted at unnatural angles.

My chest tightened. The part of me that had grown up outside the Order hurt at the sight. Cxarana's nephew, Narah's son. Just like that, he was gone.

The part of me that had spent the last few years fighting for my life saw one less enemy to worry about. I hated that part of me.

"I was Rhiadon's impossibility. He took me away from my parents when I was young and made me work as a guard under his thumb, where the Council could watch over me. I deserved better. I deserved a life. But he didn't allow me that. So I chose what Zelnick offered me… and then I made it better. If I couldn't have my life back because I was too powerful to be trusted." She smiled, a creeping, vicious thing. "So I made sure to behave in a way that would prove all of his concerns to be correct."

"A middle finger to 'the man.' I can appreciate that," Jacklyn said. "What I don't appreciate is the middle finger to us! We've been used as pawns, same as you."

"Have you not been paying attention?" Lyira asked. "I don't want to govern. I want to rule. And you were never going to let me take over, were you?"

The ego on this chick was monumental. But she wasn't all-powerful. She had to be wounded from that fall, too. Sure, she seemed to believe she was pretty damn spectacular, but she wasn't stupid. Not if she'd managed to pull the wool over our eyes from the beginning. Not if she'd outsmarted Lavinia and Zelnick. She was delaying. I'd play her game until I figured out why.

"I still won't. You'll have to kill me first," I said, flashing her a smirk.

"Gladly."

I heard the rocks before I saw them coming. Lyira had pulled back more of the crust protecting the Dawn from the Dusk. And then she aimed it at my head.

But Daddy raised a championship level runner, even without using my Aegis. Or at least… Daddy had intended to raise one.

I dashed to the side, and the rocks hit the ground with a dull thud just as I pulled from the hum of energy in the air and returned a volley of electric bolts.

She may not be an ordinary Key, but as it turned out, neither was I.

No more conserving energy. She was strong, and she was planning something. And I wasn't about to make another mistake. Not like I had with Lavinia. I still had my power, but my skill mattered more here. I needed to stay on my toes and contemplate what she was trying to get me to do.

Because she was definitely trying to get me to do something.

Lyira stumbled backward as she brought up a shield of rubble to block my electricity. She tried to play it off smoothly, but I'd rattled her. And that's why she started circling me. I followed the movement, boots crunching the gravel beneath.

"You know the Sirin resistance exalted you!" She eyed me, sizing me up. "They believed your return to the Order to be the turn of the tide. When they looked back on the closing of the Rifts, they thought you brought it about. But it was me. That Kylie girl was going nowhere. A dead end no matter how Lavinia tried. But then you returned. Zelnick enjoyed your attitude, and I enjoyed your connection with Kyp. How easily manipulated it could be."

"Yeah, yeah, you lined us up like dominoes," I grumbled, keeping a watchful eye on her hands. I knew what they could summon. It was her earth and wind powers I was most concerned with. We matched on the fire, and water was not the way to go with electricity in my repertoire.

Maybe I shouldn't have divulged that little piece of info.

She stopped in front of the Rift's opening and brought up another smattering of rocks, propelled by a push of wind. I dodged, but this time I rolled forward, ignoring the flash of pain as my hands sliced on the rubble beneath.

I needed to hurry up and get close enough to fight her short range, or she was going to pull the very floor out from under us.

I barely let my feet hit the ground before I threw a kick at her head. She parried, and we traded blow for blow. I kicked her in the jaw, but she blocked and bashed a rock against my head. Pain exploded along my jaw and my world tilted. I stumbled to the ground.

A crash pulled Lyira's attention away from me.

"You don't understand!" Caleb shouted, but his voice was muffled. "We need to get her away from the damned Rift! And you can't be the one to do it!"

"Of course not," Jordan snapped.

I worked my jaw, trying to massage away the pain. I pushed myself to my feet, listing sideways as the ground tilted beneath me. I swiped my arm over my eyes, clearing the blood dripping into them. When I looked up, I found Lyira standing over the edge of the Rift. She'd yanked a knife from somewhere, and she sliced along her forearm, holding it over the swirling red light. Her blood dripped in, and the Rift began to pull forward, cracking through the concrete.

I wrapped a hand around her arm and threw her away from the Rift, jumping after her before she could do any more damage.

I recognized Lyira's methods. She must have had enough time working with Lavinia that she'd learned a few things. She wanted me angry. Enraged. She wanted to throw me off my game. She wanted me to hate her and blindfold myself with it, to choke on it, so I couldn't think straight.

I wanted to hate Lyira. She had been the reason for everything that had happened to me since I got here. She clearly wanted me to know that. But revenge meant nothing anymore. It was a spiral.

I couldn't hate her. But I also had to stop her.

There was one thing I had that Lyira didn't, for sure. The thing that made me *me*.

My fight.

I landed on top of her, aiming punch after punch at her face, pummeling as I listened to what was happening around me.

"You see, Jordan?" Caleb's voice reached my ears as I pulled my fist back once again. "Skeleton Key blood only makes it grow. I fucked up. I know I did. But I was wrong. You said I had a place with you, so let me earn it. You and I can't seal a Rift. We never could. Lyira learned it a long time ago. She was the first. We can only open them. Zelnick lied to Lavinia when she said Jainey's blood would close the MacroRift. It never could!"

"Why take her side?" Jordan rasped.

Bones snapped beneath my fists. Cartilage shifted. I pulled back, staring at Lyira's bleeding face.

"I thought… It doesn't matter," Caleb said. "It doesn't matter. She made me think she gave a shit about me. But she never did." A sob. "I was wrong. I'm trying to fix it. I was so wrong."

Lyira's eyes were out of focus. Rocks knocked together around me, but they weren't doing much.

"I've got her," Jordan said. "I've had her for a while now."

I climbed off her, rocks scraping my knees. "She didn't Mind Block?"

"She did." Jordan stood beside me, and Caleb slightly behind, like he was using Jordan as a shield.

"Jordan couldn't do it alone, but we're Skeleton Keys. The rules don't work that way for us. It's like the thing with our blood. It doesn't close Rifts, it opens them. The only reason what you did closed the last MacroRift was because of your lifeblood. And there were two of you. I'm not sure which part helped more, now that I think about it," Caleb babbled.

I stood. "Jordan, hold her."

"On it."

I stepped directly in front of Caleb. "I'm going to close this Rift. And once I do, you can't open one again."

Tears spilled over from his pale blue eyes, running down his cheeks and cutting clean strips into the grime there. "I never opened this one. I wasn't lying about that. It was Lyira."

That was unexpected. I was sure…

"I didn't come to your house looking to betray you. Liv had made me an offer and left me to decide. I don't know if I ever really had a choice. But when I realized Kylie… my mother… was there, in Cass… I don't know, it felt horrible. I was still hoping there was some way to bring her back, like you got brought back."

"Kyp and I only came back because our bodies were thrown into the Eventide," I said, wincing at the vulnerability in his eyes.

"And my other mother was a murderer. I thought… I thought I was supposed to fight for her. Keep her from dying like Kylie had. And then she introduced me to Lyira, and she was so captivating and she had been hurt too, and couldn't rely on anybody. And I thought maybe we could rely on each other. Like she understood me. But she didn't. She lied. And the only person who ever understood me had watched me betray him by helping these awful people and I… I didn't mean to. I just kept doing the wrong thing. I never expected it to get this far. I thought you'd have killed me by now, so I didn't have to really do it."

Damn it. The little shit was making me cry, too.

"I think…" I swallowed against my parched throat. "I think sometimes we forget how young you guys are. You and Jordan have only been around for so long, even if your appearance says otherwise. We look at you and it makes us feel like we can't baby you like we do, Jainey."

"Jainey isn't even as old as she looks," Caleb corrected.

"And there's that part of you that's related to Kyp." I smiled. "We can't treat you like you're the age we were when we fell into this mess. You're very different."

Caleb stared at me, lower lip trembling, like he was waiting for me to hand down judgment.

"I'm going to kill Lyira. Not because I want to. I don't even want revenge the way I did with Lavinia. You see, I understand you, you little rage goblin. You're pissed and you want the world to know. I was that way too. But it just hurts. I never liked killing. I thought I'd relish killing Lavinia, but I didn't. You understand?"

He dropped his face into his hands. "I hated what I did. Every second of it. But… I didn't think… I didn't know."

"And now you do. So I have to ask you. Are you going to let me kill Lyira, or are you going to try to stop me? I'm prepared, either way."

He lowered his hands from his face and crossed his arms over his chest. His lower lip was caught between his teeth. It broke my heart a little, but I couldn't help but smile.

"What?" he asked, his voice taking an edge.

"It's just that you look like Kylie," I said. "I don't think she ever looked at me without at least a little bit of scorn."

Caleb huffed a humorless laugh. "Do it. I'm going to let you."

I nodded and walked toward Jordan.

"No more blood," he warned. "Some already got to the Rift. That wound she cut into her arm is bleeding pretty heavily."

The churning chasm of red did look a little wider, now that he mentioned it.

I knelt beside her, blood seeping into my leggings. She didn't move, but her face was twisted in indignant anger, her lips curled into a snarl, but her eyes were wide with terror.

There were undoubtedly more humane ways to do this. But a fight would mean more blood, and the MacroRift was already far larger than it should have been.

Tears pooled in my eyes. I was so tired. I never wanted to be this. But this was the end. The final kill.

"I'm sorry," I said as I gripped her head in my arms. A tear ran down her cheek.

The snap of her neck was a soft sound, a quick pop that normally would barely be heard over the ambient noise of the open Rift. Somehow, however, it echoed through the warehouse, swallowing up every other sound the way a black hole devours light.

It wasn't the most honorable death, but war wasn't all that honorable, as it turned out. Being a hero wasn't just about saving lives. It was about doing things nobody else could do.

A hand landed on my shoulder.

Lyira's body spilled from my arms and I whirled, ready for a fight.

Instead, I found Kyp's handsome face staring back at me.

I punched him in his arm, holding back my true strength.

"Ow."

"When the hell did you get here?"

"Just now. You didn't hear us?"

I swallowed and my throat ached. "I hate this. I hate having to kill. I hate all of it. I just…"

His arms wrapped around me, and he pulled me close. I let my head fall against his chest and cried for everything I'd done as a soldier in this war.

A war that may actually be coming to its end.

Cradled in my husband's embrace, I stared out at the tear in the ground and waited to see what else I'd be forced to lose.

THIRTY EIGHT

OPEN WOUNDS

JACKLYN

I pulled myself together, swiping at my eyes and getting my breathing under control. I gave myself no more than five minutes before stepping away from Kyp and surveying the others, each standing before the MacroRift. They all looked tired, covered in various cuts and bruises. Austin held his arm bent and close to him and Ray seemed to be nursing his ribs. Drew's hand was clamped tightly over a nasty bite in his shoulder, and Rennie appeared to be limping. Cass gripped Jainey protectively to her, all the while both looking about ready to drop from exhaustion.

"Cliff Notes version?" I asked.

"Cxarana asked us to stop Lyira and seal the Rift. She and Andaria will take the rest," Kyp explained. "And Andaria has a theory on how to seal the Rifts."

I pressed my hands to my cheeks. "Okay. Okay. What do we have to do?"

"And what are we doing about him?" Rennie asked, her chin jutting out toward Caleb, fists clenched at her side.

"Believe it or not," I said. "He's under our protection now." I looked at Jordan.

He shrugged. "I know, Ren. But trust me, he sees it. He needs us."

Rennie sighed, shaking her head, but I got the impression she knew it wasn't worth arguing about at this point. That empathy power was pretty useful sometimes.

Caleb cleared his throat. "The last MacroRift only closed because two Keys gave their life blood to close it. It had nothing to do with your relation to Jainey. This one is bigger. It will take more Keys."

"And not Skeleton Keys," Jordan cut in. "We open doors. We don't close them."

"Would three do it?" Ray asked Kyp. "If all three of us closed the Rift, would it work?"

"I don't know that it would override the whole lifeblood requirement." Kyp frowned. "I'm not sure anything will. Lifeblood has a lot of power in it. The Rituals consider it to hold a piece of our souls."

"We've done this before. We know the rules," Ray said dismissively. "We don't have time to waste. Every minute is a minute the war can come back through here. Cxarana asked us to seal it. We can't worry about the lifeblood thing. What we really need to worry about is how to seal it without it opening again."

"He's right," Kyp said. "The Senefestrian taint in my blood made it reopen."

"What about the Ritual you all did for Papa?" Jainey asked.

"It sealed the wound in him. Maybe it will seal the wound in the ground."

"I don't think it's supposed to work that way." Cass frowned.

"No, but she's right," Jordan said. "We used the Ritual to unlock the abilities in the Guardians in a way it wasn't designed to be used, and that worked. If everyone's a Key now—"

"Wait!" Caleb said. "Everyone's a Key now?"

"Feckin' yes, you gob shite! Keep up!" Ray groaned loudly, gripping his middle.

"Dad?" I reached for him, and so did Kyp, but he backed away from both of us.

"I'm fine," he grumbled. "Just banged up my ribs, is all."

"Why can't you heal them?" Zane asked, her mouth tightening.

"Because closing this Rift and doing it the right way is going to take all of us," Ray said. "We're all exhausted, and we've been using our Aegis all day. Bleeding out for this will take all I have left."

I didn't like it, and from the looks of everyone else, none of us did. But he wasn't wrong.

"Ah, come on," Ray said, clapping me and Kyp on the back. "Zane can wrap up my ribs after." He waggled his eyebrows.

"Ugh, fine," Kyp groaned. "But I don't like this."

"Do we have the ingredients to pull off the Rituals?" Cass asked.

Kyp slid Cxarana's backpack from his shoulders and settled it on a stable spot of ground. There wasn't much left in the warehouse. And it wasn't a small warehouse. There was the space they stood in and the rest of the giant field of rubble had dropped into the

MacroRift.

He unzipped the backpack, and Drew pitched in, removing each piece from the bag.

Jordan took this time to approach Rennie, but Caleb caught him by the wrist. I stiffened.

"Dude, wait. That's too close to the edge. Be careful."

Jordan smiled. "Thanks, man."

Rennie huffed impatiently. "Well, we can all hang out later. I can't become a Key, so we're pretty useless."

"Not really," Ray said. "We need someone to do the Ritual."

Drew and Austin pulled the kids aside to teach them the Ritual, since none of them had been there for the first go-round. Cass lowered Jainey to the floor, and she took off for team Skeleton Key and Rennie.

While they worked on that, the rest of us knelt on the ground in the remaining free space.

"Step on it, kiddos," Ray called. "We don't have all day."

"He's right," Kyp said. "Before we fall in the damned Rift."

"Hey!" I snapped. "You two cool it off. Better they learn it right than quickly. If it makes you feel better, I'll bust the walls down so we have more space."

"That's more Aegis than you should expend," Zane noted.

I made a face. "Fine, I'll have Jordan do it."

"Just get started, sugar," Austin shouted. "And don't cut yourself too deeply. When this gets finished, there ain't any more healin' happening."

Kyp reached into the bag and produced the gold athema blade.

"The key, no pun intended, is to each use some blood, but our numbers will mean we can avoid giving too much." He sliced into his palm, then handed it to me.

I took the gold dagger, the one I had used when first pledging myself to the Order, and I was surprised at the emotion that sparked within me. My throat hurt with the suppression of emotion required to keep me from bursting into tears. This was really it. The books were on this side. There were no Skeleton Keys on that side. Barring ours stepping out of line, closing this Rift would end it all.

Swallowing it all back, I pressed the dagger against the flesh of my palm and sliced. I hissed as the blood welled up, my palm like fire without the flames. I held my palm over the Rift and passed the dagger to Ray.

He did the same, and passed it down to Zane, who passed it to Cass, and down the line.

The Rift started to seal. Slowly, the ground ahead of us knit shut, and we crawled forward, continuing to let our blood drop into it, even when Ray, Austin, and I needed to reopen our wounds so we were still bleeding enough.

"You know," Ray said beside me once we'd crawled forward again to keep up with the shrinking Rift. "I think I was too mad at you to really impress this upon you the first time, but I want you kids to know I'm really proud of you."

Jordan stepped forward and performed the Ritual over the Rift so the Senefestian taint would heal.

"I'm proud of all of you, really. But I'm so incredibly proud of you, Kyp and Jacklyn." He smiled weakly at us.

He didn't look so good, and something panged in my chest. None of us were feeling so great. I mean, we were all bleeding a pint or two into this thing. That was all it was. He was just pale from blood loss. We probably all were.

"I left you all a mess," Ray said. "And you did your best. I started a war that left you with so many enemies and you managed to find the best fecking collection of badasses I've ever met. This family you made, they'll be with you when this is all over, and thank goodness for that, because I'm about to drop a whopper on you. And I'm about to piss you off. Which serves you right, really. You tried to piss me off last time. But that wasn't the natural order of things. A man's not supposed to watch his kids die."

"Dad." Tears welled in my eyes. "What the hell are you talking about?"

He stabbed his thumb in Kyp's direction. "He knows."

I followed his eyes to Kyp's shaking hand above the Rift. I didn't bother looking into his eyes. I didn't need to.

"What the *fuck* is he talking about, Kyp?"

"He didn't think anyone knew," Ray said. "But Andaria told him he needed lifeblood to close it. Maybe he thought enough of us were going to do this at once that we wouldn't need it. He didn't know I was so badly fecked. It's only closing because… because…"

"Ray?" Zane said.

He leaned back into her, lying down with his hand hovering over the ever-smaller Rift. "I'm sorry, Zane. I couldn't warn you. You're my best friend, you know that, yeah?"

Zane sobbed, cradling his head in her lap, and brushing his

sweaty brown curls back from his forehead. "I love you."

"Love you too," he whispered, voice raspy.

He was getting paler by the second.

Kyp leapt to his feet. I didn't even think. I followed him up.

"No!" Kyp shouted. "We're not doing this! We'll find another way, dammit. We're not!"

I stepped between my husband and my father. "Kyp, what is going on? Tell me the truth."

Ray lifted his tight black T-shirt to reveal a ragged gash along his side, which was slicked with clots of purple-tinged blood. "Shrapnel from the grenade. I didn't pull it out until you all started bleeding yourselves to close the Rift. I honestly wasn't sure I'd be quick enough. You certainly were all taking your time."

Kyp dove around me, sliding on his knees until his hand was pressed along the gash. "Jacks, quick. We need to heal him."

I was frozen, my feet rooted to the floor. My chest heaved and sweat dripped down my brow and underneath my hair until it had slicked its way down my back. I stared at my father's bright green eyes. They were dimmer by the minute. I fought down vomit.

"Don't you feckin' dare." His eyes flitted between mine and Kyp's. "Don't you dare start this nightmare again. Not for me. I meant what I did. No lookin' back now."

"Jacks, come on!"

"Please, baby girl. Let me end this. If someone has to die to end this, it should be me. Let me die to give you this dream. Our dream."

I stepped away from Kyp, tears running down my cheeks.

"Are you fucking crazy? Jacks! What are you doing?" His voice was ragged, torn. Cracking. I couldn't look at him.

My father was asking me to let him save me. He hadn't been able to before. But now…

I couldn't take this from him. He was trying to give us a gift.

"It won't close without lifeblood," Ray said, his head on Zane's lap, eyes rolling as he struggled to breathe. "You were right, son. We created you for war. We put you in the middle of battle. We were wrong. Let me set it right." His eyes drifted to the left slightly. "Get your claws out of him, you bloody witch."

"No, please. Please don't do this," Kyp cried. Tears dripped onto Ray's wound.

"Son," Ray said. "Never forget what is worth remembering, nor ever remember what is best forgotten." He flashed a shaky smile. "'Tis an old Irish blessing. Felt like it fit you most. But I'm sure you could use it too." He looked around at all of us.

I was watching my father die. I wasn't going to stop it. I could, but it would doom the world. The Rift would remain open. And it needed to close.

"Come on, Birdie," Ray said. "Give your da a hug."

"I can't," escaped on a sob, my stomach heaving as I pointed to Kyp's hand on his wound. "He'll…"

Kyp gasped for a breath and pulled his hand away. I hadn't realized it before, but everyone else was circling us now, Austin, Cass, and Drew crowding Kyp as if ready to pull him away if needed. Jordan and Jainey dropped to their knees by Ray's legs. Zane curled over his head, smoothing his hair back from his sweat-soaked forehead. She was livid, her teeth gritted, but he whispered to her and she nodded, a small sob escaping.

I stepped around them and collapsed against Ray's side, Dad's side, the side that was unwounded. I buried my face in his neck, my tears soaking into the collar of his shirt.

Ray reached forward and yanked Kyp down onto his other side. "It's not fair, I know. But it's time I faced my mess and stopped running. Woulda done it last time if I coulda."

We cried harder, throats raw and chests aching. My heart didn't exist anymore. It was disappearing with the light in my father's eyes.

"Finally, I did what I been tryin'…since…your age." His voice faded a bit. "The Order is good, kids get a normal life, yeah?" A hoarse whisper. "Love you, kiddos."

"We love you too, Daddy," I whispered into his neck.

Zane let loose a horrible sound, something that scraped against my soul, and I knew he was gone.

I looked up. Ray's green eyes, once sparkling with mischief, were now empty and cold. The red glimmer of the MacroRift was sealed.

All that surrounded us were tearful cries and the rubble of the warehouse around us.

THIRTY NINE

ONE TINY DECEPTION

KYP

It did not go down the way Kyp had expected.

They returned that night to the brownstone, after which Zane had tearfully explained that despite everything, Ray had wished to be cremated, and have his ashes spread at his childhood home, the Franklin estate, Kyp's estate.

"He said," Zane cried, but put on her best Irish brogue, "'Don't want to leave behind much. Don't wanna get dug up by someone's overzealous puppy.'"

Jacklyn had laughed.

Nobody questioned the estate. Kyp thought it was so he could be closer to Jaina, but he'd never tell Zane that.

"With everything, I didn't get to ask," Jacklyn said to Kyp, whispering in the night as they lay in bed beside each other, tangled up in one another like they would lose each other if they moved the wrong way, if they stopped touching each other. "How are you feeling? This is the first time you've ever been without your Aegis."

"It still doesn't feel real," he admitted, careful to be as honest as he could allow. "But I guess, without an Aegis, memories and knowledge would fade over time. It's not like I'd forget everything I knew overnight. How about you?"

"I feel…like I only ever called on it when I needed it," she said. "It'll probably be awhile into the future before I realize I can't just kick down walls." She huffed a breath through her nose, a laugh she couldn't quite manage.

"And what do you want to do?" he asked. "After. Where do you want to go?"

"I… I don't know. I can't stay here. I still feel him in the walls here, you know? He lived here for so long. We'll always have a home here. And maybe one day, I'll be able to come back. But not yet. Not yet."

Kyp brushed a hand through her soft, dark curls. "Then where should we go?"

"After the estate?" she asked. "I was thinking we could hit the road. The kids have never gotten to see the country, the world. We could spend the next few months traveling. And figure out where we want to settle from there. Is that crazy?"

God, he loved her, he adored her spirit, the way she was always thinking about their kids. "Not at all. Let's do this."

Kyp hadn't expected the entire Order to go along with the idea, but they all seemed to agree to the desire for a fresh start. They broke into two groups of five for the solemn drive to the estate. The

Franklins filled one car—Kyp drove, with Jacklyn in the passenger seat, Jordan, Jainey, and Caleb in the back. Austin drove the other, with Drew in the passenger seat, Zane, Rennie, and Cass filling the remaining seats.

Jacklyn held the container of her father's ashes. Kyp couldn't find much to say, given the circumstances, and the kids weren't faring well either. There was a bleakness to every one of them, an inability to move beyond the dread of what they had left to do. Granted, for some, it was deeper than most. Kyp felt like he was drowning in it.

Halfway through the ride, when Jacklyn couldn't be alone with her thoughts anymore, she called Austin on speaker. The entire team chimed in on both sides, and together they talked through their plan for once they got there. They would pack up those things they could use to start life over, keeping what they could possess legally, while Zane used her learned hacking abilities to create unique identities for all of them. Or rather, identities with their names but an actual paper trail.

Before they left, they would take a walk through the forest, spreading Ray's ashes along his and Jacklyn's favorite running trail.

It made sense to return there, to where it all began for the only true parent Kyp had ever had. The place Ray had often longed to return.

All this despite the fact that Jacklyn wished to go anywhere but there.

Jacklyn, who was probably suffering far worse than him, but who was powering through to keep him and the kids standing.

"You have to remember, sweetheart," she said to Jainey when she burst into tears near the end of the ride. "Ray isn't gone. We know he isn't. My mom and my sister, Gana, were gone long before you were born, and they were still here to protect you. They're just hanging out together, waiting to see what me and you do next. Like watching a movie starring your favorite people ever. Right, Jordan?"

"Right. Of course," Jordan answered, but his voice was thick with emotion.

"Probably somewhere around where Kylie and Ross are too," she said, looking over her shoulder at Caleb.

He smiled faintly, and Kyp's heart melted.

"You're such a good mother," Kyp said when she settled back into her seat.

"I'd better be, right?" She cracked a tired smile. "What does one do after being a superhero and going into retirement? All that talent has to go somewhere."

"You could do anything," Kyp said. "Be anyone. I'm glad you chose this. I'm glad you chose us. Despite… everything." His voice cracked, and he hated himself for it. He lowered his voice. "My brother's behavior led to… what happened…" He couldn't put words to Ray's death.

Not yet. "And you're taking in Caleb, adding him to the family like—"

"He's part of this family, as fucked up as it is," she said with a shrug. "I killed both of your parents. And his mother. When does it stop?"

"I didn't love my parents. Not the way you… we…" His throat

dried further the more he spoke.

"He needs us." She said it so simply. Like it was a given.

It helped quite a bit that Caleb had spent the evening before looking through the books and Arvokian herbs Cxarana had given Kyp, and performing a Ritual on himself that would cleanse his blood of its unique abilities.

Caleb believed it removed his Skeleton Key abilities, so he would never have the option of opening a Rift. He wanted them to trust him.

Kyp didn't know if that Ritual did what Caleb seemed to think it did, but it was a big enough display of trustworthiness that he started to feel better about Caleb joining them.

They reached the estate and started piling out of the car. It could have been about the long drive in the cramped car, or it could have been the knowledge of what they were about to do, but anxiety flooded Kyp's veins, leaving him jittery and breathless. He stretched his legs, walking around the car to where Jainey was waiting, staring out at the line of bushes surrounding the house.

"Hey, Bean. Want to go for a walk?" Kyp asked, kneeling beside her. He spiraled a finger through one of her curls.

"Okay," Jainey replied, a gloomy smile on her face.

He reached out for her hand to where she still only came up to his mid-thigh. She was so small. A lick of guilt charged through him, but he pushed it down mercilessly. This was for the best.

He led her away through the forest, along the path he'd worked through time after time to meet with Jacklyn when they'd first started it all.

He felt foggy and detached, like he was moving through a nightmare, the air stifling despite the breeze that rustled the leaves on the trees. He'd fought so hard to build this life, to get this chance, and he knew he was about to ruin it.

"It's beautiful out here today, isn't it, Bean?" He was trying to lead up to what he was about to ask of her. He knew she would overreact to his suggestion, but she was far more likely to agree than Jordan.

"It's nice, I guess." She swung their arms. "What do you really want to talk about, Papa?"

Kyp slid a look her way. "You're supposed to be less perceptive now."

"I still know what I know." Jainey shrugged. "I just won't learn that fast anymore. Or store all the information like I used to. So… it will probably fade over time."

Kyp nodded. She'd given him the perfect segue. "What if I told you it didn't have to fade?"

"But it has to," Jainey said. "The open Rifts feed our Aegis. I only get to keep my special Skeleton Key blood."

They came to a clearing in the forest. The gravestones the family had created for Jacklyn and Kyp came into view, a seedling of a willow tree planted behind it where the stump of their destroyed willow had been dug out.

He couldn't do this here. He led Jainey past it toward where a small brook ran through the woods. The brook was shored up with smoothed rocks and pebbles, many of which were large enough for them to sit down. He waved Jainey along to sit down beside him.

She primly smoothed her jacket underneath her before she sat.

Kyp lifted a thick tree limb from the ground. "What if we reopened a small Rift? I have a book with an Arvokian Ritual in it that would hide it." He used the tree limbs to sweep aside some of the undergrowth and other fallen tree limbs in front of their rock-stools.

And there it was. He'd finally said it. It was no longer just a thought in his head. He couldn't take it back now.

Jainey's head tilted, her curls bouncing. "Mama said you guys didn't want the Rifts open anymore. You don't want us to have an Aegis. You don't want to have to fight."

Kyp shrugged. "Yeah, well… I guess I had to be wrong at some point."

"You're wrong plenty," Jainey said. "I just don't point it out because I hate when you're all mopey."

"Jainey, for goodness' sake, if you can't be kind, be quiet." He sighed.

"I'm like Mama," she said simply.

Kyp kept the cringe that triggered inside. He didn't want to think about Jacks right now.

Instead, he reminded himself that doing this would insure Jainey's ability to defend herself should she ever need to. But it also meant she would never turn into a child that was just like any other child her age? Did he want her to?

What if Jordan's anxiety continued to make his abilities flare up? That wouldn't happen the way things were now. Did he want to force him to continue on that way?

He knelt in front of her. "I've seen inside your mind before. It can be dark in there. I trust you understand. They don't, but you do. God help me, I don't want to know how you understand, or what that implies. Despite your innocence, you would do anything to defend your own. You know how essential it is that we hold on to our Aegis."

"To protect our family," Jainey said. "To make sure we keep our Aegis in case of an attack."

"Right," he said, something twisting in his heart as he removed a dagger from his boot, along with a sachet of Arvokian herbs.

It didn't matter. The miniscule amount of guilt he felt would be more than made up for by the inestimable joy he felt at the continued safety of the children, of Jacklyn, of what was left of their family. He could hold them together. He could make this work. All he had to do was maintain this one tiny deception.

He handed her the dagger, his hand shaking. Her eyes met his, a frown growing as she gripped the handle. Jacklyn's dagger. The one Ray had left her. It was only fitting.

She looked at the handle for a moment, then back at him one more time. He nodded, coaching her along. He knew why she hesitated, but now was the time for action—before they lost their chance.

She sliced across her palm, blood dripping onto the ground before them. She sprinkled a selection of herbs atop the blood, and the ground split open into the tiniest glowing red scar.

He could feel his Aegis return to him in a rush, like a dog that had simply been awaiting his master's return.

"Papa." Jainey's eyes went wide. "Papa, what now? Mama's not going to be okay with this."

"I planned for that," Kyp said, his lips turning up slightly. "Now we have to perform the Ritual that will hide—"

All at once, a surge of voices.

No!

Kyp, what are you doing?

I begged you not to.

You're just like her.

You damn fool!

My son.

Spirits screamed within him, and he covered his ears on mere instinct, as though that would keep the voices in his head at bay. He fell forward onto his knees.

"Papa!"

Her voice broke through the cacophony.

And then hers.

"Well, well, well. Puzzle, puzzle. I solved the damn puzzle."

Jacklyn stood at the edge of the clearing, arms crossed over her chest.

FORTY

WHISPERS

KYP

Kyp felt the blood leave his tingling face as his eyes connected with Jacklyn's.

She sauntered closer until she stood just on the other side of the Rift. The rift between them had clearly grown bigger than the red and angry slice cut into the ground.

"Were you ever going to tell me?" she asked. "Or would you try to make me believe we'd somehow sealed the Rifts without losing our abilities?"

Kyp sighed heavily and rose. "I could make it so you never remember this. I could make it so it stays open, guarded, and you never know. And we'll live our lives and finally get free of this place."

"Papa," Jainey gasped.

"Like hell you would." Jordan emerged from where Jacklyn had entered, Caleb beside him.

"I'm not going to let you make a mistake like I did," Caleb agreed. "I know it's rich, coming from me, but those Rifts ruined my damn life. They stay closed."

The rest of the team filed through around them, each face more disappointed than the next.

"He wouldn't do that," Cass said, her chin jutting out like a challenge. "If he wanted to, he wouldn't say it. He would just do it."

He flinched. Cass really did know him well.

"I guess you're right," Jacklyn said. "He would have done it and then lied about it to my face. Like he did when he allowed the Rift we had come through when we returned from the dead and erased my memory of the Rift there. Or like he lied when I asked him why he was reading through all the Arvokian spell books, when the reason was so he could do *this*." She hurled a dagger down right through the center of the book. "You bastard. I thought we were a *team*!"

The accusation set his blood aflame. "I thought we were *too!* But you held me back from curing Ray."

"This started before that!" She waved him off. "Seal it, now."

Kyp gritted his teeth. "Seal it yourself."

"No." Tears filled her eyes. "It has to be you that closes it. Nobody here should close it. Because if I can't convince you to close it, then what's the point? You'd just find a way to open one again."

"But what if we can still bring him back?" Kyp asked, and his vision blurred. "What if we can still save him?"

"We can't," Cass said. "He's already well into the world of the spirits. I can feel him there. Can't you?"

Kyp shook his head vigorously. "I don't like looking there. I can't."

"So you're going to resent me forever for following Ray's wishes?" Jacklyn asked.

"No," he snapped. "I'm going to resent you for making it so that Ray's gone and one day I'm going to forget him."

Jacklyn softened slightly. "You're not going to forget him. You never could. And that's beside the point. You've been hiding this for far longer than that. Give me an explanation. Make me understand."

You're a failure.

"Guess I'm just exactly as power hungry as Mother was," Kyp said, though every word was bitterness dripping from his tongue. He picked at the scab on his wrist, where he'd bled himself dry over the Rift he hadn't wanted to close. "I didn't know Ray had a life-threatening wound. But he had to get all noble on us and die. Without lifeblood, the Rift would have stayed open. Just open enough."

Austin shoved a hand through his ash-blond hair. "C'mon, man. You know better than this."

"Shut it, Tex," Kyp snapped, his voice strained. "I'm thinking over here."

"You're thinking a mite too much, I'd say."

Jacklyn's gasp mirrored his shock. *Ray.*

It wasn't coming from Cass. In fact, it was projected between the two of them, a trail of smoke and shimmer vaguely shaped like the man he saw as a father.

Kyp shot a questioning look at Cass.

"I'm stronger now. You desperately wanted to see him." She shrugged, her face sheepish. "I wished Ray was here. And…" She motioned at Ray.

"Dad." Jacklyn smiled, but it was a shaky thing. "You look like a Force ghost. It's actually pretty cool. Is it boring over there?"

"Never a dull moment, Birdie. Tons of entertainment. But I'm not liking what's on this channel at the moment." He flickered slightly. "Cass wanted me to visit." He reached a hand toward her, then lowered it with a shake. "You have to learn to let people go, child."

"I'm working on it," she said, her throat tight.

He moved in front of Kyp, looking him in the eye while floating just above the tear in the earth.

"Cass thought I could talk you out of this. But she should know by now that I'm not enough to talk you out of a real bad idea once it's taken root, isn't that right?"

Kyp couldn't look at him. He focused his attention on the swirling Rift, on his shaking hands.

"So I brought a bit of backup. An expert." Ray sighed, then, in a quieter voice, he murmured, "Don't fuck this up."

"No," Jacklyn said. "No, Dad, what the fuck?"

A soft sigh and a voice like a whisper. "We're rather proficient liars in our family, aren't we, son?"

Kyp's head snapped up, his legs buckling beneath him until his knees hit the forest floor. That voice. The voice he had heard in his ears for days now, whispering. Sometimes words of comfort, sometimes vicious words of recrimination. It was *her*.

Mother.

"I understand your shock, darling. And I understand your anger at Raymond, Jacklyn. But I'm not here to cause any upset, believe it or not. I'm here to help."

"You're here to help?" Kyp rose again, steeling himself against the heartbreaking look in her spectral eyes. "You never help. You've been whispering in my ear for weeks. Telling me I can't protect my family. Confirming everything I'd already worried about. I heard you loud and clear. As little as I wanted to admit it, I heard you and you were right. I can't protect them. Not without my Aegis. And I need an open Rift to do that. So you won. You got me to do what you wanted. And I don't even disagree."

"Kyp," Drew said. "We can protect them. In the regular world, they'll be safe."

Kyp laughed, a slightly shaky, manic sound. Looking his mother in the face had any semblance of mental stability he'd held onto slipping through his fingers.

"Drew! Rennie! You both grew up outside the Order. How well were your parents able to protect you without an Aegis?"

"My mother died," Rennie snapped. "She would've protected me with her life."

"And I will threaten the safety of the world to protect you," he said. "All of you. I would give up the peace that was the only thing I ever wanted for most of my life to protect you. Do you think this is an easy choice? Do you think I don't know you'll walk away from me for this? But will your Aegis protect you? Yes, it will. And that means I'm doing the right thing here. If it means all of you leave me, I don't care. I need you alive and safe more than I need you to love me."

"I hate this," Jacklyn cried. This was the Jacklyn he loved so much. Tears streaming down her face, and still she stood bravely.

"I'm sorry," was all he could utter. "Stop me if you must."

She shook her head. "If I have to make you seal it, that's the end of it. The end of us."

Jainey scurried around the Rift, rushing to Jacklyn, and Kyp winced at the clear decision inherent in it.

She was their child, sure, but Jainey and he had a different bond. His Bean had officially changed sides on him.

But Jacklyn didn't look like she'd achieved anything. Instead, her shoulders slumped, and she shook her head, defeated.

Oddly, Mother looked the same. "Kyp, I have some things I need to tell you. Will you let me speak before you make a definitive choice?"

Hate burned through him in a way it hadn't since he'd last seen her, when she'd nearly killed him last. "If you think anything you have to say will change what I'm doing here, you're wrong."

"Before I say anything, I wish to apologize. Firstly, to Jacklyn, whose pain comes closest to the pain I've caused you." She turned to Jacklyn. "There are no words I can say to make anything better. I took away so much from you. I was a different person there than I am here. I see what I've done now very clearly. Thank you for ending my reign. I deserved everything you've given me and more."

Jacklyn watched her with a stone stare. "I don't know what you expect now, but you won't get any tearful words of forgiveness from me. You're just lucky I won't punish your sons for your actions the way you punished me for my father's."

"And yours." She smiled slightly. "You did plenty. Don't sell yourself short."

Jacklyn just sighed. "If you weren't dead already, I'd kill you again just for fun."

Lavinia huffed something like a laugh before turning back to Kyp. "I wasn't always the wicked woman who raised you, or even the one Ray swore to fight. I used to be better than that. It was the darkness. Mind Keys struggle with all that they know and all that they can't forget. Coupled with being exposed to battle far sooner than I should have been, the pressure and pain became too much for me. I started to travel down a path, a dark path, continuing until I had a choice to make. Once I made that choice, I cut away the part of myself that wanted to protect people more than I wanted power.

"I had you in a desperate attempt to hold on to my sanity. I don't know why you weren't enough to save me. It didn't work for me, it could work for you. But if you cross this line, there's no turning back."

Kyp didn't miss that. The fact that he'd been conceived to save his mother, and hadn't even been capable of that. It was just like she was always whispering in his ear. That he would never succeed. That the world would crumble at his feet because he couldn't save anyone.

"I created this in you," she said. "If you do this, it won't be out of some power grab, like it was for me. If you cross this line, it will be because closing this Rift means taking away the only weapons you have left to fight with."

The hatred still burned within him. She was still every inch

Mother. Lavinia in all her poise and posture, but it was also unfamiliar. Something he'd never known before. There was a kindness there, the kind he'd seen in small glimpses before, sure, but had never allowed himself to believe in them, because he knew they were merely glimpses of something he could never attain.

"I know I'm the one who made you need those weapons," she said. "But I'm no threat to you and yours anymore. I know I'm not the right one to tell you. I know. But you don't need your weapons anymore."

Maybe she was actually the right person to tell him this. Maybe this was what he'd needed to hear.

Or maybe not.

"You're right." He felt the way his face contorted with misery and he allowed it. Because she was playing him again. She wanted him to keep the Rifts open. She was just changing her path.

He heard her words again. *I don't know why you weren't enough to save me.*

She wanted him to fume. And she wanted him to lash out in anger, to do the opposite of what she asked. To shoot himself in the foot because she told him not to.

But he wasn't a petty creature, and she was wrong. It wasn't him who hadn't been enough.

He allowed himself to feel everything he felt without remorse or regret, in a way he never had around his mother. He allowed the anger, the rage, the fear. The love he felt for the family he'd built. He let it flow through him without any of the horror he normally felt at showing his emotions. He didn't hold it close, and he didn't allow it to burst free from him due to a lack of control.

For once, he didn't even try to hold back.

Behind her, his family crowded together. Jacklyn held Jainey close, one of Jordan's hands gripped in hers. Caleb had an arm around Jordan, whose head drooped onto Rennie's shoulder. Austin and Drew watched from behind Rennie. Zane stood by the apparition of Ray, one hand out to steady Cass. All of them were crying. Some stifled the tears, eyes red-rimmed and glossy. Others had tears streaming down their cheeks.

Mother was making the people he loved cry.

She always seemed to make the people he loved cry.

"You're right," Kyp repeated. "I'm not doing this for the reasons you were. I could never do the things you've done." The words exited in a snarl. "I could never hurt people for my own power. I was doing it to protect my own. I was allowing you to taint me, allowing the voice in my head I've been hearing this whole time to corrupt me. I was allowing the voice in my head you planted in me since, since fucking *birth*, to destroy me. I allowed you to make me believe I couldn't protect them without this and to ignore the people I could be hurting by leaving this open. I was allowing your selfishness to destroy everything I am."

He took another step closer until he was eye to eye with Lavinia, wearing the face of a mother he'd never had, one who may never have existed. "You're claiming you were good. And maybe you were at some point. But you allowed this to take over you. I won't." His eyes narrowed. "Congratulations, Mother. I'm stronger than you. You can't get to me anymore. And I don't forgive you for what you've done. We're not the same."

At his words, Lavinia dispersed into the ether as if she hadn't been there at all.

He glanced toward Ray's spirit, where it waited, watching as Gana and Jaina appeared beside him.

"You should have known better," Kyp spat.

"We did." Ray winked.

"She wanted to say her piece, so we let her." Gana grinned.

"Because we knew what she really is," Jaina said. "And we know what you are not."

Something within him warmed. He scanned the others, and they all appeared relieved, Jacklyn most of all.

"Kyp… close the Rift."

He swallowed past the lump in his throat. "There's… I'm not thinking clearly. I need help."

Jacklyn stepped around the Rift, coming to his side. She took his hand in hers, and it felt like coming home. All the secrets were gone. All the foolish secrets he had tried to keep because he'd forgotten what she'd told him all those years ago. As much as he wanted to protect her, she did not need his protection.

"I told you I can't do this for you," she said, but this time it was gentler. Her eyes met his, those beautiful hazel eyes his world had revolved around for most of his life. "It has to be you."

Her strength had never been her Aegis. Her strength was her passion. For life, for him, for everything.

Maybe his strength wasn't his Aegis, either.

"That's not what I meant," he admitted. "I meant I need help.

After. I need to shake her. Get her out of my head. So I can move forward."

"I have some contacts," Zane said. "People who had an Aegis. Who knew about the Order and happen to have a degree. I can find you someone to talk to." She exchanged a smile with Ray and Jaina, and Kyp wondered if he'd gotten it wrong.

He'd had parents. Not just Ray, but Cxarana, and Zane, and Jaina, each in their own ways. And he had people he could rely on. He just had to let himself truly rely on them. This time, he'd do better.

"Seal the Rift, Kyp," Jacklyn said again, her head leaning on his shoulder.

It didn't take much of his blood. It was a small Rift.

"I'm sorry, Jainey," he whispered as it closed in front of him, his blood knitting the earth back together.

"It's okay, Papa," she said from Cass's arms. "I'm sorry I didn't tell you it was a stupid idea."

He chuckled despite the way his head roared from the battle. He still felt relieved. Even if the fear remained.

He kissed Jacklyn's hair. She smelled like strawberry shampoo. "I always knew it would end with us here, together."

She brushed his hair from his eyes with gentle hands. "You scared me for a minute there, but really, there was never any other option."

"I'm so sorry. I forgot for a minute. We are stronger together. Sometimes I'm a little…"

"Crazy?" She smiled. "That's okay. We do that together, too."

Epilogue

Kyp

"I'm convinced kangaroos are just human men who have been cursed," Austin said as he adjusted the lid on one of their storage containers.

Jacklyn laughed out loud. "Is it because they stand like buff men?"

Sometimes Kyp found walking into a conversation between the two of them to be like falling into an icy lake and finding it as hot as a sauna. They had their own language, he swore.

"It's like they want to square up, the damned mutated boxers," Austin complained. "I'm telling you, man, there's a Rift to a whole different dimension in Australia that leads to their world."

Even Kyp couldn't avoid laughing at that.

Jacklyn moved to take a box down from the top of the pile they had made, but stumbled under the weight. "Shit, shit, shit, shit."

Kyp rushed forward, but Austin ducked under the box first, lowering it to the floor and dropping it there to check on Jacklyn.

"Girl, ya gotta quit forgetting that," Austin said, his hands fluttering about like the mother hen he was beneath all that tough guy exterior. "You're gonna detach somethin'."

"Yeah, yeah, and I don't heal as quickly as I used to anymore, I know," she said.

It was an adjustment for all of them, but perhaps even more so for Jacklyn and Kyp, since they hadn't spent a year without an Aegis just before this particular mess. But they were making it through.

Even Kyp. He was trying to be more optimistic.

"I'll get that one, ya damn fool," Austin scolded her, then he lifted the box overhead like it was feather-light, muscles rippling and all that.

Kyp rolled his eyes. It wasn't enough that the guy had muscles on his muscles or was built like a brickhouse, but he was wearing a tiny white tank top and he was all sweaty and gleaming as he headed to where Zane was popping the trunk open. Worse still was the way Cass and Drew were watching him from the hood of one of the cars, sharing a beer and sharing their views on Austin's muscles and whether his shirt would survive them.

Okay, fine, it was a little funny.

Kyp joined them, leaning against the car they were sitting on. "Is all that really necessary?"

"It might not be for you, but it's definitely necessary for me," Drew said with a laugh, bumping shoulders with Cass. "That beefcake asked me to marry him."

"He did?" Cass shrieked.

It was weird how, even without his Aegis, Kyp could feel the happiness coming off Drew in waves. "Congrats, man!"

"Thanks!"

Cass hugged Drew. Drew reached across her to awkwardly hug Kyp.

"So, do I have to worry about this from you too?" Kyp asked Cass, playfully rolling his eyes. "Now that the war is over, will you start searching for some muscle-bound cowboy for your very own?"

Cass shrugged, the smile dropping off her face for a moment. "Not really my thing."

"A cowgirl?" Drew teased. "A perfectly acceptable alternative." Cass shook her head.

"A cowperson? A non-cow person?" Kyp snorted.

"I meant the whole partner thing. It's not my thing," Cass said. "I'm good as I am."

"But no love?" Drew pouted.

Cass leveled a glare his way. "There's more than one kind of love, Drew. I've got what I need right here, and plenty waiting for me after I go." She pressed a kiss to each of their cheeks. "Besides, I've got to return to college. I have a career I'm working toward. I've heard some people might need it. It will take a while, but I'll get there."

"You'll make an amazing therapist, Cass." Kyp grinned. "Just don't pick at my brain… more than you already do."

"She makes no guarantees," Drew said.

"She doesn't." Cass stuck her tongue out at him.

"Hey, handsome," Jacklyn called. "You're needed over here."

Kyp would have been annoyed at her addition if he hadn't realized she was talking to him. His cheeks warmed.

"I think that means we're heading out soon." He tapped both of his dearest friends on their knees before turning to head to Jacklyn. He only took a single step before nearly bumping into Caleb as he went racing by him, Jordan and Rennie following closely behind.

"Sorry!" he shouted behind him as he moved, but Kyp could barely hear him over Jordan and Rennie's laughter.

It wasn't until he was past all the cars that Kyp realized Caleb held Jainey under his arm like a football. Her giggles joined his sharp peals of laughter as he sprinted to the edge of the backyard, lifting Jainey into the air and lowering her to the floor.

"Touchdown!" he called, just in time for Jordan to tackle him around his waist.

Rennie winced for a moment, watching to see any sign of anger from the boys as they rolled around. They batted each other's hands away as they tried to maneuver each other into increasingly complex wrestling moves, all of which seemed to have names that the boys shouted.

"Losers, it was football!" Rennie called after them, joining Jainey in cheering on their display.

"Try for a One-Armed Monkey Wrench!" Jainey coached.

Chuckling, Kyp walked the rest of the way to Jacklyn. She looked beautiful as always, with her brown hair tumbling in curls down her back over the loose pink tank she wore, hips swaying in her torn jeans.

She smiled when he reached her. "It's good to hear them laugh, huh?"

He huffed a laugh. "Yeah, one could even mistake them for

ordinary kids."

"They're far from ordinary," Jacklyn said, reaching out to swipe the hair back from his forehead with a soft smile.

The miasma of melancholy had cleared since that day in the woods, and Kyp could finally breathe. He still missed Ray, of course, but Ray had died to give him this, this thing he had wanted all his life and had never been able to grasp. When he thought of the way he had nearly sabotaged it, his gut twisted.

The anger toward Lavinia hadn't gone away. It probably never would. But Zane had given him some options to consider while they were on the road to Boston, a place Jordan really wanted to visit because he picked it out blindfolded on a map. There really was no other reason but that.

And why not? They could go anywhere, do anything.

He walked over to the collection of boxes with Jacklyn by his side, ready to pull some more of the weight. It had bugged him all day that he had needed to make a physical list of where things were being packed, because he had never needed a list, only his memory. The realization that it was already fading into something more… ordinary… was a revelation. But the important memories, good and bad, remained.

The memories of those he loved and lost remained, however tinged by a slight haze that hadn't existed before. His family and their love remained. Even if he had to remind himself they couldn't hear him when he merely thought about it. He vowed to tell them what they needed to know with his actual voice as often as he could. That was his penance for his error.

And he hoped it would keep the darkness teasing at the edge of his brain at bay. Every now and then he saw evidence of what his mother had made him, eating at who he was, and he had to stop himself from pushing the warmth of his life away, from hiding and letting the darkness handle everything for him.

But if he did, it would ruin everything about who he wanted to be.

So he'd fight. He wouldn't push away the love and attentiveness they offered him. And in return, they'd stand by him, giving him all the gentle and not-so-gentle nudges back onto the right path.

"So that should be it. Austin just grabbed the last box," Jacklyn declared. "Are you ready?"

He shoved his hands into the pockets of his jeans, his shoulders pushing upward from the movement in a sort of half-shrug. Then he smiled like a flower soaking up Jacklyn's light. "You know, I think I am."

JACKLYN

"A normal life," I said. "Perfectly average. Just like you always wanted."

He had wanted that. And he had nearly given that up in a foolish bid to protect us. And it was definitely foolish. But it had been foolishness that loved us. We could work with that.

Kyp returned my grin, and I believed it. I knew the way his smile looked when he lied. This was true.

He looked better these last few days. He'd slept, and he'd eaten, and he even seemed to be taking care of himself better than he had the night my father died. It wouldn't be easy. It would take work and a lot of deep diving into some pretty horrible stuff that had happened to him, that Lavinia had done to him, but we'd get there. We'd make it right.

"Come on, guys! Get to your assigned cars!" I said, waving behind me for Kyp to follow. Our fingers brushed for a moment.

"Shotgun!" Kyp shouted, taking off for our car. Jordan was too far away, but he made a play at running for the door as if he could beat Kyp there.

We were splitting up the same way we had on the ride over to the estate. It would be a long drive, but we intended to stop as much as we needed along the way. Who knew where life would take us?

I walked around to the driver's side, hand on the handle. Kyp grinned at me over the top of the car, mischief dancing in his dark eyes.

As we got settled in the car, I allowed myself a moment to worry.

What if Cxarana and Andaria lost their wars, and the interdimensionals found a way back? Well, they would have to tear the rifts open for that, wouldn't they? We were the only ones with the ancient Arvokian spells, and all of the Skeleton Keys. I was sorely tempted to burn those Arvokian books.

I probably wouldn't.

But even if someone found a way, we would still be there to stop them. Or maybe someone else would. We'd figure that out when we got there.

It wasn't perfectly safe. But things weren't perfect. They never would be. But I would always be there for this family I'd built. I'd always be there for Kyp. And he would always be there for me. Tugging each other in the right direction. Reminding each other of what really mattered.

Once my seatbelt was clicked in place and I'd checked all of my mirrors, I glanced back over at Kyp just in time to see him tip his head back, his chest expanding in a deep breath. When he opened them again, his eyes sparkled with the kind of happiness I rarely saw in him.

"A normal life," I said.

"Finally."

Yeah. We'll be okay.

I looked into the rearview mirror and watched the kids in the back of the van, then further back to where Austin drove the car behind us. I could just barely make out Austin's little wave.

I put the car in drive and set out to find our new normal.

Acknowledgements:

How can one begin to say thank you for completing a series that was in the making for most of my lifetime? There is no real way. I can thank so many people, from the first teacher who taught me the joys of writing (I remember you, Mr. Michael Shaw!) to the high school teacher who got me back on the path when I had stopped living for myself (Dr. Jonathan Dzik). From my very first fan (my mother, Doris Minners), to my newest fan (my son, Logan Manzano), to my #1 fan (my husband, Ismael Manzano). But I'll try to keep it brief by keeping it to this particular book.

I will fail because my gratitude is just that MUCH.

To MaryBeth Dalto and Laynie Bynum, the founders of Sword & Silk books: Sword & Silk became a home to me when I had just about given up on seeing my dream through to fruition. Thank you for taking a chance on me, with Brynn, yes, but particularly a chance on my series and on Jacklyn and Kyp. You saved my career and, in a way, me.

To Jennia Herold-D'Lima, my editor: You have always been able to find the strengths in my work, and to strengthen my weaknesses. You are magic.

To Emily Wright, my proofreader: You were supposed to correct my punctuation, and you did a great job, but you also managed to correct my lacking knowledge of both linguistics and eyeliner. You rock.

To Celin Chen, my cover artist and layout designer, who does beautiful work, and somehow manages to pull the vision of my book covers right out of my brain. You are fantabulous, and I've never seen you create anything less than gorgeous work. I'm blessed to have you as my book designer.

To Kristin Jacques, content creator, for always making me look good, even when I'm completely clueless. I can always count on you to come up with brilliant ideas for promotion. Thank you for bestowing your genius upon me.

To the crew and membership of WriteHive, thank you for inspiring me daily and reminding me of the beauty of the writing community. When we come together, we can do anything.

To the Witches Coven: Kia Leep, S. Kaeth, Jerusha Renee, and Hannah Kates, thank you for the daily support in writing things and literally everything else. I don't think I would have survived two of the most difficult years of my life without you. And Hannah - thank you for the fire ants bit. I'm sorry I couldn't have Lavinia eaten alive by fire ants as her actual death, but I already had a plan for her. I hope you can forgive me.

To Darrell Hon, thank you for keeping me accountable on a nearly daily basis, when I couldn't pull out of my burn out. You and the folks listed above saved my bacon. Accountabilibuddies for the win! To my other amazing writing/editing buddies, Jeni Chappelle, Liv Macy, Christie Curry, Zoraida Cordova, Beck Erixson, Paulette Kennedy, Joseph Chianakas, Jennifer Gadd, Elena Battista, Catie O'Neil, Jennifer Lewis, Casie Bazay, Gage Greenwood, the WIM crew, the Pitch2Publication crew, and the old Inkwell Council folks who have stuck around. Thank you to all of you for inspiring me and pushing me to be better.

To Maria Tureaud - you may not have been able to CP this one, since I completely screwed up my deadline time, but your advice and supportive words live inside of my head in a cozy corner with a cup of tea, and a tv tuned to K-dramas. Thank you for always being there and smacking me when the imposter syndrome gets to me.

To the Bowery crew - the first day job I've ever had that was committed to keeping me sane and being as flexible as I needed to maintain this crazy mother/wife/daughter/sister/friend/writer/editor/ non-profit board member/executive assistant life I've got going on. Cass, Mariko, Brandon, and Andrea most especially, but all of you - you guys are champs, you have no idea.

To real life family and friends, Megan Manzano and Julian Sherman, Jon Minners and Kristy Caruso, Melissa Minners and Dorothy Doremus, Allegra Starobin and Robert Fruhmann, Jennine and Anthony Carella, Victor and Christopher Berrios, J'vania Roberts-Ward, Heather Martone, Carlos Garcia and Sandra Iglesias, Miriam and Luis Rosario, Manny and Helen Manzano, the Minners aunts, uncles and cousins, and my mother, Doris Minners. The support you give to my writing, my husband, my son, and my life is unmatched. I'm a very lucky girl all around.

To the kiddos who keep the wonder and silliness in my life: Millie and Wynnie, Moira and Eowyn, Kaitlyn and Chloe, and Tucker. Thank you for loving my bonkers personality…and even encouraging it.

To Joy: my sista from anotha mista. I'm so lucky to have someone who understands me the way you do. Our lives are wild, and I could never even try to place a value on what you give to me regularly. I can only hope I return anything even close. There have probably never been two people who seem more different but are so the same on the inside. You are the green tea to my coffee, girl. Never change. Badass survivors, thrivers, and uniters forever.

To Trooper, my seventy pound lapdog. You are a blessing. Thank you for stealing Logan's heart at first sight, for cuddling up to me while I'm writing so I have an excuse to take pet breaks, and for taking your cut of my cheese snacks.

To Logan, I gained the courage to become a writer from your birth, and I gain the courage to continue writing because of your presence. Things have not always come easy to us, but we've gotten good at encouraging each other to succeed. You actually like my work and you cheering me on means so much. I can't believe you're a high schooler now. Time flies when you're obsessing over geeky stuff together. I'm so proud of who you've grown into and I can't wait to see you grow even more. As I type this you are cackling wildly while playing Fortnite with your crew, and it's driving me a little crazy, but what else is a teenage son for? Also, you just called someone a weenie because you're pretending you don't curse. It's cute, really.

To Ismael, my love, the peanut butter to my jelly, the rice to my beans, the Drew to my Austin, because I can't really say the Jacklyn to my Kyp. I'm both of them, let's face it. You have never once stopped encouraging me, supporting me, and loving me, when I was at my worst and when I was at my best, and you know me so well, you wrote my apparently predictable tears into your vows. Time lost all meaning when you came into my life, because it's somehow been twenty-six years and simultaneously no time at all. Looking forward to continuing bending the laws of time and space together.

Most importantly and finally to the readers - thank you for taking this journey with me. Jacklyn has been living in my head rent free since I was seventeen years old, if you can believe that. Finally, her story is complete, and she can move out to a very nearby apartment, where I can occasionally come visit. None of that would be possible without each and every one of you. I hope you will continue to follow me wherever I go next. I genuinely have no idea where that will be yet. But either way, know that you have been both appreciated and adored, and that you have made my art worth creating. May a little of Jacklyn always live in your head and heart forever.

With love and light,
Justine

About Justine Manzano

Justine Manzano is the geeky author of the geeky YA series *Keys & Guardians,* and geeky YA novel *Never Say Never.* Known as a Professional-Life-Ruiner-By-Antagonist, Justine's fiction is tough on the outside and sweet on the inside, like an M&M or a hard candy with a gooey center, delivered with sass and snark. A freelance editor, she also serves as an Editor-in-Residence at WriteHive. She lives in Bronx, NY with her husband, teenage son, and new puppy! She can usually be found at her website, www.justinemanzano.com or all the usual social media haunts. If you've looked in all these places and can't find her, she's probably off reading fanfiction. She'll be back soon.

Also By Justine Manzano:

Never Say Never

Brynn Stark swore off love forever.

Her friend Val is determined to change her mind, no matter the consequences.

Prickly and cynical, Brynn tries to avoid Val's attempts at setting her up, until Val reveals her true identity--Aphrodite, goddess of love, who promises to show Brynn why she shouldn't lose faith

Skeptical at first, Brynn soon realizes she's falling for Adam, Val's boyfriend. So she throws herself full-force into dating Val's picks, hoping one can lure her away.

When even that doesn't work, Brynn's forced to decide if she'll choose her goddess-given fate, or risk it all for the wrong-but-right guy.

One thing's for sure.

Love sucks.

And it's all about to blow up in their faces.

Also By Justine Manzano:

The Order of the Key
Keys & Guardians, Book 1

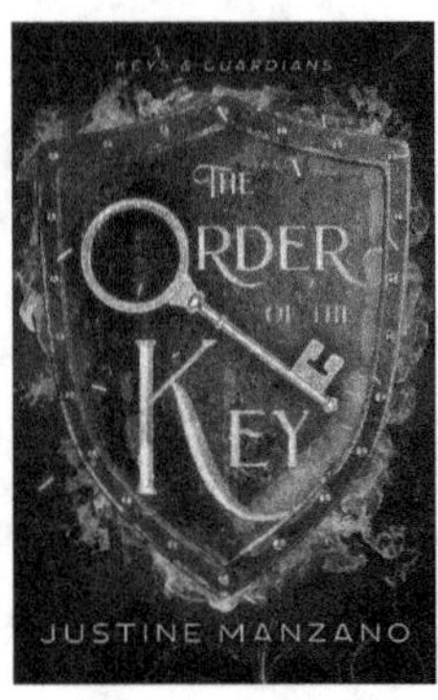

Jacklyn Madison never expected to be attacked by a beast on an evening
snack run.

Add a rescue mission enacted by a trained regiment of teenaged warriors,
and her night officially becomes just like a scene from one of her beloved
comic books. Turns out, her parents were once members of the Order of
the Key, gifted humans that protect humanity from creatures spilling
through inter-dimensional rifts. Unable to control her newfound abilities,
Jacklyn and her family rejoin the Order.

After an attack on their headquarters leaves Jacklyn questioning their
leadership, Kyp—the boy who led her initial rescue—reveals a darker
secret. The Order's leader may be corrupt, and Jacklyn's questions could
put her family in danger. Drawn into the search for proof, Jacklyn must
use her guts and magical brawn to protect her family, her friends, and
herself from the monsters spilling from rifts, and those hiding within the
Order.

ALSO BY JUSTINE MANZANO:

The Skeleton Key
Keys & Guardians, Book 2

Kyp Franklin can't move on.

One year after his mother officially declared war against him, Kyp is still struggling to find his feet as the Order of the Key's new leader. He's far too concerned about tracking her down before she causes even more damage than she already has. In fact, that's all he's been doing. Until one day, after a particularly reckless mission, he returns to find a surprising visitor on his doorstep...

Jacklyn Madison can't move on.

One year after she left the Order, she has a new team, and a new mission. She's determined to close all the interdimensional rifts between our world and the Dusk, before more people die trying to stop the creatures that pass through them. But a vision she had while on the edge of death leads her to the one place she never intended to return ...

Forced to work together, Jacklyn, Kyp, and their respective teams uncover Lavinia's next plan: an alarming mix of magic and science the likes of which has never been seen before. Jacklyn and Kyp must learn to work together again and confront the demons of their past if they're going to stop Lavinia and those assisting her before their larger plan is put into action--a plan that could bring the monsters of the Dusk to our world...forever.